"DAMN IT ALL, LASS, BUT I SWEAR YOU'VE BEWITCHED ME."

The sound of his voice and the caress in his eyes had a like effect on her. She did not resist, only trembled a little as he bent his tall head and put his lips on hers. She could not help herself. Why did he have this power over her? A power that made her knees shake and her head spin wildly.

His arms tightened about her. Beneath his mouth her quivering lips parted. His kiss was soft and tender, but as he felt her gentle response, the pressure of his mouth deepened. His arms pulled her closer and she felt herself melting against his big, hard body.

"Forgive me, Lisa," he said at last. "I warned you I was no gentleman."

50

CLOAK
OF
FATE

Eleanor Howard

A TAPESTRY BOOK
PUBLISHED BY POCKET BOOKS NEW YORK

This novel is a work of historical fiction. Names, characters, places and incidents relating to non-historical figures are either the product of the author's imagination or are used fictitiously. Any resemblance of such non-historical incidents, places or figures to actual events or locales or persons, living or dead, is entirely coincidental.

An *Original* publication of TAPESTRY BOOKS

A Tapestry Book published by
POCKET BOOKS, a Simon & Schuster division of
GULF & WESTERN CORPORATION
1230 Avenue of the Americas, New York, N.Y. 10020

ISBN: 0-671-46163-X

First Tapestry Books printing January, 1983

10 9 8 7 6 5 4 3 2 1

*To Glen
for his help,
his encouragement
and his love*

Chapter One

It was late in the afternoon when Lisa reached the outskirts of the village of Bridgeford. Hearing music and shouts of laughter, she slowed Primrose down to a walk and looked past the rustic bridge before her. She could see sharp flashes of color through the trees and as she crossed the bridge she saw the Maypole standing at the top of the gentle slope, its wooden shaft wreathed with flowers and long streamers of bright-colored ribbons.

May Day in the year 1663 was celebrated with abandon in Merry England. It was the scene of rural festivities, which, for at least one day, cheered the folk who participated in them.

> Come, lasses and lads, get leave of your dads,
> And away to the Maypole hie;
> For every fair has a sweetheart there,
> And the fiddler's standing by. . . .

The farmers and tenants of Stavely Manor and the neighboring village of Bridgeport had been gathered around the Maypole since long before noon, blending sexes and ages in a greater freedom than on any other day of the year.

Plagued by her own unhappiness, Lisa had completely forgotten what day it was, but now the gaiety of the crowd was contagious, and drew her closer. Surely, she thought, it wouldn't hurt to watch the dancing awhile. She would buy something to fill her empty stomach from the line of booths set up at the far edge of the woods.

Dismounting and securing Primrose in the trees beside the road, Lisa straightened her clothing and smoothed her long, dark hair, her blue eyes sparkling with anticipation.

She noticed that through the trees to her right, overlooking the sparkling little river, lay a stately red-brick manor house. Turreted and gabled, it showed a blending of the Tudor with an architect's fantasy of a medieval castle.

As she prepared to start up the hill, Lisa spied in the distance three somberly dressed men walking toward her. To judge from their solemn, shaven faces, they derived no pleasure from the spectacle around the Maypole. Instead, their glances held such obvious disapproval that Lisa instinctively concealed herself in some nearby shrubbery before they caught sight of her. As they drew closer, she could hear their conversation.

"'Tis time again that the saints of the Lord should put a stop to these abominations."

"Aye, it grieves me to see the tenants of Stavely Manor as merry-mad as those of any malignant."

"If Stavely be one of us, why are such heathen revelries held on his lands?"

"Fie, man! Do thee think him a fool? He does well to be very loyal, just now."

"Aye, it will not be for much longer, brother Brintnall. Thee must have patience."

Lisa felt a cold shiver go through her as these men, obviously Puritans, perhaps even Fifth Monarchy men, passed by her and over the bridge. Were they plotting against the king? For three years Charles II had been enjoying his own again. Was a new uprising being planned? Or were they just threats of a divine retribution directed to the revelers?

Still considering what she had overheard, Lisa emerged from the bushes. Her eyes went to the whirling dancers about the Maypole above her. She was young with only herself to worry about now and the lighthearted music made her push these dark, uncertain thoughts back in her mind.

Under a grand old oak, a fiddler and a clarionet player sat

scraping and blowing energetic jigs and reels. On another and longer bench were a row of old people, vicariously enjoying the sports and feasting heartily on good country fare.

In the late afternoon sun the young still danced. Many of the gowns and kirtles of the lasses were soiled and awry, their braids of hair tumbled from the neatness of the morning, while among the lads several were observed to have indulged a bit too much in the strong mead. The couples, fours and larger groups kicked up their heels in the sprightly country dances, with shouts of joy and laughter.

It was during a rousing finale of one of the dances that the music suddenly faltered, and Lisa saw that a gray-clothed man was slowly approaching the dancers.

Basil Stavely was a man of forty years, with a strong and powerful stature, but his once handsome face now showed signs of dissipation in the thickening of his features, the purply veins on his cheeks and in the heavy lines around his mouth. His hair was still thick but iron-gray, and there was gray in his heavy black brows. In fact, there was a marked absence of any color about him, except for the plume in his hat. Without it, he might still have been wearing the severe garb of the Puritans.

As Stavely drew closer, the revelers fell back and the dancing finally stopped altogether. An ominous stillness filled the air and was not broken until Lisa heard the sound of hoofbeats behind her. She turned and saw a horseman riding a magnificent black stallion galloping up the lea, heading straight in her direction!

She jumped back as quickly as she could, but the horseman reined in his coal-black mount, bringing it to a nervous, snorting halt.

For a moment Lisa could only stare up at him, into the flashing emerald eyes. He was clothed as a gentleman. She saw the gleaming leather of his silver-spurred boots and the richly tooled sword at his hip, but he had none of the foppish manner of the current gallants. Instead, he had the romantically handsome face of a rogue—cool and dangerous like that of a highwayman or a buccaneer.

She should have dropped her eyes modestly before the gaze that boldly appraised her, but she felt herself held fast and motionless like a startled doe. For a second his own eyes bore the same hazed stare as hers. Then his white teeth flashed into a wicked grin and he tore off his plumed hat and swept her a mocking bow.

CLOAK OF FATE

She blushed as he spurred his horse on past her, but her eyes remained on his golden head as he rode to the top of the rise.

The whole incident had taken barely a minute, yet Lisa had the strange feeling that those emerald eyes would be etched in her memory for a very long time to come.

Upon reaching the merrymakers, the newcomer threw himself agilely from his horse and grasped Sir Basil Stavely's reluctant hand.

The group stared at the stranger who had so suddenly appeared. Stavely addressed him as Lord Drayton. Some of the elders who were present remembered his father, who had fallen for the cause of King Charles at the bloody battle of Northampton. The former master of Stavely Manor, Sir Edmund Stavely, had also fallen in the same cause, at Naseby. With one accord, they felt Lord Drayton worthy of a more cordial welcome than the lackluster one bestowed upon him by Sir Basil.

Drayton had gained the full attention of them all with his commanding presence. A full head shorter, Basil Stavely seemed to fade into insignificance beside him.

The women shyly admired Drayton's spectacular good looks. Great shoulders stretched his fawn-colored doublet over a wide expanse of chest. His golden, shoulder-length hair, in the cut of the Cavalier, gleamed in the sunlight. He stood in an easy stance talking to Sir Basil, his bridle in one hand, his broadbrimmed hat in the other. A few words of inquiry and information were exchanged between them and an invitation, although slow in forthcoming, was extended to stay at the Manor for as long as he was in the area. In the silence that followed Drayton's acceptance, Sir Basil again became aware of the quiet bitter faces around him.

"Out of the way, you surly rascals," he growled. "Look at them, Richard. Have you ever seen such a sullen group of malcontents?"

Drayton frowned. "A pity," he said in his rich, deep voice. "A happy yeomanry is the true boast of Old England, and now that the monarchy has been restored there should be more smiles. Perhaps you are too rough on them."

Sir Basil laughed harshly, the laugh grating on Drayton's ears like a door with unoiled hinges. "They must be made to know their places, Richard, and they *will!*"

CLOAK OF FATE

"True, their places, as you say. Still . . ."

At Stavely's dark look he did not continue, but could not help but think that when a man is so disliked by his own people, then he has done something to deserve such hatred.

"Come," Stavely was saying, "we have had enough of these rustics. Let us on to the Manor. 'Tis nearly time to sup."

"Pray do me a favor and do not wait for me, Basil," answered Drayton. "Spare me a half-hour to see these people at their merriment and then I will join you at the Manor."

This suggestion met with no opposition from Stavely, who was glad of the opportunity to reach the Manor ahead of his unexpected guest, so he merely said, as he stalked away, "Do as you will, Richard, but I hardly see much merriment in these clods."

Lord Drayton, bridle still in hand, watched his host walk back toward the bridge, then he turned to the group who had begun to chatter among themselves.

"Take this bridle, some lad who wishes a bright silver groat."

The claimants for the groat among the younger boys were so many that the result was a disbursement of a half-dozen of those pieces.

There was a merry shout then from Drayton to the musicians and the group surrounding him.

"Good masters and mistresses! Let me wet my whistle and then I pray you to your places for one more dance!"

Lisa had climbed the rise as the two gentlemen stood talking and had made her way toward the line of booths. She was dressed in a skirt of blue linsey-woolsey and a white blouse which just tipped her creamy shoulders. A black stomacher was tightly laced over it, accentuating her tiny waist. With her wealth of dark, silky hair and her enchanting face, she had not approached unnoticed.

Before she could decide between a cold meat pattie or a golden leg of capon, a goblet of some sparkling fluid was thrust upon her by an admiring and bold young villager. She accepted it thirstily, drinking deeply of the strong, cool wine and smiled at him gratefully. The dazzling smile immediately reduced him to gawking speechlessness as the vision before him again put the goblet to her lips and this time drained it.

"A maid after my own heart," said a deep voice beside her,

5

proceeding to drain his own foaming flagon. Then her small hand was grasped in his large one and she was pulled forward through the pressing crowd toward the circle of dancers.

Head and shoulders above the others, he looked like a magnificent giant as he turned and gave her a disarming grin. It swept aside the rather cynical lines that etched his mouth. The emerald eyes laughed down at her.

"May I have the honor of this dance?" he drawled, giving her a little bow, but he never released her fingers and she had no time to refuse, for he was shouting: "Musicians! A lively reel, before the setting of the sun and the end of the May Day!"

The music began. All seemed in motion at once. Feet flew, arms waved, skirts spun out above shapely ankles, locks came loose and braids and combs as the dancers whirled wildly about.

Lisa found herself passed from the hands of Lord Drayton to one young man and then another before returning to Drayton again, her feet flying to the music. She was smiling, a smile of pure delight. Her cheeks were flushed, her blue eyes radiant. Her soft curtain of hair rippled down her back in shimmering waves as she threw back her head and laughed, her happy laughter blending with Drayton's as he spun her around and around. Her head reeled giddily from the effects of the wine on her empty stomach. She saw his face before her, white teeth flashing, and those emerald eyes that seemed to sear into hers. Her heart hammered wildly with the intoxicating excitement of the dance and her recent unhappiness was stripped away, making her spirits light and free. While the dance lasted, time and place ceased to exist. Here in the midst of this laughing, happy crowd, she was alone with the most extraordinary man she had ever seen, and feeling a carefree gaiety that was completely new to her.

Lord Drayton's pretty partner was causing much speculation from the others present. Who was she? Where had she come from?

Drayton was not unaware of the admiring glances cast in Lisa's direction by the other men. He knew they envied him, for there was not a lass present to equal her in grace or beauty.

The dance livened and grew more uproarious. Even the old tottered from their benches to clap their hands and keep time with their feet. Shouts of merriment arose as individuals gave their own interpretations of various steps until, at last, the music came to a halt, and, breathless and exhausted, the couples drifted off to find a drink for their parched throats.

Drayton led Lisa, unresisting, away from them to the edge of the thick woods of the park. He stopped in the shadow of the trees and let his eyes caress her.

Rich, blue-black hair tumbled to her shoulders and down her back. She was breathtakingly beautiful, with a flawless complexion and a pair of large liquid eyes that could enslave a man. Yet the maid seemed completely unaware of her beauty. There was a freshness and innocence about her. Damn appealing to one as tired and jaded as he! How delicate her features were. She must come from a purer, finer breed than the other village lasses. Why, she stood out like a thoroughbred from a plow horse!

His lips formed a cynical smile. Was this beauty the result, perhaps, of a nobleman's dalliance with a housemaid or a tenant's daughter? The smile widened as a thought crossed his mind. Perhaps old Sir Edmund . . .

"I am not one of the villagers," she said as if in response to his unspoken question. She wondered why she had bothered to explain this to him. Under his intense scrutiny her soft voice trembled a little. "I must go."

He lifted an eyebrow. She did not have a country accent. Her voice was cultured, refined. Now, who the devil was she? Egad, but her eyes were so dark they were almost violet.

"Not yet," he said, his voice warm and deep, his eyes never leaving her. Those emerald eyes had now lost their fire and had become disturbingly sensuous. How astonishingly long and dark his lashes were for one so fair!

She attempted to go by him, but he grasped her tightly by the wrist.

"Let me go!" she demanded, a little frightened now.

"Nay, I beg only a moment."

"I am afraid you are no gentleman, my lord," she declared hotly.

"I agree. I am a scoundrel. But you are so delectable."

In a split second he had pulled her to him and tilting her face up to his, he kissed her trembling lips.

Lisa had never dreamed a kiss could be like that. Starting with gentleness and restraint—so that she had no fear but slowly succumbed to the tender sweetness of it. And then it changed, became more demanding, so that she felt her own involuntary response as her mind gave way and her body took over. She had never felt desire before—it was an unknown emotion to her—but she felt it now and she knew, as he released her, that because of this encounter she was never going to be quite the same again.

Blushing furiously, she looked up into eyes that stared down at her. They were not brazen or smiling with self-satisfaction, but with a querying look in them as if he did not quite believe what had happened himself.

The next second, without looking back, Lisa was gone, moving wildly away from him as fast as she could go, running frantically down the lea, ignoring his cry of "Wait!"

She was shaken and angry with herself. Shaken by the kiss that had sparked an unknown flame deep within herself; angry with the scoundrel and the liberties he had taken and angrier with herself for letting him. What had possessed her? Against all she had been told about men, she had let that rogue lead her off by herself; had let him kiss her. He was big and powerful, but she could have stopped him. He had not forced her.

Her thoughts in a turmoil, she crossed the little bridge, unaware that two young revelers were following her.

She untied Primrose and climbed gracefully up into the saddle, directing the horse back to the road.

What a magnificent stallion he had ridden, she thought. And why not? He was a lord. Lord Drayton. She had heard someone call him that. He had looked like a crusading knight galloping up the hill!

"You must forget what happened!" She warned herself. "You will never see that scoundrel again!" But though a scoundrel he might be, she had to admit that she had been drawn to him. There was something commanding in his maleness, something disturbing in the way he had held her. It had frightened her, that was true, but it had also thrilled her. She had felt a strange stirring deep within her. She had wanted to clutch him back, to feel again his lips on hers. What was the matter with her? A lady should not feel that way and she had been raised a lady. She must put Lord Drayton out of her mind! She had a purpose and nothing must interfere with it.

Chapter Two

As Lisa rode on she thought again of her purpose in coming to this part of the country. It had only been two days before that she had made her solemn resolution.

Her mother, Valerie Manning, had lain dying in the wooden caravan that was their home, a caravan camped outside a town in Suffolk where the Manning Shakespearian Players were performing.

Lisa had sent for a local physician. He examined the poor, wasted shell who lay on the narrow bed before him and shook his head in sorrow. He recognized the signs: the cough and the hemorrhage of the lungs. Valerie Manning was in the final stages of consumption and there was nothing he could do for her. He took Lisa aside as he explained this to her.

"How long has she . . . ?" Lisa asked him, her deep blue eyes desolate.

The physician was honest with her, recognizing the strength beneath the delicate beauty.

"Her time is short. A few days—a week at most."

Lisa's lips trembled, but she took it well. He was right. She was not the type to swoon or break into wrenching sobs.

Was there a family home, the physician asked her, where her mother could be taken to end her days more comfortably?

9

Lisa shook her head. "Mama ran away from her family many years ago in order to marry my father. They disowned her and I know naught of them. Not even their name."

So that was how Valerie Manning had become one of the first respected actresses on the stage, the physician thought. Before her, most females in the acting profession were considered little better than prostitutes, but it was evident that Valerie Manning was well-born and her young daughter had the same refined, ladylike manner.

Lisa sighed as he departed. He had offered no advice, but the medication she had obtained from Zada, the old gypsy woman, at least seemed to alleviate the violent coughing fits and help her mother sleep.

Zada had been with the acting troupe since the beginning, following them in her own caravan and telling fortunes where they played. When Valerie married Evan Manning and joined the players, Zada appointed herself personal maid and attendant to her. Upon Lisa's arrival, she became the child's nurse as well.

Despite their itinerant way of life, Lisa had been raised as a lady, her mother teaching her the manners of polite society. Her father had passed on to her his great love of literature and had taught her to sit a horse well.

Lisa had known that she would never be an actress of the same stature as Valerie, who possessed a certain magic whenever she stepped onto the stage, but she had discovered that she did have an innate talent for making the character she portrayed believable to an audience.

The day the doctor came had been a hectic one for Lisa. *Hamlet* had had to be cancelled, due to Valerie's illness, and following the afternoon performance of *Midsummer Night's Dream,* the troupe had packed up the set and headed back to the caravan encampment. All but the leading actor, Phillip O'Brien. Furious that *Hamlet* had been canceled—that he'd missed the opportunity to play the Prince of Denmark for the first time—he had stayed at the village inn and drank steadily while he recited his favorite soliloquy.

Phillip O'Brien barged into the caravan while Lisa sat at the table worrying over the fate of the struggling troupe. A handsome, ambitious young actor, he accosted Lisa with a proposal. She should marry him, and he would take charge of the troupe now that her mother was incapacitated.

10

He laughed at Lisa when she defiantly claimed that she could manage things quite well by herself.

"You?" he sneered. "A mere slip of a maid? Who would listen to *you?* You have been sheltered by your mama far too much. You live apart from us in this caravan. You don't even eat with us. Zada makes all your meals. Even when you act with us we must be on our best behavior because your mama is hovering close by, ready to swoop down like an avenging angel if someone becomes too familiar."

But it was the avenging angel who again managed to come to Lisa's rescue a few minutes later, when Phillip decided to take matters into his own hands. He made an unexpected grab for Lisa, flinging her down on the nearby couch that served as her bed.

She fought him valiantly, inflicting a scratch down one cheek and a blow to the side of his head, but he held her fast until Valerie's sudden intervention.

Wearing only her flannel nightdress and holding herself erect by grasping the back of a chair, she had never looked more regal or imperious as she ordered Phillip from the caravan and dismissed him from the acting troupe. Her frail body seemed to exude strength and authority. Lisa was filled with admiration for the magnificent actress her mother was!

However, with the disappearance of a cursing Phillip out the door, Valerie's body seemed to shrink and grow limp and Lisa barely caught her before she collapsed.

Settled again in her bed, Valerie weakly insisted that she be propped up on her pillows. There was much she wished to say to her daughter and so little time.

She put a hand to Lisa's cheek and her eyes filled with tears. "You are so beautiful, child, and soon you will have no one to watch over you."

"I am not a child any more, Mama. I am seventeen. I can look after myself. Zada has talked to me about men, warned me. I just never dreamed that Phillip . . . with you so close by . . ."

"You must *never* be alone with a man unless you know him well and he has earned your trust," Valerie cautioned her. "Oh, Lisa, I pray you will find someone like your papa to care for you." She grasped Lisa's hand, her lovely eyes entreating. "Promise me you will save yourself for the man you will love. One day soon he will appear and awaken you as a woman. Wait and be sure he is the right one." The slim fingers tightened. "When I die, I want you to leave the company immediately. I will talk to Barlow about it in the morning. I am sure he will accompany you. Take what belongs to us in the small strong box. Then go to the village and obtain passage on the first coach going north. My family lives near Chatsworth in Norfolk. There is a letter in the box which I have written to them. I know they will take you in and do their best for you and I will rest content, knowing you will be under their protection."

"But you are not going to die! And I would *never* go to them! Never! Not after they had disowned you for marrying Papa."

Valerie sighed heavily. "Hush, child. I have more to say and little breath."

She began to cough and when she put a crumpled handkerchief up to her mouth, Lisa saw that it was stained with bright flecks of blood. It was another moment or two before Valerie could go on. "You have always known that you were not our natural child, Lisa, but I want to tell you something you are unaware of—something I should have told you long ago— something about your true background. . . ."

In the morning, Valerie Manning was dead.

It had been Lisa's duty to inform the acting troupe. She had stood before them, proudly erect, not breaking down until after a small memorial service had been conducted by a local vicar and she was able to return to her caravan.

Zada had comforted her and she had finally fallen asleep, only to be awakened in the middle of the night by the anxious gypsy.

Lisa had immediately awoken. Phillip, hearing of Valerie Manning's death, had returned. He had brought wine and spirits for a true Irish wake. Declaring himself the new leader of the troupe, he was loudly declaring that Lisa had agreed to marry him. His voice was ugly and full of menace.

"You must leave," Zada had whispered to Lisa. "Phillip will be here soon."

"But I can't go away now," Lisa had argued. "Mama wished to be buried beside Papa. 'Tis twenty miles distant. I planned to leave in the morning."

"I will see that your mother's body is taken to its resting place.

"But—"

"No buts, Lisa," the old gypsy said firmly. "Time is short."

Lisa dressed quickly and gathered up her few belongings into a bundle. She put the money and papers into a leather pouch around her waist. Zada's black eyes watched her.

"So young and so vulnerable," the gypsy thought, "so brave but so unknowing."

She pressed a small, deadly looking dagger into Lisa's hand, to place in the waistband of her petticoat for protection.

"You will go straight to your mother's people," Zada was instructing Lisa when there was a fierce knocking at the door of the caravan. Phillip's thick voice bellowed out for Lisa to open up to him.

With only seconds to spare before the old lock gave way, Lisa managed to escape through the door at the back of the caravan. Into the woods she ran to where the old gypsy had Primrose saddled and waiting for her.

Perplexed, Lord Drayton stood looking after Lisa as she fled away from him down the lea. Never in his thirty-three years had he ever been thrown so offbalance by a wench. It was not only disturbing, it was damned uncanny. Was the maid a witch?

He had ridden north from London that morning with his manservant, heading in the direction of his family estate. They had reached the village of Bridgeford in the late afternoon and Drayton had decided to stop at the local inn and spend the night, instead of pressing on. Observing the May-Day festivities, he left his servant to engage suitable accommodation and rode off toward the merrymaking.

Now, as he strode over to where his horse was being held, Ned quietly intercepted him.

"I have obtained rooms at the inn, m'lord," he said, "and unloaded the baggage."

"I am afraid you will have to return and collect it," Drayton murmured distractedly. He was still gazing off in the direction Lisa had taken.

"I beg pardon, m'lord?"

"I have been invited to stay at the manor house yonder," Drayton indicated the red-brick structure just visible through the trees.

"Very good, m'lord. I will fetch the baggage."

Drayton again started toward his horse, when this time he

13

was familiarly slapped on the shoulder. Angered by the affrontery, he spun around, a sharp reprimand ready on his lips.

"Has Lord Drayton left his memory behind among the Monseers? Dang it, thee be a great man now, but thee was a boy once, and then thee didn't mind a sturdy slap from Matthew Chester!"

"What! Matthew Chester indeed, as I live!" exclaimed Drayton, at last recognizing one of the old servants of Stavely Manor.

He was a man of fifty years or so, with a shock of brown hair showing little gray and a bronzed and weathered face. From his brown hose and jerkin, broad cap and knife at belt, he was now evidently the keeper of the chase.

"You are quite right, Matthew. I did not mind a sturdy slap, then, nor does it irk me now," responded Drayton, heartily gripping the man's broad hand.

"I hope thee don't mind my liberty, m'lord," said Matthew, a little ashamed now and belatedly removing his cap, "but I was so glad to see thee that I forgot—"

"Not another word, Matthew, and replace your cap before I *do* grow angry," said Drayton, looking around them and drawing the man beyond the earshot of the now dispersing group. "You seem to be the only thing not changed at Stavely Manor, old friend. Tell me, how does Basil Stavely come to be the master of the Manor, and does he manage well?"

"M'lord, it wouldn't do for me to—" the forester hesitated, looking over his shoulder.

"Matthew Chester, if you do not answer me I shall pay back that slap with interest!" Drayton grinned.

"I *am* glad to see thee, m'lord," Matthew smiled. "Dang it, we be so on our guard here now. If thee must know about—"

"Begin at the beginning," Drayton broke in, "and speak rapidly, my good man, because supper is waiting me at the Manor, but before I step within its doors, I would like to know more of Basil Stavely. Remember that I have been away a long time and everything has changed."

"Aye, it has changed all right. Thee remembers when Sir Edmund Stavely fell at Naseby and perhaps thee heard that his poor wife, my lady, died shortly after."

"Aye, I know that much, although I was young in the wars then."

"Well, when Cromwell was giving away all the lands of the

old families to his psalm-singing crop-ears, Basil Stavely, who, thee knows, was a cousin of Sir Edmund's—"

"Aye, I know that much, too," again interrupted Drayton, "and I knew the lady whom he married, Mary Ellsbury."

"Well," pursued Matthew, "Basil Stavely somehow managed to be on the right side, though, dang it, he had done naught to help any side, except drinking and gaming and wenching, and Stavely Manor fell into his hands. I'll speak plainly, m'lord, it was a sad day for all of us when he came to be master, with his overpowering ways, and the fields ha' never smiled since, the way they did when good Sir Edmund was alive."

"Aye, I can well believe you," replied Drayton, reflectively. "But now that the king has his own again, where is Sir Edmund's heir? And how does Basil Stavely manage to be on the right side again—with Cromwell gone to hell?"

"Sir Edmund had two children if thee remember, a lad and a lass, but now Basil Stavely is the only Stavely left. He manages, somehow, to be on all sides, so men say. He is a king's man now, and much joy may the king have o' him!"

"But what happened to the two children?"

"When Sir Edmund was gone and their mother died broken-hearted after Naseby, and when Basil Stavely held all these lands from the Parliament, the lad and lass were taken in by Squire Prescott, a relative of Sir Edmund's lady."

"And?" Drayton asked impatiently.

"It was a dreadful thing that happened. The house was fired by the Parliamentary troopers in the middle of the night and all therein died in their beds!"

"My God! It sounds as if there were foul dealings there."

"Pray, m'lord, don't 'ee ask me anything more. Supper is waiting at the Manor for thee. Men do talk, when they have had a dram or two and when those two young 'uns was out of the way, Basil Stavely was clear the next heir and neither king nor Parliament would dispute the title with him now."

"Hmmm," was all Drayton said. Then, after a moment of pause, he added, "and Lady Stavely—does she live in happiness and comfort with this black-browed man?"

"M'lord is going to the Manor. Thee can see better with thine own eyes than with old Matthew's tongue," was the cautious reply.

CLOAK OF FATE

Lord Drayton motioned for his horse and as he set foot in the stirrup he said, "You are a good and honest fellow, Matthew Chester, and do not fear that you have spoken a word too many."

With a wave of his hand and a nudge to the big stallion's flanks, he was away down the lea.

Chapter Three

MARY STAVELY STARED AT HER REFLECTION IN HER DRESSING-TABLE mirror. At thirty-one she knew her beauty was fading. Her auburn hair bore streaks of gray and her brown eyes had a sad, resigned look about them.

She twisted a last curl into place and pinched her cheeks. She had not had a maid of her own since little Annie had run off in the middle of the night. Lady Stavely had her suspicions why the girl had left so abruptly, but she kept them to herself. She got to her feet, arranging her skirts becomingly. She wore an exquisite gown of pale-green figured silk, the bodice seams outlined by delicate *point de Gesne* lace trimming, which was repeated up the center front of the skirt. A dainty lace collar encircled the off-the-shoulder neckline.

Lady Stavely tried a smile, but her lips trembled. Apart from dressing her like a queen—solely to show her off to his friends, she was sure—her husband, Basil, ignored her. Aye, he ignored her except for once a week, when he tore himself away from his gambling friends and other women and came to her to perform his "duty."

Other *women!* Young maids they were for the most part—some hardly more than innocent children—servant girls, tenant and farmers' daughters—oh, she knew about most of them. It made her feel ashamed and humiliated as she was sure he meant her to feel. Others had borne him children, he was quick to point out to her, but she, his beautiful, noble wife, could not give him an heir. The only reason he came to her bed at all, she knew, was in order to try again. He was determined to father a legitimate offspring.

Mary Stavely had carried only one child to full term, and it had been a breech birth which had nearly killed her as it had the poor child. Basil had never let her forget that the babe had been a son. Since then she had suffered through six miscarriages, which had done little to make the prospect of his weekly visit pleasant. He was usually half-drunk when he came to her and the act was completed as speedily as possible so that he could get back to his cronies and their card and dice games.

Basil had come to her bedchamber a half-hour before to tell her they had a guest and she must look her best. He would not tell her who it was, but he did not look too pleased at the prospect.

"Try to act a *little* animated tonight, m'deàr," he had said in his usual sneering tone. "I believe a hostess is supposed to entertain her guests, not bore them to death."

She wondered who this guest might be. A wealthy merchant, perhaps, or a squire from a nearby village. Cavaliers were noticeably absent from their table. Old friends of the family had long since ceased to call. Only her brother, Peter, visited twice a year despite sensing Basil's animosity toward him. His visits were all she had to look forward to.

Lady Stavely sighed again and sprinkled a little cologne onto a lace-trimmed handkerchief. For a moment she held it up to her nose. The scent reminded her of a happier time in her life, a time before she had married Basil Stavely and had been little Mary Ellsbury. She had been considered quite a beauty and had been courted and admired by many of the most wealthy and titled men in the country. There had been parties and balls and music and laughter. But that had been so long ago—before the Protectorate. Tears sprang to her eyes.

Nay! She admonished herself. It was too late for tears. They did not help. Nothing helped. She moved toward the door. Basil would be angry if she did not hurry and she trembled at the thought of incurring his wrath.

Lady Stavely descended the wide staircase that rose through the center of the Manor. Made of heavy black oak, she thought it as dark and ugly as the paneled walls of the great hall below where the weaponry of past generations was displayed in grim reminder of bloody battles won or lost.

As she crossed the empty hall toward the long gallery, a figure stepped out of the shadows and startled her.

"Beg pardon, m'lady, but may I ha' a word wi' thee?"

It was Matthew Chester, the keeper of the chase, and he brought forward a young girl, her hair matted with dirt and her clothing torn and muddied.

"Knowing how kind thee be, I had to bring this lass to see thee, m'lady," Matthew was continuing.

"But what happened to the poor child?" Lady Stavely was instantly sympathetic as she viewed the sorry state of the slim figure before her. Lisa had not raised her head, but she stood several inches taller than the diminutive Lady Stavely.

"She was at the May-Day merrymaking, m'lady. I saw her dancing there, though I ha' ne'er seen her hereabouts 'afore this. On the way back to the Manor I came upon two young ruffians who ha' waylaid her on the road and pulled her into a ditch. They were up to no good wi' her, m'lady." Matthew stopped, his face reddening.

Mary Stavely's soft eyes turned to Lisa who stood with one hand clutching the neck of her blouse where it had been torn open. All thought of her husband and guest left her mind. Her heart went out to this young unfortunate. Men were nothing but beasts! Filthy, lusting animals!

Lisa's long dark hair lay half over her face, mud-caked and tangled. She still had not spoken. Shocked, poor, simple child, Lady Stavely thought, and little wonder! Regardless of ruining her gown, she put her arms around her.

"'Tis all right now, my dear. You are quite safe with me." She nodded to Matthew. "Pray send Mrs. Pottle here, and Matthew, do get Nelly to put some healing salve on your knuckles. They are badly scraped." Her mouth turned up a little. "I can see you took good care of those ruffians."

He grinned, looking a trifle sheepish. "Aye, m'lady, that I did."

When he had left, Lady Stavely drew Lisa closer to the light of a candelabrum. Gently, she tilted up her head, and brushing the hair back from her face gave a little gasp at what she saw. Even covered with dirt, the exquisite beauty was evident.

"Are you all right?" she asked.

Lisa nodded her head. She appeared so young, so untouched by life. Mary Stavely bit her lip. Why were there always brutes around to try and destroy such purity and loveliness?

"Those ruffians did not . . . ?"

Lisa shook her head.

"Thank God for sending Matthew in time," Lady Stavely sighed with relief. "Where is your home, my dear?"

"I have no home," Lisa spoke for the first time, her voice so flat and expressionless that Lady Stavely was not aware of its refinement. "My parents are dead."

"You have no place to go?"

"No. Those men . . . they stole everything I had."

Mary Stavely looked distressed. "I would put you in service here," she said, "but . . ." But Basil would see you and that would be the end of you, she thought.

"What is this?" exclaimed a booming voice and Lady Stavely started visibly, not having heard her husband enter the hall. Sir Basil had been drinking; his face was flushed and his eyes were glittering with anger.

"We are awaiting you, wife," he growled. "What is this that has delayed you?"

"A young maid, Basil, in need of help," Lady Stavely managed, though the insidious, snakelike fear was running through her body. "I know the household is full, but—"

Sir Basil's eyes swept over Lisa and he smiled.

"A beauty in dirt and rags, by the bones of old Noll!" He turned to a gaunt-faced woman dressed in somber black bombazine who had quietly joined them. "We are in need of another scullery maid, Mrs. Pottle. Wash this lass and put her to work with Polly," he commanded.

"Wi-with Polly?" Lady Stavely stammered. "But what about the little Irish maid—Brydie?"

Mrs. Pottle's hard gray eyes regarded Sir Basil for a second before turning to her mistress. "I sent her back to her family yesterday, m'lady," she said, giving an eloquent sniff.

"Back home? But why? I was not consulted. What was the reason for her dismissal?"

"She is with child, m'lady," Mrs. Pottle said quietly, clicking her tongue in indignation.

Mary Stavely's face blanched, yet she forced herself to look up at Sir Basil. He shrugged his shoulders indifferently, but she caught the smug pursing of his thick lips. She uttered a little cry, which she smothered with her own hand. Her reaction amused her husband. He put back his head and roared with laughter.

"No doubt she will have a son," he said. "A big, strong, strapping lad."

"Please, Basil, I beg of you," she implored him, "not in front . . ."

He turned his back on her. "Mrs. Pottle," he said, "take this little lass below stairs and wash her."

Mary Stavely looked despairingly at Lisa, so beautiful even in her filth and rags. God help you, she thought, but even in the midst of her own humiliation, her motherly instincts, so long dormant, came out and she addressed the young maid. "Do not be frightened, my dear. No one will harm you." Her chin even managed to rise a little in defiance. "I will see to that myself."

Sir Basil snorted. "Of course. Her ladyship will attach you to *her* household."

My household, Lady Stavely thought, seeing the derision in Mrs. Pottle's eyes. Oh, Father in heaven!

"Thank you," Lisa whispered and made a curtsy.

"Come now," Sir Basil barked at his wife. "We must see to our guest." He took her arm roughly and drew her away, but not before Lisa had seen the tears that filled the soft brown eyes of Mary Stavely.

Lisa had been in shock. It had taken Sir Basil Stavely's flagrant behavior to his wife, his humiliation of the poor woman before the servants to bring her out of it. Anger had been her panacea. It swept the bleakness from her mind as she followed the straight-backed Mrs. Pottle across the hall and down a corridor to the rear of the house. An intense rage rose in her at this man who had thrown his patent infidelity in the face of his gentle wife. Here was another lecherous pig like Phillip O'Brien and those two ruffians! She had seen the lust in his eyes when he had looked at her. There was no mistaking that wicked gleam. Dear God, was the whole world filled with such as he? Were there no honorable men left? Then she remembered the handsome, golden-haired Cavalier who had kissed her that afternoon. Somehow, she felt sure, that although Lord Drayton might kiss a maid, he would never take her against her will. But then, she considered, he would hardly have to. She could picture maidens prostrating themselves before him, eager for his caresses. How many had he kissed the way he had kissed her? She wondered where he had come from and where he had been headed and then was angry at herself for wondering. She must not think of him! She turned her mind back to the present.

If she decided to stay at Stavely Manor, she would have to beware of Sir Basil—that was evident—but this could prove to be the perfect opportunity for her. How strange that the fates should place her here in Stavely Manor; here where purpose and determination had led her despite her mama's wishes.

When her money and possessions had been stolen from her, she had lost the proof to convince the authorities and thereby confront Basil Stavely to his face. But, she straightened her slim shoulders, perhaps here in Stavely Manor, even if she were forced to work as a servant, she might uncover further proof. There was also the matter of Sir Basil's connection with the three Puritans who had appeared to be plotting something against the king. Sir Basil Stavely's downfall might be right here, within her grasp. Her blue eyes hardened as she thought of how sweet that revenge would be.

Lord Drayton smiled at Mary Stavely across the table. By his expression, one would never have guessed how deeply shocked he was by her changed appearance.

The slender body which used to be carried with such grace was thin to the point of gauntness. The slight shoulders drooped as if they had been forced to support too great a weight. The rich auburn hair—and he remembered its gleaming, golden highlights—had faded to gray-streaked lifelessness and the sparkling eyes had a defeated look in their tawny depths.

She and Sir Basil had no children, so Mary had not been aged by childbearing, he thought. Therefore it must be Stavely, himself, who had caused this pitiful transformation. It was not difficult to imagine. Basil Stavely was an arrogant, pompous bastard! Interested only in power and wealth, it was obvious that he controlled his wife and tenants through fear. He had told Drayton proudly that he kept a tight rein. There was no question of his farmers being late with their rent or his tenants allowed any grace. He had even boasted of stringing up a thieving farmer in the village square and whipping him until his back lay open, as an example to all who might contemplate keeping more grain for themselves than was their due.

"Perhaps he had a large family to feed," was Drayton's quiet comment.

"Thirteen children," Basil had laughed. "A lesson to all not to dip their wicks so often if they cannot afford to feed the result."

Yet after another brandy he was boasting to Drayton of his own wenching and how his bastards must now succeed even the king's in number. Then his face had darkened. "My wife is another matter. No good for breeding, that one. No good at all."

Drayton regarded him with contempt. Apparently all Stavely wanted in a wife was a brooding mare. Poor Mary, he thought. He could imagine what her life was like with Basil Stavely.

Giving her his full attention when she appeared, Drayton had made Mary blush with his compliments, made her smile with his reminiscences of people and events they had both known and experienced, for he had been a frequent guest in her parent's home, being a close friend of her brother, Peter. He had even made her laugh, remembering pranks he and Peter had pulled when they were youngsters.

Mary's eyes had slowly come alive again and she added to the conversation, mentioning other happy times, asking him if he knew what had become of this person and that.

She could not help appraising him in the soft candlelight. What an arresting-looking man Richard Drayton was. The years had only added to his good looks, making him more self-assured, giving a new strength to his broad shoulders, his firm jaw. He looked like a golden lion in his suit of bronze satin. In comparison, Basil reminded her of a surly bear. Richard's startling green eyes gleamed with laughter, Basil's dark ones glowered.

If the war had not come along, would she have had a chance to marry Richard? He had always been so attractive to women. She remembered the one time he had kissed her. It had been at a ball at Lord and Lady Bingham's. He had taken her for a walk in the garden. She had worn a pink satin gown caught up with little seed pearls. For weeks afterward she could think of no one but him, yet then she had caught him kissing her best friend in a darkened hallway and disillusionment had set in. She had even hated him for a while after that. No, she doubted Richard could ever be true to anyone for long. It was probably just as well he had never married.

But now he was telling them both why he had come to Essex; why after the army he had found Whitehall diverting for a time, but that now he wished to attend to the reconstruction of his home and estates which lay some miles to the west of Stavely Manor.

"But surely you do not wish to leave the life at court for any length of time," Sir Basil said, pouring himself another glass of wine.

"I grew up in the country, Basil, and was a soldier for many years," Drayton said, his jaw hardening. "I much prefer the company of honest, hard-working men to the rich London gallants with their artfully curled wigs and affected manners and speech. Oh, I will return to Whitehall, but I plan to live in the country for most of the year."

"I still cannot see you settling down to the life of a country gentleman, Richard," Mary Stavely said in her soft voice. "But perhaps you are keeping something from us. Do you have plans to marry?"

"Marry!" he laughed. "Marriage, my lady, is farthest from my mind." But while he said the words, the memory of a beautiful oval face flashed before his eyes. The guileless expression, the lovely violet-blue eyes, the cloud of soft dark hair.

"No doubt Richard has mistresses enough not to have need of a wife," Sir Basil smirked.

Drayton raised an eyebrow. Such matters were never discussed before a lady. The remark only added to his poor opinion of Stavely.

"Perhaps I would marry," he said with an engaging smile in Mary's direction, "if I could find a wife as beautiful and charming as yours, Basil. I envy you. It seems that nowadays if a lady be beautiful her background is suspect, and yet if she be of noble birth beauty seems abysmally absent." He pulled a long face. "Thus I remain a lonely bachelor."

"Somehow I cannot feel very sorry for you," Mary Stavely laughed. "I do not believe you have tried overhard to find a wife."

Richard then turned the conversation to the court and its diversions, regaling them both with tales of the amazing wagers in the gambling houses in Haymarket, amusing anecdotes of Whitehall's more famous personages, the latest extravagant fashions and the new theatrical endeavors at Covent Garden.

His stories were quite suitable for Lady Stavely's ears and yet witty and entertaining. Mary laughed more than she had in years and even Sir Basil appeared less unpleasant, though she caught him looking at her down the length of the table several times as if bemused by her behavior.

Mary was basking in the thought that Richard had promised to make Stavely Manor his headquarters in the weeks to come, while he traveled back and forth to his own estate. It was very pleasant to contemplate.

Chapter Four

AFTER THE LONG DAY, LORD DRAYTON WAS GLAD TO AT LAST RE-
tire to his room. When he entered his bedchamber, it was to
find a servant girl passing a warming-pan between the sheets of
his oversized bed.

Even the ill-fitting dress could not disguise the perfection of
her figure, and when she lifted her head he was amazed to see
that she was the maid from the fair!

She was even lovelier than he remembered, despite the ugly
mobcap covering her luxuriant hair. His eyes flickered over her
deliberately. Perhaps she would not be adverse to warming his
bed with more than the warming-pan.

"So we meet again." There was a mocking tone to his deep
voice.

"You!" she exclaimed and then remembering her place, Lisa
curtsied, but he noticed by the way she held herself that there
was little of the suppliant in the gesture.

Drayton's eyes did not leave her as he strode purposely
toward her, his tall presence so imposing, the candlelight gilding
him in its glow from his golden head to his bronze satin coat and
pantaloons.

Lisa lowered her gaze before his. She was afraid her admiration must be clearly apparent in her eyes. He was even more wildly handsome than she remembered.

"What is your name?" he asked, stopping before her.

"It is Elizabeth Manning, my lord, but I am called Lisa."

"A pretty name for a pretty maid."

"Thank you, my lord." A faint blush suffused her cheeks, but there was no answering coquetry in the violet-blue eyes. She removed the warming-pan from the bed and placed it on the hearth before the fireplace. She walked proudly, he noticed, and yet there was a demure, untouched air about her. This maid would not easily submit to a man, Drayton pondered, and yet she had let him kiss her at the fair. Why? Could it be that she felt a like attraction to him?

Lisa turned before she reached the door. "Your fireplace appears to be smoking a little, my lord. Would you like me to ask someone to—"

"The fireplace be damned!" he broke in. "Come here!"

"But my lord, I am needed down—"

"Come here!"

Obviously apprehensive, she did not immediately obey him.

"I won't bite you," he said with exasperation. "I just want to know more about you. How came you to Stavely Manor?"

She gave a helpless little glance at the door and then looked back at him. Hesitantly, she took a few steps in his direction.

"I have been at Stavely Manor but a few hours. On continuing to the village after the fair, I was waylaid by two young ruffians." She paused. "I lost my horse and my money and possessions were stolen from me," she finished quietly.

"Good lord!"

"A kind man by the name of Matthew Chester came to my aid, just as . . . just in time. He brought me here and my lady took pity on me."

So it was Matthew who had brought this maid to Stavely Manor, Drayton thought. What a fool thing for him to do! He should never have brought anyone as lovely as she within sight of Basil Stavely's lecherous eye.

"I am sorry such a thing should have happened to you, Lisa, but you should know better than to go about the countryside alone. What of your parents? Would they not—"

"They are both dead, my lord." She swallowed hard. "Now I have lost everything that was left to me." Despite herself, Lisa's soft eyes filled with tears.

"Perhaps something can be recovered. I will speak to Matthew," he said gently, coming toward her, wanting somehow to comfort her, yet noticing that she drew back at his approach.

"You do not trust me, do you?" He shook his golden, leonine head. "Apparently you haven't forgiven me for kissing you this afternoon."

"I should not have let you."

"Why not? Did you not enjoy it? I found it most delightful myself."

"You think to charm me again, my lord, but you will not," her chin rose and she made again for the door.

"You are very lovely, Lisa. One cannot help but try to charm you." His deep voice had an intimate, caressing tone to it now.

In a few strides he was beside her, towering over her, his big hand covering hers on the latch of the door.

At the touch of his hand, she felt a strange sensation surge through her. He was so powerfully built and she was alone with him in his bedchamber. The wide eyes looked up at him fearfully.

"I have upset you," he said, removing his hand. "I have no wish to detain you against your will or frighten you. You simply intrigued me and I was curious to learn more about you."

Lisa wanted to run away from him, to escape from the feeling that, although he had not done so, his arms were already around her. She had felt the strength of those arms and now she realized that the power that seemed to exude from him was stronger still.

She stared at him, seeing the glimmer of amusement in the emerald eyes. It was as though he had read her mind. She wrenched open the door and fled.

Drayton was still standing in the same spot a moment later when his manservant knocked and entered.

"I can attend myself," Drayton gestured him away. "Get some sleep, Ned."

As the door closed, he sighed and crossed to the bed. He shed his clothing quickly and draped it over a chair before climbing between the warmed sheets. There would be no impatient young body to claim him tonight.

Chapter Five

AFTER LEAVING SIR BASIL AND LADY STAVELY, MRS. POTTLE HAD taken Lisa down to the laundry room.

"Thee can use one of them tubs to wash up in," she said gruffly, "but thee will have to haul the hot water from the kitchen thyself."

Lisa had obeyed, struggling down the stone steps with several heavy kettles of water before the cook complained that it was suppertime and she could spare no more.

Lisa bathed herself using a cake of strong soap that reddened her soft skin. While she washed her hair, she considered whether she should enter into the servant's role completely. She had a good ear and it would not be difficult for her to affect the country accent in her speech or to be convincing in the part of scullery maid. Yet she realized that her only hope of learning more about Stavely Manor was to be placed in a position above the kitchen. She decided not to change her natural speaking voice or manner. Lady Stavely, Lisa was sure, would soon recognize this fact and elevate her to a more responsible position.

When she pulled on the servant's dress that Mrs. Pottle had left for her, Lisa found that it was much too big, but when she tied on the apron it brought the dress tighter about her slim waist. She had not time to dry her hair, for Mrs. Pottle was calling her name, so she just stuck it up, still damp, under the mobcap, and carrying the kettles ran back up to the kitchen.

Lisa was quickly put to work helping with the supper and the cleaning up afterward. It was dark by the time everything was finished, yet Mrs. Pottle muttered to her about being shorthanded due to May Day and extra chores she would need Lisa for later in the evening.

Another housemaid, Polly, a buxom lass in her early twenties, showed Lisa where she was to sleep. It was a dark room down a hall behind the pantry. It had two beds—little more than pallets—with a small clothes chest between them and a rush mat on the floor. There was a high window that faced the stables and a distinct odor permeated the room from that direction.

Polly occupied the other bed in the room. She was a slatternly girl with brown hair straggling out from under her mobcap. That she was not very tidy was evidenced by her unmade bed and several articles of clothing lying about on the floor.

Lisa looked around the little bedchamber and wondered what she was supposed to wear to bed.

"Wha's the matter?" Polly stood in the doorway, her hands on her hips. "'Tis not grand 'nough for 'ee?"

"I have no nightdress," Lisa explained. "My clothing was all stolen."

Polly walked over to the clothes chest and lifted the lid.

"Wear Brydie's," she said. "There's also a 'ousedress o' 'ers left 'ere."

Lisa looked in the chest and saw some clothing nicely laundered and folded on one side. On the other, obviously Polly's side, clothes had been stuffed in helter-skelter.

Polly spied Lisa's neck as she straightened up. A dark, ugly bruise was evident at the neckline of her dress.

"'ear 'ee was put upon on the road," she said. "Was it Matthew who rescued 'ee?"

Lisa nodded, then shuddered, remembering. "I lost everything I had. My clothes, my money—"

"But not thy maiden'ood, eh?" Polly grinned. "Or 'ave 'ee already lost that?"

Lisa could not prevent the blush that spread over her cheeks. She shook her head.

"Still a virgin?" Polly looked incredulous. "At thy age?"

Lisa's chin went up at that. "Aye," she said proudly.

"'ow long are 'ee goin' to 'ang on t' it?" Polly sneered.

"I don't see that that is any of your concern."

"Oh, pardon *me!*" Polly stuck her nose in the air.

"I just believe in saving myself for the man I marry."

Polly burst out laughing. "An' who's 'e t' be? A prince on a white charger?" She laughed even harder at the scarlet-faced Lisa. "I was goin' to ask 'ee t' join me at the May-Day romp tonight at the stables," she snorted, "but 'alf the fun's the rollin' in the 'ay."

Polly ignored her then as she changed from her servant's dress to a not-too-clean blouse that revealed a good deal of her ample white breasts. A brightly colored skirt was pulled on over her well-rounded hips. A wooden comb was used to comb out her lank hair.

"Don't expect me 'afore dawn," she laughed as she flounced out the door.

Soon after Polly had left, Mrs. Pottle called Lisa to accompany her upstairs. The little upstairs maid had disappeared soon after supper, and the housekeeper was afraid that in her haste to depart she might not have properly attended to the guest bedchamber.

Lisa followed Mrs. Pottle up the sturdy oaken staircase and across the upper gallery. After living in the confines of a small caravan most of her life, the manor house seemed vast indeed to her.

The bedchamber was spacious and the furniture large and comfortable. It was clearly a room for a gentleman.

The housekeeper immediately noticed that soap and water had not been provided and Lisa was sent to fetch them from below stairs. She did not envy the little upstairs maid. She could imagine the tongue-lashing that one would receive in the morning.

Checking that everything was to her satisfaction, Mrs. Pottle departed, leaving Lisa to warm the bed. It was at this task, a moment later, that Lord Drayton had found her.

After her encounter with him, Lisa had run back to her room, her heart pounding. As she lay trying to sleep on her hard little bed, Polly's taunting words kept going around and around in her head. "Who's 'e t' be? A prince on a white charger?"

No, she thought, not a prince. But he did have a title and he rode a magnificent stallion. How tall and handsome he was with his golden hair and flashing green eyes. She put a hand to her mouth, remembering the wonder of his kiss. There was a soft smile on her lips when she finally fell asleep.

Chapter Six

THE NEXT MORNING LADY STAVELY AND LORD DRAYTON HAD breakfast together. Drayton intended to leave for his estates directly after the meal.

"I hope you will not think it rude of me," he was saying, "if I make an early departure. 'Tis a fair ride."

"Of course not. No doubt you are eager to see your old home and what can be done to restore it."

"I am," he agreed, smiling at her, "but I intend to return in time to dine with you this evening."

She looked at him a little shyly. "I don't want you to feel you must restrict your movements while you are with us. I hope you will feel free to come and go as you please. It—it means so much just to have an old friend near—" she stopped, extending her hand to him.

Drayton rose and gallantly bowed over the delicate little hand. "Your kindness is most reassuring, Mary. It makes me hope there may be others from my boyhood who have not forgotten me. You may be sure," he added with sincerity, "that I will always remain your loyal friend." He kissed the cold fingertips.

"Ah, Richard," she sighed, as he resumed his seat across from her, "I only wish you could remember Mary Ellsbury as you had last seen her—young and happy—then the present Mary Stavely—so aged and weary. What was it you said? Friend? How sweet the name when one has none."

"What is this, Mary? You are the mistress of Stavely Manor. You have a husband who cares for you and—"

"Cares for me!" she interrupted, the blood rushing to her pale cheeks. "Are you blind, Richard, that you cannot see how he treats me? My husband! I doubt he has *ever* loved me. I merely passed the first two requirements he wished for in a wife. I had noble blood and was not unpleasant to look at. But I have failed the third requirement badly, I am afraid, and as a result I bear days of anguish and nights of fear. And yet you speak as if in him I could find a friend!" Her soft voice had risen and her hands were shaking so that she had to put down her knife and fork. "What can you mean—"

"I mean," said Drayton, leaning closer to her, his voice deep and earnest, "that I have dared force from you what I had already surmised. I am so sorry, Mary. I want you to know that in me you have a friend who will be there if ever he is needed."

"Oh, Richard!" Mary's face lit up with joy and she put a hand over his. Then, an instant later the pale gray pallor came down again upon her face and she said entreatingly, "Nay! I should not have spoken out. 'Twill only cause trouble for you."

Drayton grinned at this. "And do you not think I have been in trouble before? Basil Stavely does not frighten me, Mary."

"But he should!" Her voice dropped to a hoarse whisper. "He is not a good man. I have heard ugly rumors. There are strangers he meets in secret and . . . and I do not believe he rightfully came to Stavely Manor."

So Matthew Chester had been right, Drayton thought to himself.

"There is much I would discern here, but I will be discreet," he assured her. "Above all else, one acquires discretion at the Court of Whitehall."

They ate in silence for a few minutes and then Mary spoke again. "There is one other thing you should know, Richard. Basil has . . . he has other women," she admitted, color staining her cheeks.

"A mistress?" he asked.

"No. There are many. I don't really mind," she said hastily, "since it means he leaves me alone most of the time. You see, I have miscarried six children and another was stillborn and—"

"Mary," his deep voice was very gentle, "you don't have to tell me—"

"But I want you to know what hurts me much more than the fact that Basil is unfaithful. 'Tis . . . 'tis that he often forces himself on young, innocent girls—the housemaids—the workers' daughters—nothing young and even passably pretty is safe from him. These girls are not willing, but they are too afraid, too terrified to do anything about it."

"Surely some have fathers or brothers who would—"

Mary shook her head. "Times are hard, Richard. The men are afraid they will lose their own positions or be turned off the land if they complain."

No wonder their surliness to Stavely at the May-Day festivities, Drayton thought. Aloud he growled, "The man doesn't deserve to be master of a dog!"

"No," Mary said, meeting his blazing eyes, "he does not. Though I betray him by saying it." She bowed her head and began clasping and unclasping her hands. Her voice when she spoke again was so low that Drayton had to bend toward her to catch her words.

"Basil is a beast, Richard. I have seen what he has done to some of those girls. I have nursed . . ." She started to cry.

"Mary." He put a sympathetic hand over hers. "Have you never told your brother about this?"

"Aye," she sniffed, "and once Peter tried to speak to Basil. . . . That is why he is only welcome here twice a year, although he does not live that far away. He comes for my birthday and at Christmas."

"You must not think about—" Richard paused, hearing steps outside the room. "Someone is coming. You are agitated. Perhaps . . ."

"Aye. I had best retire. I will see you this evening."

Without a moment's hesitation, Lady Stavely arose and hurried across the room to the servant's door. Even as she disappeared through it, the opposite door opened and Basil Stavely strode in.

"Was that Mary leaving?" he demanded.

"Aye, it was, Basil. She said she had something to attend to in the kitchen." Drayton calmly continued with his breakfast, outwardly composed but inwardly seething at his host.

"Mary is a very domestic little mouse." Basil's laugh was sardonic.

CLOAK OF FATE

"A pleasing quality in a wife." -

"True, but there are other qualities men like you and I might find *more* pleasing," Stavely gave a meaningful wink as he sat down at the head of the table.

Drayton said nothing as Master Pottle, Stavely's steward of the household, immediately appeared with Sir Basil's breakfast.

Pottle was a stout but imposing figure and took his position very seriously.

Sir Basil dove into his food like a starving animal, stuffing his mouth just before he spoke, so that it was difficult for Drayton to comprehend his first words.

"Enjoy' y' tales o' Whi'hall las' even', Richar'." He swallowed a great gulp of ale and his words became clearer. "As a loyal Royalist," he said, his eyes never leaving his plate, "what is the current feeling in London? Is everyone well-pleased with the king, or is the honeymoon of the Restoration over?"

Drayton frowned as he regarded his host. What was on Basil Stavely's mind? He had tried to sound casual, but Drayton had the distinct feeling that there was something more behind his question. He must not underestimate this man. Stavely was no fool, though he might play the part. He was a cunning and clever schemer who had become master of Stavely Manor by his own manipulative means.

"Charles still retains his popularity," Drayton drawled. "At least the people are left to live their lives as they please. Cromwell didn't allow that with his stern Puritan restrictions and bans. Of course there are those who would wish the king would become more moderate in his spending and perhaps devote more time to the government and less to his mistresses."

"And what are your feelings, Richard?"

"Charles lived in exile for many years with little money. It must be a great temptation for him to overspend."

"But there is still widespread religious intolerance."

"The king himself has no desire to persecute people, but he must support the established church."

"The taxes get higher every year."

"He has paid out much to reward his loyal followers for losing all they had in support of him."

"Humph! You paint a different picture than most."

"Most do not know him as I do. Charles has his weaknesses, but he is a kind and generous man."

"Perhaps one day I will have the good fortune to meet him. I have heard it mentioned that he may visit Watford this spring. 'Tis not many miles hence."

Drayton shrugged. "I have no idea of the royal itinerary."

Sir Basil grew silent. He had hoped Drayton might have more knowledge of the king's activities, but if he did he was being closemouthed about them. Perhaps during Drayton's stay he might succeed in gaining his confidence.

"I am afraid I must ask you to excuse me," his guest was saying. "I should be on my way."

"You are off for the day?"

"Aye. I want to view Calderwood. See if there is anything worth saving or whether it should be completely torn down and rebuilt."

"A tragedy it was destroyed. A real tragedy. Mary tells me 'twas built in your grandfather's time."

"It was designed, in the Italianate style, by the architect Inigo Jones."

"Was it besieged in the war?"

"Aye. My mother, who was widowed by then, and my brother and sister had taken in some wounded Royalists. They tried, with some loyal tenants and servants, to hold it against Cromwell's troopers, but muskets were no match against cannon," Drayton recounted bitterly.

"Were they *all* killed?" Basil asked, rather insensitively, as he chewed loudly on a piece of meat.

"Aye," Drayton replied, his voice cold and hard. "The house was virtually cut down on top of them."

Stavely let out an oath, and Drayton's head came up at the loud exclamation. Were Basil's feelings so vehement against the Roundheads? But that had apparently not been the reason for his outburst. Drayton watched in astonishment as Stavely rose, picked up his plate and flung it against the fireplace. The pewter plate bounced off the gray stone, leaving a spreading stain of meat and gravy which dripped and ran down onto the hearth.

"Tough as saddle leather," Stavely growled. "Mary will hear about this!" Without another word he strode furiously from the hall, slamming the door behind him.

A minute later Master Pottle silently entered the room, took a frowning look at the fireplace and withdrew. As Drayton rose from the table, a housemaid entered with a scrub brush and pail. She quietly knelt down before the fireplace and began to scrub the splattered stones.

"Does this happen often?" Drayton inquired, still astonished by the tantrum he had just witnessed.

"I would not know, my lord."

He recognized the soft, cultured voice.

"Good lord, are they making you do every menial task about this house?"

"We are shorthanded," Lisa answered, continuing her scrubbing.

"Come here!" he demanded.

She hesitated a moment, then rose to her feet and approached him, the dripping scrub brush still clasped in one hand.

"Come closer!"

The bright morning light coming through the diamond-leaded glass windows illumined the flawless skin, the fine-boned features. There was a rosy tint to her cheeks caused by her exertions. The soft violet-blue eyes met his and he was startled by their candor, their lack of servility. He had been right then. This lass was not of the servant class.

He towered over her, so magnificent in his well-fitting riding clothes and long, soft leather boots. His eyes were so incredibly green, she thought. She felt so breathless beneath his gaze, yet she did not look away.

Drayton frowned suddenly. "Does Lady Stavely know you are of gentle birth?" he said quietly.

"Gentle birth?"

"Do not deny it. It is obvious by the way you speak—by your every gesture."

"I was raised and educated as a gentlewoman," Lisa admitted, "but I have worked for my living for three years."

He reached for one of her hands, turning it over so that the recent blisters on the palm were clearly evident.

"But not with your hands."

"There are other ways."

The green eyes darkened for a second as he regarded her. Was her apparent innocence a mockery—a deceiving mask?

Heat suffused Lisa's cheeks at his cynical appraisal. "How *dare* you think that of me?" she said indignantly, forgetting her position.

He lifted an eyebrow. "Think *what* of you?" There was now a twitch to the corner of his lips.

"You—you know." She was flustered now and the color in her cheeks had deepened.

"Tell me what I thought?" he asked, not able to resist teasing her. How breathtakingly beautiful she was as she proudly tossed her little head at him, those huge violet eyes ablaze with anger.

"You thought I was no better than I should be," she declared hotly.

He burst out laughing. "If I did, the thought was quickly dispelled. Unfortunately, deviousness to me is synonymous with women and innocence an unknown quality. I should have remembered how you trembled when I kissed you at the fair and that whores do not blush so easily."

Her eyes were black with anger. "You are . . . you are despicable!" She turned her back on him and went back to work at the fireplace.

He let out a roar of laughter. "Quite true. And insufferable and contemptible and unspeakable. I've been called them all."

Her mouth quirked a little at that, but she continued her scrubbing.

He walked over to stand beside her. "May I have a guess at your profession?" He considered a moment. "I would say your work might have leaned toward the academic—something very proper and bookish." He rubbed his chin.

"Then you would be wrong, my lord. I was an actress," she said proudly, rising to her feet, a challenging look in her eyes.

"An actress!"

"Aye. My father had a theatrical troupe, 'The Manning Shakesperean Players.' We toured most of England."

"How extraordinary!"

"Not really. My father was a wonderful actor and my mother—" Lisa stopped. "They are both gone now."

"I am sorry," he said. Obviously the lass had been left destitute. He changed the subject. "Will you tell me something, Lisa? Was it Lady Stavely who offered you a position here?"

"Nay, it was not. I think my lady wished to, but something held her back. 'Twas Sir Basil who hired me."

Drayton stared down at her. It was obvious to him why Basil Stavely had given her a position. The bastard was probably waiting his chance to get his hands on her. He resolved to speak to Mary upon his return that evening. The lass must be put somewhere out of Stavely's reach.

His eyes did not leave Lisa as she set to work again. He would like to have learned more about her. The girl was an enigma. That she was innocent, he had no doubt. She was a beautiful, ingenuous creature with no self-consciousness in her frank eyes. He was puzzled. How could she have been an actress? His knowledge of actresses was that they were usually from the lower classes and not of the highest moral character. Why, most were little better than common prostitutes.

Drayton pondered over the girl as he waited in the empty hall for Ned to bring the horses around. Lisa was clearly a mystery, a mystery he thought might prove quite delightful to solve.

He paced the oaken floor, his spurs keeping a sort of clinking time to his steps and the whip in his hand occasionally tapping the soft buff leather of the thigh-high riding boots.

Stavely Manor was a house of mysteries. Perhaps if he stayed long enough he might unravel some and at the same time help poor, gentle Mary. Yet, he wondered, if he meddled in Basil Stavely's affairs he might add to the poor lady's troubles. Should he leave well enough alone? He frowned and the whip came down with a gesture of force on the Spanish leather at his thigh. To hell with Basil Stavely! He would do all he could to alleviate Mary's troubles and if Stavely tried to take it out on her, he had best beware. Drayton had dealt with worse enemies.

The handsome black stallion was being stubborn this morning. He pawed the ground angrily as Lord Drayton strode down the front steps of the manor house and approached him. Taking the reins from Ned, he swung up easily into the saddle.

The stallion at once threw up his head and reared in a wild attempt to throw the man from his back. Drayton hung on.

From the dining-hall window, Lisa watched admiringly as Lord Drayton controlled the spirited horse fearlessly and skillfully before setting off down the road at a gallop.

As he disappeared from view, Lisa gathered up her brush and pail. Perhaps she would have a moment to explore a little more of the Manor before returning to the kitchen.

Chapter Seven

THE PARTY AT THE STABLES HAD BEEN WILD AND NOISY AND THE drunken laughter and lusty singing had kept Lisa awake until the wee hours of the morning.

Lisa felt she had only been asleep a moment when she awoke with a dishevelled Polly staggering against her bed. There were bits of straw in the girl's tangled hair and her blouse was ripped from one shoulder. She was so drunk that Lisa had to get up and help her, but before she could undress Polly, the girl had fallen back on her bed and was soon fast asleep. Lisa covered her up and went back to her own bed just as Polly began to snore loudly and wheezily. She burrowed under her pillow and again closed her eyes. Before she knew it, daylight was filtering through the tiny window of the bedchamber and she was being shaken awake by Mrs. Pottle.

"Get that lazy Polly up," the woman said to Lisa. " 'Tis her job to light the fires an' yer t' help her."

Lisa tried her best to wake Polly, but it was no use. The girl only groaned and turned over. In the end, Lisa told Mrs. Pottle and the others who had gathered in the kitchen that Polly appeared to be ill. This remark was greeted by rude snorts of laughter.

As Nelly, the cook, had already got the fires going, Mrs. Pottle put Lisa to work with the mop and broom. It was not until late in the morning, long after Lisa's encounter with Lord Drayton in the dining hall, that Polly finally appeared to help her.

"Bitch!" Polly spat. "Why didn't 'ee wake me? Thought t' get me in trouble, did 'ee?"

Lisa's blue eyes flared. "Why, you ungrateful little—"

"So 'ee do ha' some spirit after all," Polly scowled. "'ee hide it well before old Pottle. Tryin' t' get on her good side?"

"No. I am just trying to do my job. You should thank me. I told her you were sick."

"Ayé, that I am," Polly grunted. "Got a 'ead on me like a strikin' anvil."

"Then why don't you go back to bed? I will manage the rest of the cleaning."

"'ee would, wouldn't 'ee? And get me in *more* trouble. Maybe me wages docked this time."

Lisa sighed wearily. Polly was not going to make things easy for her, she could see that. "I only thought if you were ill—"

"I only thought if you were ill—" Polly imitated her in a high affected voice. "Look, Miss 'igh n' mighty, give me that bloomin' broom. I'll sweep the 'all, thank 'ee, and 'ee can go and scrub down the kitchen."

It was a long and exhausting day for Lisa, who was not used to hard physical work. She had scrubbed the entire floor of the stone-flagged passage to the kitchen, the kitchen itself and the pantry. Her hands were rough and red and the blisters had broken on her palms and were sore and painful. How she wished she had some of the soothing balm Zada used to make from cowslips for Valerie's tender skin.

Yet, despite her weariness and discomfort, never once did Lisa waver in her determination to stay on at Stavely Manor. Although Polly had been in an ugly temper all day and Mrs. Pottle had chided her on her slowness, there had been one who had been kind to her. Plump Nelly, the cook, with her round flushed face and laughing blue eyes. She had even managed to save her some soup at noontime when Lisa had been late to the table.

Matthew appeared in the kitchen just before supper and Lisa caught him giving Nelly a squeeze in the corner, beneath a string of onions and drying herbs. She had already learned that they were planning to wed at Michaelmas.

"So there thee are," he said, reddening when he realized she had observed him. "I ha' some news for thee."

Lisa's eyes lit up. "Is it about my things?" she asked.

He shook his head. "No trace ha' been found of that pouch with your money, lass, but I ha' a surprise for thee outside." He nodded toward the door.

"I must help Nelly, Matthew—"

"Go along wi' 'ee lass," said that woman, turning back to basting some chickens on a spit over the fire. "But be quick about it."

Matthew took Lisa out a back door and around the side of the house to where he had secured a horse to a hitching post.

"That be your mare?"

"It's Primrose!" Lisa cried as soon as she caught sight of the horse. Rushing over to it she threw her arms around the mare's neck, burying her nose in its gray mane.

"Thank you, Matthew," she said, turning at last to the smiling man.

"A nice little mare she is." He nodded, but his face had gone solemn. "How did thee come by her?" he asked.

"Don't you worry, Matthew, I didn't steal her. She belongs to me. I brought her from . . ." And then she told him about the acting troupe and her mother's death and having to leave in such a hurry.

"But thee should not be working here as a scullery maid," he said, frowning.

"I have no money now, and it is honest work."

"Dang it, working with the likes of Polly and some o' the others ain't right somehow . . . not for someone like thee."

"And who is someone like me?" she smiled.

"A good lass. Don't take much to see that."

"Thank you," she said, "but don't worry about me."

"Can't help it. Thee reminds me o' me daughter, Jane. A good lass she be too, bringing' up the other children when their mother died."

"How big a family do you have, Matthew?"

"Four young 'uns, countin' Jane."

Lisa patted the horse's nose. "Would you be able to keep Primrose for me, Matthew? At your home? The children are welcome to ride her if they would like."

"I would be glad to look after her for thee," Matthew agreed, smiling down at her. "An' whenever thee would like to ride her, I'll have 'er ready."

He unfastened a bag from the saddle and handed it to her.

"Here be thy belongings. Take care now and . . ." He looked around him and lowered his voice. "Stay clear o' the master. He fancys pretty young 'uns like thee."

"Thank you again, Matthew." Lisa stood on tiptoe and kissed the weathered cheek.

It was nearly twilight when Lord Drayton came in sight of Stavely Manor.

It had been a bleak day for him, a day of lamenting over a black and empty ruin that had once been a home. Staring at the stark remains, he had almost heard again the familiar sounds that had once resounded through the lofty rooms. The cries of his brother and sister and the scampering of their feet on the stairs, the happy music and laughter and the joys and sorrows of a closely knit family who had loved one another dearly.

Now he was the only one left to mourn.

It hurt Drayton to remember the splendidly designed structure and to see such beauty despoiled. The mansion was like a ravished woman. Could she ever return to her former innocence and charm? Would there not always be bitter memories there? Would it not be better to pull it down completely and start afresh—not from the old plans but a totally new residence?

Drayton mulled over these thoughts as he and Ned retraced their route to Stavely Manor. On the morrow he would return and tour his land completely. He needed a balm to his spirit and he felt the beauty of the countryside and the green open fields would supply it.

As they reached the bridge below the lea, Drayton looked up to see the Maypole still standing on the rise, a few ragged streamers clinging bravely to it in the breeze. It made him think of the maid, Lisa, and realize that it was not the first time that day that she had entered his mind. He kept seeing those beautiful eyes, so vivid and intense. Their color defied description. Not blue in the true sense—darker—huge and luminous and soft as velvet. When he had taken her small hand that morning, he had seen how delicately shaped her fingers were. Those hands should not be scrubbing a rough, stone hearth. Their only labor should be in working embroidery or soothing the brow of a fevered child. They were so like his mother's hands—cool and soft and gentle.

He was suddenly angry. Why was such a beautiful creature forced to do such common labor, slaving for such a licentious bastard as Basil Stavely? He must speak to Mary. Tell her about Lisa. Get the maid placed under Mary's protection. Mary's protection? What could poor, gentle Mary do to stop Basil from taking the maid if he wanted her?

"M'lord!" Ned was shouting at him and he turned his head to see his manservant dismounting from his horse and hastening over to the river's edge.

Drayton turned the stallion's head and went back, tethering both horses to a nearby tree before he joined Ned beside the river.

The man was struggling to pull something from the water. It looked like . . . it was . . . a body! The body of a woman! Drayton saw the long wet strands of hair. His heart turned over. The hair was dark like Lisa's and she wore the same sort of servant's dress he had seen Lisa wearing! Oh God, no! Drayton dropped down beside the body and turned it over. He pushed back the dripping tentacles that clung to her face. He had never seen the maid before! He felt himself let out his breath, unaware that he had been holding it. The maid was young and, he judged, had not been in the water more than a day. As his eyes moved lower, he saw the rounded belly. It was evident she had been expecting a child.

Was this the work of Basil Stavely? He wondered. He remembered Mary's words that morning: "Nothing young and even passably pretty is safe from him." Had this poor maid been ravished and then become so distraught over her condition that she had taken her own life?

"Place her across your saddle, Ned," he said in a tight voice. "We will take her up to the manor house. Perhaps they can identify her there."

Chapter Eight

THE LIBRARY WALLS AND CEILING WERE PANELED IN STAINED OAK and the room was always dark, even in the daytime. Now it was after midnight and at the library table sat the three men Lisa had overheard at the fair, awaiting their host.

Two rushlights at either end of the oak table barely illuminated their faces. The men all wore hats and their swords were buckled to their sides as if they might at any moment be called to set down their wine goblets and grasp their blades.

They had been sitting in silence for a time, carefully listening. It was Timotheus Webster (plain "Timothy" before the Puritan era) who spoke first. He was a short, burly man with a red, heavy-joweled face. There was an impatient tone to his voice.

"'Tis after midnight. What is keeping our host?"

"Our host!" echoed Thomas Carver with a snort of contempt. Carver was of a different appearance to the good-living Webster or to the other man present, Jonathan Brintnall, who was tall and gaunt with a perpetually righteous expression. Carver's face and build were strong, like that of a soldier. He had been known and dreaded even in Cromwell's time, having many dangerous adventures to his credit.

"Methinks," he went on, "that *we* hold nearly as good a title to be 'hosts' in Stavely Manor as *he!* If this enterprise succeeds

46

and Charles Stuart dies, we hold Stavely and its wealth in our hands. If it fails, his fear of the headsman will drive him hence—and then who shall be 'host' here, eh, brother Brintnall?"

"Nevertheless, I like not this place without his presence," was the anxious reply. "He should have escaped all prying eyes by this time."

"Hark! Perhaps that be his step now?"

"Let us hope so," said Carver and as he spoke the door behind them opened with a certain care and little noise and Basil Stavely entered, closing and locking it behind him with a caution foreign to his nature.

"You are late, brother Stavely," was the quiet comment of Brintnall, as the host flung himself into one of the heavy leather chairs at the table.

"Aye! I have a curst Cavalier staying with me. Had to be careful he was safe abed."

"It appears thee have joined him in more than one tankard," said Carver, his eyes contemptuously sizing up his host.

"It be a wonder I'm not foxed, surrounded by a household such as mine. Well-nigh having fits over a little scullery maid who drowned herself in yon river."

"What! A drowning! A bad time to call attention to this house."

"No fault of mine," Stavely growled. "'Twas Lord Drayton, my guest, who found the body and brought it to the Manor."

Carver was looking at Sir Basil closely. "Thee seem nervous, Stavely. 'Tis possible thee be at the cause of this little maid's drowning?"

Stavely struggled to his feet, his hand clutching his sword hilt. "Your pardon, sir!"

Carver put up a hand. "Here now, no offense, but it *has* been rumored hereabouts that thee have a certain—er—fondness for pretty young wenches." His smile was a trifle too familiar. "Perhaps this one did not want to mother thy bastard."

"Who told you that lie? Who dares to spread such falseness? I have just suffered an evening of accusing faces and wifely tears over one who was no better than she should be. A strumpet, plain and simple."

Stavely grabbed the huge half-demijohn of wine from the center of the table and poured himself a gobletful, swallowing near half of it in a single gulp.

"Libertine!" murmured Brintnall under his breath. "Can we trust a man when his own family—"

Stavely hit the table with one of his big fists.

"My house may, for the day, harbor hostility to me, but trust me to cut it off when it is time."

Sir Basil might not have made this threat if he had known that there was someone just outside the library door with an ear pressed carefully to it.

"Time passes," Webster was saying. "Will you confer with us now, Stavely?"

Sir Basil nodded, rubbing a hand across his eyes. "Have you arranged the plan?"

"Yes, we have," murmured Brintnall, taking a thin packet of papers from his doublet and spreading them out upon the table. "We have learned that Charles Stuart will be coming to Watford the beginning of June, accompanied by some of his court. The plan is for our men to lie hidden in the woods beyond Watford Heath, and on the day when the king and his brother James pass by on their way thither, we will rush forth from the woods in a surprise attack."

"Humph!" said Stavely, examining the opened papers of the plan, though with no great care. "The arrangements seem good, but what of these men of yours? Can you vouch for their mettle? Remember there is always the possibility that not *all* will escape, and no triflers should be trusted with our necks as well as their own."

"Good men and true, as ever butchered a Cavalier!" was Thomas Carver's blunt assurance.

"Four of them were in Ireton's regiment at Naseby," corroborated Webster.

"And the rest?"

"Have all been under my command before," Carver said.

"When will you know the actual day for the ambush?"

"We will be informed when the royal party leaves London."

"That will give us very little time," Stavely pondered. "Lord Drayton, my guest, has many respected friends at court. Perhaps, if I keep an ear pealed, I may be able to obtain from him the actual day the king will be expected at Watford."

Carver's eyes lit up. "That would go much in thy favor," he assured Stavely.

"So much for the plan," Sir Basil said hastily. "Have you the bond, for without it I stir not a step in the matter?"

"Aye, it is here," replied Webster, in his turn taking papers from his doublet and throwing them upon the table, where they were at once grasped by Stavely and examined with much more care than the others had been.

His eyes swept over the list, counting the names appended. "Aye, it appears they are all here, except your own names and mine. There!" He grasped a pen from a ready inkhorn and dashed off his signature boldly. "Remember, my friends, I am not a fool and I know that the risk is a desperate one, yet I dare it. I have staked enough, aye, lost enough, thanks to you and others. Now I am putting my head on the block."

"Aye, thy head, but *our* necks!" said Carver, with his usual boldness. He seized the pen and scrawled his name beneath the other. "Thy head, Stavely, because thou art a gentleman, but the hangman for us who are of the people. There *is* a difference."

"Nay. What difference, one death or another?" said Brintnall, and slowly and laboriously he affixed his signature. "The monarchy must be destroyed and the righteous men possess the earth."

"And now," said Sir Basil rising, "take your plan again, Master Brintnall, for I have no need of it. But this"—he indicated the bond—"I will place in yonder oaken chest, well-locked, and it will lie safely till the time it shall be brought to use. Drink, all of us, in this burgundy, red as the blood that will soon flow for this night's work." He filled the goblets and each grasped one as he spoke: "Drink to the hands that will strike down old Rowley and erase the monarchy once and for all!"

The whole household was shocked by the apparent suicide of little Brydie, the young Irish housemaid.

Finishing up in the kitchen after supper, Nelly said angrily, "The master be as guilty of Brydie's death as if he had thrown her into the river himself."

Polly looked over her shoulder. "Shhh! 'E *is* the master, Nelly. 'E can do as 'e likes."

"He should not be allowed to," Lisa said quietly.

"Really?" Polly snorted. "Who's to stop 'im? 'ee with thy fine speech and ladylike airs? 'e'll bring 'ee down too, 'e will. See if 'e don't."

"I'd rather die first!"

"That's just what Brydie said." Polly shook her head. "But

she died *afterward*. Fancy 'er takin' 'er own life and she a good Catholic too. Doomed 'er soul to 'ell she did and why I say?"

"She must have been at her wit's end, poor thing."

Lisa had been asleep for only an hour when she awoke, her heart pounding. She opened her eyes to just slits and saw a large dark shape holding a lantern move from the doorway in the direction of Polly's bed. The big man stumbled over a shoe and cursed under his breath. The noise did not wake Polly, who still continued to snore noisily.

The figure set down the lantern and came closer to the bed. One large hand shook Polly's shoulder.

The girl came awake then, rubbing at her eyes. "'O is it?" she exclaimed. "Wha's the matter?"

"Got something here for you, girl," chuckled a deep voice.

To Lisa's horror, she recognized the man. It was Sir Basil, tearing open his breeches, his rigid organ ready.

"Wha' about 'er?" Polly nodded in Lisa's direction. "Wouldn't 'ee rather ha' the little virgin?" There was a malicious hiss to the words that made Lisa freeze.

"Hell with wailing virgins. Want an eager wench for once." The voice was louder, slurred with drink, as he yanked the covers from the buxom maid.

Polly giggled and thrust her nightdress up above her waist, lewdly spreading her sturdy white legs.

"Come on then, Sir Stallion," she laughed. "Polly's always eager."

Without even removing his boots, Sir Basil fell on her, his clumsy fingers fumbling for one of the pendulant breasts.

"'ey! Easy there," Polly cried. "Give us a chance."

The bodies thrashed about, the small bed protesting under them.

Lisa's eyes were shut tight now, her head thrust under the covers, but she heard Polly's gasp as Sir Basil drove into her and desperately she tried to cover her ears. Still, she could not escape the grunting, urgent noises of their copulation so close beside her, the hoarse breathing, the squeak of the bed moving with the rhythm of his thrusts, faster, faster, until the convulsive completion.

Oh God, they were no better than animals! Lisa thought. Never, never would she let a man use her that way. Her body was her own, and she swore she would keep it inviolate. Only the man that claimed her love would ever possess it.

She lay awake a long time before sleep claimed her again, but Polly was snoring almost before Sir Basil's heavy footsteps disappeared down the hall.

Lisa was summoned to Lady Stavely's bedchamber the next morning. Mrs. Pottle led her to the door and knocked. With the answering "Come in," they entered the bright, spacious room.

The bedchamber was attractively decorated in shades of dusty green and mauve. The coverlet of the huge four-poster bed was of a soft mauve silk damask as were the draperies of the room. A delicately colored carpet that looked like a field of flowers covered the floor. It was apparent that Lady Stavely had made the room as charming as she could despite the dark wood-paneled walls and heavy furniture.

She sat before her dressing table finishing her toilet. As Lisa entered the room behind Mrs. Pottle, Lady Stavely turned and smiled at her. "Have you talent for arranging hair?" she asked. "I am rather hopeless at it."

"I think so, my lady," Lisa replied with a curtsy. How often she had watched Zada arrange Valerie's hair for her different acting roles and had tried to copy the styles herself.

"Then do come here, my dear, and set to work. My hair is so fine and since Annie left me I have had no one to help me." She nodded in the housekeeper's direction. "That will be all, Mrs. Pottle. I'm afraid you must find someone else to help Polly downstairs. I have decided that Lisa is to be my new lady's maid. Would you see that her things are moved into the little room next to mine?"

Mrs. Pottle's eyebrows rose slightly and two spots of red appeared in her colorless cheeks, but she nodded and departed silently from the room.

Mary Stavely smiled to herself. She had done it! For the first time she had asserted her authority over Mrs. Pottle and she had won! Richard's presence, his firm avowal of his friendship, had given her all the assurance she needed.

Lisa set to work brushing her mistress' hair. "'Tis very kind of you to offer me this position," she said to Lady Stavely. "Thank you, my lady."

"You might also wish to thank Lord Drayton," Lady Stavely smiled. "He was most anxious about you."

A slight pink suffused Lisa's cheeks as she continued her brushing.

"He told me," Lady Stavely went on, "that you were not raised as a servant and should not be doing menial tasks. It was witless of me not to discern that for myself."

Lisa smiled. "How could you have known that, my lady? I was in rags and covered with mud when first you saw me."

"Your speech should have told me your station. You are obviously a gentlewoman, Lisa. How come you to Bridgeford?"

Lisa did not answer immediately, taking time, under the guise of concentrating on her work, to formulate the exact story she would tell Lady Stavely. She decided to tell her the truth—up to a point—the very point of her question.

As Lady Stavely's hair became arranged in a becoming fashion, Lisa began telling that kind and gentle soul all about Valerie and Evan Manning and the acting troupe, her mother's death and her abrupt departure in the middle of the night.

"But why did you not go to your mother's people when she died?" Lady Stavely asked, plainly puzzled.

"I could not go to people who had disowned my own mother, my lady," Lisa said bitterly. "How could I find happiness with them?"

Mary Stavely nodded. "I understand," she said, "but the alternative seems even worse to me. Aren't you fearful to be entirely on your own? Do you expect to find happiness here, working as a servant? Surely when you ran away you had something else in mind—some destination?"

"Aye," Lisa admitted, "I had a destination, but then all my money was stolen from me and my horse was gone. . . ."

Lady Stavely saw that remembering what had happened had caused a cloud to cover Lisa's face and quickly said, "You must forget about all that, my dear. Just thank God that Matthew came along in time to save you from a fate one would hate to contemplate." She shuddered.

"I will always be grateful to him," Lisa murmured. Securing a last strand of hair with a bodkin, she stood back to survey her work.

Mary Stavely looked at her reflection in the mirror, turning her head from side to side. She smiled at Lisa. "How nimble your fingers are," she said. "You have arranged my hair most becomingly. I have a feeling that I will bless the day you came to me."

Lisa left Lady Stavely's bedchamber with a small pile of laundry in her arms. She was headed down the corridor in the direction of the servant's stairway, when a door opened and Lord Drayton, dressed in riding clothes, strode out of his room.

He smiled when he saw her. "Good morrow, Lisa," he said, in his rich deep voice.

"Good morrow, my lord." She gave a little curtsy. "I wish to thank you," she said sincerely. "Lady Stavely has elevated me to lady's maid. She told me it was at your suggestion."

Drayton stood staring down into her lovely face and the moment seemed to stretch out until he quickly recovered himself and said, "I did not think you were suited to the scullery."

"It was kind of you."

Her pulse quickened as his eyes held hers fast. She could not look away. Why did this man disturb her so?

"Will you do me a favor?" he asked, a teasing smile now playing at the corners of his mouth.

"If I can, my lord." Why did he have to stand so close to her? So close that she could almost feel the warmth of his body. . . .

"Will you take off that damned cap?" his eyes twinkled. "You have the most incredibly beautiful hair. I deem it a crime to conceal it."

Disconcerted by his remark, she did not readily move, so he put out his hand and snatched the cap from her head. A wealth of hair, soft and silky and black as midnight, cascaded down about her shoulders.

"That's better." Something flared in the emerald eyes as he looked at her. "Damn it all, Lisa, but you're an enchantress. I swear you have bewitched me."

The sound of his vibrant voice and the caress in his eyes had a like effect on her. She stood and watched in a trancelike way as he tossed aside the laundry she carried and drew her into his arms.

She did not resist, only trembled a little as he bent his tall head and put his lips on hers.

A voice came to her as if from afar. You should not be letting him do this! And yet she could not help herself. Why did he have this power over her? A power that made her knees shake and her head spin wildly.

His arms tightened about her. Beneath his mouth her quivering lips parted. His kiss was soft and tender, but as he felt her gentle response the pressure of his mouth deepened. His arms pulled her closer and she felt herself melting against his big, hard body.

Drayton's kiss was far from light now, awakening her dormant senses, making them come frighteningly alive.

Then, with the same unexpectedness with which he had begun, he broke away from her and stepped back. Only his brilliant green eyes still held her, searching her face intently, as though he were trying to see within her.

"Are you really as innocent as you seem?" he murmured in a voice oddly thick. "Or are you just a damned good actress?"

"I—I don't—" Lisa stammered, looking utterly bewildered, her heart still hammering in her breast, her cheeks pink, her lips soft with uncertainty.

His manner changed as his penetrating eyes accepted the confused, hurt expression harbored in the luminous depths.

"Forgive me, Lisa," he said at last, and now his voice was harsh, self-deprecating. "I warned you I was no gentleman."

He left her standing in the middle of the corridor, the laundry scattered at her feet.

Chapter Nine

LISA DASHED OUT INTO THE BRIGHT, SUNNY AFTERNOON, TAKING deep breaths of the warm, spring air as she made her way down the pathway. Cooped up in the house for two days, she had longed to be outside.

Lisa had not gone far along the road before she heard the sound of Matthew's axe. The forester was working to fell a dead elm and just as Lisa came upon him the tree came crashing down, so close it startled her.

Matthew Chester was shocked when he saw Lisa standing there, her face quite white.

"Don't thee know enough not to come close to a man choppin' down a tree?" he scolded her. "Dang it, lass, you could ha' been killed!"

"I'm sorry, Matthew. It was stupid of me." She was instantly contrite. "It was just that I was in such a hurry to find you. Lady Stavely has given me some time off and I so longed to take Primrose for a ride in the fresh air. I did not know where you had her stabled and—"

"Slow down there, lass," he grinned. "I rode the mare over meself this mornin' to give her some exercise. Left her behind the stables. Come with me and I'll fetch her for thee."

It wasn't many minutes later that Matthew Chester watched as Lisa galloped off across the fields beyond Stavely Manor.

"That lass be a real beauty," he said to himself, shaking his head as he turned to go back to his work.

The wind blew Lisa's long hair straight out behind her as she rode at a gallop across the green open fields. Her blue eyes shone with delight and fresh color came to her cheeks. Lisa's mind was moving as quickly as Primrose.

It had been pure coincidence that she had been crossing the great hall the night before. She'd seen the front door quietly open and three dark figures stealthily slip in. She had instinctively pulled back into the shadows, recognizing the three Puritan sympathizers she had seen at the fair.

Following them at a discreet distance, Lisa saw them enter the library and close the door. She put her ear to the door and found that she could just make out what they were saying. They were waiting, it seemed, for Sir Basil. She melted into the darkness of the hallway, prepared to wait there until Sir Basil appeared.

When Stavely at last joined the men, the conversation Lisa overheard justified the long wait. Now she wondered what she should do with this vital information.

She thought of Lord Drayton. Lisa had learned from the servants how he had fought valiantly for the king and had followed him into exile. There was no doubt that he was a Royalist and a loyal subject of Charles II. Was he the one she should approach with her knowledge of the treasonous plan?

She hesitated only because she remembered his reaction that morning in the upper hallway. She felt her pulse quicken at the very thought. Why had she let him kiss her again? Why the strange attraction to this man that made her unable or too weak to resist him?

Lisa knew that even if Lord Drayton had kissed her, it probably meant nothing to him. He had undoubtedly kissed dozens of maids! Yet when he had looked at her, the look had been so wonderfully tender. He had said she had bewitched him. Did he know she shared that feeling? No! She would not care for him! She must not!

They had been drawn together, two strangers, but it was only a physical attraction. What did she really know of him or he of her? It was only desire that had made him kiss her. Nothing more. A great lord did not fall in love with a servant. And he knew her only as a servant. No. A man such as he might use such a maid to relieve his passions, but that was all. She must not be just an obliging pair of lips or (she blushed at the thought) an accomodating body. He was a courtier, a breed of men who held love and fidelity in mocking contempt. She must avoid seeing him again—she did not trust herself. Her heart beat faster even at the thought of those teasing green eyes, those soft, demanding lips.

Lisa returned from her ride by way of the road near where Matthew Chester was now busy cutting up the tree he had felled. He insisted upon returning to the manor house with her and chatted as he walked beside her around to the back of the group of low stone buildings which comprised the stables. The area smelled of fresh hay and manure and pitch.

"Thank you, Matthew, for taking such good care of Primrose," Lisa smiled at him as she handed him the reins. "I have enjoyed my ride so much. I could not bear being locked up inside that house much longer on such a beautiful day. Growing up in a caravan has made me love the fresh air."

"She be a good little mare," Matthew said, patting the horse's flank. It was when he returned his hand to his pocket that he gave a snort. "Why, I nearly forgot. Spied this by the side of the road this morning." He drew out a dirty little leather pouch and handed it to her. "Be this thy lost money pouch? Figure those ruffians must ha' dropped it after they shared the coins."

Lisa took the bag from Matthew eagerly and pulled it open.

"Only some papers left in there," he said. "Can't read, so they meant naught to me."

They did mean something to Lisa, however, and she thanked him gratefully. The ride had brought color to Lisa's cheeks, and with her long dark hair tied back by a bright ribbon and her blue eyes shining, she made a very pretty picture.

When the head groom now appeared from around a corner, Matthew motioned him over. "Lisa, this be Master Trent," Matthew said. "Lisa be m'lady's new maid."

Thomas Trent touched his cap. He was a wiry, sandy-haired man in his late forties and knew his job well. "There is an extra stall at the end of the stable, miss," he said quietly. "I'd be happy to put thy mare in it and Sir Basil will ne'er be the wiser."

She smiled at him. "That is very kind of you, Master Trent," she said, "but I promised Matthew his children could ride her and—"

"I be a bit afeared for them to, if I may say so, Lisa," Matthew broke in. "They be used to riding naught but an old plow horse and the mare is a bit spirited. Keep her here. You will want her close by now that you have time to ride."

Lisa's face lit up. "Oh, I would like that. You are sure you would not get into trouble if I kept her here, Master Trent?"

At that point he would have agreed to keep the mare on the lawn if she had asked him. He nodded. "I'd be pleased to, and I will have her saddled for thee every afternoon if thee wish." He was looking at the sidesaddle. His brow furrowed. "Do thee be a lady, miss?"

"I am only Lady Stavely's maid, Master Trent."

"By thy speech you are no servant," he insisted. "No little housemaid I ever knowed owned such a fine animal."

Lisa regarded him. "Primrose is all I have left," she said quietly. "All my money was stolen—"

"I told 'ee about those ruffians," Matthew broke in.

"I'm that sorry, miss," Master Trent said, and feeling ill at ease he turned back to Matthew. "Ha' you seen Lord Drayton's black stallion? 'Tis the most beautiful beast I ever seen. Seventeen and a half hands tall he be."

After an animated discussion between the two men on the equestrian merits of Lord Drayton, Lisa and Matthew went on to the Manor.

"I saw his lordship control that stallion yesterday with so little effort," Lisa said, unaware that her voice betrayed her feelings. "He was magnificent!"

Matthew glanced sharply at the girl. "Ha' you had words wi' his lordship?" he asked.

"Aye, we have talked several times. It was he who suggested me to Lady Stavely for her maid."

Matthew put a hand on Lisa's arm and stopped her, staring down into the guileless eyes that looked up questioningly into his. Someone had to tell her, he thought, and cleared his throat.

"Lisa, thee be a beautiful lass. Thee must know that 'ee draw the male eye. But mind thee. Rich men with titles and feathers and whatnot are not for thee." His voice roughened. "Thee saw what became of poor little Brydie. That be all such men want from the likes of thee. Just to take their pleasure."

"Lord Drayton is not like Sir Basil," Lisa protested.

"Nay, thee be right there. I have known m'lord since a boy and he be a good and kind man, but he be a rich man after all and rich men are used to havin' their own way like, especially with the lasses."

Lisa became indignant. "Lord Drayton would *never* take a maid against her will!"

Matthew sighed. "M'lord is handsome and has a way with him. Might she not grow to care for him and be quite willin'?"

Lisa was silent.

"Stay away from him," he warned her and his eyes were kind as they gazed at the beautiful young girl. "Mixin' above thy station will only cause thee heartache."

It was time for Lisa to help her mistress dress for supper. As she approached the door to Lady Stavely's bedchamber, she heard the sound of raised voices from within.

"I admit the chit was carrying my child, but it was not I who killed her," Sir Basil growled.

"Surely, Basil, you must feel some responsibility for her death. Just to send her body back to her people with your manservant and no word of condolence, no—"

"John took a heavy purse with him. He will explain to them where she was found."

"And the swollenness of her body? Will he also explain that?"

"'Od's blood, woman, it is not your place to question me in such matters," Sir Basil thundered. "I'll hear no more about it!"

But Lady Stavely had the temerity to continue. "Basil, I beg of you, from now on leave the young innocents alone."

The slap was loud, vicious. "I am the master here. Don't tell me what to do!"

Angrily Sir Basil stormed out of the Manor, leaving by coach to join his cronies for a night of cards and dice and drinking in Waltham.

Lord Drayton sent word that he would not be returning that night. He had spent the day in the saddle inspecting the vast areas of his estate and had decided to accept the invitation of his agent and stay overnight, rather than make a further journey back to Stavely Manor.

Mary Stavely hardly touched the light supper sent to her room. Lisa applied cloths dampened with vinegar to her bruised and swollen cheek. Neither made any reference as to why they were needed.

Lisa's heart bled for the unhappy woman. She did everything she could to make her comfortable, ending up by sitting by the wide bed and reading to her in the soft candlelight.

"You have a lovely voice, Lisa."

"Thank you, my lady."

"It does not seem right, somehow, that a young lady as well-educated as you should be a servant. I wish, Lisa, that you could be more than that to me." She paused and her eyes filled with tears. "It has been years since I have had a close friend—a woman friend—someone I could trust—"

She started to cry and Lisa impulsively put her arms about the frail shoulders and held her close, letting Mary Stavely cry it all out against her.

"I'm sorry, Lisa," she finally sniffed, drawing back and wiping at her eyes with her lace handkerchief. "I forgot myself before you. Sometimes, you see, it gets to be too much. . . ."

Lisa said nothing as she straightened the pillows behind her mistress' head, but when she met Mary Stavely's eyes for a moment, the latter saw that the girl's own eyes were wet with tears.

"Why—why you care about me," she whispered, quite unnerved by the sight. "You really *do* care."

Lisa nodded. "I only wish there was something I could say—something I could do to help you."

"There is nothing, Lisa." Lady Stavely shook her head resignedly. "Although you have been but two days at Stavely Manor, I am sure you are aware of . . . many things."

"Aye, my lady."

"My husband, Sir Basil is . . . a violent man . . . a lustful man. Keep out of his sight as much as possible. You are very beautiful and . . ." Her hands went up. "I want you to understand that I am saying this not because I am a jealous woman. Heaven forbid!" She shuddered. "I am saying it for your own good."

"Thank you, my lady."

"Don't thank me. You may wish you had never come to Stavely Manor. In fact, if I were not so selfish, I would suggest that it would be better for you to leave this cursed house this instant." Mary Stavely gripped Lisa's hands in hers. "Oh Lisa, I need more than a lady's maid. More than anything else, I need a companion. Will you be my companion? It is obvious to me that you are a gentlewoman. It would be a more fitting position for you. All that you would be required to do is to sit with me and read to me and eat your meals with me when Basil is not at home."

"But Sir Basil . . . would he not object?"

"So long as I am here when he wants me, he objects to nothing I do within this house."

"You are sure, my lady?"

"I am sure." She nodded, a smile lighting up her tired face. "But on two conditions. One, that when we are alone you will call me Mary, and two, that you do not wear that horrid dress and cap again!"

Lisa laughed.

"I will see that you have some appropriate gowns made," Lady Stavely continued. The prospect of having someone there to keep her company brightened her whole being. She need never be lonely again! "You have made me very happy, Lisa. Perhaps there was a divine purpose that brought you to Stavely Manor."

Lisa's smile faded. "Perhaps there was," she replied, a cryptic look appearing in her eyes.

Chapter Ten

It was late evening and all had retired—all but Sir Basil, who had still not returned to Stavely Manor.

Candle in hand, Lisa crept down the wide staircase, merged with the shadows and hastened in the direction of the library. She closed the door quickly behind her and crossed the room to where the carved oak chest sat on a stand in the corner. She tried to open it, but it was securely locked.

Lisa began to search the room for the key, opening and closing drawers and cabinets. Then she remembered that Sir Basil, had walked right over to the chest and opened it that night. Perhaps the key was hidden between the chest and its stand. She went back to it and strained to lift a corner of the heavy chest. The key was there!

Nervously she threw back the ornately carved lid, quickly taking the papers from the chest and carrying them over to the table where she had placed her candle. She examined them with eagerness, murmuring to herself as she looked at them.

Lisa glanced first at the will. It had been made before Sir Edmund had gone away to fight for his king and in it he had left all to his wife and children. Tears filled Lisa's eyes as she read the firm, bold script. Her father's handwriting! With Valerie

Manning's deathbed confession that Lisa was in truth Elizabeth Stavely, the daughter of the late Sir Edmund, Lisa had been fired with a fierce resolve to claim her rightful inheritance.

Basil Stavely had usurped her lands and possessions. He might even have been responsible for her brother's fiery death. Though she had no memory of it, Valerie Manning had told her that she had run into the woods behind the burning house to where the Manning Shakespearian Players were camped. Zada had found the pitiful dazed child. Though only four years of age, Lisa had managed to tell them her name and enough about herself for Evan Manning to make inquiries in the neighboring village. He had learned that it had been Parliamentary men who had fired the squire's house. Obviously, someone had wanted all within the house to die.

It was then that the Mannings had decided to keep Elizabeth's identity a secret. She had become Lisa Manning and her true name had never been mentioned again. She herself remembered nothing of her past life. Valerie Manning gave her the papers that her husband had carefully compiled regarding her true identity and heritage.

"Your papa," Valerie told her, "was of the opinion that Sir Basil Stavely, who was a distant cousin of your father, was behind the plot to murder you and your brother. It was clear that he wanted to claim the lands and title for himself. He's still master of Stavely Manor. It is best that he never know of your existence, for I am sure he would do everything in his power to get rid of you."

Instead of frightening Lisa, Valerie's statement had only intensified her resolve. She was determined, by whatever means she must employ, to regain her true heritage!

If it had been her brother who had lived, she was sure that he would have stood up to Sir Basil. Just because she was female did not mean that she lacked courage. If she went to the authorities, she now had the identity papers and the will to support her claim, but might only be able to turn Basil Stavely off the land—and then she would have to live the rest of her days in fear of his retribution!

There was no proof that he had been involved with the Parliamentarians during the war, had arranged with them to fire the squire's house. Unless . . . unless it could be proven that he was still working with them—was even planning regicide with them. The bond was what Lisa was after now. The bond to murder the king, which she knew Sir Basil and his friends had signed!

Lisa knew she must be quick. She had little time, and prayed that it would be enough.

The pen was in the inkhorn and a folded paper came from the wide pocket of her oversized dress. Lisa bent over the table, the dangerous compact spread out before her, copying the words as fast as she could.

For many minutes she wrote rapidly, stopping ever so often to listen in fear that some interruption might come before the completion of a task for which this might be her only opportunity.

At length there were muffled sounds of a door slamming and heavy footsteps crossing the great hall beyond the library. The master of Stavely Manor had returned!

With danger of discovery threatening, Lisa quickly locked the papers away and hid the key once more. She blew out the candle and stood still and trembling by the table, her heart beating wildly.

No other sound came from the great hall outside. Lisa waited in silence as the minutes crawled by. Had he climbed the stairs?

At last she crept to the door and opened it cautiously. The great hall was in darkness except for a flickering candelabra on a post at the foot of the stairs.

Lisa quietly stepped from the room and closed the door. Tiptoeing across the hall, she made for the stairway. She was about to start up it, when someone sprang from the shadows and clutched her wrist!

She gasped at the sight of Sir Basil! He had obviously been drinking heavily. His garments were in disorder, his face flushed, and his eyes glittered dangerously.

"How now, wench! What do you here?" he demanded roughly.

"Oh, my lord," Lisa exclaimed, putting a hand to her heart. "How you frightened me!"

"What do you in my library? I saw the light. Who gave you the right, wench, to be elsewhere in Stavely Manor but in the scullery?"

"I have become my lady's companion," Lisa explained to him, rubbing the wrist he had released. "I was but returning a book to the library for her. My lady had trouble sleeping and so I read to her until quite late."

"Could the book not have been returned in the morning?" Sir Basil raised a black brow.

"Aye, it was stupid of me. I am so new and—and I did not think."

"You should make an excellent companion to Lady Stavely," he snorted. "Having a like intelligence."

The light from the candelabra was illuminating the perfect oval of her face, the ebony hair no longer restrained by a cap but curling over one slim shoulder, the wide blue eyes that held a touch of fear.

That fear was heightened by the softening of Sir Basil's voice, his lascivious smile. "What is your name, wench?"

"Lisa, sir."

Instinctively she began withdrawing from him, managing one step backward.

"So you have learned to read?"

She nodded. "I have, sir."

Suddenly, his big hand darted out and grasped her arm again, pulling her roughly back to him. His voice had thickened.

"You are a comely chit. There is something else I would have you learn."

Lisa tried to break away, but the ironlike arms tightened about her body. She struggled to avoid his lips, catching the sour odor of brandy on his breath as he forced her head back. The full, wet lips covered hers, pressing them open.

Her mind raced. Scream, it said. Scream! But who would come to her rescue if she did? She knew none of the servants would dare to interfere. Lord Drayton was miles away, and Lady Stavely had not the strength. Her fate was in her own hands this time. Instantly she had an inspiration.

Sir Basil had seized upon what he thought was an innocent victim, but suddenly that victim's manner changed. When he raised his head from hers, she smiled tantalizingly up at him. It took every shred of her acting ability to make that smile soft and inviting.

"Are you going to stop at a kiss?" she whispered, making an upward gesture with her head toward the second floor.

In the surprise of the moment, Sir Basil dropped his arms from about her.

Another surprise followed, for the minute she was free, Lisa turned and with the speed of light darted up the stairs. If she could only make it to her room and bolt the door!

But Basil Stavely, though drunk, moved quickly. When Lisa stumbled on the turn at the first landing, he leaped on her. A cry of despair sprang from her lips. A cry that brought Lady Mary out of her bedchamber. Clutching the stout oak balustrade, she looked down and saw Lisa trying desperately to beat off Sir Basil, her fists pummeling his chest. He was laughing as he held her down.

"I like a wench with spirit."

"Release me!" she demanded, kicking and flailing.

He laughed again and bent over her, seeking her lips, but with one hand she raked at his face.

He struck her so viciously that her head snapped back, hitting the edge of a stair. An explosion of light erupted before her eyes and blurred her vision.

"Little bitch!" Savagely he groped and wrenched up her skirts. His big hands were all over her then, kneading, probing. "You want it. You know you do." He fumbled with his breeches. He would have her here and now!

"Take your hands off that girl!"

Sir Basil's head shot up in amazement. Was that Mary's voice? He squinted into the shadows at the top of the stairs.

"I said, take your hands off her!" The voice was stronger.

"Mary?" he asked, gazing up to see his wife's petite form appear on the stairs above.

He grinned. "Jealous, my dear?" he laughed. "Don't fret yourself. I am a vigorous man. I will attend to you as soon as I am through with this one."

"You swine!" Lady Stavely cried, anger and shame giving her courage. "Release her immediately! Is no innocent maid safe in this house? Is one death on your hands not enough?"

"You watch your tongue, woman," Sir Basil roared, lunging in his wife's direction, but in that moment Lady Stavely brought forth a pistol that she had been holding hidden in the folds of her nightdress.

Taking advantage of Sir Basil's surprise, Lisa squirmed free of him. Not taking his eyes from the pistol in his wife's hands, he smashed out sideways at Lisa with his fist. The blow glanced off the side of her jaw. She lurched to the left, striking her head as she fell against the sturdy oak bannister. Losing consciousness, she crumpled in a heap on the landing.

She was struggling through a tunnel of swirling darkness. In the distance, Mary Stavely's face floated above her. Now Mary was backing slowly up the stairs. Her menacing husband was in pursuit. Unexpectedly he struck out, wrenching the pistol from her shaking hands. It flew over the railing and Lisa heard it land with a dull thump on the floor below.

Sir Basil growled, "You may wish, my jealous little wife, that you had remained in your room."

"Nay, Basil!" Lady Stavely's cry was pitiful as he scooped her up in his arms and strode heavily up the stairs.

Lisa closed her eyes. Her head was spinning wildly. How had this happened? Sir Basil would now take out his rage and frustration on fragile Mary Stavely.

Lisa heard a heavy door slam shut above her. Reaching for a stairpost, she began to pull herself up to her knees—then to her feet. She reached for the bannister and grasped it with both hands, steadying her swaying body. Slowly, one step at a time, she moved up the stairs, holding on heavily, heading in the direction of her little room.

She was almost at her door when she heard a heartrending cry from Lady Stavely's bedchamber. What was that drunken brute doing to her? Out of her splitting pain came a growing rage. She must do something! She fumbled with the doorlatch and it opened so quickly she almost fell into her tiny room. Staggering through inky darkness to find the heavy candlestick she sought as a weapon, her foot hit the side of the bed and she lost her balance and pitched forward across it. The fall caused a fresh wave of nausea to flow over her and once more Lisa knew nothing as she sank into a sea of soft and welcoming darkness.

Chapter Eleven

WHEN LISA OPENED HER EYES AGAIN IT WAS EARLY DAWN. THE first gray light was entering her room from the small uncurtained window. She was conscious of pain and when she raised her head the room swam hazily about her. Still there was something inside that kept nagging at her—urging her to do something.

The room grew brighter. She looked about her. Where was she? Why was she lying fully clothed on top of the bed? Then she remembered. It all came rushing back, and she could not help but let out a cry of anguish at the memory.

Mary Stavely! She must go to her!

She tried to sit up. A wave of nausea swept over her, which she strove to control. The pain was unbelievable.

Slowly, she thrust her legs over the edge of the bed. She took a few steps toward the small chest at the end of the room and gazed at her reflection in the mirror above it. Wild eyes looked back into hers, eyes with dark circles beneath them. An ugly blue bruise covered half her jaw and spread up her cheek.

With slow, measured steps she crossed the room to the door. She let herself silently out into the corridor and made her way along it to Lady Stavely's bedchamber.

Lisa listened outside the door. There was no sound. Dared

she knock? No! She would try the door first. If it were open she would peek in and see if Lady Stavely were alone.

The latch lifted and she quietly pushed the door inward, peering into the darkened room. She moved silently toward the bed.

Lady Stavely was alone. She lay in bed looking very white and still. Just as Lisa was about to touch her shoulder, she moved and let out a pitiful little moan.

"Mary?" Gone was the servile address Lisa had once used. Mary had proved indeed to be a dear friend to her.

The woman seemed to cringe from the sound of a voice and struggled to move to the other side of the bed.

"No!" she whimpered. "No more! I cannot bear . . ."

"'Tis Lisa, Mary," the girl said softly.

Lady Stavely turned her head and her eyes slowly opened. Pain was mirrored there—pain and undisguised fear.

"Is he gone?"

"Aye, Mary."

Lady Stavely gave a ragged sigh.

"Are you all right?" Lisa asked anxiously.

"I think," she murmured, "I have lost another child." Her eyes closed again.

"Oh, no!" Lisa bent over her and gently pulled back the covers.

Mary Stavely lay naked in a pool of blood. Even in the dim light Lisa could see that her petite body had been beaten, for she was covered with ugly bruises and welts.

"Oh, my God!" Lisa cried out at the sight, fighting the wave of nausea that threatened to overcome her.

"Lisa," Lady Stavely whispered, "you should not be seeing this. Get Mrs. Pottle for me. She knows what to do."

Lisa ran from the room, her head pounding with every step. She found Mrs. Pottle in the kitchen with Nelly. She had no idea how wild she looked with her bruised face, her unkempt hair and torn dress. Nelly rushed forward when she saw her.

"What happened to thee, girl?" she exclaimed.

"I'm all right," Lisa assured her. "'Tis my lady. Please come, Mrs. Pottle. I fear she has lost another child. There is so much blood. . . ."

Mrs. Pottle was instantly on her feet. "You wait, girl. Get some hot water," she instructed Lisa and rushed from the room.

The cook crossed immediately to the hearth where a large kettle was boiling. "Can thee manage it, lass? You look mighty poorly."

"Now what is going on?" drawled a voice from the doorway. Polly was standing there, her hands on her rounded hips. "The master up afore dawn bellowin' at everyone because 'e's decided all o' sudden to 'ead to London. Poor John, only a moment back from taking Brydie's body 'ome must tear about packin' for 'im and fetchin' the coach. And off goes the master as if the devil 'imself is after 'im."

Lisa took the kettle from Nelly and made for the door. "My lady may have lost another child."

"Another!" Polly lifted her eyebrows. Then, seeing Lisa's face, she asked, "And what, pray, 'appened t' 'ee?"

"I had a fall," Lisa murmured, pushing past her.

"Looks more like a fight t' me," Polly laughed. "Did the old lecher get wha' 'e wanted?"

Lisa ignored her and hurried as fast as she could with the heavy kettle down the hall.

"The bleeding has stopped," Mrs. Pottle said, washing her hands in the basin by the bed.

"Thank God," Lisa murmured, pushing a lock of hair back from her face. She had been busy tearing up a sheet and making pads from it. After changing the bedding, Mrs. Pottle had packed poor Lady Stavely with clean linen pads to staunch the flow of blood.

"Aye, she's very weak—lost a good deal this time. I figure the child came away sometime during the night."

"During the night! Do you mean she has been lying here in this condition ever since?"

Mrs. Pottle nodded. "Never seen the master lay a hand on her before. Methinks he caused the loss of this one himself."

"He's a monster!" Lisa cried, tears filling her eyes. "Lady Stavely was only protecting *me.*"

"Humph! So that was it," Mrs. Pottle snorted. "By the look of thee I figured something of the sort."

Mary Stavely moaned in her sleep.

"She's so little and gentle," Lisa said softly, looking down at her friend. "How could that brute do this to her?"

"He is the master here and it is not your place to call him

names and speak out against him," Mrs. Pottle said reprovingly, pursing her lips as she cleaned up around the bed.

"You can say *that* after what you have just seen?"

"Men have a right to do with their wives as they wish."

Lisa was incredulous. "I doubt you would feel that way if Master Pottle beat *you!*"

"Insolent troublemaker!" Mrs. Pottle picked up the dirty linen and shoved the bundle at Lisa. "Take this downstairs to Emma in the laundry. I will see to m'lady. I have experience in such matters."

Emma, a big, raw-boned, red-armed girl took the bloodied sheets from Lisa and made a clicking sound with her tongue.

"Poor m'lady. I hear she lost another. Don't seem right somehow that some has more than they can feed and others can't bear a live 'un."

Lisa nodded, took the clean pile of laundry she was handed and went up to the kitchen. Her head was aching and she was glad to sit down at the table, but she had little appetite for the breakfast Nelly set before her.

"M'lady very bad?" the cook asked sympathetically. She thought the girl looked on the point of fainting herself.

"She lost a lot of blood," Lisa said.

"And what o' thee?"

"My own fault. I was warned about him."

Nelly nodded. "So 'twas the master. I thought as much."

"Lady Stavely saved me, Nelly. That sweet-faced little lady saved me. And at what a terrible cost to her!" Tears again filled Lisa's eyes. "He beat her and heaven knows what else. Oh Nelly, he's an animal! A vile animal!"

"Aye, that he be, lass, and I care not who hears me say it. Perhaps he'll be gone a while. The last time he went t' London he stayed a fortnight."

And when he does come back to Stavely Manor I will expose him, Lisa thought, clenching her fists. I now have all the proof I need. I will wait no longer.

She managed only a few spoonfuls of porridge. Her head was throbbing so much her only wish now was to lie down.

Opening the door, she looked up to see Polly standing at the landing, flirting with one of the manservants. Not wanting to be confronted with a string of questions, Lisa decided to go through the house to the main staircase.

She had just entered the great hall when the front door was flung open and Lord Drayton strode in. Seeing Lisa alone, he grabbed her about the waist and swung her around, bringing her close to him. So close, that the warm masculine smells of leather and horses that clung to him filled her nostrils. But the swinging motion had made her dizzy. Her head spun even after he had set her down and a ringing filled her ears. She barely heard the deep voice say, "Why is it every time I get my hands on you, you are carrying laundry? This must be a deucedly clean household."

He was grinning as he looked down at her, but the smile quickly vanished from his face at the sight of her bruises.

"What devil did that to you?" he roared. The anger made his eyes flash like green fire. They were the last thing she remembered before she lost consciousness.

When Lisa opened her eyes, she was lying on a sofa in the gallery. Lord Drayton was bending over her, holding a goblet of brandy to her lips.

"Drink!" he commanded.

She swallowed a little, feeling it burn all the way down her throat, but it seemed to give her a little more strength.

"Thank you," she whispered.

"Don't raise your head. I felt the lump and I think you have a mild concussion. You should be in bed."

"I'll be all right if I lie here a moment."

"Of course you will and then you can get up and scrub the whole bloody manor house," he growled.

"You're angry. . . ."

"You're damn right I'm angry. I'm away from this house one night and when I come back I find you bruised and battered and fainting dead away. Was it Stavely? Did he do this to you? By God, if I get my hands on that filthy swine, I'll—"

"Aye," she said, "it was Sir Basil, but it was partly my own fault. I should not have left my room."

"Tell me what happened." He placed another cushion beneath her head, his big hands amazingly gentle as he lifted her.

She told him the whole story of Sir Basil catching her on the stairs, of Lady Stavely coming to her aid with the pistol and the terrible result of her defiance.

"Where is the bastard now?" Drayton's voice was hard and cold.

"He left at dawn for London."

Drayton snorted. "Ran away did he? Cowardly bully. I had a feeling I should have come back last night. Something told me—" Cursing Stavely he slapped his right fist into the palm of his other hand. "Wouldn't be back this morning," he said, "but I wished to ride out and see Lady Stavely's brother on a matter concerning the rebuilding of my home. He lives fifteen miles north of here. Thought I would stop by here first and see if Mary had a message for him."

"I'm sure she would like to see you, if you can wait until she awakens."

"I have no intention of leaving now. It will make little difference to my plans if I wait a day or two."

Gently he smoothed the tangled hair from her brow and touched her cheek.

"That's an ugly bruise." His voice roughened. "You can believe I will make Basil answer for that."

"My lord—"

"I'm going to carry you up to your bed now," his deep voice was soft and comforting. "I want you to rest there for the remainder of the day."

"But who will attend my lady? Mrs. Pottle—"

"Will care for her," Lord Drayton interrupted, lifting her effortlessly in his powerful arms. "I will see to everything now."

Pressed close to his muscled chest, letting her head fall back against his wide shoulder, Lisa relaxed. How wonderful it was to feel those protective arms about her, carrying her like a babe, keeping her safe. How easily this strong yet gentle man allayed her fears.

When at last he placed her down on her bed, she clung to him a moment, not wanting him to leave her.

"Are you all right?" his voice was anxious.

"Aye, my lord." But she felt so tired. So very tired. She closed her eyes.

He pulled the coverlet over her and stood looking down at her with a tenderness in his cynical green eyes that his friends would not have recognized.

"Lovely, lovely Lisa," he whispered, but she did not hear him. She was fast asleep.

* * *

Lisa slept most of the day. She awoke toward evening and slowly sat up in bed. The lightheadedness seemed to have gone. She felt only a dull ache where before there had been a pounding in her head. Gingerly she felt the lump at her hairline. It seemed to have receded a little and was not so tender to the touch.

She got out of bed and regarded herself in the little mirror. What a sight she was! The bruise on her face seemed almost purple in color now.

It was when Lisa began to change her clothing that she discovered the copy of the bond that she had made the night before. She placed it in the pocket of the plain daygown she had just drawn over her head.

Her hair needed attention, but she found she had to be very careful as she drew a brush through its tangled mass. Brushing it seemed to increase the ache and in the end she left it unbound down her back.

Lady Mary was awake when Lisa knocked at her door and gave a weak smile as the girl entered the room.

"Lisa!" she murmured. "I have been worried about you, although Richard assured me that you were all right and only needed rest." Her soft, sensitive eyes appraised the girl. "Oh, my dear, what a dreadful bruise!"

"But how are you, my lady?"

"I feel a little stronger. I have just had some of Nelly's good broth."

"I'm glad to hear that. Mrs. Pottle, do go down and get your own supper," Lisa said to that woman. "I'll stay with my lady now."

Mrs. Pottle rose from her chair by the bed and picked up the tray. She eyed Lisa's unservile appearance with displeasure before heading for the door.

"If you should need me, m'lady . . ." she said, before opening it.

"Lisa will look after me now, Mrs. Pottle," Lady Mary assured her. "You have been very kind."

She sighed when the door was closed. "Mrs. Pottle is a good woman, but she is so cold and superior. Oh Lisa, I was very anxious for you."

"For me? But you—"

"Richard told me that you had fainted and he had put you to

bed. He feels badly that he was not here last night, but what could he have done?"

"He could have stopped Sir Basil from laying his hands on you. Oh, Mary, you have been through so much." The suffering suffusing Mary's thin white face, filled her with pain.

"At least the child was not far along. I was not even sure of it. I had not told Basil." She looked at Lisa. "Has he really gone away . . . to London?"

"Aye. I believe he's expected to be away for sometime."

"A reprieve. A blessed reprieve!"

Lisa sat down in the chair vacated by Mrs. Pottle and reached out to clasp Mary Stavely's hand.

"I have never seen Basil as angry as he was last night," the fragile woman went on, and her voice shook at the memory.

"Don't think about it," Lisa said firmly, afraid that Mary would upset herself.

"How can I forget it? Ever! He was like a wild man! He beat me and forced me to—No! You should not hear of such things. He is wicked and evil and God in heaven help me, but how can I go on living with such a man?"

You will not have to for long, Lisa thought, setting her chin, but aloud she said, "Pray do not upset yourself, Mary. Lord Drayton will see to him."

"What can he do?" Mary Stavely cried despairingly. "I am Basil's wife. I have no recourse. A man has a right to do as he wishes with his wife."

There was a knock at the door and Lisa rose to answer it. She was surprised to see Polly standing there with a tray in her hands. The housemaid thrust it rudely at her.

"Nelly sent this up to 'ee. Why 'ee should be so pampered is beyond me." She tossed her head and marched back down the hall.

Lisa closed the door and stood for a moment with the tray in her hands.

"Come sit by me," Lady Stavely said, "and have your supper. You must be very hungry."

Lisa discovered that she was hungrier than she had supposed. While she ate, Mary Stavely talked to her about Lord Drayton and told her how he and her brother, Peter, had grown up together.

"Then you have known my lord a long time?" Lisa said, more interested than she cared to admit.

"Since I was a child."

"And is he Sir Basil's friend as well?"

"No. Oh, Basil knew him, of course, but they were never friends. Richard was so young when he went away, you see. Only a boy."

A boy soldier, Lisa thought.

"He was with the king most of the time. Richard described to us the other evening his return with Charles to England after his father's execution. A fearful time! They were fugitives after the disastrous battle of Worchester. Hiding out. Finally escaping back to France."

"What's all this?" asked a deep voice, surprising the women. Drayton stood in the doorway, the height and breadth of him seeming to fill it completely. He grinned his lazy grin at them.

"I was just telling Lisa what a brave soldier you were," Lady Stavely smiled.

"More a foodhardy one," Drayton laughed, crossing the room in a few strides. "When one is young everything seems a great adventure." He smiled down at Mary Stavely. "How are you feeling this evening?"

"Much better than when I saw you earlier."

"Still, you look as if you could do with some sleep."

"I admit my eyes are beginning to feel a little heavy."

"Then we should leave you to rest. Lisa will be back. I just want a word with her."

He took Lisa's elbow and ushered her to the door.

"Where can we talk that we won't be overheard?" he whispered as they entered the hall.

"I don't know." Lisa looked around her. "Perhaps . . . the nursery? 'Tis just down the hall."

She remembered her mother's words: "Never be alone with a man unless you know him well and he has earned your trust." She knew then that she did trust Lord Drayton. He did not lust over her as Sir Basil had and although he had kissed her, it had never been against her will. He was a gentleman, in the truest sense of the word.

It was almost twilight when they entered the nursery and a bit eerie to see, in the growing shadows, a cradle and a rocking chair and several toys that had never felt or seen or known a child.

CLOAK OF FATE

"We won't be long, so I won't light a candle," Drayton said.

His eyes swept over Lisa approvingly. "'Tis nice to see you wearing something that becomes you."

The simplicity of the violet gown Zada had had made for her did nothing to hide the perfection of Lisa's figure. The full, young breasts, the hand-spanning waist, the tantalizing curve of her hips were clearly apparent despite the demure bodice and plainly draped skirt.

Her eyes sparkled. "I felt the shade a perfect match to my bruise."

He laughed his deep laugh. "You must be feeling better to make light of it."

"I am, thank you." She smiled up at him a little shyly. "I am very much obliged to you, my lord. You were very kind."

He was smiling as he stared down at her and then the smile faded and an intent, searching look took its place.

"I think you owe me an explanation," he said. "That is why I wished to speak with you."

"Oh? What is it I must explain?"

"What were you doing downstairs at such a late hour last night?"

The question had been plaguing him since she had told him where she had encountered Sir Basil. Had she been secretly meeting someone downstairs? he had wondered. He was totally unprepared for her answer.

"This was why." She reached into the pocket of her gown and drew out a folded paper. "I have thought carefully about this. I believe you to be a true and loyal supporter of the king and so I am entrusting it into your hands."

"What is it?"

"Sir Basil met with some rough men a few nights ago in the library. I overheard them plotting this dastardly act. They all signed a bond. Last night I went down to the library and copied it. Fortunately Sir Basil did not discover it on me."

Drayton frowned at her. "Lisa, you realize you had no right—"

"Read it!" she ordered.

He took the paper from her and walked over to the fading light of the window. As he glanced over the page, his expression changed. His handsome features hardened. "My God! An agreement to murder King Charles and the Duke of York on their way to Watford!" He read on. "It is signed by Basil Stavely and half a score of the malcontents!"

"I thought it would interest you," Lisa said quietly. "When I overheard them that night, Sir Basil said he was putting the bond in the chest. I could not open it at first, but I finally located the key under the corner of the chest. I just had time to copy the bond and return it."

Drayton shook his head. "The copy, I'm afraid, is of little use. I will need the actual bond to convict these traitors. Pray that 'tis still in the chest, Lisa."

"The copy is not proof enough?"

"No, my dear, I will need their own signatures."

"The authorities will not take *my* word?"

He regarded her. "I am afraid 'tis only the word of a servant against her master."

"But I am not—" She stopped herself. It was not yet time to reveal her true identity. She must curb her impatience to tell him the truth.

"What were you going to say?"

She shrugged. "I see what you mean. They would never believe me."

"Unfortunately not. Especially as Sir Basil has ill-treated you. The authorities would think you were accusing him on that account. Lisa, I *must* have that bond!"

He folded up the paper and slipped it inside his doublet.

"I will see you later," he said, starting for the door. Then he paused. "You have not spoken of this to anyone else? Lady Stavely?"

"No." She shook her head. "It would only have upset her more. You are the only one I could trust with it."

"I thank you for that trust," he said, his voice very deep.

"I knew you were a member of the court—a loyal friend of the king."

"Aye, Lisa. I would die for him," he said gravely. Then he grinned. "And I nearly *have* several times."

She waited a few minutes in the darkening nursery before she followed Drayton out the door and hastened back to Lady Stavely's side.

An hour later, having settled Mary Stavely for the night, Lisa left her sleeping peacefully. No one was in the dimly lit hallway as she hurried to her own little room. She opened the door and a tall, dark figure arose from where he had been seated on the edge of the bed. She gasped.

"Lisa, it's Drayton," he whispered. "I've been waiting for you."

He lit a candle.

"Did you get the bond?" she whispered back.

"No. The chest was empty except for a will belonging to the late Sir Edmund."

"You are sure?"

Gruffly. "Of course I am sure. Stavely must have taken the bond with him. Perhaps he was afraid to leave it here. I've only just remembered that he questioned me the other morning at breakfast about the king paying a visit to Watford this spring. The plan you overheard for the attack to come from the woods beyond Watford Heath seems logical. I must depart first thing in the morning for Whitehall and sound a warning. I don't want anyone to know where I am going. Let them think I have gone back to my estate. I'll return here as quickly as I can."

"God go with you." Lisa tried to keep her response casual as she moved to open the door, but he reached out and grasped her hand, turning her around to face him.

They said nothing as their eyes met. There was no need for words. He bent his head and his fingers were gentle on her fine-boned chin as he raised it and found her lips. When he drew back, she looked up at him, her eyes large and soft and luminous. He couldn't resist her innocent appeal and kissed her again.

Lisa could feel her heart race as he drew her to him. The floor seemed to rock beneath her feet. There was an overpowering magnetism about this man that seemed to pull her until her body came vibrantly alive, responding to the possessive demands of his mouth. Embarrassed by her eager reaction to him she strained to free herself. She felt the movement of his muscles beneath his doublet as he released her. The eyes that looked down into hers had grown dark with passion and frightened her.

"Please go," she whispered.

"Aye," he said hoarsely. "I had better."

He looked back from the doorway. Lisa's lips were still parted; her eyes glowed like deep violet pools. He felt a pressure rising in his loins. God, how he wanted her!

He fought the impulse. If he kissed her again he knew he could have her. It would be a simple matter to move her gently toward the bed. But she seemed so young and helpless, so vulnerable. It would be unfair to take such advantage. Unfair and dishonorable. He hoped to God he had not sunk *that* low.

"I am leaving tonight," he said thickly, making the sudden decision. "It will be better if I can slip in and out of London without being seen."

Mutely she nodded. "Godspeed, my lord."

He grinned. "Don't you think it high time you called me Richard?"

Chapter Twelve

THE OLD PALACE OF WHITEHALL LAY UPSTREAM ON THE Thames from the city of London. It was made up of an ill-sorted collection of buildings, constructed over many periods and in many styles. These buildings housed everyone connected with the Court from the king himself and the ministers of the crown down through an entourage of friends, relatives, parasites, schemers and opportunists, servants and prostitutes. All went to make up the ribald and covetous Court of Whitehall.

Here, the king conducted his government, entertained visiting dignitaries and made love to his mistresses.

On this gray, dismal morning, Lord Drayton was heading upstream for a private audience with the king. Few of his friends would have recognized him. His clothes were of a dark, plain cut; his boots, usually so highly polished, were splattered with mud. A heavy cloak of gray was pulled about his wide shoulders and a large black hat with a wet, drooping feather covered the dark periwig he wore to conceal his fair hair. He had even blackened his moustache.

The tilt boat now nudged into shore. The rain had begun to fall more heavily and the waterman held the boat steady as Drayton stepped out onto the slippery platform at the bottom of the Privy Stairs.

He was greeted by the king's page, Will Chiffinch, who peered hard at him and then, satisfied by the roguish grin that he was indeed Lord Drayton, climbed the stairs ahead to lead the way.

They passed the little courtyard and went through a low door that led up to the king's apartments. At the top of these steps, the page knocked at the door to announce Drayton's arrival, took his dripping hat and cloak from him and gestured for him to enter the royal bedchamber.

Drayton gave a low bow to his monarch who had risen to greet him.

"Delighted to see you, Richard," Charles said, grasping his shoulder.

"And you, Your Majesty."

"By God, Drayton, you could almost pass for me in that wig. Your moustache is a little larger than mine though," he said, touching his upper lip. "How did you manage to darken it?"

"Boot black, sire." Drayton grinned and Charles laughed aloud.

Crossing the room, the king took a chair by the window and indicated another close by for Drayton.

Richard threw himself into it, stretching out his long legs.

"What is this urgent business you had to see me about?" Charles asked.

Drayton wasted no time on preliminaries. "While in Essex, Your Majesty, I managed to learn of a plot—"

"'Oddsfish, who the devil is plotting to kill me now?" Charles laughed.

Drayton did not join him. Instead he pulled the bond Lisa had copied from his coat pocket and handed it to the king.

Charles perused it swiftly. "Stavely, eh? Just met the man last evening at Arlington's party. Claimed to be a good friend of yours, Richard, so I took the time for a few words with him."

Drayton shook his head. "He is no friend of mine, sire."

"Glad to hear it. A sour-faced villain if ever I saw one."

Drayton explained to Charles how Stavely had inherited the title and land under questionable circumstances and the reasons why he was feared and disliked by all who worked for him.

"I believe he has come to London solely for one purpose," he said.

"And that?"

"To ascertain the day you plan to leave for Watford, Your Majesty. Then he will alert the other men who signed that bond to carry out their plan of attack."

"What would you have me do, Richard?" Charles asked, his melancholy eyes regarding the other closely.

"Nothing," Drayton said succinctly. He had worked out his own plan carefully. "Let Stavely and his friends think you are still traveling to Watford. Name the day. I will secretly arrive here on the eve of your journey. I hope to have with me Roger Francis, my old adjutant in the army. I plan to pose as yourself and have Roger pose as the Duke of York. In the morning, we will go out by coach from Whitehall bearing your standard and head for Watford."

"And certain death. That's a damn foolhardy plan, Richard, unless you are keen to meet your maker."

"I would be a pretty poor soldier, sire, if I did not have the malcontents surrounded at Watford Heath before our arrival. For that purpose, I plan to gather as many of my old regiment together as I can muster. The plan must be carefully timed and executed. None must escape."

"You plan to return to Essex then?" the king said thoughtfully. He bent down to stroke the ears of a spaniel that had curled up at his feet.

"Today," Drayton said. "I came only to alert you."

"There is only one I would take into my confidence concerning this matter—Clarendon, my Lord Chancellor. My brother need not be informed until the last minute."

Drayton nodded in agreement and seeing Charles rise, got to his own feet. The audience was ended.

"There is no one better I would trust with my life than you, Richard," Charles said to him as he stood by the door.

"Thank you, Your Majesty," Drayton replied, deeply moved.

"You have seen Lady Grenville?" the king smiled.

"No, sire, I wished no one to know I was in London."

"Very wise. But take my advice. Do not delay too long in the country. The lady misses you."

"Really?" Drayton caught the implication. "She did not waste much time."

"A mere dalliance, Richard, no more."

Drayton grinned in his insouciant manner. "God help the poor bastard if he lacks stamina."

Charles's hearty laugh followed him even after he had descended the narrow stairway to where Will Chiffinch awaited him.

Before he left London that night, Lord Drayton had a meeting with Roger Francis. Francis had fought on the continent with Drayton after the Restoration and returned to England with him. Now he was happily married and running a profitable wool business in London.

They met in a tavern on the outskirts of the city and after quaffing a few jugs of ale and reminiscing over old times, Drayton quietly outlined his plan to his friend.

Francis was eager to help. He had found life a bit tame lately and was anxious for some excitement.

"How many of the men do you think you can muster?" Drayton asked him.

"Twenty at least—perhaps twenty-five."

"That should be plenty. Remember the king's own soldiers will themselves open fire at the first sign of attack."

"They are not to know they are guarding imposters?"

"No. Nor will our own men. Only the king and Clarendon and later the Duke of York will be aware that you and I are taking the place of Charles and his brother James. The fewer who know about it the less risk to our plan."

Francis nodded in agreement.

"You will arrange a meeting with the men a fortnight from now. Some place off the main road to London. I leave that up to your own discretion. A barn, perhaps, or a deserted house. You can send word to me at Stavely Manor in Bridgeford of the location."

Lord Drayton arrived back at the Manor very late. Lisa awoke with the sound of his firm footsteps crossing the upper gallery and going down the hallway. She heard a clock in the distance faintly strike two o'clock. For some reason she knew he had accomplished his mission. She turned over and went back to sleep.

Lisa met Lord Drayton outside Lady Stavely's bedchamber just before noon the next day. "Your bruise is fading," he smiled. "How is the pain in your head?"

"Much better, thank you." She lowered her voice. "Was your visit to London successful?"

"Everything has been attended to," he answered, but he did not tell her of the plan he had devised. When Mrs. Pottle appeared unexpectedly, he adeptly swung the conversation around to the warmer change in the weather.

With Mary Stavely recovering in bed, Lisa found herself pretty well confined to the house. In the days that followed, she ran into Lord Drayton several times. A chance meeting on the stairs, another in the great hall, once crossing the upper gallery. Each time Drayton asked after her health and seemed pleased to see her, but she noticed that he always moved away first. It was as if he were anxious not to get more involved with her.

And then one sunny afternoon when Lisa slipped downstairs at Lady Stavely's naptime, prepared to take Primrose for a short afternoon ride, Lord Drayton met her on the path outside the manor house. They were both surprised to see one another. Lord Drayton recovered first.

"Good afternoon, Lisa."

"My lord," she acknowledged him, "I thought you away for the day."

"No. I have just spent the morning writing some letters." He smiled down at her. "Are you off somewhere?"

"Just to take the air. Lady Stavely is having her nap."

"Will you join me in a walk in the garden?" He surprised himself by asking her. Since the night he had left for London he had vowed to himself that he would stay away from this girl. Her beauty tempted him and he was not used to resisting temptation. Besides, he knew women, and was aware, without conceit, that she was not unaffected by his kisses. Beneath the innocence, he felt, lay a passion that the girl seemed unaware she possessed. Like a knight of old, he felt he must protect her honor from those who might defame it—not the least of these being his own baser self.

Lisa agreed to join him and soon they were walking down a secluded path behind the house. On one side was a high hedge that prevented them from being seen from the Manor, on the other, the fragrant, well-designed gardens.

Curious to know more about her, Drayton encouraged Lisa to talk about herself. He became charmed as much by her total lack of artifice as by the happiness that emanated from her as she described her life with the acting troupe. She found herself opening up quite easily to him.

"Mama was a lady in name as well as in manner," she told him. (So that was where she got her grace and refinement, he thought.) "She gave up a great deal to marry my papa."

"And what of him?"

"He was very well-read. The son of an impoverished vicar. He adored Shakespeare and Jonson and could quote from them by the hour." She paused. "I suppose he was a dreamer. I doubt there was a practical bone in his body, but he was handsome and charming and Mama adored him." She smiled, remembering. "He had a deep, rich voice—rather like yours. I can still hear him reading from the Bible. He loved Ecclesiastes."

" 'To every thing there is a season, and a time to every purpose under the heaven,' " Drayton quoted.

" 'A time to be born, and a time to die,' " Lisa continued in her soft, musical voice. " 'A time to plant, and a time to pluck up that which is planted.' "

He smiled. "I wish I could have seen you on the stage," he said. "Did you enjoy acting?"

"Aye," she nodded.

"Then why did you leave the troupe?"

She hesitated a moment before answering. "After Mama died, the leading actor wanted to—to take over and he—he—"

"Wanted *you* as well," Drayton finished in a low voice.

She stopped walking to look up at him in amazement. "But how did *you* know?"

He laughed. "It wasn't difficult to determine. You are very beautiful, Lisa." The look in his green eyes made the color mount in her face. "And so you ran away," he finished, as they resumed their walk.

"Aye. My mother had wished me to go to her people, but I refused to go. My grandfather, you see, had disowned Mama for marrying Papa." Her eyes flashed. "I would *never* ask for their charity! Never!"

"You are a very courageous young lady to start out on your own."

"But a very stupid one in the ways of the world. Now I am penniless, but at least Matthew found my mare the next day. I have been keeping her in the Manor stables, thanks to Master Trent."

"Both he and Matthew are good men," Drayton said. "When Calderwood is rebuilt I would like to offer them both positions on my estate. Trent is exceptional with horses. Do you get much chance to ride your mare?"

"Sometimes in the early morning before Lady Stavely awakens, or at this time of day." She smiled. "Now you know most everything about me, my lord."

Drayton stopped walking and turned to put his hands on her shoulders and look down at her. "Lisa, I want to establish something right now. We are on equal terms, you and I. I want no more, 'my lord' this or 'my lord' that. My name is Richard. I want you to call me that, as I have been calling you by your first name. Will you do that for me?"

"If you wish . . . Richard." His name was new and strange on her lips.

"Good. Then that is settled."

They walked on a little further and then he led her over to a bench against the garden wall, in the shade of an ancient yew tree. For a moment after they sat down Lisa admired the garden before them, the brilliant color of the azaleas against the mauve, white and purple of the fragrant lilacs, but then she was caught up by Richard's rich voice. He was gazing at the rose garden to the right of where they sat. It reminded him of one his mother had cherished.

"When I came home from France," he said bitterly, "and saw the ruin of my home, I—well, I didn't want anything to do with Calderwood just then. I had had too much of death and destruction. I left my estate in the hands of an excellent agent and took up residence in London. But now I have had enough of Whitehall. It is like a rotten egg, Lisa. It looks good enough until you crack it open and smell what is inside."

"I have always held a glittering picture of life at court."

He snorted. "I hate to be the one to disillusion you, but your picture is pretty tarnished. Tarnished by intrigue and opportunism, by gambling and debauchery. After the army I found it a very empty life. That is why I have elected to leave Whitehall and attend to the reconstruction of my home and the running of my estates."

"It sounds very worthwhile."

"Much more so than my life in London, I can assure you," he said positively. "I look forward to the day when I can live permanently at Calderwood and put some of my ideas into operation."

"The house—will you rebuild it as it was?"

"I thought so at first, but now I have changed my mind. I have decided to start over—to have a new home designed entirely for me." He smiled. "I must be like my grandfather. He had a new Calderwood built for him. It was designed by the great architect, Inigo Jones. But I doubt that you have heard—"

"But of course I have heard of Inigo Jones," she exclaimed, her eyes sparkling. "He was originally a theatrical designer of costumes and scenery for court masques in King James' time."

He grinned at her. "It rather astounds me how well-informed you are."

"I don't know if I should be flattered or offended by that remark."

"Flattered. I think you are the first young lady I have ever really conversed with."

"Tell me more about Calderwood," she urged him.

"Inigo Jones went to the continent in 1613 with the Earl of Arundal, who was a friend of my grandfather's. When they returned, they visited him at his estate. Grandfather, having been to Italy himself, was impressed by Jones' enthusiasm over the beauties of the Italian architecture of antiquity and commissioned him to design a new Calderwood."

"I have heard that his design of the banqueting house at Whitehall is a masterpiece."

"It is." He regarded her. "Have you never been to London?"

"No. We were country players. We never entertained in the cities."

As Drayton reminisced over his old home, Lisa noticed that a proud shine came to his eyes.

"Jones used the same system of related proportions to Calderwood as he did to the banqueting house. It was a perfect example of the Italianate style and very beautiful." His green eyes grew very dark. "Cromwell's troops destroyed and vandalized it."

Lisa shook her head. "And yet they left so many ugly dwellings intact. It doesn't make sense."

"In this case they cared not for the building," Drayton said bitterly. "It was what was inside they wished to destroy."

After that first meeting, Richard joined Lisa quite often in the garden. Rules and protocol might prevent them from being together in the Manor, but they were both free to walk and converse in the garden. They talked about everything and Lisa found that the flowers and the trees and the hedges about her dissolved completely and all she was aware of was the tall man who walked by her side.

She became lost in Richard's voice, his teasing green eyes, his laughter. It was so easy and natural to banter with him and so enjoyable. A new brightness came to her face and to his as well. It was clearly apparent that a rare and special connection had been made between the two of them. They were so in tune that sometimes they would both begin to speak at once, the same thoughts coming to their minds.

Drayton's fascination for Lisa was not merely that she was beautiful, but bright and intelligent to talk with. She utterly enchanted him! Her manner was so refreshingly natural and honest, unlike any other female of his acquaintance. He had been to Oxford, yet her reading was almost as extensive as his. And what she had read she had thought about and enjoyed discussing. Her opinions were always her own, so sometimes he found himself arguing with her, but other times he was in complete agreement.

Lisa discovered that Richard was not as black and white about life as her papa had been. Perhaps it was because he had traveled so extensively and had found himself in so many situations. He took events and people as he found them and not as they should be and most times he could find humor in what he found.

The two of them discovered they could say almost anything to one another with two exceptions. He never spoke of the annihilation of his family. It was too painful for him—and he felt that something perhaps as painful might be true in her past, for there was a barrier there of which he was aware, and she would not yet reveal to him.

Drayton wanted her desperately, but that sense of innocence in her, that total trust in him, made it impossible for him to take advantage of her. It was not easy. Her constant nearness, the soft sound of her voice, the sweet scent of lavender that constantly surrounded her—all nearly drove him wild. Not being a celibate man, he was unused to parrying such tempting provocation. The fact that at the age of thirty-three he should find himself enamored with a young innocent almost half his age was hard for him to believe. Yet Lisa was so entirely different from any female he had ever encountered. One of his mistresses had once referred to him as a ruthless rake. She would have been surprised at how gentle and considerate and controlled he was with Lisa.

Chapter Thirteen

IT WAS A BEAUTIFUL MAY MORNING. THERE WAS A BLUE CLOUD-
less sky, a warm sun and a faint breeze rustled through the
treetops.

Lisa had awakened early and decided upon a ride before
breakfast. As she waited for Primrose to be saddled, Drayton's
deep voice came to her.

"Good morrow, Lisa." He tried to sound surprised. "You
ride very early."

Somehow she knew he had hoped for her appearance. She
smiled up at him. "Good morrow, my lord." (This last for the
ears of the young groom who was approaching with her horse.)
"Lady Stavely does not wake early. I find this a delightful time
to ride."

"May I join you?" he asked, as the mare was led up beside
them.

"By all means. I would enjoy the company."

Drayton helped Lisa mount, noticing how gracefully she
settled herself in the awkward sidesaddle. Her riding dress was
of a soft blue and she had secured her lustrous hair beneath a
little blue hat with a jaunty pheasant feather. Her riding attire
had once belonged to Lady Stavely and had been made over

for her, with some other gowns, by that lady's seamstress. Lisa looked very fetching as she smiled down at Lord Drayton, patting Primrose's neck.

He turned from her as his own horse was brought out, prancing and tossing its long black mane. Its coat was glossy and sleek in the morning sun.

"What a beautiful animal!" Lisa said with admiration, running her gaze over the stallion's lines.

"His name is Blackguard and believe me he can often be a knave."

Before he mounted, Lisa saw Richard give the young groom some coins. For services rendered, she wondered, or was he buying the lad's silence?

They set off at a canter down the road. The air was mild and filled with the sweet perfume of spring. There was no struggle this morning between Drayton and his horse. He sat astride Blackguard with complete ease. Apparently the stallion had at last learned that he bore someone on his back who was clearly his master.

Before long they crossed a clover-covered meadow in the opposite direction from the Manor and the village. Cattle grazed in the distance, birds sang. It was a peaceful, pastoral scene.

"How people can be content to live in crowded cities when they can have this beauty I will never understand," Drayton said, gesturing around him.

Lisa smiled. "It is plain to see you were raised in the country, Richard. But London must be very colorful and exciting. I've always imagined it to be a city of gilded coaches, beautiful buildings and richly dressed lords and ladies."

"Humph!" he uttered cynically. "Someday I shall tell you about the real London."

"Tell me now."

He shrugged, carefully slowing his horse to a walk.

"I suppose when I think of London, I think of clamor. 'Tis a very noisy and bustling city. The hawkers—coalmen, milkmaids, tinkers, flower and vegetable sellers—all hawk their goods along the cobbled streets, crying, 'Fine strawberries,' 'Fresh cockles' or whatever. Their combined shouting makes a raucous din."

"Go on," she said, picturing it vividly.

"The shops are small and most have signs displayed outside,

such as the one outside Mr. Farr's tobacco shop. It reads: 'The Best Tobacco by Farr.'"

Lisa laughed at this.

"A little further away is the shop of his rival," Drayton continued. "This man's sign reads: 'Far Better Tobacco Than the Best Tobacco by Farr.'"

They both laughed.

"One has to have a sense of humor to exist there, and the people do enjoy poking fun at themselves. The city itself, you see, is pretty dismal. The dwellings are wooden and dangerous, reaching out across the narrow streets, as overhanging stories have been added by succeeding generations. Mark my words, if a fire ever gets a start it will sweep through the whole of London in no time."

Lisa shuddered at the thought.

"It is wise never to go out alone after dark. The narrow streets are unlit and thieving footpads lurk in the passageways. In wet weather the passages become open sewers and a breeding place for disease. Ladies hold rosemary or a perfumed glove to their noses to try and block out the stench when they go out into the streets. And over all of London is the polluted smoky air obscuring churches and palaces."

"What a gloomy picture you paint."

"An accurate one, I'm afraid. Now, let us forget the filthy city and enjoy this verdant countryside."

Drayton had been doing his best to curb his skittish black stallion, but now he decided to give the horse its head and the animal took off at a gallop over the gently rolling meadowland.

Not to be undone, Lisa raced Primrose after him and they streaked across the open fields. It took the utmost of her skill in horsemanship to try and keep pace with Drayton and his magnificent steed, but at last she had to concede and let him gallop on ahead.

At the end of the field he turned and came trotting back to where Lisa and Primrose had pulled up beside a low stone fence. He admired the way she had handled her horse.

"Papa taught me to ride when I was quite small," she smiled. "Have we not time to sit down a minute before we head back?"

"Why not?" he agreed. He leaped agilely from the saddle and helped her to dismount, tethering the two horses to some nearby shrubbery.

Lisa settled herself on top of the low fence and Drayton sat down beside her, stretching out and crossing his long legs at the ankle.

"What a beautiful day it is," he sighed, opening the neck of his shirt.

"And much fresher than London," she smiled. "You have made it sound positively horrid."

"'Tis that," he grinned.

"Then speak no more of the city. Tell me instead about the king. Did you see him when you went up to London with the copy of the bond?"

"Aye. I gave it to him to read."

"Did it upset him?"

"Charles?" he laughed. "There have already been dozens of plots on his life. Nevertheless, he agreed to my plan."

"Won't you tell me what it is?"

"Perhaps. When the time comes."

"What does the king look like in person?"

Drayton shrugged. "He is a tall man and athletically built, rather swarthy in complexion. Some think him ugly, but nevertheless, the ladies find him very charming."

"So I have heard."

"And from that stems his biggest problem. Money. The gifts and titles showered on his mistresses and illegitimate children are a constant drain on the royal finances."

"I have heard that the morals at court are very loose."

Drayton clicked his tongue and touched a finger to her nose. "It is considered very improper for a young lady to discuss such a subject."

Lisa brushed his finger aside a little angrily. "Why should it be? The king is the monarch of this country. His example can influence his people greatly. When Cromwell was in power his parliament punished adultery by death, but Charles, I have heard, ridicules chastity and faithfulness. Is that true?"

"Well, he is no saint, but—"

"Don't you see? The people are bound to ape him, preferring laxness and immorality to the vigorous discipline of Cromwell."

"True," he admitted, looking out over the field before him. The cynical lines seemed to have deepened in his face. "The old views of morality have gone as much out of fashion as high-necked gowns."

Her gaze centered on the riding crop she clasped in her delicate gloved hands. "Has the royal example affected *you*, Richard?" she asked him in a small voice.

He turned to look at her, a twitch forming at the corners of his mouth as he saw she was blushing.

"Are you asking me how many women I have made love to?"

The blush spread. "Nay! Forgive me. I had no right—"

"Hundreds."

The violet eyes widened and then she saw he was laughing at her and she laughed, too. Quite suddenly they both stopped. His clear green eyes searched her face and she met his gaze with her own, equally intent.

Lisa felt something rise in her, a desire to feel his lips on hers, his strong arms around her. She began to tremble.

Something inside him was warning him that he was moving into something far more entangling than the casual liaisons he was used to. Yet he could not help himself. A bright emotion had come alive in his eyes. He reached out a hand and removed her little hat, his fingers pulling out the bone bodkins that held her hair, loosening it until the soft black cloud descended about her shoulders.

"You are so beautiful, Lisa," he said thickly. "So damned beautiful." He kissed the hollow of her throat, and she could feel the blood run as hot as a flame along her veins.

"Richard . . ." She uttered his name in a barely audible sigh.

He began to cover her face with kisses. Then his mouth found hers and he was holding her, caressing her, kissing her, as her heart pounded within her. Impulsively, she wound her arms around him, feeling the strong, corded muscles that ran down his back. Where his shirt opened she could see the golden hairs on his chest. She rested her cheek there and sighed contentedly.

"Lisa?" His deep voice was husky as he gently swept a silky strand of hair back from her face.

She said nothing and he lifted her chin with his fingers and kissed her again.

"You really have bewitched me," he whispered. "No other woman has ever had this affect on me. I swear it! I've wanted them, yes. Had them, too." He laughed. "Not hundreds, but too damn many to count." It was as if he felt compelled to purge himself of all the faceless females in his past. He wanted to tell her of the tavern wenches and the unfaithful wives, the camp followers and the amorous courtesans, but her hand came up and covered his mouth.

"I don't want to know about the others," she cried. "Just hold me, Richard. Just hold me and kiss me."

She lifted her mouth to his and his kiss was gentle, almost too gentle—as if he did not trust himself.

"I felt something from the first moment I laid eyes on you riding up the lea," she murmured. "'Twas as if I had been waiting for you. Can you understand what I mean?" She shook her head a little sadly. "How foolish I am. I know nothing can come—"

"Hush!" His eyes devoured her. "You're what I've looked for all my life."

Of course it was what she had wanted to hear. She had almost been about to admit to him that she was not who she seemed, but now it did not matter. He cared for her, was bothered not a bit by her station.

This time his kiss was long and hard and passionate. She kissed him back, her soft lips clinging to his, her hands moving over his wide shoulders, fastening in his golden curls, pulling his head down, his lips closer.

It was then she should have ceased, for the alchemy between them was much too strong, and her own body was responding with a trembling awareness, new sensations bursting into flower. He thrust her roughly from him.

"Nay!" he groaned, jumping to his feet. "We are going back. NOW!"

Lisa rose slowly from the fence and reached for her feathered hat that had tumbled onto the grass. She could not look at Richard. The excitement in her veins had turned to shame. Tears of humiliation filled her eyes.

Did he think she had behaved like a wanton? Had thrown herself at him? Trembling with an emotion she took for anger, she rushed to mount her horse. She took off quickly, galloping fiercely across the field.

He caught up to her on the road before the Manor and grabbed for her reins, drawing Primrose up so abruptly that Lisa nearly tumbled from the saddle.

"I apologize for what happened," he said, roughly.

"Why?" she said angrily. "'Tis quite obvious you blamed me."

"You!" His eyebrows rose. His voice when he spoke again was filled with self-mockery. "On the contrary, Lisa. I blame only myself. I'm a bit of a bastard, but until now my depravity has never sunk to Basil Stavely's level."

"What do you mean?"

"I mean this is the first time I have ever been tempted to tamper with the young and innocent." He saluted her. "In the future, my dear, I will endeavor to see that we are never alone again."

Lisa's face paled. "Do you mean we can no longer be friends?"

"Friends?" He gave a hollow laugh. "You call me your *friend?*"

"Aye," she nodded. "I've never had a friend before. Someone I could talk with so easily. Someone who seemed to understand me and the way I thought. I know there were times when we argued, but we always laughed at the same things."

She had completely disarmed him. "So we did," he said softly.

"Is that all to be over then?"

"Oh God, Lisa," he growled. "Can't you see that we have gone beyond friendship? To me you are a beautiful, desirable creature whom I want more than anything in the world to make love to. I'm a man, Lisa. I've denied myself few pleasures. I dare not see you alone any more. In my lax moral code I draw the line at very little, but I do not seduce and dishonor virgins."

Before she could say another word he was gone, galloping off down the road.

Lisa sat in stunned silence, listening to the retreating hoof-beats.

"Oh, Richard!" she murmured. She felt again the strength of his arms about her, those warm, hard lips pressing against hers. Deep inside her was an indisputable awareness—rich, warm and complete. She had fallen in love with him. She had fallen totally and irrevocably in love with Richard Drayton!

But it was not until that night, when she tossed and turned in her bed, that she finally admitted to herself that she desired him as much as he desired her. "More than anything in the world," he had said. But he was not ready for marriage. That was obvious. And so he had pushed her away.

Her mama had warned her and left no doubt in her mind of

the sinfulness of submitting to a man before marriage. But love was such a powerful emotion. Richard was right. She must avoid his company . . . evade any encounter until he was ready. Perhaps when Calderwood was reconstructed, when everything was as he wanted it to be he would ask her to be his bride. But that might be years and years!

Chapter Fourteen

DRAYTON WAS GONE FOR NEARLY A WEEK. HE DID A GREAT deal of thinking in that period and Lisa was at the center of his thoughts.

It was time he married. He knew that. But what did he as Lord Drayton require in a wife? Well, for one thing she need not be rich, for he was wealthy enough himself. Beautiful, then? Yes. That went without saying. A virgin? Yes, that too. Innocent and beautiful—Lisa was both of these, but there was one thing she was not. The difficulty was that this one thing was unsurmountable. Lisa was not of noble birth. Drayton had a responsibility. He was the last of his line. His wife's lineage must be impeccable.

True, Lisa had said her mother had had noble blood, but her father had been a lowly actor—a ne'er-do-well. Who knew if her parents had even been legally married? She might be illegitimate. Damn his infernal pride! Why should this matter? But it had been drummed into him all his life. His family history was traceable to the days of William the Conqueror. He was the heir. He would be Lord Drayton, Baron of Calderwood, someday. He must not marry beneath him.

"Marriage and love are often two very different things," his father had told him. "'Tis a question of putting family and duty first."

"But didn't you love Mother?" the young Richard had asked him.

"I had only seen her once before our marriage," his father had admitted. "I did not know her. I grew to love her afterward. Your mother and I, you see, were very fortunate. It does not always happen that way."

"But what if I should fall in love with someone unsuitable?"

His father had sighed. "Then, if she agrees, you may place her under your protection."

"What does that mean?"

"She would become your mistress."

"Did you ever have a mistress, Father?"

The older man had nodded. "Aye," he had said slowly. "Before I was married."

"Did you love her?"

"I thought so at the time. Now, that is quite enough of that, my boy." And his father had quickly changed the subject.

Lisa found herself growing more and more concerned about Mary Stavely. She seemed slow to recover her health and strength. For long hours she lay motionless staring up at the ceiling above her bed.

Lisa tried to talk to her and to read to her but nothing held her attention for long. Day by day, although she became stronger in body, her apathy remained.

One night Lisa awoke with a strange feeling of unease. It was the same feeling she had felt the night of her mama's death and she shivered, remembering how she had told Zada of it the next morning after they had found Valerie Manning dead.

"Perhaps you possess the gift, child," the old gypsy had said.

Yet Lisa had never had visions. She was no soothsayer. It was only an odd presentiment that had filled her then and filled her now.

Mary! She felt sure it had to do with Mary! She rose quickly from her bed and pulling on her wrapper, rushed from her room.

Mary's bedchamber was lit by only a candle and upon entering the room, Lisa felt an instant chill. The tall, mullioned windows at the end of the room stood open to the small stone balcony beyond. Cold, damp air was rushing in, billowing out the curtains.

Lisa glanced at the bed and as she had somehow known, it was empty.

"Oh, Mary, no!" Lisa's heart began to pound as she raced for the windows.

A strong wind was blowing and threatened to push Lisa back into the room as she stumbled out onto the balcony.

She looked frantically about for Mary.

In the dim candlelight from the bedchamber behind her, Lisa made out a thin tiny form trying desperately to climb up onto the stone railing.

She stopped herself from crying out and instead moved cautiously but steadily forward in Mary's direction. She must not frighten her and yet she must get to her before . . .

She was just behind her now. Mary had managed to get one knee up on the balustrade and was trying to pull herself up.

Lisa reached out and grasped the petite woman around the waist, prepared to pull her back.

Mary gave a start. "No! Let me go!" she screamed, holding onto the railing with surprising strength.

"Mary, please don't!" Lisa grabbed at her with icy fingers, trying to dislodge her hold.

The wind whipped around them, cold and damp and of almost gale force. Lisa was quickly frozen in her light wrapper and imagined how cold Mary must be since she was clad only in her nightdress!

Suddenly the railing began to crumble beneath Mary's clutching hands! Lisa made a frantic grab for a firmer hold, her muscles straining, as she fought to draw them both back from the edge of the balcony. An opening of several feet had appeared before their eyes as the stone crumbled away to the ground beneath.

The two women struggled on the dark, windswept balcony. Mary squirmed and twisted in Lisa's grasp, trying to free herself and plunge through the gap now open before her. Their long hair whipped around their heads, their clothing blew out about their bodies.

Lisa felt she could not hold on much longer. She must try something!

She made a sudden lunge backward, taking Mary with her,

and they went down in a heap on the hard stone floor of the balcony.

Lisa struggled to her feet, pulling Mary back with her toward the open windows. With difficulty she got her back into the bedchamber. Mary fought her all the way. Leaving the exhausted woman lying on the carpet, Lisa quickly shut the windows against the wind.

She went back to Mary, helping her to her feet and half carrying her back to bed.

"You must be chilled to the bone," she said, covering her up. "I will build up the fire and get the warming pan." As she did this, the blood began to circulate more readily in Lisa's own shivering body.

Mary was crying hysterically now.

"Pray don't cry, Mary," Lisa soothed. "It's all right now."

"Nay! You don't understand," Mary moaned. "It took me so long to get up the courage and then you . . . you stopped me."

"I had to, Mary!"

"Why? What have I to live for? I have been lying here hour after hour, thinking about Brydie, about her taking her own life because Basil had taken her without her consent." She gave a short gulping laugh. "Basil *always* takes me without my consent. Not one of the children I have miscarried was ever conceived in love! That is why they don't live." Her voice rose, and she began trembling alarmingly. "And Basil will continue taking me and I will continue losing my babies and I cannot bear to go through that any more! I would rather be dead!"

"Oh, Mary, don't—" Lisa put her arms about the frail shoulders and Mary Stavely sobbed against her.

"Not all my miscarriages were like this last one, Lisa," Mary went on, blinking back the tears. "Some were farther along. Then they are more than blood and a few clumps. The water bursts and then the baby comes and it is still attached by the cord and it has to be cut. Oh God, once I had to do it myself. It was alive, Lisa, and I had to cut that cord and kill my baby! 'Twas so little and well formed and clean because it came out with the water. It had tiny eyes and tiny fingers and toes and—"

"*Don't*, Mary! Don't think about it!" Lisa was beginning to fear for Mary's sanity.

"Why, Lisa? Why am I being punished? What have I done? I am so tired of it all—so very tired."

"Of course you are tired, Mary. You have been through a

great deal, but I promise you things are going to change. Don't ask me how I know. Just have faith, Mary. This will never happen to you again. Never!"

It took a little while, but Lisa at last managed to settle Mary down. She rang for the upstairs maid to bring some brandy and hot tea. As Lisa sat by Mary's bed reassuring her and sipping the hot tea, she made Mary promise to go out in the spring sunshine with her the next day.

"Aye, Lisa, I will come," she sighed. "Although I am afraid it will do me little good."

"I am only anxious for you to get well, Mary. We all are."

"Has Richard sent word when he will return?"

"No, Mary."

"It was so strange of him going off that way—so unlike him. Can he be at his estate all this time?"

"I don't know, Mary."

Lisa didn't know where Richard was, but she missed him terribly. She missed the walks in the garden with him and their talks and his deep laugh. She thought of him so often—sometimes quite unwillingly. He had a way of creeping into her thoughts and dreams and she had to fight to push him away.

What would she do when he did return? What would she say? If only she could go away for a time and think things out. But she could not leave Stavely Manor. Originally there had been only Sir Basil and her inheritance to consider but now there was Mary as well.

"What is the matter, Lisa?"

"Nothing, Mary." Lisa forced a smile. "I think it's time you got some sleep. I won't leave you. I will sleep right here on the sofa."

Chapter Fifteen

IT WAS LATE THE NEXT AFTERNOON WHEN LORD DRAYTON RE-
turned to Stavely Manor.

Lisa had escorted Mary Stavely out to the garden that
morning. They had sat in the sun admiring the flowers and
talking for over an hour. Mary had looked much better for her
outing.

Drayton immediately went to see Mary upon his arrival. He
knocked on the door of her bedchamber and both women
uttered their surprise as he strode into the room.

Lisa felt that Mary must surely hear the wild beating of her
heart at the sight of him. He was magnificent in green doublet
and breeches and long, soft leather boots. No other man, she
thought, had his width of shoulders, his great height, his
disarming smile. He had clearly spent some time out-of-doors,
as his face seemed bronzed by the sun, making the green of his
eyes even more piercing in their intensity.

"Good afternoon," he grinned at them both and to Mary he
gave a low bow. "My profound apologies, Mary, for my
rudeness. I am afraid I woefully abused your hospitality. I
disappeared with no explanation and now I reappear without
the courtesy of informing you. Pray forgive me and my bad
manners, but I bear good news."

"Good news?" Mary Stavely asked questioningly.

"Aye. I have been visiting your brother, Peter, for several days and a good time the two of us had catching up on all the years apart. We've done some hawking together and some hare coursing and talked ourselves hoarse over a tankard or two."

"Or three or four," Mary added with a twitch of her lips.

It was good to see Mary smile again, Lisa thought. But then Richard Drayton had that affect on women. There was no question he was a charmer. He grinned at Mary.

"I told Peter how I thought the sight of his face would do you the world of good and he is coming to visit you."

Her eyes lit up at his words. "Oh Richard, how wonderful! When?"

"The day after tomorrow."

"So soon!"

"Aye. So you must get out of that bed of yours and be up and about for him."

"Oh, I will," Mary Stavely assured him. "Lisa had me outside today for the first time. We sat in the garden and I am sure the fresh air was very beneficial."

For the first time Drayton let himself regard Lisa.

"How well you are looking," he said, glancing at her. "I'm glad to see that the bruises have completely disappeared." His voice had been under control, but his eyes never quite met hers.

It seemed a miracle at how quickly Mary Stavely's spirits spiraled upward at the thought of Peter's impending visit. Apathy was replaced with a new vitality as she anticipated his arrival.

The next morning, while sitting in the garden, Lord Drayton joined Mary and Lisa.

"How long is Peter planning to visit?" Mary asked him.

"A week I should think. I understand he hasn't seen you since Christmas."

"Aye." Mary's face darkened. "I wanted him to stay longer then, but Basil . . ."

Lord Drayton nodded and changed the subject. "I am surprised Peter hasn't married again. How long has he been a widower?"

"Four—no I believe it is five years now."

"I was sorry to hear about his wife."

"He told you how she died in childbirth?"

"Aye."

"She was a timid little thing—so sweet and gentle. The little boy lived but a day."

Drayton shook his head. "He, said they had been married only eleven months."

"That is so. A tragedy. He has become quieter now than he used to be—more serious," Mary Stavely mused.

"I could see that," Drayton smiled, "but I soon got him laughing about the old times. He hasn't lost that droll sense of humor of his."

All the while they talked, Drayton's eyes kept straying to Lisa, sitting so quietly beside Mary.

How lovely she looked this morning, he thought. So fresh and young in her light flowered gown and face-framing straw sunshade. Her eyes seemed as blue as the primroses and violets that lined the path, but they were lacking something. The sparkle he had grown used to seeing was missing. Had he hurt her? He cursed himself. Of course he had, but it had been for her own good . . . hadn't it? She had been constantly in his thoughts from the day he had ridden off not knowing or caring what direction he took.

His visit to Peter had never completely taken his mind off her, for she had a way of returning to his thoughts. The simplest things reminded him of her. The sound of a nightingale singing in the evening. A copy of Shakespeare's sonnets lying beside Peter's chair. A young housemaid wearing a mobcap.

"I asked you a question, Richard?"

"I'm sorry, Mary."

"Do you think I could have a party with Basil away? Just a small supper party while Peter is here?"

Drayton considered. "Why not? Your friends would be delighted. Peter tells me they never get a chance to see you."

Mary Stavely smiled. "Oh, 'twould be so lovely to have some of our old friends here without Basil to ruin—" She stopped, and then rushed on. "Just friends who grew up with you and Peter and me."

"But would it be too much for you, Mary? You are still not very strong."

"'Twould do me a world of good." Mary Stavely's eyes shone. "Just a small party. Supper and some card playing afterward. Perhaps a little dancing."

"What is your opinion?" Richard asked Lisa offhandedly.

"I see no harm as long as Lady Stavely does not overexert herself."

"We must all see that she doesn't," Drayton said to her.

"I will enjoy making the plans, Richard," Mary Stavely assured him, "and you and Lisa, I am sure, will help me carry them out."

Sir Peter Ellsbury was not what Lisa had expected. She had visualized him as being small of stature like his sister. Instead, he was quite tall, though lean of build, and had chestnut-colored hair and friendly brown eyes with pleasant crinkles at the corners.

"This is Elizabeth Manning, Peter. She is called Lisa." Mary Stavely introduced them. "Lisa recently lost her mother and has come to live at Stavely Manor as my companion."

Ellsbury bowed gracefully over Lisa's hand. "I am delighted," he said, and smiled at her kindly. "Delighted to meet such a lovely young lady and delighted my sister has at last found a friend."

They dined in the flickering candlelight. Lisa was dressed in a gown of soft yellow that Mary had had made over for her. It showed off her creamy neck and shoulders and tiny waist.

It did not take long for Mary to notice that her brother's eyes turned to Lisa with interest and pleasure whenever she spoke, but Lisa seemed oblivious to this. Peter and his sister sat at either end of the table, flanked on either side by Lisa and Lord Drayton.

Lisa was enjoying Peter's attention, but was forever conscious of the blond giant's searing green cat eyes appraising her over his wineglass.

Mary Stavely glowed with happiness, her little face shining in the light from the two candelabra.

It was not an elaborate supper. There was a chine of roast beef, a loin of veal, two dishes of larks, one of neats' tongues and a plate of neat's feet and mustard—which was apparently a favorite of Peter's—some tansies and a fine claret.

The conversation was light and amusing.

"I've always wondered," Mary said, the claret making her pale cheeks pink, "why the king has the nickname of 'Old Rowley.'"

Peter cleared his throat as Richard laughed.

"Will you tell her or shall I?"

"Little sister. The name is taken from one of the stallions in the royal stud."

"Oh," said Mary, waxing crimson. "I'm glad I did not pose the question to a stranger."

They all laughed.

To cover her embarrassment Mary went on to tell Peter about the party she had planned in his honor.

"'Twill be this Saturday evening, and they have all accepted my invitation, Peter. I am so looking forward to seeing our old friends again."

Peter smiled at her. "Mary, you look more radiant than you have in years. I don't know if it's Lisa's influence or Basil's absence, or both, but I would like to offer a toast." He rose, as did Lisa and Richard. "To our hostess, my favorite sister, Mary."

It was plain in the next day or two that Lisa had not only charmed, but completely captivated Peter Ellsbury. He had known many beautiful women in his life, but Lisa was the most exquisite creature he had ever seen. He hung around her even when she was not attending Mary and jumped to assist her at every opportunity. At mealtimes, she often felt his eyes on her and he gave her quiet little compliments, quite unaware of his friend's growing jealousy.

Lisa knew Richard had observed Peter's attentions to her, but when her eyes tried to communicate to him her lack of interest in Peter, he only grinned in that insouciant manner that infuriated her.

Inside, however, Drayton felt far from indifferent. Peter, he knew, was a gentleman and his attentions to Lisa would therefore be quite honorable. Eventually, he might even offer her marriage. Would Lisa accept him? Why did the thought of another man possessing her bother him so much?

"Forget the damn wench!" he told himself angrily. "If there is no affinity, no tenderness, no love in a marriage of convenience, then that is the price I must be prepared to pay." Hadn't the king told him not to expect to find delight and duty in the same bed? Yet, for the first time in his life, he found himself wishing that he were not of the peerage. Although it might be frowned upon, Peter Ellsbury, being but a knight, was free to marry whom he wished. He envied him.

Each evening after the four of them had dined, they would sit talking and laughing around the table. The three old friends made sure Lisa was never excluded from the conversation for long, although it was natural for them to reminisce.

"Have you decided what to do about Calderwood, Richard?" Mary asked one evening.

"Aye. I am going up to London next week to speak with a man by the name of Christopher Wren."

"Isn't he a friend of yours, Peter?"

"Aye. We are both fascinated by astronomy. He was appointed Professor of Astronomy at Oxford a few years ago. I have attended meetings there a number of times."

Mary looked puzzled. "But what has astronomy to do with rebuilding Richard's home?"

"Wren is very interested in architecture and Inigo Jones in particular. I am sure when Richard tells him that Jones designed Calderwood, he will be anxious to see the remains and possibly take on the job of planning the reconstruction."

"Or design a completely new structure," Drayton added. "That is now what I have in mind."

"Really?" Mary said. "But 'twas such a beautiful residence. I remember the last party I attended there. . . ."

"So do I," laughed Peter. "Your father took me aside, Richard, and asked me directly if I knew whether you were enamored with anyone of the fair sex. Methinks he was trying to arrange a future marriage between you and Lady Letitia Galt."

"That cow?" Drayton exclaimed. "Pray excuse me, Mary, but she had a face like a plum pudding. Little raisin eyes—"

Mary laughed. "That may be, Richard, but she has produced four sons since she married Lord Haversham. You may be sorry she did not become Lady Drayton."

"Never!"

"Methinks Richard may have someone in mind for that role," Peter teased. "Why else this sudden interest in settling down?"

"Is that so?" Mary asked. "Shame on you, Richard, you have never said a word. Who is to become Lady Drayton?"

"Peter jests, Mary," Richard glared at his friend. "I have no intention of considering marriage until Calderwood is rebuilt and my estates have been developed as I would like to see them."

So she had been right, Lisa thought. Marriage was far from Richard's mind. It might be years before he considered it and by that time he would have been sought by dozens of suitable beauties. Being both handsome and wealthy his choice would be wide. Why should she even think he would consider her?

The thought was an agonizing one. Lisa knew that she loved Richard Drayton, that she wanted no more in life than to be his wife. But for the time being, there was nothing she could do about it.

"You look sad this evening, Lisa," Peter whispered to her later. "Is something making you unhappy?"

"No," she hastened to assure him. "I have enjoyed these last few days very much."

"So have I," he said, his brown eyes warm as they regarded her. "I only wish . . . I know so little about you, Lisa. I would like the opportunity to get to know you better."

"There is very little I can tell you," Lisa smiled. "I have lived a very quiet life. Cut off from society."

"Mary tells me that with your parents dead, you are quite alone. I am sorry that you did not get the full protection you needed here."

"I beg your pardon?"

"I know about Sir Basil—his unwanted advances and abuse to you. I want you to know that I intend to call him out on his return."

"Does Mary know this?"

"I would not have her worry on my account."

"Richard, I understand, is of the same mind."

"Then I must speak with him. It is my duty alone as a member of the family."

"Then take care, Peter," Lisa said, laying a hand on his arm. "For I do not believe Sir Basil would engage in a fair fight."

Peter glanced down at her hand. A hope flared in him that this beautiful young girl might have begun to care for him. He intended then and there to pursue her in earnest.

Richard, entering the room just then, stiffened.

Lisa and Peter were standing close together. She had a hand on his arm which, at that moment, Peter clasped and brought to his lips. It was as he leaned forward to whisper something in her ear that Richard slipped unobserved back out the door.

Chapter Sixteen

AT LADY STAVELY'S REQUEST, HER SEAMSTRESS HAD BEEN SUM-moned as soon as the date of the party had been set to fashion a gown for Lisa to wear. Two simple gowns for everyday wear were also ordered for her and Mary had had several others of her own made over for Lisa. The girl's gratitude and pleasure clearly delighted Mary Stavely.

Mary had become as fond of Lisa as if she had been the younger sister she had never had and treated her with as much warmth and affection. Lisa's natural reciprocation of this often brought tears to Mary's eyes.

The night of the party arrived. Peter Ellsbury, tall and distinguished in cream satin, watched Lisa's descent down the wide stairway and was struck again by her incredible beauty.

The gown she wore was of a pale-blue silk that bore almost a mauve cast. The softly draped neckline was lowered off her shoulders, accentuating the natural fullness of her breasts. The gown's simplicity, together with Lisa's young and regal bearing, gave it a classical beauty unmatched by any of the more richly dressed and jeweled ladies who had already begun to fill the hall.

"Lisa, my dear," Peter said, kissing her hand. "You look enchanting."

"The gown is a perfect shade for you," Mary Stavely said, greeting Lisa with a gentle smile.

Mary was a woman utterly lacking in envy, despite realizing immediately that she would be completely eclipsed by her radiant young companion.

Her own gown was of a soft rose shade, the neckline draped with transparent gauze, caught at intervals with tassels of pearls. A long string of pearls was looped around her neck and she wore earrings of pearl drops.

"More guests are arriving, Mary," Peter broke in. "If you will excuse us, Lisa," he said a little regretfully. "Richard, I am sure, will attend you."

Lisa followed Peter's gaze back up the stairway. Lord Drayton was casually descending, looking magnificent in dove-gray brocade trimmed with silver. His coat was expertly cut to emphasize his broad shoulders and narrow waist. At his neck frothed a lace cravat which matched the cuffs of his wrists. Unlike Peter, he wore no wig, and his golden hair shone in the light from the overhead chandelier, which smoked and glowed with dozens of candles.

Candles also ringed the walls of the lower hall and lit the gallery and dining hall. The dark old Manor had never seemed so bright and alive.

Richard's green eyes admired the picture Lisa made at the foot of the staircase. Her dark, lustrous hair was piled up in soft curls, with one allowed to descend over a creamy shoulder. Her delicate, slender neck thus revealed made her features resemble a beautiful cameo. Her violet eyes, so large in the perfect oval of her face, mirrored the color of her gown.

"Good evening, Lisa," he said, assuming his recent air of amused indifference. "You look very lovely. A most becoming gown."

"Thank you. Lady Stavely had her seamstress make it for me especially for tonight."

As he came closer to her, Lisa could not help but feel her heart quicken.

"No doubt you will have all the gentlemen at your feet by the end of the evening," he said dryly, his eyes coming to rest on the soft curves of her breasts as they rose above the lowered neckline of her gown.

Lisa blushed under his insolent stare. "I do not wish—" she began.

"But of course you do," he interrupted. "All beauties long to be the center of attraction." His gaze swept the hall. "There is none to equal you here tonight. See the two young gallants over there pawing the ground? That's how anxious they are for an introduction."

"Why are you talking to me this way?" she asked him, hurt by his remarks and the cynical twist of his lips.

"Just a warning," he shrugged. "It is only natural for men to wish to be near beautiful women, Lisa. You have succeeded in beguiling Peter, and there will be many others who will fall under your spell this evening." His voice roughened. "Just don't go off alone with any of them."

"I don't need *you* to tell me that," she flared, angered now by his arrogance. Why was he trying to ruin this evening for her when she had been looking forward to it so much?

"Perhaps not, but just don't expect *me* to rescue you from any compromising situation in which you may find yourself."

The nerve of him! "You need have no fear of that," she snapped back, her violet eyes now blazing.

Mary Stavely appeared at this juncture, Peter and she having by now received most of the guests. She frowned at Lisa and Richard as if she had caught the exchange between them and drew Lisa away to meet several of her old friends. When Lisa looked back through the milling crowd, Richard had resumed his lazy, indifferent manner as he conversed with the two young gallants who were staring in her direction and clearly questioning him about her.

Lisa smiled automatically as she was brought forward by Mary to meet several people, but she could not help but feel her spirits rise as she was accepted graciously by one and all. She found herself conversing easily without a trace of the shyness she had expected she might experience.

Mary Stavely's idea of a small supper party consisted of over forty people. Lisa was soon surrounded by most of the eligible young gentlemen present excluding Richard Drayton, whom she saw standing against one of the walls and eyeing her, a half-mocking smile on his lips. He raised the goblet in his hand in a salute to her and she looked quickly away.

Before the first hour was over, Lisa felt herself blossoming under the abundant compliments she was receiving. Those men who were not married or had not escorted someone to the party actually jostled one another in their eagerness to gain her attention. Lisa caught Mary's little sign to her, and with some difficulty extracted herself from the group who surrounded her.

"I am going to sit in the gallery with some of the ladies whose husbands have adjourned to play cards. Don't feel you must sit with me. Stay with the young people and enjoy yourself. The dancing is about to begin."

Peter appeared just then at Lisa's elbow and maneuvered her off to one side of the hall. He mopped at his brow with his handkerchief. The warm spring evening and the many candles burning in the great hall had caused it to become quite hot.

"Would you care for a glass of wine?" he asked her.

She agreed, thanking him. She did feel thirsty.

Peter had barely disappeared through the crowd when Lisa again found herself encircled. She tried to concentrate on what one of the young gallants was telling her about the horse racing at Newmarket, but her gaze unwittingly sought out Richard Drayton. When she finally caught sight of him, he was no longer alone.

A lady with red hair and an extremely low-cut gown was clinging to his arm and as Lisa watched, she gave him a seductive smile from beneath her long lashes and said something that made him put back his handsome head and roar with laughter. Before Lisa could look away, he glanced across the hallway at her, as if his catlike instinct had sensed her eyes on him. Lisa's glance immediately shifted to the returning Peter Ellsbury and she bestowed upon him a devastating smile as she took the wine glass he offered her.

The musicians could now be heard tuning up their instruments in the gallery and immediately Lisa was bombarded with requests for a dance.

She granted the first to Peter and they made their way through the crowd and into the gallery. The night being warm and pleasant, the long gallery windows had been thrown open wide and the sweet smell of honeysuckle was soon wafting inside.

Lisa found herself dancing one dance after another. She never seemed to stop talking or laughing or spinning around, first with one young gentleman and then another as the evening quickly passed.

Peter appeared often at her side and she was flattered by his attentiveness, yet her eyes often strayed to see if Richard had entered the gallery.

Finally she saw him. His height and the breadth of his shoulders always gave him such presence. He stood alone, ignoring the ladies who threw him inviting glances. He was swilling the liquid around in his goblet, indolently watching as Lisa and Peter danced the galliard.

His thoughts were not as self-composed. Damn the girl! She had never looked more lovely. The brandy he had consumed hoping to bring about a small degree of insensibility seemed merely to have inflamed his desire for her.

Lisa danced until she could dance no more, spinning endlessly like a humming top, and when she finally ceased she laughed and chattered with only pause to drink a sip or two of wine.

The evening was drawing to a close when Richard at last appeared beside her, smiling down at her with his lazy, amused grin.

"May I have the pleasure of the next dance?" he asked.

"If you wish," she said coolly. "I wondered why you were not dancing."

He lifted an eyebrow. "I am surprised that you had time to wonder about anything—least of all *me*. You seemed to be so busy enjoying yourself."

"I have been enjoying myself—very much."

He didn't speak as he led her out onto the floor and because she felt piqued by his silence, she added, "Everyone has been so very kind to me."

"The gentlemen, I presume you mean. I told you there was no one here to equal you." The green eyes glittered as he moved closer to her and took her hand for the dance.

Their whispered conversation became broken as they came together and then apart following the intricate steps of the minuet.

"How gracefully you dance, Mistress Manning, but doubtless you have heard that compliment many times this evening."

"I admit I have and I usually reply that it is due to my having such an excellent partner."

"But not in this case since he is quite foxed."

"Foxed! You? I don't believe it."

"Then take a look at Peter's face. He is outraged that, considering my condition, I had the blatant effrontery to approach you for a dance."

"He *does* seem to be watching us."

"Seem to be? He hasn't taken his eyes from you."

"Nor has the red-haired lady by the window removed her gaze from you."

"Who? . . . Oh, Sylvia Montague . . . an old friend."

A murmur. "More than an old friend, I'll warrant."

A laugh. "That was most unseemly of you, Mistress Manning."

"But honest. With you I dare to speak my mind instead of the inanities I have had to engage in all evening."

"Really? Even with the estimable Peter?"

"Particularly with Peter. Do you know what he said? 'You should not bother your pretty little head about such matters, Lisa.'"

"May I ask the topic of your conversation?"

"The Dutch."

"The Dutch!"

"Aye. Whether the fierce commercial rivalry with them might lead to war."

A roar of laughter.

"You think that amusing?"

"Lisa, Peter is not the slightest bit interested in your intellect."

"Why not?"

"Because he, like most men, seeks only beauty and complacency in a woman."

"I don't believe it."

"Ask him. A spirited woman would frighten him to death."

"And would she frighten *you*?"

"What do *you* think?"

"I think you like a woman to have a mind of her own."

"I do—except in one place."

"Where is that?"

"In my bed."

Lisa blushed scarlet as Drayton grinned his infuriating grin.

The two of them were quite oblivious to the attention they were receiving from those on the sidelines. They made a very handsome couple, but it seemed evident to anyone watching them closely that there was a certain tension between them. Lisa's large eyes had flashed at Richard several times, although he seemed to view her testiness with amused indulgence.

"I think you had better smile, Lisa," he finally realized. "Mary is looking at us rather oddly."

"Is she? I wonder why?"

"I think she feels she should have warned you about me."

116

"Mary has no need to warn me about *you!*"

The dance ended, to Richard's apparent relief. The constant bowing and turning about had not done his head any good. He led Lisa back to where Mary and her brother now stood together, silently watching their approach.

"Oh-oh," Richard said and quickly bowed over Lisa's hand. "I believe I will disappear and fetch you a glass of wine."

"I think Lisa might prefer some supper," Peter said, over-hearing him. "The buffet has been laid out. Er—would you care to join us?" he added reluctantly, willing the other to refuse.

"Richard has already dined," Mary interceded.

Drayton grinned at Peter. "Your sister saw to that. Thought me a trifle foxed and in need of sustenance of a different sort."

"But you ate scarcely a morsel," Mary reminded him.

"One must not take the edge off your excellent brandy, Mary."

"You wretch!" But she smiled at him. It was that latent charm of his, Lisa thought, watching his mouth twitch as he bowed to her and Mary and then with a wink at Peter, strode away through the crowd.

The supper was a sumptuous affair. The long oak table was lit by many branched candelabrums and sparkled with silver and crystal. Two huge bouquets of roses were at either end.

Pottle and two other manservants helped to serve the food which Nelly and her helpers had been preparing in the kitchen for days. There were jowls of salmon, prauns and oysters in a cream and wine sauce, a fricandeau of veal, fowl, pullets and larks. For dessert there was a syllabub, plus a selection of trifles, tarts and cheese.

As Lisa nibbled at her supper, Peter apologized for his friend. "Richard has not been himself lately."

"And what is himself?" Lisa inquired.

"A kind and loyal friend—generous, understanding. Although he has not confided in me, I believe that at the moment he is disturbed by something."

"And consequently takes out his ill humor on other people."

"I wish you did not dislike him so much. If you could only get over your initial antagonism—"

"Antagonism?"

"Aye. I am afraid you have made it rather obvious, Lisa."

She stared at him. Was that what he thought? What Mary thought? Well, perhaps it was just as well. Yet, here she stood with no appetite, pushing the food about her plate and wondering about the very man they thought she hated.

Where had he gone? Was he with his red-haired lady friend? Had he taken her off somewhere and was even at that minute making love to her? A lump formed in her throat. She put down her fork. She could no longer eat or make polite conversation with Peter. She must get away by herself for a time, away from all these people and the noise and the heat of the stuffy room. If she did not get a breath of fresh air soon she felt she would suffocate.

"Pray excuse me for a moment, Peter," Lisa begged of him and slipped quietly away through the crowd.

Chapter Seventeen

THE GARDENS SEEMED TO BE DESERTED. THE THICK SCENT OF honeysuckle hung in the still night air. It was a clear night. The stars above shone brightly and the moon was but a few days past its fullness. Lisa drew a deep breath of the cool air, savoring the feel of it on her heated cheeks.

She wandered slowly down the path she and Richard had so often trod, remembering the many animated conversations they had shared, the frankness that had come so naturally—the honesty.

She now smelled the scent of roses from the rose garden, somehow so much more potent on the evening air.

There was the bench they had sat upon so often. She passed it by, continuing on down a second path, stopping only when she reached a great cedar-of-Lebanon. It was scarred and broken by the centuries, but still vigorous and throwing wide its branches of clustering spikes as it had done for the previous five hundred years. Richard had told her that the shoot or seed had probably been brought from Syria by one of the returning Crusaders.

As she stood looking up at the tree, a dark shape stepped out of the shadows beside it and moved toward her.

She started and backed up, suddenly wishing she had not wandered quite so far from the safety of the house. Then she recognized him by his size.

"It's much more pleasant out here, isn't it?" Richard said, his face still hidden in shadow.

She could not see his expression, but her senses were suddenly alive—taut and expectant.

"Aye," she managed. "It is."

She heard him sigh. "We discussed a great deal in this garden—politics, religion, literature. . . ."

"Aye," she said. "We did."

"Do you miss those discussions?"

"Very much," she admitted.

"'Tis good to find someone with whom one can easily converse. Rather rare between a man and woman."

There was a slight thickness to his speech and as he moved closer to her, Lisa caught the distinct odor of brandy about him. It frightened her. She had reason not to trust men who had been drinking.

"I must return." Lisa backed away from him.

"Of course," he scoffed. "Peter will be waiting."

"'Tis not that."

"What is it then?"

"I—I am afraid," she said honestly.

"Of me?" His voice was soft.

"No . . . yes . . . I don't know," she shook her head at her own indecision.

Drayton stared at her as she stood there in a silver patch of moonlight. She looked young and helpless and so breathtakingly beautiful he fought to keep his hands from her.

"You should be," he growled. "I'm deep in my cups and if you know what's good for you you'll hasten back to the party as quickly as you can."

She didn't move at first. She was trembling now at his nearness, her body filled with contradictory emotions. At last she turned away.

"No!" he groaned. "Don't go!" He reached out and pulled her back to him, gently enfolding her in his arms. He buried his face in the hollow of her neck and began to press feverish kisses along her throat. When he found her mouth he gave a muted curse. Gone was the cool, indifferent facade he had been striving so hard to maintain.

"Why?" he murmured hoarsely. "Why? 'Tis not just your beauty, although God knows that is reason enough. But 'tis everything about you: the way you walk as if you were a queen; your voice, as soft and as musical as the wind in the trees. Your eyes—your lips—oh God, Lisa, I ache from wanting you and yet I dare not touch you because you are so damn innocent and pure that I would feel like Satan himself desecrating an angel."

"Oh, Richard"—tears filled her eyes—"surely you must know that I want you, too."

His lips crushed hers, began moving, searching, until her own began to tremble. The trembling seemed to spread throughout her body as he drew her closer to him. She felt herself melting against him. Her hands moved up around his neck, her fingers working through his thick golden hair.

He parted her lips and his kiss was suddenly scalding, fiercely demanding. She sensed the danger and yet an aching desire was filling her. A desire to belong to him completely. No longer was she so sure that she could control her emotions; no longer was she so proud of her virtue. She had become someone she did not even recognize. In Richard's arms all her moral resistance was shattered. She wanted him, urgently, desperately, whatever the cost.

His lips moved downward from her mouth to the pulse in her neck, to the hollow between her breasts. He felt her quick, passionate response and knew that he had not been mistaken in her. Beneath her innocence something smoldered, ready to burst into flame. The thought sobered him. He wanted Lisa. He wanted her as no other. He wanted to be the one to introduce her to love.

His hands slid over her breasts and she shuddered. She felt a strange physical ache, deep between her loins, as he caressed her. Things began to blur as the sensation arose. All rational thinking ceased. Her breathing came in shaken, ragged gasps and she moaned softly, wondering at the new feelings that were flowing through her.

"Tell me to stop!" he growled. "For God's sake, Lisa, tell me to stop!"

But she was beyond the point of turning back. All she wanted was for him to continue.

She shook her head, and he drew her closer against him. So close she could feel the hardness of his desire. Involuntarily she jerked back and he could sense the warfare within her, the fierce demanding passion struggling with the fear and modesty. Had he the right to continue? Although he was not acting against her will, he knew that he was nonetheless seducing her—but the brandy had succeeded in deadening his conscience.

His lips continued their descent between her breasts, gently pushing downward until one exquisite white globe was nearly exposed. His tongue thrust beneath the blue silk and gently traced the nipple, feeling it grow hard and erect at his touch.

"Let me love you," he whispered and she murmured her assent.

She could not fight the weakness that now pervaded her body. She took his hands, moving them to the laces at the back of her bodice. She felt him begin to loosen them with fingers that she knew were no amateur to the task.

"Come," he nodded toward the shadows beneath the tree.

She looked up at him, her blue eyes soft and filled with a sweetness and a poignant longing that tore at his heart. Her beautiful face looked almost ethereal in the moonlight.

It was as he paused that a voice called out on the still night air.

"Lisa! Are you out there?"

It was Mary Stavely.

Reality quickly returned. Blushing furiously, Lisa hastened with trembling fingers to reach the laces at the back of her bodice. A strange feeling swept over her. Was it relief? It had to be relief. It couldn't be disappointment. Yet she knew in her heart that it was. She had been quite prepared to give herself to Richard Drayton!

"I'll fasten them," he said, his deep voice calm as he tried to help her. She would have pushed him away, but she knew there was no way she could do up her gown by herself. The very touch of his fingers on her flesh excited her.

What has happened to me? she asked herself. The way he kissed me, making me so weak, making me want more. I didn't want Richard to stop kissing me, she thought. I didn't want him to stop at all!

"It need not be goodnight," he murmured, turning her to face him. His voice was low and intimate, his lips so very close to hers. "Come to me later," he begged.

She dragged herself from his arms and picking up her skirts, ran in the direction of the manor house.

Lisa watched as Mary and Peter bid farewell to the last departing guests. Most of the guests who were staying for the night had already retired. Except Sylvia Montague. She had paused purposely on the bottom step of the stairway.

"I wonder where Richard has disappeared to?" she asked Peter as he led Mary toward the stairs.

"I have no idea. Haven't seen him in hours."

"Have you looked in the library?" Mary suggested.

"He could be sleeping it off somewhere," Peter grinned. "He was imbibing rather freely."

"Richard can hold a great deal and never show it, as you well know, Peter," Sylvia said tightly.

"Perhaps he has already retired," Mary sighed. She was looking a little pale. It had been a long evening for her.

"Then let us all follow his example," Peter urged, slipping an arm about his sister's frail waist.

Sylvia Montague shrugged and hurried up the stairs ahead of them.

Lisa followed behind Mary and Peter and after Peter had said goodnight to his sister, he turned to Lisa.

"You charmed everyone tonight, Lisa," he said, his brown eyes warm and soft. "I hope you enjoyed yourself."

"I had a lovely time," she smiled up at him.

He had a sudden longing to take this beautiful girl in his arms and kiss her, but he restrained himself. He didn't want to frighten her. Instead, he bowed over her hand and took his leave.

Mary Stavely had started to undress herself by the time Lisa entered her bedchamber.

"I am so tired, Lisa. I can hardly wait to get into bed," she wearily confessed.

"I do hope you did not overdo it."

"If I did and I have to spend tomorrow in bed, it was worth every moment," Mary smiled. "I enjoyed myself so much. The party was a success, wasn't it, Lisa?"

"It was very successful," she replied, helping Mary to remove the rest of her clothing.

"You must have danced every dance," Mary teased her. "You never lacked for a partner."

"Thank you for including me in the party," Lisa said, "and for my beautiful gown."

"You are most welcome," Mary touched her cheek, "but there is something I wish to say to you before you leave me."

She slipped into her nightdress and Lisa drew back the covers of her bed. When she was settled against the pillow she spoke again.

"You and Richard seemed to be having words this evening. I want you to be honest with me. Was he being too . . . familiar?"

"Why, no." Lisa felt the heat rise in her cheeks.

"I only say this because he seemed, for some reason, to be drinking a bit heavily. Richard is a gentleman, but I am afraid he is known to be rather a rake with the fair sex. I should have warned you about him."

Remembering Richard's words to this effect, Lisa had to hide a smile.

"He did not make unwanted overtures to me," she said truthfully.

"I should hope not. I would order him from this house if he had," Mary said indignantly. "Although Peter and Richard are the best of friends, there is a vast difference between them. Peter's wife was his first love and he has looked at no other since." She shook her head. "I would hate to count Richard's conquests. Yet, being the handsome devil he is, he doubtless convinced each and every one that she was the love of his life."

Lisa's heart sank at Mary's words. Had Richard professed to care for her only in order to seduce her? She could not believe it. Why, he had even begged her to stop him.

"And yet Richard is such a charming rogue," Mary was continuing, "that even when a romance is over the lady still cares for him. Look how that Montague woman acted this evening. Completely brazen! I wouldn't be at all surprised if she stole into his room tonight."

Lisa caught her breath. "Would she do that?"

Mary misread the shock in Lisa's eyes. "She has never got over him, although she has had two husbands since Richard dallied with her."

"If he is no longer interested in her, surely he would send her away."

Mary shook her head. "You *are* a little innocent, aren't you, dear? Nay, do not be angry, I am not belittling you. Stay that way, Lisa. That is what is so appealing about you." She grasped the girl's arm. "Keep yourself pure and clean. Don't let men take you and dirty you like I have been dirtied. 'Tis so ugly and debasing for a woman," she said vehemently, her face flushing, her fingers biting into Lisa's flesh.

"Don't think about it," Lisa soothed her, afraid Mary was becoming overwrought. "You are very tired. You must get your sleep now."

Poor Mary, she thought. The act without love could be ugly and debasing. She had only to remember Polly and Sir Basil's coupling to agree with that. Without love? Did Richard really *love* her, or did he want only to possess her? He had never told her he loved her.

When at last Lisa had settled Mary for the night, she went to her own room. The happiness she had felt in Richard's arms, the joy and the wonder had all faded.

She took off her clothes and stood before the mirror. His warm hands had caressed those breasts, arousing her as never before. Were those same hands arousing Sylvia at this very moment? Caressing her? Was he pressing his strong, hard body against her? She let out a little cry. No! Mary Stavely was wrong! He would never do such a thing so soon after holding *her*, telling *her* what she meant to him. She refused to believe it.

Then go to him yourself, a voice inside urged her. He asked you to come. Go and prove to yourself that he wants you and only you. Go and see if he is alone.

But she could not move. She did not want to know. If she would but admit it to herself, she was *afraid* to know.

Finally, she drew on her nightgown and crept between the covers. She lay in an agony of doubt until dawn, when sleep at last overcame her.

Chapter Eighteen

SYLVIA MONTAGUE LEFT THE NEXT MORNING AND THE OTHER guests had all departed by the afternoon. Lisa had had no chance to speak with Richard. In fact, she had hardly seen him. He had breakfasted late, after she had left the dining hall, and at luncheon he was seated at the other end of the long table from her.

Peter had spent the day trying to monopolize Lisa's time and had succeeded in doing so. He made no attempt to hide the fact that he admired her and did his best to keep her amused.

As Mary and Lisa descended the stairs before supper, Mary said, "I've seated you beside Peter tonight, Lisa. Do be especially nice to him as he has talked of nothing but you all day. If you don't I shall suffer for his ill temper!"

Lisa smiled. "I am sure Peter is never ill-tempered. He has the most agreeable nature I have ever encountered."

"Aye, he is a kind and considerate man." Mary patted her hand. "I am glad you are getting along so well. I only wish Basil—"

"Have you had word of your husband?" Richard interrupted, coming over to them as they reached the foot of the stairs. "Forgive me, but I thought I heard his name mentioned."

"I have not heard from him directly, Richard," Mary said, "but I had a letter from a friend of my mother in London. She said she had seen him. That was all."

"I see." Drayton turned to Lisa as Mary went over to speak to Pottle. "Good evening, Lisa," he said stiffly. "I'm afraid I must apologize for my unforgivable behavior last evening. I offer no excuse except that I was deep in my cups. I assure you such an occurrence will not happen again." He bowed, and before she could make a rejoinder he was halfway across the hall.

"Did that old reprobate say something to disturb you, Lisa?" Peter frowned, coming up to her.

"Not at all," Lisa managed, but her eyes still followed Richard.

"Well, I do wish you two would try to get along better. You always seem to be quarreling about something."

Mary excused herself after supper, begging fatigue. It was evident the party the night before had exhausted her, although she had spent the entire meal exclaiming about this person and that and how much she had enjoyed seeing her old friends.

She had barely departed when Richard downed what was left of his brandy and rose to his feet.

"I am sure you two would be only too happy to excuse me as well," he said with a sideways grin at Peter.

"Not at all," Peter said. "Sit down, Richard. I want you to hear what I have in mind for tomorrow."

Richard's eyebrows rose. "I thought you and I were leaving for Calderwood."

"We are, but I wondered if Lisa would like to ride out with us and view your estate. I am sure Mary wouldn't mind."

Lisa looked at Richard.

"I doubt that it would interest Mistress Manning." His words were clipped.

"But of course it would, wouldn't it, Lisa? You told me you enjoyed riding and the weather has been perfect."

He was bound he was going to get these two together to settle their differences.

"Perhaps Richard would prefer it to be just the two of you this time," Lisa said tactfully.

"Not at all." Drayton's tone was a bit too hearty. "I would enjoy showing you both what is left of my home. You may tell Mary we will be back in time for dinner, Lisa."

* * *

CLOAK OF FATE

They started out from the manor house right after breakfast the next morning. It was a beautiful day and they took their time, the three of them riding abreast on the main road.

Lisa looked entrancing in her blue riding dress and matching hat and Peter could hardly keep his eyes from her. Richard, however, joined very little in the animated conversation that passed between Peter and Lisa. Passing through the village of Bridgeford, they were soon out in open country.

Peter's pleasant voice was upraised in a gentle monologue for some miles on his hobby of astronomy which Lisa had questioned him about. She asked him such pertinent questions, in fact, that he was quite amazed by her erudition.

It was close to the middle of the morning when the road narrowed and Peter graciously fell back.

Richard turned to Lisa, lowering his voice. "Still using your feminine wiles on old Peter, I see." He grinned, but there was a harsh quality to his mocking tone that did not quite match the way the green eyes looked at her.

"What do you mean?" Lisa asked sharply.

"Now don't tell me you have suddenly developed an all-consuming interest in astronomy."

"How do you know that I haven't?" she snapped.

"Do you take me for a fool? Flattering another admirer is all *you* are interested in."

"How dare you!"

"What is the matter with you two?" Peter asked, riding up to join them again. "You are always having words."

Nothing was explained to him. Instead, Richard and Lisa rode on in straight-backed, tight-lipped silence.

It was about half an hour later when they heard a shout behind them and slowed their horses to look around.

Matthew Chester was galloping toward them and waving his arms. He drew up beside where they had stopped at the side of the road.

"A man has arrived at the manor house from your estate, sir," Matthew gasped, addressing Peter. "He says he has urgent business wi' thee."

"Did he say his name?"

"Boxton, sir."

"Boxton manages my dairy herds. 'Oddsfish, he's a terrible worrywart," Peter groaned. "Doubtless it is something to do with the cows."

128

"Are you returning?" Drayton asked him.

"I'm afraid I must. You two go on and if it is something I can settle with the man, I will rejoin you later." His lips twisted. "And for heaven's sake try not to scrap!"

Peter turned his horse around and they heard him say to Matthew, "They are like two old ladies, always bickering."

Matthew, however, looked back as they rode off, and his face bore a worried frown. He didn't like the idea of Lisa being alone with Lord Drayton. The girl was a darn sight too pretty.

It was almost noon when Lisa and Richard rode into the village of Swantree, some seven miles west of the main road. They had spoken little since Peter had left with Matthew.

"We'll stop for luncheon at the inn yonder." Richard inclined his head toward a black and white timbered building. "The fare at The White Swan is usually good."

The inn was cool inside and they sat at a little oak table in the square, low-pitched parlor with its stone-paved floor and mullioned windows closed against the noonday heat. They ate cold roast beef and fresh crusty bread and Cheshire cheese, all washed down with tankards of ale.

Lisa only picked at her food. She was conscious of the green eyes that always seemed to be regarding her when she looked up from her plate.

Finally Richard spoke, breaking the uncomfortable silence that had enveloped them since they had entered the inn.

"Have you the slightest idea what hell you put me through the night of the party?"

"Put you through—"

"I stayed awake for hours—willing you to come."

"Really? I thought Sylvia would have done her best to satisfy you."

"Sylvia?" he roared. "Why on earth—"

"She was very anxious to find you."

"And you thought—"

"Aye. I stayed awake too. Thinking of her with you."

"You were wrong."

"So were you."

Their eyes met and held across the little table. Lisa could feel her heart beginning to beat furiously. Richard covered one slim little hand with his own.

"I've become damn jealous of Peter," he admitted.

129

"Peter? Whatever for?"

"You keep giving him such enchanting smiles and flirting outrageously—"

"I haven't flirted."

"But you don't discourage him. Aren't you aware that he has fallen head over heels in love with you?"

"Peter? Why he treats me like a sister. He has never done more than kiss my hand."

"He is a gentleman. He would not dare."

"You dared."

He laughed hollowly. "But I am no gentleman."

They were silent for a moment, both remembering the intimate moments beneath a spreading cedar in the manor house garden.

"We must go," Lisa said, the color rising in her cheeks. "Have we much further to ride?"

"No. It will take but another half-hour or so," he said.

A few fleecy clouds dotted the clear blue sky as they mounted their horses again, but the sun still shone uncommonly hot for May.

Richard opened his shirt at the neck and Lisa, after a few miles, undid the top buttons of her riding jacket, showing the pretty white lace of her blouse. The sun filtering through the thick leaves of the trees that bordered the road cast a shimmering glow about her. Richard had never seen her look so lovely.

"Calderwood, or what is left of it, is on the other side of the village," he explained.

They rode along the road for another few miles before they came to a long stone wall, covered with ivy. Continuing along it, they eventually reached a gateway. The gate stood open, hanging sadly on one hinge at an odd angle. It was also covered with ivy.

Lisa turned her horse to follow Richard's through the desolate gateway and onto a rutted gravel drive. They continued down it toward a line of trees.

"You will see the house in a minute," Richard said. "Every time I come here I feel a hope at this point that I will see it as it once was. Of course that is ridiculous." He pointed ahead. "There! My roofless, windowless ruin."

Calderwood stood before them on its magnificent weed and bramble-filled lawn, the carefully terraced gardens choked and overrun. The mansion itself was a fire-blackened, hollow stone shell, with a section of one wing all that was left intact.

"How terrible," Lisa murmured, bringing Primrose to a halt and staring at the ruins. "It's dreadful to see such beauty destroyed." She looked at Richard and understood the agony he must feel.

Drayton had paused beside her. He said nothing for a moment.

"You are not going to restore it?" she asked. "You are going to have a completely new house built?"

"Aye."

"But what an enormous undertaking! Wouldn't it be easier to restore it on its old foundations?"

"No. I would rather start with something new. I view it a little like the monarchy," he said. "Charles I might have been restored to the throne, had luck been on his side, but there were too many bad memories and I don't think he had changed his stand one whit, despite his trials and tribulations. How much better, when the monarchy was restored, that it was his son who became king. Someone new and promising who is popular with the people and has no delusions that *he* is Divine.

"You have a good point," she agreed. "Perhaps 'tis best to start fresh."

She watched as Richard looked over the gutted ruins, his eyes glittering as he saw something she could not see, his mouth smiling triumphantly. Lisa sensed he was seeing it already finished.

He noticed that she was watching him and spurred his horse ahead. Lisa followed on Primrose, aware now of several dark clouds that were gathering in the sky.

Shortly, the sun was blocked from view and the air became a little cooler, but Lisa still felt her skin damp beneath the warmth of her riding jacket.

As they drew closer to the neglected pile of stone and rubble, Richard turned back to her.

"I'll tether the horses under the portico—or what's left of it. It looks as if we might have some rain."

When they had dismounted, Lisa removed her riding jacket and in skirt and blouse followed a silent Richard as he tramped around the ruined structure. Stone slabs marked the places where once beautiful rooms had been. He could not bear to point out to her where the great hall, the drawing and dining rooms, the kitchens or the bedrooms had been. Of the wing that had been left mostly intact, many of the windows had been smashed. Tattered remnants of draperies still fluttered behind the broken glass.

"Can we go in?" Lisa asked.

"I would rather not."

"Have you ever entered since—"

"No."

"Do you mind if *I* do?"

"Of course not."

Lisa did not know what compulsion made her want to see inside the ruins. She lifted her skirt and Richard helped her climb up through a low broken window. She entered what had once been the dining room.

As Lisa looked about her, the sun suddenly broke through the heavy clouds outside and cast its rays on what was left of the beautifully carved wainscotting.

Wanton damage could be seen everywhere. The Parliamentary troopers had thrust their pikes into the paneling and stripped the hangings from the walls. Broken window casements hung by their hinges, creaking in the soft breeze.

The huge table had been smashed in two and the stuffing ripped from the damask-covered chairs. A door was a splintered pile of debris and the hall beyond loomed black and empty. Pieces of floorboards had been pried up. Swords had pierced and sliced the carpeting; portraits were slashed, the canvas hanging in strips. The scene was of complete desolation and ruin.

"Why did they do this?" Lisa cried, tears filling her eyes. "To what purpose?"

"They were destroying symbols," Drayton said. He had come in and was standing quietly behind her. "Symbols of wealth and power."

"Oh Richard, it had been so beautiful," she said, seeing the stricken look in his eyes.

"'Tis dead now. Let us leave it in peace."

She followed him out the window and put a hand on his arm after he had helped her down.

"I'm sorry. I should not have gone in. You would not have seen . . . it only made it worse for you."

"Nay. I only saw the ruin. Not what it once had been." There was anger now in his eyes, and hate. She had never seen such a look before on his face. It must have been the way he had looked when he had fought in the wars, she thought. The emerald eyes as hard and glittering as the steel of his sword, the jaw so rigid. In looking up into his face her glance chanced to fall on the upper windows of the wing. She looked more closely. As far as she could tell they did not look as damaged.

"Was there any way for the troopers to get upstairs?" she asked.

"Why do you ask?" His voice was a bit sharp.

"Because it looks from here as if little damage had been done there."

His eyes followed hers. "The main staircase was destroyed," he said slowly. "There was no way they could reach . . . unless . . ."

The sun had completely disappeared. Black storm clouds now covered the whole sky and a few drops of rain had begun to fall.

"Come inside," Richard said, helping Lisa to again enter the ravaged dining room. "We may as well get out of the rain. I don't think the storm will last long."

They were barely inside the room when the rain came pelting down. They moved further into the room away from the broken windows. Lisa felt herself shiver as the cool breeze swept around her.

Richard did not notice; he was advancing across the room toward the fireplace, a strange look in his eyes.

"I wonder if they discovered the hidden staircase?" he exclaimed.

He began to feel along a panel in the wainscotting, and slowly it slid back and a small doorway appeared!

"The stairs lead upward to an upper corridor or downward and into the garden through a door hidden in the shrubbery," Richard said to Lisa, who was now by his side, her eyes large with wonder.

"Shall we go up?" she asked.

"It will be dark. I used to leave a candle just inside, for when I returned late and didn't want to run into my parents."

Drayton bent his head and stepped into the opening, returning a moment later with a dusty candlestick in his hand. He lit it with a flint from his pocket.

"I will go first in case the steps are damaged." His voice mirrored the tumult of his feelings as he helped her into the opening.

They started up the stairs, brushing aside cobwebs as they went. Richard held the candle before him, examining the way. At last they reached the top and he paused for a minute before touching his hand to a panel to the right of the small landing.

"I'm almost afraid of what we will find," he admitted.

"Would you rather not see it?"

"No. I have a feeling everything is going to be just the way it was. As if the clock had just been stopped all those years ago."

He pressed the panel and it slid open. They were now in a small corridor. The once shining wood floor was covered with a layer of dust.

"What is that door to the right?" Lisa asked.

"Nanny's bedroom," he smiled. "The nursery is just beyond."

He opened the door. It was a neat little room, with not a thing out of place. The bed was made as if expecting its occupant to return for the night. A quilt was folded at the end of it. There was a Bible beside the bed on a little table with a candle. A washstand with a mirror above it and a small rocking chair were the only other articles of furniture. There was another door on the far wall, leading, Lisa supposed, to the nursery.

"Nanny died while I was away at Oxford," Richard said quietly. "It was as well she never saw the destruction."

He closed the door and they continued a few steps further down the corridor.

"The linen closet," Richard nodded at a door to the left of them. Their feet had stirred up a small cloud of plaster dust along the corridor and Richard raised the flickering candle. "The ceiling has fallen down in places here. Watch your step."

They turned a corner and Lisa noticed another door to the right.

"This is the nursery," Richard said, swinging it open.

Another room that was left intact, Lisa thought, surveying it.

Despite the dampness discoloring the walls, it was a bright, cheerful room with a windowseat under the two large windows. One of the windows had been broken and a pile of dry leaves lay on the seat and were scattered over the floor. A large beech tree stood outside the window and Lisa could imagine Richard shimmying down it as a boy.

She looked at the lonely and forgotten toys lying about the room. But unlike the toys in the nursery at Stavely Manor, these had been played with and were well-loved.

The rocking horse had lost its paint and a headless doll lay limply outside a perfect little dollhouse with miniature furniture. There was a cradle with another doll carefully covered up inside it. Two play swords lay on a bookcase that contained a top and several balls as well as books and slates. Had Richard played with the swords as a child? Perhaps engaging in an imaginary battle with Peter Ellsbury?

"How many brothers and sisters did you have?" Lisa asked quietly. Richard had not said a word as he stood in the doorway looking around him.

"Two. A younger sister and brother." It came out of him slowly, then in a rush as if he had been holding it in for too long. "My father was killed at Northampton in '47 defending the king. I was sixteen at the time and suddenly found myself the head of the family. I was at Oxford and enjoying the life there but anxious to join the Royalist cause. Some of us trained secretly, engaging in minor skirmishes. Peter was with me. I should have gone home, as he did, to look after my family, but instead I engaged in one skirmish too many and was lucky to escape unharmed to the Continent.

"I always thought Calderwood would be safe. 'Twas not on the main road, but I didn't realize it was in the very heart of an area of Royalist supporters. Cromwell, himself, directed that it be taken for a local headquarters.

"When the first troopers arrived, my young brother went for help. He never returned. They found him with a pike through his chest in a ditch." Richard's strong voice faltered a moment.

"My mother and sister had taken in some wounded Royalist friends. When they refused to surrender the house to the Parliamentarians, the troopers brought a cannon in. You have seen the result. Friends found the bodies later. My mother and sister and brother were all buried in a common grave. I had them moved to the little chapel cemetery behind the house when I returned a year ago."

"There was nothing more you could have done, Richard," Lisa said gently.

"I could have been *here!*" he declared, his voice raw. He closed the door and they continued down the dark corridor.

"There is only one room at the front of the wing," Richard said. "My bedchamber."

He paused for a moment outside the carved oak door before he pressed the latch and pushed it in.

Lisa stood back, letting him survey the room by himself and only approached the door when he stepped inside.

The room was warm and smelled musty and close. The windows had not been broken and there was only a light coating of dust over the furniture. The huge four-poster bed had a green silk damask coverlet over it that matched the faded hangings that draped the tall, mullioned windows.

Lisa looked around her, thinking that as a young man Richard had occupied this room. She noticed a wooden carving of a horse on a low oak table. A beautiful carving that showed the strong muscled legs and body, the proud head. Beside it were a small pair of spurs and a small riding crop—both souvenirs, she was sure, of Richard's boyhood. Over the fireplace was a sword with an exquisite jeweled hilt. She wondered if it had belonged to Richard's father. He stood now before it, running his fingers along its blade.

On either side of the fireplace were two paintings. One of a broad-shouldered man with the smile and the flashing green eyes that his son had inherited, for Lisa had no doubt it was Richard's father. The other was of a sweet-faced golden-haired woman with soft blue eyes. Richard had stood back, looking at the portraits. Now, unexpectedly, he beat his fist against the stone of the fireplace.

"Why the devil was *I* left?" he cried aloud, and when he turned to face Lisa she could see that there were tears in his eyes. She made a move to retire and leave him with his grief, but he motioned her toward a small chair.

Lisa said nothing as she slipped into it, but her eyes were filled with understanding and compassion. She realized this had been bottled up for a long time inside of him—this grief and this anger—and now he must get it out—all of it—like an ugly infection. Only then would the wound heal.

"My father was a big, vital man, full of life and humor. He was a good sportsman and athlete, a wonderful horseman. My mother was gentle and soft-spoken. She had a lovely singing voice. Her religion meant a good deal to her, as it did to my sister. They were very alike. My brother—" He cleared his throat. "My brother was not like me. He was quiet and easygoing and always thinking of others. He would not go hunting with me or with father. Instead he was forever bringing home birds with broken wings, or small animals that he nursed back to health. He would have made a wonderful physician."

Richard walked over to the window nearest him and pulled back the draperies, looking out at the rain. For a few moments he stood in silence. When he spoke again his voice seemed deeper, almost impassioned.

"I was the rapscallion of the family—the black sheep if you will. I grew up wanting to excel my father in everything he did. Particularly in sportsmanship. I never refused a challenge. By the time I was twelve I had been close to death several times." He shook his head. "My poor mother. I entered any contest that was dangerous. I did everything and most to excess. I remember Mother saying to Father before he left for the last time, 'Let him sow his wild oats now, James. He will settle down.'" Richard gave a self-deprecating snort. "She was wrong. I never have."

Lisa's eyes swept over the tall figure who stood unmoving by the window.

"Until now," she said. "You are ready for it now, aren't you?"

He turned to face her. "Aye," he said, nodding his head. "Aye, I think I am."

For the first time since Lisa had met him he looked vulnerable. His deep voice was anxious as he asked. "Do you think it is too late?"

"No," she whispered, rising and going to stand before him.

He smiled down at her. "Thank you, Lisa," he said quietly. "Entering this house and coming up here has forced me to come to terms with myself. 'Twas all your doing." He indicated the portraits of his parents. "Up until now I have tried to forget what happened. Thinking of it was always too painful for me. There was too much guilt involved—too much . . ."

He stopped talking. He had placed his hands on her shoulders and was looking down at her. It was very quiet except for the sound of the rain on the windows and the soft sigh of the wind in the fireplace chimney. Neither of them moved for a moment, but their eyes spoke for them.

He drew her gently to him and kissed her upturned face. It was a kiss filled with infinite tenderness, yet despite this a thrill coursed through her body. She trembled.

"Don't," he said, drawing her closer. The trembling ceased. She stood within his strong arms, her slender waist encircled, her dark head against his shoulder. He felt the softness of her body, saw the smooth curve of her cheek.

She looked up at him, her violet eyes soft and warm as they met his intent gaze.

At that instant she sensed everything had changed for them. The barriers had all disappeared. Neither could deny their feelings a moment longer.

"Lisa," he whispered, all his love for her wrapped up in that one hoarsely spoken word.

The knowledge of his caring broke the last dam of emotion within her, sweeping her away. Her upbringing, the warnings, all the taboos by which she had lived were as nothing.

Chapter Nineteen

GENTLY RICHARD'S HANDS CUPPED LISA'S FACE AND HE KISSED her brow, her eyelids, her lips, the hollow of her slender throat.

"I love you so much." His voice was low, slightly husky, and the emerald eyes repeated his words.

"Oh, Richard," she whispered, "I love you, too!"

His kiss became more demanding, hungrily parting her lips. Slowly he searched the sweetness of her mouth and a warmth began to rise within her, moving up through her body, engulfing her. Her arms went compulsively around his neck and she clung to him, meeting his burning lips with her own.

Their kisses became more and more frenzied until they broke apart, looking helplessly at one another, both of them trembling, breathing hard.

His eyes searched her face, and then with a cry of triumph he caught her to him, sweeping her up into his powerful arms, carrying her to the bed. He tore back the dusty coverlet and gently laid her down.

For weeks he had ached to make love to this beautiful creature who had tortured him from the first moment he had laid eyes on her. Now that the time was at last at hand he was aware he must be patient with her.

His hands moved over her with feather lightness, his lips

gentle as they kissed her eager mouth and nibbled at her ears and throat. His ardor slowly increased, his kisses becoming deeper, warmer, hardening into passion. Lisa opened her lips to him, her senses swimming.

Gently, whispering sweet love words, she felt him unloosening her blouse and a flame flared up within her at his touch. He kissed the creamy shoulders, his mouth descending in a trail of fire to the exquisite upthrust breasts he had uncovered.

"So very beautiful," he murmured.

A wave of pleasure burst through her as his teasing tongue made the nipples spring to life. Again his hot mouth possessed her willing lips as his fingers moved lovingly over her silken flesh.

Her heart began to pound as his hands moved lower, swiftly and skillfully removing the rest of her clothing.

She lay naked before him, not moving, hearing him catch his breath, seeing the desire that sprang to his eyes. She watched as he stripped off his own clothing, curiosity mingling with desire as his hard, muscular body was revealed to her. How magnificent he was! She shivered with fear and anticipation as he lay down beside her.

With tenderness and amazing restraint, he continued to delicately caress her, not wanting to rush her, wanting to be sure she was ready.

Delightful tremors ran through her body as his hands explored the soft curves and hollows more and more intimately, until she could have wept with joy!

Thrilled by these new sensations, she writhed against him, all modesty behind her now, destroyed by her need of him. A need to become one with this man whom she loved so deeply.

She pressed her firm, young breasts against his chest, feeling the heat of his body, the prickle of the golden hair against her tender skin. As she molded herself closer to him, she felt his rigid member throbbing against her burning flesh.

Prolonging the sweet agony, he continued his soft caressing, his fingers arousing her in fiery waves. She shuddered as they moved to stroke and part the soft flesh between her legs, gently exploring, and her mouth opened in a silent cry, her eyes misty and glazed with passion.

At his touch, her thighs fell open and he shifted his weight over her. Kissing her tenderly, lovingly, he entered her, slowly stretching the delicate softness until he felt the virginal obstruction. Gently but firmly, he pressed on, thrusting forward until the fragile membrane gave way. She gasped at the sudden, sharp pain, but as Richard began to move within her she felt a sensation so full of blinding pleasure that she clutched him to her, pressing him even more deeply into her as if delighting in her own deflowering.

A moan escaped her lips as he sheathed his full length within her, expanding and filling her completely. She tried to muffle the sound with one hand, but he murmured, "Nay. Hold nothing back."

Unconsciously her body began to move in unison with his and she responded with increasing ardency to Richard's experienced lovemaking.

Caught up with him, she urged him on, aware of nothing but the hard body plumbing her own and the frenzied pleasure it evoked.

She felt herself rising, moving toward a bright, blazing light, rising, rising, until everything exploded around her and she drifted back to earth in a sensual haze, floating slowly down like a feather. Her face was wet with tears. She had given the man she loved her most precious gift.

"How do you feel?" he asked, wiping the tears from her flushed cheeks. "I'm afraid I hurt you."

Although he had tried his best to be gentle, his big body had wanted her so badly that he had taken her more fiercely than he had intended.

"I love you more than ever," she whispered.

"Lisa . . . Lisa . . ." He kissed her tenderly. "You are mine now."

He cradled her in his arms, her hair a dark lavender-scented curtain falling over his chest. "You're not sorry?" he asked, wrapping a finger around a silky strand.

She looked up into his face. There were no doubts, no regrets in the violet eyes as soft as velvet. "No." She gave a little sigh of pure happiness and contentment.

He kissed her forehead, his lips moving down her cheek until they again closed over her mouth. He felt as if he had been searching for this perfection all his life, like the knights of old for the holy grail. Several times he had thought he had found it, only to discover it was still beyond his reach. This time he knew with quiet certainty it was his. The ambrosia taste of lips, nipples, belly—none had ever been as soft, as sweet, as pure. No other woman possessed this perfection.

One hand caressed a softly rounded hip, pulling her closer against him. His mouth covered hers in a kiss that slowly changed from tender sweetness to fierce desire. Her love-bruised lips were parted to let him claim the honey that lay within. Once tasted he could not leave her alone. He wanted her again.

She felt the proof of this as she brushed against him, feeling the swelling pressure of his manhood. A surge of triumph spread through her as she realized it was she alone who had aroused him and could appease his need. She longed to give him the utmost pleasure.

Hesitantly, her untaught hands began to skim lightly over his body, moving from his face to his wide shoulders to his muscled expanse of chest. Her soft, moist lips followed her fingers from his mouth to the strong column of his neck, down the golden mat to the firm, flat belly.

Her own body was reacting to the feel and the smell and the taste of him. A wild surge of emotion coursed through her veins as her fingers continued their exploration. When they shyly paused, Richard guided her hand to him and boldly she encircled the rigid, pulsating hardness.

"Some day I will show you how to please me," he growled. "But now—"

He rolled over her, his kiss fierce, almost brutal, as he began his own searing assault on her senses, burning a pathway down the satin-smooth skin.

Lisa gasped with throbbing delight, her body moving of its own will, letting him do with it as he wished. His caresses were so gentle. It was as if he were learning her an inch at a time, plucking her nerves to a fever pitch with his expert manipulations.

She wanted to ask him where he had learned to please a woman so, but all rational thought disappeared as he planted soft kisses down the inside of one thigh.

She could stand it no longer. Aching to become one with him again she reached for him.

Their bodies seemed to melt into one another as he slid deep into the welcoming softness. She knew what to do now. She arched her back to receive his thrusts, clasped him eagerly without restraint or fear, and responded with a rhythm and ferocity that fully matched his own. She found herself quickening with him, gloriously rising and plunging, crying out with joy as the huge bubble of ecstasy burst and they both convulsed together.

"Ah, Lisa," Richard gasped unbelievingly, as they lay panting in one another's arms. "You are all I dreamed you'd be—and more."

She smiled contentedly. "I love you so," she murmured.

"And I you, my dearest love."

His lips again captured hers in a thorough kiss that left her limp and content to lie back, luxuriating in the feel of his nakedness pressed so close to hers.

Satiated and replete Richard drifted into sleep. Lisa heard his even breathing and raised her head from his shoulder to study his face. How peaceful he looked. Relaxed, the lines that etched his mouth had softened. The golden locks lay tumbled about his head and he looked utterly defenseless. Richard, so big and strong and sure of himself, slept like a child. She felt a lump in her throat as she leaned over him and pressed her lips to his. He slept on.

Curled up beside the man she loved, Lisa sighed and nestled more deeply into the warm curve of his body. Soon she also slept. It was Richard's deep voice that finally awakened her.

"Oh, sweet child, what are you doing in bed with a bastard like me?"

She opened her eyes to see him staring down at her, an unspeakable tenderness in the mold of his mouth, the green eyes full of sadness.

She put a soft hand up to stroke his cheek. "Don't say that. You have turned me into a woman." She stretched herself and sighed. "A deliriously happy woman."

"Lisa, I don't—"

"Nay! Don't have any regrets. I have none at all."

"You should. Mary would have my hide if she knew, and as for Peter. . . ."

Lisa had to giggle. "But he kept hoping we would stop bickering and get to like one another."

"I don't think this was quite what he had in mind."

She reached up to fasten her fingers in the golden hair and brought his face down to hers.

"Stop talking and kiss me," she demanded.

He didn't dare. Instead he tenderly pressed his lips to her brow and drew away.

"'Tis growing late," he said.

"Oh, Richard, I don't want this afternoon to end!"

He smiled. "It won't end for us," he said, brushing a tendril of hair back from her cheek. "'Tis only the beginning." He turned from her, forcing himself to throw his legs over the side of the bed and get to his feet.

Lisa felt suddenly cold now that he had left her side. She wanted him to come back to her, to make love to her again. She could not bear it all to end. She wanted Richard with her always.

"Can't we wait until it stops raining?"

"Nay. We must consider your reputation, my love. Mary will be anxious for you."

Like waking from a lovely dream, Lisa hated to return to reality, but she knew she must.

As they left the ruin of Calderwood behind them, she shivered, although she was wrapped in Richard's cloak. The rain was reduced now to a gentle drizzle, but the tiny drops that slid down her cheeks felt like falling tears. She was overwhelmed with an odd sadness, the sadness of loss. Not for her maidenhood, but for the end of an afternoon she would remember all her life, an afternoon of such happiness and fulfillment that she wondered if she would ever experience its equal.

Richard rode quietly beside her, smiling over at her now and then, throwing her a kiss. She knew he loved her. He had not mentioned marriage, but she never doubted that after what had happened that afternoon he, as a gentleman, would ask her. Then they would become husband and wife in the eyes of the world, as well as in the eyes of God.

They arrived back at Stavely Manor just before nine o'clock.

It had rained heavily most of the afternoon and Mary Stavely was not surprised by their lateness. She insisted, however, on bustling Lisa upstairs to a warm bath.

After eating some supper on a tray in her room, Lisa declared that rest was all she wanted and at last she was left alone.

She lay in her little bed, her eyes wide open, the events of the day making sleep impossible.

In her mind she could still see Richard's bedchamber in the razed mansion, see the dust fly from the bed covering as he impatiently stripped it off, hear him whisper her name. Her newly awakened body began to tremble, remembering the touch of his hands, his lips. Her heart hammered in her breast. How she loved him! She tried to recapture that moment when he had first possessed her and felt again the burning longing.

We were born for each other, she thought. I must have known that from the first moment when he looked down at me from horseback and our eyes met. And when he kissed me—I was sure.

When would he ask her to marry him? She had almost expected him to tell Mary when she had welcomed them back.

"Mary, Lisa and I have fallen in love. We are going to be married." But, instead, he had asked after Peter, had seemed disappointed to hear that, worried about his herd, Peter had headed straight back to his estate. Instead, Richard had told Mary that they had gone into Calderwood and had been caught in the rainstorm while exploring the one remaining wing left standing. He had not lied, but it had all come so easily to his lips—as if deception were not new to him. While she wanted to shout it from the rooftops, it was apparent that Richard wanted to keep their love a secret—at least for the time being. Perhaps he was right. Mary might not have approved.

Poor Mary! If she could but know how beautiful the act was with the man you loved. Richard was so patient and gentle and yet could be fierce and demanding. She shivered and hugged herself, remembering the indescribable delight of his lovemaking.

How would she be able to treat him as a casual friend in Mary's presence? She would have to call upon every ounce of her acting ability, she was sure.

Acting made Lisa think of her mother and what she had said the night before she died.

"Save yourself for the man you will love. One day soon he will appear and awaken you as a woman."

It had happened just as she had said, except for one thing. She had given herself to Richard before they were married. But they loved each other; they'd soon be man and wife, wouldn't they?

For the first time a small, insidious doubt assailed her mind, and although she brushed it aside, it took a while for her to fall asleep.

Richard lay awake. He couldn't believe how happy he felt.

Lisa was the cause, of course. Beautiful, beautiful Lisa, who had given herself to him with such fire and passion. How he loved her! Never before had he felt this way about a woman. Never! It was impossible to think of a future without her.

He groaned as he thought of his mistress, Christina. He would have to tell her when he went up to London. Settle some money on her. He knew she would not take it well. He shuddered as he imagined the scene she would make. But he was resolute. He wished to place Lisa under his protection as soon as possible. Then she would be his in everything but name and because they both loved one another, that would be of no consequence. The only thing important was their love. Such a love, he was convinced, was so rare as to come only once in a lifetime. He would adore and protect her the rest of his days. Richard Drayton fell into a deep, untroubled sleep.

Chapter Twenty

THE NEXT MORNING AT BREAKFAST LISA AND RICHARD AVOIDED looking at one another lest their glances reveal their true feelings.

Mary noticed no change in their relationship except that now they seemed less quarrelsome. Peter, then, had been right in encouraging their friendship. He had been convinced that if they became better acquainted they would grow to like one another and he wanted them to be friends.

"I had hoped Peter might convince you to go home with him," Richard was saying to her.

"He spoke to me of it," Mary replied, "but of course I told him that it was impossible."

"Impossible? Why?"

"This is my home, Richard," she said proudly, looking around her. "It may be a rather dark and ugly old manor house, but I am the mistress here. With Basil away, it is now my word that counts."

"Does that mean so much to you?" He was clearly puzzled.

"It has taken me a long time." Mary smiled. "I see you do not understand, Richard, so I will explain. In my childhood home, where Peter is now the master, I was of little consequence—

merely the youngest daughter. The youngest daughter does not count for very much at all. Here, you see, I am the mistress of the Manor." Her little chin rose as she spoke the last words.

Neither Mary nor Richard was aware of the cloud that crossed Lisa's face. She had been determined to confront Basil on his return to Stavely Manor and reveal her true identity while unmasking him for the traitor he was. Now she realized what it would do to Mary to be forced to leave her home. If she went to live with Peter, she would no doubt act as his chatelaine, but Lisa now wondered if that would be enough for Mary.

"Basil will return, you must realize that," Richard was saying to her.

"I am not going to think about that," Mary said, stubbornly. "I am just going to enjoy every day that he is gone."

"That is not being very realistic—" Richard began, but Lisa hushed him and quickly changed the subject.

As if by agreement, although they had not spoken, both Lisa and Richard appeared in the garden that afternoon.

Lisa started off down the familiar pathway, hardly looking from left to right.

Drayton was already walking in the garden, admiring the world about him. It seemed a brighter place for him today. The grass seemed greener, the flowers smelled sweeter and the sky was bluer. Even the sun seemed to shine brighter. There was purpose in his step as he walked back along the path. He had not even seen her when he sensed her presence and stopped to watch her approach.

Because of the warm day, Lisa wore a light sea-green silk gown, plainly cut, but with a low, boat-shaped neckline. It emphasized her soft white shoulders and high young breasts. A straw sunshade covered her ebony hair and was tied beneath her chin with green ribbons. She looked cool and calm and very lovely.

"You read my mind," he smiled, as she stopped before him. "I was hoping you would come."

She supposed that unconsciously she had wanted to see him, had even dressed especially for him, but now she hesitated, seeing a look of intensity in those green eyes that quite took her breath away.

"Come," he said simply, taking her slim hand in his big one and leading her across the green lawn to an unfamiliar path that wound downward until it stopped before a tiny pavilion in a hollow below, its columns covered with climbing vines. It overlooked another garden beyond, a garden filled with cherry and plum trees in full bloom. The perfume from lilac bushes nearby was heavenly.

"Oh Richard, how beautiful!" Lisa exclaimed, her face alight with pleasure as he led her down to the tiny pavilion.

Inside the pavilion were two rustic benches and a table. They sat down on a bench that gave the best view of the garden below them. But Richard did not look at the garden. His green eyes, as they gazed at Lisa, darkened with desire and slowly he undid the ribbons beneath her chin and drew off her hat, placing it on the nearby table. He put his hands beneath the weight of her hair and fanned it out about her shoulders.

"That is how I love to see you," he whispered. His thumbs drew gentle circles in the sensitive hollows below her ears as he cupped her face and brought it up to his.

He kissed her deeply, the heat of his mouth making her suddenly weak, helpless. His nearness excited her so. Her heart was already pounding.

Richard's hands trembled a little as they caressed her shoulders and then he gave a little growl and drew her roughly to him, locking her tightly in his arms. She could hardly breathe.

"Oh, Lisa, my darling, I want you so," his deep voice was ragged as he covered her throat with kisses and took her lips once more.

She tried to struggle against him as his strong fingers slid beneath the low neckline of her gown, stroking her swelling breasts.

"Nay, Richard, I pray you. Not here. Not again. It is wrong—a sin."

"Is it? Then let me hear you deny that you want me."

He was so sure of himself! She had vowed she would not let him take her again—not until they were married—but the fervency of his kiss soon drove all thoughts of resistance from her head.

Deftly he unfastened the laces of her bodice, freeing her breasts for his skillful manipulation. His touch was so incredibly gentle as he exposed her breasts, cupping them in his two big hands, his thumbs caressing the hardening nipples. He bent his head, his lips closing over one pink-tipped globe and then the other.

She became like butter in his hands. Every argument she had

formed in her mind seemed to fade away as her need for him grew stronger.

She was clinging to him now, returning his kisses as hotly as he gave them, sliding her hands beneath his shirt, stroking his chest, her fingers moving slowly down his sides to his waist, drawing him closer.

She felt again the hungry longing, the ache to become one with him and experience the ecstasy she had felt before. He was doing what he wanted with her body, his hands beneath her skirts, thrusting them up as he laid her back on the bench.

Oh God, she thought, the shame and depravity to be taken so, like a little trollop, with her clothes on, in broad daylight. Yet, he was making love to her in such joyous ways, with his lips and his hands, making her want it, making her cry out for it with a need as fierce as his own! She wanted him desperately now. She cared about nothing but her need to become one with him again.

He sensed her urgency, yet continued to arouse her with more and more delirious sensations, until, her desire unbearable, she seized him, hoarsely directing his searing entrance.

Passion carried Lisa beyond any thought of shame. Richard was all that mattered. Only Richard and the ecstasy of their love!

Afterward, they lay still on the bench, their bodies still entwined. She could hear the rapid beat of his heart, or was it hers?

"Lisa, Lisa," he murmured, kissing her flushed cheeks before he found her mouth again. "If you could only know what indescribable joy you give me!"

He withdrew from her and then he was helping her to sit up, carefully arranging his breeches as she straightened her gown. He put his arm about her and she leaned her head against his broad chest. For what seemed a long time they sat, silent and unmoving, in each other's arms.

A sound in the bushes close by disturbed their reverie. They broke guiltily apart only to see a quail emerge and dart across an open space of lawn.

"I must go back," Lisa whispered. "Mary will be wakening and wondering where I am."

Richard nodded and skillfully began to relace her bodice. The feel of his warm fingers pressing intimately against her breasts brought renewed joy and, blushing, she pushed him away. He laughed his deep laugh and grasping her hand he placed it against the hard, swelling length that again strained his breeches.

"Our bodies speak for us, Lisa," he said, drawing her to her feet. "We cannot deny them or our hearts."

"What are we to do?" she asked, praying for him to propose something more definite between them.

"Follow our instincts," he murmured, kissing her a final time. "Just love me, my beautiful, Lisa. Just love me always."

They parted: Richard to exercise his horse and Lisa to return to Mary.

She slipped into the house through the kitchen. It was empty at this time of day, but she smelled something delicious simmering over the fire.

As she passed the door to the pantry, Polly stepped out into the hallway. She had a round silver tray in her hand that she was polishing. She grinned at Lisa.

"Good afternoon, Miss High and Mighty," she scoffed.

Lisa tried to brush by her, but she put out a hand to stop her.

"That's a right pretty dress. Makes 'ee look much less the prudish virgin." Then she thrust her face close to Lisa's, whispering hoarsely, her little black eyes glittering. "But thee's no longer that, is thee?"

Lisa stared at her, the color rising unbidden in her cheeks. "What do you mean?"

"Thee knows full well what I mean," Polly grinned. "I seen 'ee go to the summer 'ouse with Lord Drayton."

She must not panic. Perhaps Polly was only surmising.

"That's right," Lisa said, keeping her voice cool. "He wished to speak with me about my lady."

"Oh 'e did, did 'e?" the scullery maid let out a bawdy laugh. "I saw 'ee go down to the summer'ouse with 'is arm about 'ee and would ha' followed 'ee, had I not remembered that Nelly told me t' take some pies from yon oven, so I 'ad to scurry back."

Lisa could not help her sigh of relief.

"Ah, but I went back again, I did." Polly grinned, waving a dirty finger beneath Lisa's nose. "Just in time t' see 'im tuckin' 'is big pecker back in his breeches."

Lisa closed her eyes at the triumph in Polly's face. Humiliation was burning through her whole body.

"Now don't 'ee worry," the girl was going on. "I don't tattle, not me. Why would I tell on 'ee? It would be a shame for m'lady to learn 'ee be not the sweet little innocent she thinks 'ee to be, wouldn't it now?"

Lisa began to tremble. She could imagine Mary's reaction if Polly should tell her.

"M'lady might not want 'ee as 'er companion no longer. She might even send 'ee back to the scullery," the maid's lips twitched as she continued to polish the tray, rubbing at it and breathing on it and rubbing it some more. "'ee got some pretty things now, Lisa. I rather fancy that there dress 'ee be wearin'."

She stopped rubbing at the tray. The hallway was very still. Then Lisa forced herself to smile.

"Do you?" she said, a sick feeling rising within her. "If you should do something for me, Polly, I will give it to you gladly."

"Will 'ee? I always knew 'ee was kind, Lisa. Ever since that day you told 'em I was sick and—"

"Nothing will be said, Polly?" Lisa's voice was low, shaking, as she clutched the girl's hand. "To *anyone?*"

"Course not. I be no blabber." The maid started to grin. "Bet 'e was good, eh?" She winked. "The size o' him and all. I'd give a thousand green gowns t' be 'umped by such as him, I would."

Humped! Was a good humping with an eager wench all it had been to Richard? Oh, God in heaven, no!

Lisa ran down the hallway without looking back, hearing Polly's loud guffaw behind her.

Chapter Twenty-one

IT WAS NO USE. DESPITE LISA'S GUILT AT DECEIVING MARY, despite having to bribe Polly, despite her uncertainty over Richard's interpretation of the word "love" and his lack of promises, she could not stay away from him.

Drayton himself suffered twinges of guilt when he was reminded of Lisa's innocence. Innocence? That was what had intrigued him in the first place. Her innocence had shaken him and bound him closer to her when he had robbed her of it. He could no more stop seeing her than he could stop breathing.

Since the rainy afternoon in Richard's bedchamber at Calderwood, when Lisa and he had first made love, there was no quenching their thirst for one another. They kissed in shadowy corners and deserted hallways, eager for a touch, a caress. Lisa's bedchamber being so close to Mary's, Richard dared not go to her there, so, at his urging, she went to him in the darkness, unashamed of her own desire, a desire as feverish as his own.

Forgotten was her purpose for being at Stavely Manor. She rationalized that nothing could be done until Basil Stavely's return, but her love for Richard was now all that filled her mind.

It was evening, a few days later, when Mary Stavely called Lisa into her room. The two of them had supped together in the dark dining hall, Drayton having gone off for the day to his estates. Lisa had ascended the stairs ahead of Mary, who had gone to the library to chose a book. She was quietly sewing in her room when she was summoned to join Lady Stavely. She might be Mary's companion, Lisa thought, but she was still summoned like a servant. How much longer must she keep up this subservient role?

Mary gestured to the sofa before the window, and after Lisa was seated came over to stand before her.

There was a stern look on her sad face and Lisa was at once wary. Had Mary found out about her and Richard? She braced herself for the denunciation she knew would follow that knowledge.

"After leaving the library this evening, I sought out Master Pottle to have him take a look at the ladder for the upper bookshelves in the library. It seems very rickety. I nearly took a tumble from it. In the back hallway, I came face to face with Polly, the scullery maid."

Here it comes! Lisa thought.

"She was wearing your green gown, Lisa! Fair bursting out of it she was, and when I asked her about it, she said you had given it to her. Was she telling the truth?"

Lisa nodded, letting out her breath. "Aye, she was," she said quietly.

Mary Stavely sighed. "'Tis nice to be generous, Lisa, but you must realize that when I chose to make you my companion, I put you above the scullery. To be frank, Polly is not the kind of friend I think suitable for you. Her morals are not . . ." Mary struggled for words.

"I realize what you are trying to say, Mary," Lisa helped her. "But I—I just felt sorry for her."

"Sorry for her! Why the girl will give herself to anything in breeches! Even Basil . . ." She stopped, seeing something flare in Lisa's eyes. It came to her then. It made perfect sense. She should have known that Lisa was not the type to make an intimate of such a girl as Polly. Mary swallowed hard.

"You and Polly shared a room when you first came, did you not?"

Lisa nodded, aware of the anguish that was building in Mary's eyes.

"The night Brydie's body was discovered . . . Basil had been drinking heavily. . . . He . . . he went to your room, didn't he?" she asked.

"Mary, don't . . ." Lisa got up from the sofa and put her arms about Lady Stavely's slim shoulders. "Don't upset yourself. It is all over."

"'Tis very clear to me now," Mary said, almost to herself, as she forced herself to ask, "He wanted *you*, didn't he? And Polly offered herself instead. Isn't that so?"

"Mary, he—"

"Did Basil take Polly? Tell me, Lisa!" Mary demanded.

"Aye," Lisa sighed. "He did."

"And you were trying to repay her kindness. . . . Oh, Lisa, I'm so sorry. So very sorry." She began to weep.

"Mary, it was not . . . pray do not take on so," Lisa soothed.

"But, dear God, he must have taken her right there beside you. . . ." She wept all the harder.

"That was lust, not love. Love and lust are two such different things."

Mary looked up at her. "What can you possibly know about love?"

"My parents were very much in love," Lisa answered truthfully. "I swore years ago that I would never give myself away until I found a man for whom I could feel such love."

Mary shook her head. "One can never be sure. I truly believed I loved Basil when I married him and look where that has got me?" She broke into fresh tears.

"Mary, it is all over now. Don't you see? All the humiliation you have suffered at his hands. All over."

If only she could tell Mary the truth, tell her that as soon as Basil Stavely returned, she would reveal him for what he was, but instead she said, "Peter will deal with Sir Basil when he returns. You will see."

"But that must not happen!" Mary cried, her voice rising hysterically. "Basil would kill Peter! Peter does not understand a man like him. He is too honorable. If Peter challenged him to a duel, you can be sure Basil would not obey the rules!"

It took a long time for Lisa to settle Mary down that evening. She finally got her into bed and calmed her by reading to her, until, totally exhausted, Mary at last fell asleep.

Lisa closed the book and got slowly to her feet, stretching her tired shoulders. She had not felt as weary in a long time, but then her nights had lately been disturbed by her secretive sojourns in Richard's bed.

She left Mary's bedchamber and hastened to her own room. About to open the door, she heard footsteps coming toward her down the darkened corridor. She knew that step.

Richard appeared from the shadows. He looked concerned. "So late to bed?"

"I've been reading to Mary. She was a little upset tonight."

"Has she had word of Basil?"

"Nay, but she is worried again about his return."

"She need not. I intend to remain here until I have had a chance to confront him."

"I thought Peter wanted that honor."

"He does, and I have agreed to send for him upon Basil's return, but I am afraid things will come to a head long before Peter arrives."

Lisa looked concerned. "Mary does not think Basil would act honorably in a confrontation."

Richard grinned. "Nor do I. That is why it should be me who confronts him. Peter is too much of a gentleman."

"Why are you always so self-deprecating?" Lisa exclaimed, angrily. "You, too, are a gentleman in the truest sense of the word, yet you declare that you are not and refer to yourself as a scoundrel . . . or even worse."

He drew her into his arms and kissed her tenderly. "Bastard was the word that would not pass your lips, my sweet Lisa, and a bastard I am. Any man who seduces an innocent virgin and then begs her to come to his bed, night after night, is a bastard through and through."

"And what is she who cannot stay away from him then? A wanton . . . a trollop . . ."

"Hush!" A look of pain crossed his face as he looked down at her. "Is that what you think I have made of you?"

"Nay." She placed her hands on either side of his face and brought it down to hers, kissing him deeply. "You have made me happy beyond words."

"I love you to distraction, Lisa. You know that."

"And I love you, Richard."

The green eyes regarded her closely in the candlelight. "You look tired." He smoothed her cheek with the back of his hand. "Go to bed now and sleep the night through. Tomorrow you and I are going to take a picnic lunch and go off by ourselves for the whole afternoon."

"But how can we?"

"Leave it to me. You need time away from this dreary house. Pray for a sunny day."

"I will," she smiled, and after a goodnight kiss, she pulled herself away from him and ran quickly into her room.

"We have had no word of Basil Stavely in over a fortnight, Brother Brintnall," scowled the burly Timotheus Webster.

"He remains in London until he can send us the exact time and date of Old Rowley's departure."

"If the fool ever learns it. From what I have heard all he is doing is drinking and dicing and whoring," sneered Thomas Carver.

"But it is from those that reside in that sinful den of iniquity—Whitehall—from which he will gain the news," Brintnall assured him. "Much can be learned from a drink-loosened tongue."

"Or on a harlot's pillow," Webster guffawed.

"I admit it goes against my better judgment to trust such a libertine," said Brintnall, "but we have no choice."

"Do we not?" Carver considered. "I wonder. Richard Drayton still resides at Stavely Manor, so I am told."

"Aye, and rides back and forth to his own estate most every day."

"There is a rumor afoot in London that he is mustering some of his old regiment together."

"That is naught to do with us."

"Perhaps not. But one wonders what his purpose might be."

"What have thee in mind, brother Carver?"

"I would like to conceal a man by the London road to follow Drayton if he should head that way. To see what he is up to."

"Thee would need more than one man to be there night and day."

"Three men then, to relieve one another."

"Are there three who would recognize Drayton?"

"I will make sure of that."

"Then so be it."

* * *

Basil Stavely awoke with the sound of church bells pealing in his ears. The gray light of Sunday morning streamed through the dingy dirt-encrusted window of the bedchamber.

His head was pounding. Where the hell was he?

He looked about him at the paint peeling from the moisture-covered walls, at the crude, battered furniture, the torn and stained coverlet on the bed.

He vaguely remembered a room above a tavern off Fleet Street, where he had ended up after a night of carousing in many other taverns. He could not remember the name of this tavern or even what the wench had looked like who had shared his bed.

There had been a wench. He was sure of that. There was still an indentation beside him, where she had lain, but she was nowhere in sight.

A dreaded thought seized him and he rolled from the bed, cursing loudly as he surveyed what was left of his clothing hanging over the back of a chair in the corner.

His brocaded satin coat was gone, and it had been nearly new and damned expensive. He let out a string of invectives, knowing, instinctively, that with it had gone everything else of value—his money, of course, but also his sword—even the gold buckles from his shoes! The bitch had left him only his breeches and shirt!

In a spate of fury, he dressed and clumped heavily down the narrow stairs to the tavern below. Bellowing for the owner to fetch him a coach, he had to suffer the indignity of the dupe.

"The little whore give ye the slip, did she, gov?" The tavern owner grinned, undismayed by the size of the black-browed man who glared down at him. "Just pray that she didn't give ye a good dose of the clap as well!"

Chapter Twenty-two

THE NEXT MORNING LISA AND RICHARD DIRECTED THEIR HORSES westward off the main roads and ventured more deeply into the verdant countryside. They passed by rolling meadows and sparse woodlands and continued on until they came to a little-used track through thick woods.

They continued along this for a few miles, finally emerging from the forest. Below them lay a small valley, completely carpeted with wild flowers. Enchanted, Lisa exclaimed over its beauty as they started down the hill, negotiating it carefully. As they descended, Lisa spied a small stream meandering lazily through the meadow. Bullrushes grew along its banks and on one side several willows dipped their branches into the clear water.

"I came upon this spot quite accidentally," Richard said, drawing up his horse. "I thought it would make a nice secluded place for a picnic."

They both dismounted and Drayton tethered the horses and unfastened a wicker hamper that was secured to his saddle.

"It's lovely here," Lisa smiled, opening her arms wide. "So quiet and away from everything."

Richard led her back from the stream to a spreading beech

tree, hung with drooping clusters of purple blossoms. It was cooler in its shade, and he spread his riding cloak for them.

"You must forgive me, Lisa. I rose early and am starved," he said, withdrawing a wine bottle and beginning to unpack the food that Nelly had carefully wrapped in linen packets. He opened the wine, producing a pewter tankard in which to pour it.

"No delicate goblet, I'm afraid. Nonetheless, it's the finest mead," he grinned, handing it to her.

Thirsty after her hot ride, Lisa took several deep swallows of the potent wine while Drayton put back his head and managed a long draught from the bottle itself.

They lunched hungrily on legs of chicken and crusty bread and butter.

Richard refilled Lisa's tankard and she began to feel the relaxing effect the mead was having upon her.

"Will you have some cheese?" he asked.

"Nay, I have had quite enough," she murmured, her gaze seeming a little fuzzy as she stared up at the clear blue sky through the branches of the beech tree.

She could feel Richard's eyes on her as a lark trilled high up in the tree.

"'Shall I compare thee to a summer's day?'" he quoted. "'Thou art more lovely and more temperate.'"

"So you are also familiar with Shakespeare's sonnets," she smiled.

"I've been reading them again," he said quietly.

The green eyes seemed to darken as he surveyed her. She was leaning back against the trunk of the tree, her proud young breasts rising and falling beneath the light blouse she wore. Her lustrous hair was caught at the back with a ribbon, allowing the long tail of shining ebony to cascade down her back.

"'Tis as if we were alone in our own corner of paradise," she sighed.

"We are," he said, thrusting the remaining food back into the hamper and setting it aside. He pulled her into his arms.

"Today we are part of nature. Free and unrestrained. An Adam and an Eve."

He reached out and untied the ribbon and released her hair.

Teasing him, she avoided his hands as they went to go around her again and jumped to her feet, wriggling out of her shoes and removing her stockings. Then, lifting her skirts, she ran barefoot across the grass, her beautiful raven hair flying about her head, her laughter spontaneous and unaffected.

Richard quickly discarded cravat and boots and in only breeches and shirt, chest and feet bare, ran after her.

He chased her through the long green grass and she managed to outmaneuver him at first, running in circles until they both began to laugh hysterically. He had never felt so foolish in his life. It brought back his boyhood and made him feel half his age.

She ducked behind the beech tree, but he did not follow her, and instead tiptoed to the opposite side and grabbed her as she darted out. Capturing her at last, he threw her down beneath the sweeping branches.

They were out of the blazing sunlight, but their clothes still clung to them with the heat of their play. They were both panting and Richard noticed how the perspiration pearled the skin at the neck of Lisa's blouse.

He kissed her there, pulling her over onto the sweet-smelling grass. A ray of sun burned down hot on the back of his neck, making more warmth spread through him as his face moved down to kiss the cleavage he was rapidly displaying by unloosening the laces.

"You are overdressed for such a hot day," he murmured.

"So are you," she laughed, lifting his shirt above his head.

Impatient to claim each other more fully, they began to fumble with one another's clothes, tumbling about in the long grass.

Lisa's breasts were quickly bared and Richard bent his head to them. She moaned and her arms went about his neck, pulling his big body closer. Her lips parted beneath his and his kiss deepened, caressing her tongue with his own.

The hot sun poured down as his hands moved lightly over the flawless alabaster skin he had uncovered.

"Lisa, Lisa," he whispered, his fingers continuing to caress her. Shivers of desire coursed through her and she made little cries of pleasure, begging him not to stop.

" 'Under the greenwood tree, who loves to lie with me,' " he grinned, kissing her gently.

"I don't remember the rest," she breathed, feeling quite lightheaded from the wine and his touch.

" 'Come hither, come hither, come hither,' " he growled, imprisoning her in his arms.

The sun hung overhead in shimmering brilliance. The air was heavy with its heat. Languidly they lay side by side in the warm grass beneath the beech tree. It was very hot and their joyous coupling had covered their naked bodies with a light sheen of perspiration.

Lisa felt a longing to bathe herself. She stretched her arms above her head and opened her eyes.

Richard lay on his back beside her, breathing evenly. She was sure he was asleep.

She got slowly and quietly to her feet, not wanting to wake him and ran lightly over to the stream bank.

The water below was like glass, clear and inviting. The bottom was mud-covered—a soft, warm earth color. A minnow darted by, then disappeared in the shadow of a bullrush.

Lisa stepped from the bank and waded out into the water. It was shallow, coming halfway up her calves, but so delightfully cool. The soft mud squished up between her toes and she laughed with pleasure. After making love they had drained the wine bottle together and she felt a little tipsy from the potent mead. The hot sun didn't help the dizziness in her head. She stumbled in a hole and lost her balance. There was a splash and the next thing she knew she was sitting down on the bottom of the stream. She laughed at herself and began to trace lazy patterns in the clear water with her fingers. How delightful it felt, she thought, and slid down slowly, lying back in the coolness, her long hair rippling out around her head like dark, waving grass.

Sighing, she closed her eyes against the glaring sun and let the water lap over her body. It felt so soft and soothing as it caressed her skin.

"What have we here, a mermaid?" asked a deep, amused voice, and opening her eyes she raised her neck to see Richard on the stream bank opposite her. The sun was just behind his head, making his hair look like burnished gold. How magnificent he was! she thought. Standing there as unashamedly naked as a satyr. She let her eyes move over the width of his massive shoulders, powerful chest, his narrow hips and long, firmly muscled thighs.

"Well?" he grinned. "What is the verdict?"

"You will do," she smiled, "and you can join me if you don't stir up the mud."

He waded in quite carefully and then he was sliding down beside her to lie back in the tepid water.

"Doesn't that feel wonderful?" she asked. "Like lying on a smooth silk coverlet on a soft featherbed."

"Mmmm. But not as soft as you." He leaned over her, one big hand reaching to support her head as his mouth closed over hers, drinking deeply of its sweetness.

The water lapped gently over the soft mounds of her upthrust breasts. He lowered his face into its coolness, gently licking at the pink tips with his tongue. Lisa shivered with delight.

"You are an enchantress," he said hoarsely, "a beautiful Lorelei." He slipped his arm beneath her back, raising her to him, his lips warm against the sleek, wet skin of her shoulders.

She wanted him to make love to her right there in the soft mud of the stream bed! Not the quick, fierce love they had had tumbling in the warm grass, delightful as it had been, but slower—a lazy, sensuous, primitive love.

She began to explore him slowly, running her fingers tantalizingly down his strongly muscled back and in turn his mouth and hands gently caressed her trembling body, making her shudder beneath his expert touch. His fingers moved over her flat stomach, downward to slip between her thighs, arousing her with delicious torment. She moaned as they intimately probed and began to move in rhythm to her writhing body.

He covered her mouth with his, his lips and tongue spreading liquid fire. He was taking his time, awakening every inch of her body! She felt a hungry, throbbing ache deep within her. If he didn't take her soon she thought she would die.

She arched against him, feeling the swollen hardness of his desire pressed demandingly against her. She reached for the throbbing shaft, but he grasped her hand.

"Patience, my love, patience." He grinned, his other hand continuing to caress her softness. She was engulfed in pleasure as the agony rose. She cried aloud and twisted against him, feverishly straining, wanting more—more!

He moved over her, pressing her down into the soft mud. It oozed up around her body, warm and spongy, cradling her like a womblike sac. She let out a ragged sigh of relief as he at last slid inside her, finding her as smooth and slippery as the mud she lay upon. Slowly and with the utmost control, Richard moved within her, drawing a rising response.

Lisa tangled her fingers in the golden hair, kissing him deeply. An accomplished lover, Richard was able to take his time, intensifying the pleasure for them both by deliberately holding back. The water rippled around them as he plunged in slow, sensual rhythm.

Lisa was full of him, part of him; their fiery bodies melded together, rising and falling as one. Waves of pleasure seared through her. She met his thrusts and urged him on, moving beneath him in the satin-smooth depths of the shallow stream.

A fierce hunger now rose between them and he put his hands under her tight little buttocks, pressing her closer, driving even deeper.

She became like a wild thing, moaning and beating upon his back, mindless with ecstasy. She arched her body so that her legs wound high above his waist. He was so deep in her she felt he would pierce right through her.

Suddenly, she grasped him with her knees and they rolled languorously over in the mud. For a moment she straddled him, her fingers digging into his shoulders, riding him hard as she would ride Primrose, her head thrown back, her raven hair plastered to her head, her eyes glazed, her mouth open wide in a silent cry. They rolled again in the spongy mire, his tempo now increasing—faster—ever faster—a man and a woman entwined as one in passionate frenzy—a wondrous, panting, thrashing, water-creature!

They erupted together in a shattering explosion so great that she wept as his warm seed emptied into her.

For a long time they lay there locked together, the stirred-up mud and water gradually settling to the bottom of the stream again.

My God! he thought. Was there ever a woman such as this? She made all the others he had known fade into oblivion; all the other couplings seem like weak travesties in comparison.

He shifted his body, withdrawing from her, and propped himself on one elbow, looking down at her.

Lisa's eyes were closed. Her face soft with the drowsy aftermath of love. She was so beautiful. A ravishingly beautiful water nymph, who had already enslaved him with her powers.

How he loved her! It was an emotion so totally new to him he had yet to fully understand it.

He had known passion before, but this was a day-after-day steady fire that had totally consumed him. Beneath the flame lay such sweetness, such tenderness—that he had thought never to discover.

Lisa opened her eyes and saw him and suddenly the violet depths darkened, a dawning sense of shame replacing the warm contentment.

She scrambled to her feet, and before Richard knew it she was off, splashing down the stream as quickly as she could go. Stunned by her reaction, he rose and followed after her.

A quarter of a mile further on, the stream ran down into a little hollow, making a sheltered pond at one end. There he discovered Lisa bathing and washing her hair.

The water was deeper here and he dove under the surface, swimming underwater to where she bathed, but when he got to the spot where she had been standing, she was gone. His head and shoulders burst up out of the water and he looked around him.

Lisa was almost at the bank, wading as quickly as she could through the tall rushes.

"Stop!" he called, swimming after her, but she was out on the grass now and beginning to run back in the direction of their picnic spot.

She had finished dressing and was combing her long hair when he reached her.

She would not look at him. He pulled on his breeches and boots and approached her.

"What's the matter?" he asked gently, sitting down beside her on the grass.

She did not answer him, but when he looked at her he could see that she had been crying. The tears were still shiny and wet in her violet eyes.

"Tell me!" he demanded, clearly upset. "Was it something I did?"

"Nay," she shook her head. "I don't know what came over me. Perhaps it was the wine. I—I behaved so shamelessly—so wantonly. . . ."

His lips broke into their insolent grin as Richard gently lifted her chin with his fingers.

"Aye, you did," he agreed, meeting her eyes, his mouth twitching. "And I loved every minute of it."

"You are only saying that." Her eyes, those wonderful, big beautiful eyes, were luminous. "I did not behave like a lady. Oh, Richard, I'm so ashamed."

His face sobered. "Don't be ashamed, my love. You gave yourself wholly to me, with no reservations. It quite humbles me, because it shows how much you love me. It wasn't wrong, Lisa. It was beautiful and right."

"I love you so," she murmured, her lips trembling.

"And I love you with all my heart," he said huskily. "In my whole life I have never known such happiness as you have given me."

The black midnight curtain of her hair drifted over him as he kissed her and her lips were warm and soft beneath his.

He propped her up against the tree trunk and lay down with his head resting between the upthrust hills of her breasts.

He sighed as she stroked his forehead. Her soft skin had a fragrance about it that always enchanted him. He pulled her hand down and kissed the palm.

"What is your mistress like?" she asked him, so unexpectedly that he started.

A frown creased his brow. "What mistress?"

"Your mistress in London."

"How do you know that I have one?"

"Doesn't every man at court?"

"Nay. That is only a rumor spread by the Puritans."

She traced a finger in the golden curls on his chest. "You are evading my question, Richard. What is she like?"

He decided to be honest with her. "She is small and fair and hasn't a brain in her head. Doubtless by now Christina has found herself a new protector."

"I doubt that very much. Not after she has had a lover such as you."

He grinned. "And have you had so much experience you can compare?" he teased.

"I know what you do to *me*," she said softly. "How long has she been your mistress?"

"I don't remember. Five or six months. Lisa, must we—"

"Is she bearing your child?"

"Good lord, no!" Richard sat up abruptly. "Why the devil are you questioning me like this?"

"Because I love you and want to know more about you."
She met his eyes.

"Christina is *not* bearing my child. She—" He was about to
say that Christina was barren, but she interrupted him.

"Do you have any sideslips at all?"

"Sideslips?" He grinned. "Not to my knowledge." Then his
eyes brightened. "Surely 'tis too soon for *you* to think—"

The color rose in her cheeks. "Nay! That was not why I
asked."

He put an arm about her shoulders. "But you *did* wonder
what I would do if it *should* happen, didn't you?"

Lisa was about to deny it, and then she nodded.

"Don't you know me well enough to know that if you should
ever have a child by me that I would always look after it?"

"Look after—" She was suddenly full of uncertainty. What
was he saying? She tried to read the expression in his eyes.

"I love you, Lisa, as I swear I have never loved another
woman," he said, his voice very deep. "And I want you as I
have never wanted another woman. Before I left today, I
received word that I will have to go to London in the morning.
I do not know how long I will be gone, so I have sent word to
Peter, hoping he will come and stay with Mary in my absence.
I—"

"Why are you going?" Her thoughts were suddenly diverted.
"'Tis the plot, isn't it? 'Tis close to the time of the king's visit
to Watford and you are planning to spring a trap for the
traitors."

"Do you read minds?" he grinned. "Aye, I am going to
London to give final instructions to those involved." His voice
softened. "Come with me, Lisa. I don't want to be parted from
you again. Come with me, live with me, now and always."

Lisa's great eyes widened as the full impact of his words
reached her. She drew away from him, shaking her head, her
heart thudding within her.

"Live with you?" she echoed his words. Her body had
suddenly become cold and rigid. She felt betrayed, humiliated.
She had given herself to him, thinking that because he loved
her he would naturally propose marriage.

"I love you and you love me. I cannot bear to be apart from
you. I want you beside me."

"Nay, Richard," she managed, her voice very cold as she
raised her head haughtily. "I do not doubt that you love me, but

I believe you interpret the word differently. How can I possibly live with a man who does not honor me enough to offer me marriage?"

"Marriage?" he exclaimed. "Surely you have always known I could not promise you that."

"Why? Am I not good enough to be your wife? Is my lineage not noble enough?"

Several times Lisa had thought she would confess to Richard her true identity, but she knew what he would do and she did not want him to fight her battles. She wished to confront Sir Basil herself in her own way and in her own time. Her vengeance on Basil Stavely had been carefully planned.

If she told Richard now that she was Elizabeth Stavely and her family was as old and as honorable as his, he might offer her his name, but did she want it under those conditions? If he did not love her enough to forget pride and family as Valerie Manning had done, then surely it was not a deep-enough love.

"In the world in which I live, marriage and love are two totally different things," Richard was explaining to her. "'Tis a question of putting family first. 'Tis a duty that was implanted in me as a boy. And now that I am the last of the line, I simply cannot—"

"Marry a nobody."

"Lisa, pray do not be hurt by what I am saying. If I did not have a family obligation, I would marry you tomorrow." His deep voice lowered in the intimate, caressing way that always thrilled her. "What I feel for you will always be something quite apart from that which I might feel for a wife. Whenever I decide to marry, it will only be a *mariage de convenance,* as the French say."

Silence.

"Can't you see, Lisa, you are mine right now in everything but name, and as we love one another, what possible difference can that make? I will always look after you. Give you anything you might desire."

"Nay!" Anger surged in the violet eyes.

"Damn it, Lisa, what more *do* you want?"

"Put that way, a whole lot more!" she lashed out at him.

He reached for her, but she pushed him away from her, jumping to her feet. "I am sorry, *my lord,* but the love you offer is simply not good enough for me."

She turned to run toward her horse, but Richard had risen to his feet. He caught her in his arms and pulled her roughly against him, kissing her with a fierce deliberateness that, despite her firm resolve, brought all of her senses vibrantly alive.

"Nay!" She fought him frantically, finally bringing a hand up to give his face a resounding slap.

"Don't fight me, Lisa," he said quietly, as the mark reddened his cheek. "You know that we belong together. You can no more resist me than I can resist you."

Still she struggled in his arms.

"I have been searching for too long for a love such as this. Now that I have found you and possessed you, I have not the slightest intention of letting you go." •

She broke loose from him and ran away across the field. Releasing Primrose, she climbed awkwardly up into the saddle unassisted, and without a backward glance at Richard, galloped off across the meadow and up the hill beyond.

Lisa had escaped to her small room in the manor house, claiming illness, but she was not to be left alone. A concerned Mary came to her as soon as she heard and anxiously inquired if there was anything that she could do to help.

Little acting was required on her part as Lisa assured her that all she wished for was rest. She had a pounding headache, she told Mary, and thought she must have suffered too much sun riding to and from Matthew's cottage.

Mary admonished her, having noticed that Lisa had ridden off without her hat, but as it was apparent that Lisa was indeed ill, she ceased her scolding. Lisa's face was very pale and her eyes were red as if from weeping. Mary asked her if she would like Nelly to fix her anything to eat or drink. Perhaps just a little broth?

Lisa thanked her but declined any nourishment. She just needed rest, she begged, and at last Mary took her leave with a worried frown creasing her brow.

Lisa sighed when the door had closed behind Mary and got up from her bed to go over and thrust in the lock. She did not wish to be disturbed again. Dear God, all she wanted was to be left alone!

She pressed her fingers to her temples. Her head throbbed unbearably. The hot sun might be partly to blame, plus the potent mead, but the real reason was what had transpired at the end of the afternoon. It had been so wonderful up until then.

An afternoon of laughter and love and (she blushed to herself) unrestrained passion in a soft, warm stream bed. Now everything seemed ugly and shameful!

What a lovesick little fool she had been! Willingly she had allowed Richard to seduce her. She threw herself down on her bed and began to sob into her pillow. He had never had the least intention of marrying her. He was just satisfying his own selfish desires. But, a voice inside her insisted, he said he loved you. Fool! How many others had heard him say those very same words? Sylvia Montague, his mistress, Christina, and how many more?

She was tortured with her thoughts, so tortured by them that she began to build up a profound hatred of Richard Drayton. She pounded her fist into her pillow and vowed he would never lay a hand on her again. Her room had darkened before, exhausted, she finally fell into a restless sleep.

When Lisa awoke, the first gray light of dawn was creeping through her window. She stretched her cramped limbs. The sound of horse's hooves could be heard outside on the still morning air. No doubt that was what had awakened her.

She got up and quickly went to the window. Below her, she saw a dark shape swing himself into the saddle and ride off down the gravel driveway. There was no mistaking those broad shoulders. She watched him until he was out of sight.

"Go back to London!" she almost cried aloud. "Lie tonight in Christina's arms, you deceiving bastard!" (There, she had said the word—if only to herself.)

But as she sat still by the window, watching the sun begin to rise, she was forced to face the real truth. Richard had never tried to deceive her. He had never promised her anything. The fact that he had seduced her was as much her fault as his. If she would only admit it to herself, it was completely her fault. He had tried his best to keep away from her. "Tell me to stop!" she remembered him groaning as he held her in his arms in the garden. But she had made it known to him that she wanted him as much as he wanted her; she had encouraged him by her very submissiveness. He had never forced her. He had never mentioned marriage. It was just that she had thought that a gentleman always married a lady if he . . . if they. . . .

He was no gentleman! He had said as much several times. All he had wanted was a new conquest. She wondered how long it would have taken before he had tired of her. She felt a terrible sense of betrayal. She had given the man she loved her body, her soul, everything she possessed. He had sworn he loved her and yet, if this were so, he had not loved her enough to forget the barriers of class and ask her to be his wife. She was not good enough for him!

If only, she wondered. If only she had confided her secret to him long ago, at the time she had told him of the plot on the king's life. Would it have made a difference in their relationship? Would they have fallen in love? Would he have asked her to marry him? Would he have taken her before the wedding? She would never know, but she did know that if Richard rejected her as plain Lisa Manning, he could not possibly love her enough. Perhaps it was just as well she had found this out now. She certainly had no wish to marry such a pompous and arrogant man, a man who only considered marriage an institution for cementing titles and propagating bloodlines. In fact, she wished she never had to lay eyes upon him again!

Perhaps, she considered, she didn't have to. She could leave Stavely Manor even now, go to her mama's parents as Valerie Manning had wished her to do. But could she so easily give up her heritage to the man who had been responsible for her brother's death? Who even now was plotting the king's extinction? Was she so heartless to leave Mary, the friend who had suffered so much in her defense, in Basil Stavely's cruel hands?

Chapter Twenty-three

As Drayton set out along the main road to London, the gray dawn lifted and a bright sun appeared. It would be another scorching day, he thought. The last few days had been unaccountably warm for May.

How hot it had been the day before, lying in the sunshine of a flower-covered meadow. His thoughts went back to those blissful hours of lovemaking with Lisa and so deep in thought was he that he did not notice a man on horseback had fallen in behind him, keeping a discreet distance between them but always managing to have the big black stallion within his sight.

At first Drayton had not understood Lisa's anger at his proposition. She had considered it an insult, and yet he had told her he loved her. Had shown her in a hundred different ways. He had forgotten how innocent she was of his world. How naive. To her marriage followed naturally when two people declared their love. If only it could all be so easy, so uncomplicated.

He thought of Ned who had gone on ahead the night before to arrange things for him in London. He envied his manservant. The man might choose whoever he pleased for a wife, but men of his own station rarely married for love. How had he let himself fall in love with this girl? Now, by God, he had to have her. She had become a part of him. But what the devil was he going to do about her?

He recalled the sweet pressure of her lips beneath his, her velvet-soft eyes that could haunt a man's soul, the eager response of her passionate little body when they made love, and he knew that Lisa could make him forget everything—his family—his title—his very heritage. Yet he had to have her! Damn it, he admitted to himself, life would not be worth living without her!

Drayton only took the time to wash the travel dust from himself and change his clothing before he was on his way to see Christina.

Her little French maid opened the door to him.

"Oh, m'lord," she said, clearly agitated upon seeing him, "m'lady is not at home, *cet après-midi.*"

"If you don't mind, Yvette, since I pay the rent, I will check for myself."

He took the stairs three at a time and pushed open the door to Christina's bedchamber. He would not have been surprised to have caught her in the arms of her new lover, and almost wished he had—for it would have made the parting from her a great deal easier. The room, however, was deserted.

Evidence of Christina's untidiness lay all around him as he stepped across the threshold. Little piles of her clothing were draped over bed and chairs and scattered over the floor. Her dressing table was covered with a jumbled assortment of bottles and jars and spilled powder, discarded jewelry and other finery.

"I believe you are paid to take care of this." He indicated the untidy room to the breathless maid who had followed him.

"*Oui*, m'lord, I was just about—"

"Where is she?" he growled.

"M'lady is attending a luncheon party at Lady Swinford's."

"Which will end in her playing cards and losing another hundred pounds," he muttered.

"She will be sorry to have missed you."

"She won't miss me. I will await her return in the drawing room."

"But m'lord, I—"

"In the drawing room, Yvette, and bring me a brandy."

What was wrong with the girl? he wondered. She had blanched paler than the white apron she wore.

173

He strode down the stairs and flung open the drawing-room door.

A good-looking young gentleman who had been reclining in a chair before the fireplace sprang to his feet.

"Tina, I couldn't wait—" he began, then blushed scarlet at the sight of Lord Drayton standing in the doorway.

"Really?" Richard drawled, raising an eyebrow. "I am afraid you are going to have to wait a little longer. . . . Hetherington, isn't it? I know your father."

He crossed the room and seated himself comfortably in the chair opposite to the one the young man had just vacated.

"Do sit down." Richard waved a hand at Hetherington. "You look damned ridiculous standing there with your mouth open."

"T-thank you, m'lord," the young man stuttered and reseated himself hesitantly on the edge of his chair.

"Am I to gather, Hetherington, that you have been seeing Christina in my absence?" Drayton asked him.

"Why, I—" The young man gulped. "The lady bestowed upon me the honor of escorting her to a few entertainments in your absence."

"I see. And did the lady also bestow upon you the honor of sharing her bed?"

"M'lord!" Hetherington jumped to his feet. His hand trembled at his sword hilt before dropping away. "I have no wish to be called out. I know you are a swordsman of the highest order and I—"

"'Tis a little late to think of that now, isn't it, Hetherington?"

"I would never—I did not mean—m'lord, you must understand, the lady bewitched me. She is so enchantingly beautiful, so gay and amusing. I—I could not stay away from her." He was pleading now, perspiration beginning to roll from beneath his foppish periwig down his forehead to cheeks that had hardly felt the blade of a razor.

Drayton guessed his age to be around eighteen. Tina was discovering the younger bucks now. No doubt the older men, knowing she was under his protection, would be too wary to approach her with him liable to return to London at any moment. Drayton was known to have never lost a duel. It was a high deterrent to dalliance with the fair Christina.

"Go home, Hetherington," Drayton sighed, waving his hand in the air as if to indicate that the incident meant little to him.

There was a timid knock at the door and Yvette entered with a decanter of brandy and two goblets on a tray.

The young gentleman stared at Richard as the servant placed the tray at Drayton's elbow and hurried from the room.

He spoke again when she had departed. "You mean you . . . you would not . . ."

"No. Let this be a lesson to you, Hetherington. Do not trifle with other men's whores."

Anger flared in the young man's face. "Christina is not . . ." he dared to contradict. "She is a lady, m'lord."

"She is a whore, sir. And for the time being she is *my* whore. Get out of here before I try and whip some sense into you!" Drayton rose ominously from his chair and Hetherington made a hurried exit, crashing against the edge of the doorway as he opened the door and plunged through.

Drayton waited only until the young man had closed the front door behind him before breaking into a cynical laugh. Was I ever that young? he wondered, as he poured himself a brandy. Was I ever that green?

He was glowering into the fire when a few minutes later the front door burst open and Christina's voice was heard in the hall.

"Yvette! Where are you?"

There was a swish of skirts as Christina approached the open doorway to the drawing room. She saw him immediately.

"Richard! You are home!"

Arms outstretched, she ran toward him across the carpet, a vision in pink silk and lace.

He rose from his chair and his bigness seemed to fill the whole room. She had almost forgotten how wonderfully handsome he was. When she got close to him he grasped her elbows to prevent an embrace.

"Good afternoon, Tina," he said, his deep voice very low.

She could not read his expression, but she knew something was wrong. There was a taunting gleam in the emerald eyes as they surveyed her.

"I'm so glad you have returned," she whispered, smiling up at him beguilingly. "I missed you so."

"Did you?" His mouth quirked in its cynical smile. "Then of course you remained faithful to me."

She tried to extricate her arms to move closer to him.

"I have never looked at another man," she assured him, her voice husky. Just one glance at this big, golden-haired giant and she longed to bed with him!

"Perhaps not a man," he said consideringly. "But a boy . . . ?"

He knew! Dear God, he knew! A cold chill ran down her spine, though a quick denial sprang to her lips.

"'Tis little use lying to me, Tina. He was here when I arrived. Young Hetherington. Mooning over you."

Richard had let go her arms and she stood before him, her face paling under his harsh gaze.

"Wh-what did you do?"

"What would a gentleman in my position do under the circumstances?"

"You called him out?" A gleam of triumph appeared in her blue eyes. "You are going to fight a duel over me?"

Richard's face darkened, the green eyes becoming nearly black with anger. His two large hands reached out, imprisoning her slender white neck between them.

"So that would please you, would it? It would please your damned vanity for me to kill that poor besotted fool because of you!" He flung her away from him. "How could I have ever taken up with such a self-centered, unfeeling little baggage."

He strode toward the door. "You have until the end of June to find yourself a new protector. The rent has been paid until then."

"No!" She ran after him, throwing herself down at his feet. "Nay, Richard, you cannot do this to me! I love you! I cannot live without you!"

He looked down at her and there was no sign of softening in his face.

"I have been told you managed to run up some exorbitant bills in the past weeks. They will be paid and I will settle a thousand pounds on you. Considering your perfidy, I believe this to be very generous. Goodbye, Tina."

Despite the secrecy enshrouding the meeting place, Lord Drayton and his men were unfortunately spied upon that evening.

The man who had followed Drayton to London had informed his superior of his arrival and it was Carver, himself, who trailed Drayton to the old barn a few miles from the northern outskirts of the city.

Roger Francis was already there with twenty hand-picked men, and all were delighted to welcome their former commanding officer and be together again.

Carver hid himself in the shadows beside the barn, close enough to the unglazed window that he could hear what was being said within.

After much back-slapping and catching up of news, Drayton finally stood up before them and cleared his throat.

"You have been asked to come here tonight because of your loyalty to His Majesty and your skill with sword and pistol. The king has been informed of a plot upon the life of himself and his brother." Many exclamations followed this remark. "The attack," Drayton continued, "is expected to take place when the king and his party depart from London next week on a journey northward. We have been informed of the planned place of attack and you men will close in on the traitors there, after they have assembled. They will therefore be apprehended before they get a chance to lift a sword against the king."

There was a cheer from the men and Richard waited until they had settled down before he continued.

"Francis and I will not be with you, but will be traveling with the party itself. I have placed Braddock in charge. He will inform you of when and where you are to assemble. Just remember that your monarch is staking his life on your ability. Tell no one. The success of this venture lies entirely in your hands."

Drayton reported on the meeting to the king and it was agreed that Roger Francis and he would arrive at the Privy Stairs at Whitehall just before dawn on the fourth of June.

In all, Drayton was away from Stavely Manor for five days. On his last day in London, he was visited by Christopher Wren, the young professor of astronomy and friend of Peter Ellsbury.

Drayton was immediately taken with his sensitivity and interest in Calderwood and its reconstruction. He was a small man in stature, slight and lively in movement—almost wrenlike—Richard thought, grinning to himself.

Only a month before the Royal Society had seen Wren's design for the Sheldonian Theatre and asked him to deposit a description of it in the archives. He was just finishing this for them, he explained to Drayton.

The Royal Society, he said, was concerned with every aspect of life to which scientific methods of constructive reasoning could be applied. The king's interest in the Royal Society was much more than nominal, he added, his bright eyes gleaming, and at the present time he was making plans for the installation of his own telescope and laboratory at Whitehall.

Drayton was fascinated by this man and succeeded in maneuvering the conversation around to a discussion of Inigo Jones' work, explaining how that man had come to design the original Calderwood.

Wren expressed a desire to see the ruins of the mansion, but would not commit himself as to whether he would take on the task of designing its reconstruction. Drayton had to be content with the fact that Wren was planning to visit Peter Ellsbury in a few day's time and promised to ride over to see Calderwood while he was there.

Drayton persuaded Wren to stay for luncheon, but when he left shortly afterward, shouted for Ned, and within the hour they were on their way back to Stavely Manor.

Mary and Lisa and Peter Ellsbury were enjoying a glass of claret in the gallery before they dined, when Pottle entered the room and announced Lord Drayton.

He strode in with his boots ringing on the floorboards in that brisk way he had, totally unconscious of himself or the effect he produced.

Lisa's heart began to pound rapidly within her, but she turned her eyes to Peter as he sprang to his feet and hurried across the room, hand outstretched.

"Richard! I'm so glad you returned before I had to leave. I was afraid I would miss you."

"Do sit down," Mary invited, but Drayton declined, saying he was still booted and spurred and must change from his dusty clothing before joining them. His eyes still sought those of Lisa's, but those soft violet eyes had clouded and turned away from him to focus on Peter.

Had Ellsbury spent this time at Stavely Manor pursuing his courtship of Lisa? He wondered this as he crossed the wide hall and headed up the stairs.

His brief glance at Lisa had shown him that she had not

forgiven him. Where she had looked hurt the first time he had left Stavely Manor, this time there was a touch of bitterness in those wide, expressive eyes. There were also dark smudges under them, as if she had not been sleeping too well. Somehow they only served to make her look more defenseless. He longed to put his arms about her.

Peter returned to his chair after Richard had strolled from the room. He was clearly delighted that he would have an evening with his old friend. They had much to discuss and would have the time together over brandy later in the evening.

Lisa sat quietly, feeling the pain that the sight of Richard had reawakened in her. Since he had made his insulting proposition to her, she had been trying to convince herself that she never wanted to see him again, that it was all over between them.

Peter had arrived the next day, and she had tried her best to forget Richard by allowing him to entertain her. He was a droll and easygoing companion and she found that she enjoyed being with him. Mary appeared to countenance their friendship and left them alone on several occasions. Just that afternoon, Peter had taken her hands as they had walked in the garden.

"How long have I known you?" he had asked Lisa, stopping to look down at her.

"Several weeks."

"I don't need any longer to convince myself I am in love with you." His voice had lowered to a hoarse whisper. "I have never known anyone more beautiful—and it is not just an external beauty. You are beautiful inside as well as out, Lisa. You are so warm and understanding—so good for Mary."

"Thank you, Peter."

She felt suddenly ashamed of her deception. Both Peter and Mary thought her to be sweet and innocent—but she was neither. She was bitter and used and all because of their friend, Richard Drayton. Still it was gratifying to have this kind and handsome man tell her that he loved her. Perhaps in time he could manage to cure her forever of thoughts of Richard.

But now that she had seen Richard again she knew it would not be that easy. He affected her as no other man could.

Lisa was quiet through supper and let the men and Mary do most of the talking. When the ladies withdrew afterward to the gallery, leaving the men at the dining table with their brandy, Mary mentioned this.

"Are you still not well, dear? You really don't seem to have been yourself since the day you suffered from the sun."

"I am fine, Mary."

"I have been hoping Peter would be able to lift your spirits. I am sure you are aware that he has grown very fond of you." Mary regarded her closely as she picked up her embroidery.

"He has spoken to me of it."

"And do you also care for him?"

"I am fond of Peter, but . . ." she paused.

"But you are not in love with him."

"I have not known him long, Mary."

"Of course," Mary nodded. "And you are very young. He would make a good husband, Lisa. He is kind and gentle. Not at all like . . . like Basil."

Lisa jumped up, unexpectedly. "I don't want to be rushed," she said, unwanted tears filling her eyes as she turned away from Mary.

She felt the other's soft hands on her shoulders. "Is it because of me, Lisa?" Mary asked softly. "Has the horror of my miscarriage, Basil's lust with Polly—has it all made you frightened and afraid of the intimacies of marriage?"

Lisa shook her head. "That is not it, Mary."

"Are you sure? Those two ruffians and then Basil trying to force themselves on you. It would make any young girl apprehensive. I will tell Peter he must be patient with you. Give you more time. It would make me so happy, Lisa, if you could grow to love my brother—to marry him." Mary's face lit up. "Then we would be sisters!"

Peter stopped Lisa outside her bedchamber door that evening and before she knew it he had drawn her into his arms.

Had the brandy given him extra courage? she wondered, smelling it on his breath. He and Richard had lingered for a long time together in the dining hall before joining the ladies. Richard had apologized, explaining that they had been discussing Christopher Wren and his coming visit to Peter's home.

"I leave early in the morning," Peter said now to Lisa. "Might I be so bold as to claim a goodbye kiss?"

She did not answer and he pulled her closer. His mouth was soft and warm on hers. He held her as if she were infinitely precious and fragile—not in the hard, possessive way Richard did.

"I love you, Lisa," he whispered, and then he was gone from her, down the darkened hallway to his room.

Lisa stood there a moment, a hand to her lips. Peter would ask her to marry him, she felt sure. He did not care what her background was. It was enough that he loved her. Tears filled her eyes.

"How quickly you change affections, Mistress Manning," said a deep, sardonic voice.

Richard came out of the shadows and stood glaring down at her. By God, he was thinking, is she no better than Tina?

"'Twas not what you think."

"Really? And am I to suppose you have not encouraged him at all?"

"And what if I have?" she flared. "Peter loves me and would marry me, despite my lack of *noble* blood."

Richard grasped her arm, his strong fingers pressing deeply into her soft flesh.

"Let me go!" she cried. "There is nothing more for us to say to one another."

"I think there is. Nothing can change the fact that we love one another, Lisa."

At that moment, seeing the dark emotion in his eyes, Lisa almost allowed herself to be swept into his strong arms. Her body ached to feel him against her. Her lips burned for his kiss.

"Do we?" she demanded. "I do not remember any exchange of vows between us, any promises." She felt herself shaking. Even her voice. "Let me alone, Richard. You know I don't really mean anything to you. I am just another conquest."

"Conquest?" he growled, his green eyes searing into hers. "Damn it, Lisa, ever since I met you you've been like a thorn under my skin, tormenting me, constantly on my mind."

His words touched a responsive chord deep within her and seeing the softening of her eyes he pulled her roughly against his chest. His mouth closed ruthlessly over hers, but as the kiss warmed and deepened into scalding desire, she managed to twist from his embrace. Flinging open the door of her room, she stumbled inside, slamming and locking the door behind her.

Shaken by his kiss and the wild urge that had flared up in her to return it and give way to the passion that surged through her, she sank down onto her bed.

Why, why did he affect her the way he did? Was it those

181

green predator's eyes of his which seemed to look so deep into her soul? Was it that aura of virility he exuded, or the magnetism of his personality? His very nearness, she knew, completely disarmed her, made her weak—made her forget all her firm resolves.

How could she marry Peter or any other man? She belonged to Richard just as surely as if he had enchained her.

Chapter Twenty-four

IT WAS LATE THE NEXT AFTERNOON, AND DRAYTON HAD JUST RE-turned from a day spent at his estate. He had left Stavely Manor even before Peter that morning and was tired and more than a little agitated by Lisa's behavior the previous night.

He had changed his clothing and was just about to descend the wide stairway when he heard what sounded like weeping coming from behind Mary Stavely's bedchamber door.

He crossed the upper gallery and knocked on the heavy panel.

"'Tis Richard, Mary, Is there anything I can do?"

There was silence for a moment and then Mary's small voice said, "Come in, Richard."

He entered her bedchamber to find her curled up on the sofa before the window. What looked like a letter was clutched in one hand and in the other was a white ball of a handkerchief. Her eyes were red from weeping.

"Whatever is the matter, Mary?"

"This letter came just now. 'Tis from Basil. He will be returning in a few days." She burst into another flood of tears.

"Mary," Richard said softly, sitting down beside her. "'Twill be all right. I will be here."

"'Tis just," she gulped, "I have been so happy these past weeks. It has been almost like 'twas before the Civil War, when you and Peter and I . . ."

"I know. I know." She felt the comforting gentleness of his arm around her. Why, oh why, could Basil not be more like Richard? She started to sob and he pulled her closer. It seemed the most natural thing in the world for her to turn to him, to sob against his broad chest, to be held in his strong arms.

Caring for Mary, Richard made no move to take advantage of her vulnerability. But, all at once, everything changed for *her*. Comfort turned to want. This was what she had always longed for—someone gentle and compassionate to turn to—to lean on. She put her arms about his neck and strained against him, her heart pounding in her slight body. For the first time since her wedding night she began to feel an ache—a longing—deep within her. She wanted a taste of what love could really be like—just a taste! She raised her lips to his, but his big hands had gone to her thin shoulders and he was tenderly pushing her away.

"This isn't what you want, Mary," he said softly.

"Yes," she murmured, hoarsely. "Oh yes, Richard, yes!"

He kissed the tear-filled eyes as he extricated himself from her arms and got to his feet.

After a moment she looked up at him, a blush staining her pale cheeks crimson. "What you must think of me!" she cried, putting her hands over her face.

"I think only that you are unhappy and needed comforting," he said quietly.

"Forgive me—"

"Speak no more about it, Mary."

As Richard left her bedchamber, he thought he saw a flash of Pottle's maroon livery disappearing around the corner of the hallway, but he shrugged and continued down the stairs.

He dined alone that evening. Neither Mary nor Lisa joined him at supper in the dining hall. He found he had little appetite and drank only sparingly before returning to his own bedchamber.

The day had been gray and gloomy and darkness came early. With it came also the sound of rain upon the windows. It was a welcome sound. The day had been hot and humid without the slightest breeze, causing a very oppressive feeling. Now, a deep rumbling sound could be heard, growing steadily louder and louder until the storm finally broke, battering at the old manor house in all its fury. Lightning crackled and filled the evening with its startling fingers of glaring light.

Mary lay on her bed thinking of Richard. Why had he come back into her life now? The man who had been the first to make her heart flutter all those years ago. In a few minutes on the sofa in his arms she had seen how different things might have been for her. She wondered what it would have been like if he had *not* been a gentleman and had taken advantage of her weakness and made love to her. Somehow she knew that Richard would not have just pounded into her, anxious only for his own release. He would have been gentle and loving, giving her pleasure; giving her the ecstasy and fulfillment she had never experienced.

Basil always took her without words, clumsily and quickly. She hated his heavy, gasping breathing while she lay there and willed it all to be over. With Richard, she felt sure, it would have been different, but now she would never, never know. The thunder deadened the sound of her renewed weeping.

Lisa was wide-awake in her bed, listening to the howling of the wind, the rumble of the thunder.

She lay there fighting the conflicting emotions that surged within. Her body wanted Richard, wanted to go to him and be wrapped in his strong arms, wanted to feel the warmth of him hard against her. She felt such a need of him. Such a shameless, wanton need!

How expertly Richard had awakened her innocent body to the intimate pleasures of lovemaking. By a kiss, a simple touch, he had made her forget everything and respond to him as eagerly and abandonedly as any trollop would.

She tried to focus her thoughts on the storm that crashed about the manor house, but the fury of it only made the pressure rise within her own body. She could almost feel Richard's gentle hands caressing her flesh, his lips buried in her hair, his fierce possession of her.

She fought to blot him from her mind, but it was useless. Oh, God, would she always have this ache in her heart for him, this ache that only he could heal—with his arms, his lips, his body.

The nature of the thunderstorm had risen. Lisa was caught up as much in the turbulence that raged outside as that which raged within her.

A warmth had risen in her body, suffusing her. Her heart was pounding furiously. She could not lie there a moment longer. She had to do something!

She rose from her bed and without putting a robe over her fine lawn nightdress, she left the confines of her stuffy room.

She paused only long enough for a flash of lightning to illuminate her way before her bare feet padded soundlessly down the corridor.

At the back of the upper gallery above the stairs was a large arched window. Lisa found herself standing before it, looking out at the magnificence of the storm. It was at its height now. The flashes of lightning followed each other so swiftly they lit up the whole sky, making the garden below the window as bright as day. The thunder crackled deafeningly as the storm moved overhead.

Lisa's breathing had quickened. Her face was flushed, her body strung out so taut she wanted to scream.

All at once, she began to struggle to open the window latches and straining against them, she found herself pulling, pulling, until they finally gave way and jarred open. Lisa flung back the double panes of the big window, allowing the wind and the rain to rage in at her, whipping and lashing at her body, soaking her to the skin in seconds. She did not care.

She put her arms out to receive the full blast of it, delighting in the chill raindrops that cooled her heated body, the wild wind that almost knocked her from her feet.

Suddenly, strong hands reached out and pulled her roughly back, fought to close the windows. Powerful arms wrapped her in a tight embrace and scooped her up as a deep, familiar voice said harshly, "Little fool! Do you want to catch a fever?"

"Put me down!" she cried, shaking her head so that water flew from her long wet strands of hair into his face.

Richard paid her no mind, striding purposely down the hall to his bedchamber, pushing open the door and kicking it closed behind him.

He threw her down on the tumbled bed and proceeded to tear off her sodden nightdress and begin to towel her down with a soft wool coverlet. His large hands moved deftly over her entire body until her skin was pink and tingling with a warm glow.

"I couldn't sleep either," he said. "Always prowl about when there's a storm."

As she watched, he calmly removed his robe and tossed it in

the direction of a chair. He was naked beneath it and his muscles rippled as he lay down beside her, never taking his eyes from her face. He drew her against his warm length, one big hand stroking the still damp hair that fanned out about her head.

"Better?" he asked, huskily.

She began to protest, to try to push away his hands as they started to move over her slowly and skillfully, arousing in her the trembling sensations she had tried so hard to forget.

"Nay!" she cried, pummeling his chest with her fists in a desperate attempt to escape.

"I hunger for you, Lisa," he murmured, dragging her wrists above her head and pinioning them there as he continued to fondle her, to place a blazing trail of hot, demanding kisses from her mouth to her breasts. The nipples hardened and grew taut beneath his ministrations and he grinned down at her with satisfaction.

"You lecherous beast!" she hissed. "Why can't you leave me alone! Didn't Christina satisfy your lusts enough for you?"

He raised an eyebrow. "Why, Lisa, do I detect a note of jealousy?"

"Jealousy!" she snapped. "You flatter yourself. I care not who you bed!"

"And you haven't missed me?"

"Missed you! Whyever would I do that? I have been much too occupied."

"Occupied?" A muscle worked in his jaw. "Has Peter then been so attentive?"

"Aye, he has."

"And you never thought of me at all?"

"Never!"

"What a little liar you are," he chuckled, resuming his soft caresses. "Despite it not being of interest to you, I will tell you that I was not unfaithful with Christina or any other wench while away from you. I returned completely virtuous and panting with desire for you, and what do you do? Reject me and slam your blasted door in my face."

"I will not be your mistress, Richard," she cried. "I will not be any man's whore. I will not—"

"Methinks the lady doth protest too much." He pressed his hot mouth over hers, his kisses growing deeper, his searching tongue arousing her still more.

Her eyes filled with tears as the desire rose within her traitorous body and she found herself responding to his expert lovemaking. Tormented by his hands, his mouth, she opened to accept rather than reject the throbbing length, urgently directing its invasion, desperate to feel the longed-for thrust.

She gasped with joy as he slid deep within her. It felt so easy, so right. Slowly, deliberately and with the utmost control, he moved inside her, taking her to the very heights of pleasure.

She moaned and writhed against him, the passion of her pent-up emotions rising as the fury of the storm outside reached its last crescendo. The pressure within her mounted as he plunged deeper and in a flash of lightning, she saw his eyes. They were intensely green, the pupils like large black orbs, completely engulfing her.

The tension grew to a frenzied pitch as his tempo increased and wave after wave of ecstasy swept over her. The tumult burst loose and Lisa cried aloud, her cry lost in a simultaneous crash of thunder.

Richard held her close, feeling the tremors within her slowly subside.

She said nothing, but the glow in her lovely violet eyes spoke for her. He brushed a damp lock of hair from her face.

They lay in contented silence until Lisa sighed, admitting her defeat. "You've won, Richard."

"Won?"

She nodded. "I am yours to do with as you will. I require no promises, no conditions, no wedding ring or fine house to be set up in." Her eyes were suddenly luminous. "Denying I love you is as useless as denying the beating of my heart."

"I had to have you, can you understand that?" he murmured, softly pressing his lips against her throat. "Forgive me, Lisa. I could not help . . . I just love you so!"

The rest of the night was spent finding new ways to express their love, each seeking to please and arouse the other to new and glorious heights. Finally, exhausted, they lay in one another's arms, overcome by sleep as the eastern sky spread its first band of light across the horizon.

Richard awoke first. It was morning. A bright sun was shining through the uncovered casement windows, illuminating the bedchamber. He sat up quickly. What was the hour? Lisa lay beside him fast asleep, her eyes shadowed with fatigue. He reached out and touched a dark curl that lay on the pillow and was filled with a strange emotion. Acute happiness, touched with awe. Awe that such a beautiful creature could return his love so deeply. What the devil had he done to deserve her? He kissed her soft cheek.

"Mmmm," she murmured, with a little half-smile. She did not open her eyes.

"I must take you back to your own bed, my love," he whispered.

He arose and drew on his robe and wrapping her up in the coverlet, he carried the sleeping Lisa back to her room and tucked her into her own little bed.

But his clandestine movements had not gone unnoticed.

Peter had left one of his manservants, a man by the name of Styles, at Stavely Manor, to look out for his sister when Drayton should be absent from the house. Styles was instructed to send immediate word to Peter in the event of Basil Stavely's return, and to act as Mary's protector until his arrival. There was also Lisa to consider. His swine of a brother-in-law must not be allowed near her. Styles was big and rugged and Peter was sure he would be a good match for Basil in a confrontation.

It had not taken Polly long to discover the handsome new manservant. The gifts from Lisa and her jealousy of the girl had made her more conscious of her appearance, and Styles was soon attracted to her obvious charms.

It was after a nightly visit to Polly's room that he had risen early and ascended the servants' stairs to the second floor to make his regular morning reconnaissance. It was then that he had seen Drayton leave his bedchamber with Lisa in his arms. Her long dark hair told Styles who she was, because he had admired her from a distance.

So! he thought to himself. Mistress Manning was not the sweet little innocent his master supposed her to be. He must ask Polly more about Lady Stavely's young companion.

Chapter Twenty-five

DRAYTON STOOD WITH CHRISTOPHER WREN BEFORE THE RUINS OF Calderwood.

"Where I would differ with Jones," Wren was saying, "is that I believe the fronts ought to be elevated in the middle, not the corners, because the middle is the place of greatest dignity and first arrests the eye."

Drayton nodded in agreement.

"Jones' columns are Ionic below and Corinthian above," Wren continued, indicating the remaining wing. "I like rich surface texture. I would use Corinthian above, with carving at the top of each pair of columns. The effect of the design of any building, m'lord, lies chiefly on the balance of horizontals and verticals."

"As I mentioned to you before, Wren, having seen your designs, I would be delighted to give you free rein—"

"I can see splendid wrought-iron gates round a semicircle with a fountain in the center," Wren was saying, pointing back down the drive from the proposed mansion. "Magnificent terraced gardens . . ."

Drayton grinned. "You will take the commission then? You will design a new Calderwood?"

"I have already begun," Wren smiled. "'Tis already taking shape in my mind."

It was late evening on June the third. Lisa tiptoed into Richard's room to find him standing in the dark, by the window, gazing out into the night.

She was instantly aware of his tenseness.

"What's the matter?" she whispered, coming up behind him to slip her arms about his waist.

"I am leaving in a few hours, Lisa," he said quietly.

"Leaving?" Her heart gave a lurch. "Oh God, the time has come, hasn't it?"

"Hush!" he warned her. "Speak not of it. We have such a short time together before I go, why must we waste it in talking?" He turned to her, gathering her to him.

"You're right," she shivered, a cold chill running through her body. "Let us not talk. Just make love to me."

Their lovemaking that night was a little frantic, a little desperate, and afterward they clung together as if it might be their last time in one another's arms.

"Take no chances," she murmured, tears clouding her eyes. "Will you be actually guarding the king?"

He hesitated a moment, wondering if he should tell her of the plan. But if it had not been for Lisa overhearing Stavely and the others, of making the copy of the bond, nothing could have been done to prevent the traitors from attempting and quite probably carrying out the regicide.

Lying there, with Lisa's head against his chest, he quietly told her of the arrangements. How he and Roger Francis were to take the places of Charles and James and how his men were to intercept the Fifth Monarchy men before the king's party arrived at Watford.

Lisa shuddered, seized by a terrible premonition as the plan was revealed to her.

"I don't like it!" she cried, sitting up and looking down at him. "'Tis too much of a risk. What if the traitors decide to attack you somewhere else on the road?"

Drayton shook his head. "That is doubtful. Watford Heath is the obvious spot."

"Nevertheless, Richard, be on your guard, I beg of you!"

"I will, my love." He kissed her nose. "Don't worry. Tomorrow night I will be back here in this very bed, holding you again in my arms."

Tears filled her eyes and she turned her face from him so he would not see.

"We are always parting," she managed.

"Let us hope this will be the last time. If Basil dares to be present at Watford tomorrow, and is captured, all will be over for him."

"What will happen to him?"

"His punishment will depend on the king. He could be hanged. Stavely Manor will certainly be forfeited to the crown if Basil is proved to be a traitor."

"Forfeited!" Lisa exclaimed.

"Of course. Why does that worry you? Mary will be more comfortable and happy living with Peter."

"'Tis just . . ."

"I know you must be wondering what would become of you." He smiled at her, pulling her back down to him. "There is a small house on my estate which I hope to have made habitable by the autumn. We can live there quite comfortably until Calderwood is completed."

"And in the meantime?"

"You will come with me to London," he smoothed the furrow that had formed between her brows. "I promise you we will be very happy together, Lisa."

She lay quietly beside him, looking up at the ceiling.

"Will I ever see Mary or Peter again?"

"What an odd question. Of course you will."

"But 'twill not be the same, will it?" She turned her violet eyes to his. "They will not think ill of *you*, Richard," her voice cracked a little. "No one thinks ill of a man because he takes a mistress. 'Tis accepted in our society and you will not be ostracized by your friends."

Puzzled, Richard stared down at her. "And you will be?"

She nodded. "I am very fond of Mary. She is the first woman friend I have ever had. I—I value her friendship, but I know that her moral standards are such that she would never allow our friendship to continue. I hate the thought of losing it."

"And Peter's friendship? What of it?" he lashed out, quite unreasonably. "Perhaps losing his fond regard would disturb you even more."

"That's not fair!" she declared, pushing herself away from him. "'Tis only natural not to wish to drop in anyone's estimation. 'Tis not *you* who will be branded the whore!"

"Lisa!"

She could not help it. She burst into a flood of tears that were caused not only by the situation in which he would place her, but also, though she as yet did not admit it, by the premonitory fear for Richard and what the morrow would bring.

He gathered her into his arms and wiping the tears from her cheeks, tried to comfort her.

"I am to blame for all your unhappiness," he whispered. "I am a selfish cad, wanting you so much I could not see what I was doing to you, what I was making you become in your own and others' eyes."

He kissed her gently and then after a moment he gave a deep sigh. "All right. I have no family left to answer to. I will put aside my infernal pride and marry you."

"What!" Lisa let out a cry of fury as she scrambled from his arms and flung herself from the bed. Anger and resentment blazed up in her. These were the words she had been longing to hear, but not spoken like that . . . not like that! She fought to control herself and her voice was strong and sure as she spat the words at him. "I would not marry you if you were the last man on earth, Richard Drayton!"

How magnificent she looked in her nakedness, the candlelight playing on her heaving breasts, her flashing eyes. She struggled to pull on her robe.

"Damn it, Lisa, what the devil is the matter with you? Isn't marriage what you want?"

The fury mounted in her face. "I suppose you quite expected me to go down on my knees and thank you for even considering to make such an insignificant little nobody your wife! Why, you arrogant . . . pompous . . ." She flung the words at him. "As far as I am concerned, you and your precious title and all that goes with it can go to the devil!"

Lisa paced her room when she returned to it, the anger still seething within her. How dare he! How dare he treat her as if she were some little trollop he had picked up out of the gutter and had deigned to bestow his affections upon!

Why had she ever let herself fall in love with such a pretentious . . . insufferable brute! Why couldn't she have loved Peter instead? He was so different. He treated her like a lady and was always so considerate of her feelings. Yet he was no milksop. She had felt the latent strength in him when he had taken her in his arms the other night and told her of his love for her. Yet she knew he would never use his strength to subdue her as Richard did—yanking her roughly into his arms, kissing her savagely, arousing her to such passion that she became the wild, writhing little whore he wanted. Oh God, why had she let Richard become such an obsession with her? Why? Why?

It was then that she heard the sounds of departure below her window, the beat of horse's hooves on the driveway as someone rode off. Richard. She remembered with horror where he was going.

What if her dark premonition had been right? What if the fears she had felt became a reality and she never saw him again? What if he were killed?

It all went according to plan. Six emblazoned coaches left Whitehall for Watford, filled with what appeared to be the king and his brother, plus a number of representatives of the court. Twelve of the king's armed troopers accompanied the party.

Drayton, the same big build as the king, had darkened his skin to match Charles' olive complexion. Dressed in the king's elegant clothes and with one of his periwigs on his head and his hat pulled low, none had pierced his disguise.

Roger Francis, on the other hand, was slightly heavier than James, but fortunately his coloring was vastly similar. As he was not likely to attract as much attention as Drayton, his disguise also had not been penetrated.

They moved at a slow but regular pace along the main road leading from London, adding color to the dismal gray of the morning.

Drayton greeted the people who flocked out to see and cheer their king in every village through which they passed. He waved to them as jovially as he knew Charles himself would have done.

They lunched in Falconbrook as planned and started out again. The towns were growing further apart and the road became more winding and forest began to close in around them. They had passed no one on the road for some time and were now traveling through a dense section of woods.

We must be about five miles from Watford Heath, Richard was thinking, when, suddenly, a volley of shots burst out on either side of them and two columns of men rode swiftly forth from the woods.

Some of the troopers returned their fire, while others charged at the attackers, brandishing their swords. Richard saw an enemy horseman drop down close beside their coach. He had already cocked his own pistol.

The Fifth Monarchy men had the advantage of an unexpected ambush and had picked out their men before they attacked. The road was already dotted with the bodies of at least five of the troopers as the traitors whirled their horses among those who were left, shouting, "God with us!" over the clashing swords and the screams of the dying men. The king's men were clearly outnumbered two to one.

The air was filled with black gunpowder and Richard could discern very little. His own men, he knew, were miles away. Would they have heard the gunfire?

One of the coachmen of the king's coach had been killed as was one of the footmen. The remaining two were trying desperately to guard the doors of the coach that contained who they thought to be the king and his brother. When Richard made an attempt to open his door and get out into the battle, he was gently, but firmly, pushed back inside.

The enemy was certainly greater in number than he had been led to believe, Richard thought. The fighting continued, violent and bloody, all around them.

"By God, Roger, I can't just sit here when I'm needed out there," Richard exclaimed. "What about you? Perhaps if we both made a concentrated effort on one door. . . ."

He looked back at his friend and his eyes widened in horror as he saw a dark stain of blood flowing out from a wound in the man's chest!

"Roger!" he cried, tearing open the green silk coat and the ruffled shirt beneath. He yanked off his own cravat, rolling it into a pad to place hard against the bloodied hole, hoping to staunch the flow of life-giving fluid.

He quickly realized that his friend must have been hit by one of the first shots that had been fired at the coach.

"Richard . . ."

Roger was trying to speak, but his voice was so weak that Drayton could hardly hear it above the tumult outside.

"I'm here, Roger. Hang on. Don't talk. Save your breath."

"No use." The breathing was labored, seeming to rattle in his chest. He grasped Drayton's hand. "Who knew?" he rasped. "Who knew about our plans besides the king and Clarendon?"

"No one, Roger."

"Someone betrayed us . . . someone . . ."

He was gone. Drayton laid him gently down upon the seat.

Who had betrayed them? Who had caused Roger's death? A sudden thought pained him. Lisa. Oh God, *not* Lisa! Yet she was the only other person who knew of the plan. The only one!

The haze had settled outside his window. Richard could see one of the Fifth Monarchy men quite clearly. He was one of their leaders, it seemed, for he was directing his men from a rise beside the road.

Drayton was filled with rage. He could stay out of the battle no longer.

With a shove of one of his great shoulders, he threw open the door of the coach and rolled out onto the road and down into the ditch that paralleled it. He had observed a riderless horse heading across the ditch toward the woods and got up swiftly to lunge toward it and leap up onto its back as it came abreast of him.

He raised his sword and started up the rise toward the enemy leader who, at the last minute, saw him coming and charged down at him.

Richard was ready for him and the two swords clanged together as they connected, the steel flashing in the sunlight that had just broken through the clouds.

"The king himself!" Thomas Carver yelled triumphantly, seeming to recognize his opponent. He lashed out at Richard so recklessly that Drayton was able to counter his thrust and with all his strength he then came down in a sweep at Carver's naked wrist. With less than a second to spare, the man jerked back, preventing the severance of his hand, but the sword was torn from his grasp.

Carver whirled his horse about with lightning speed and galloped back into the woods.

Digging his heels into the horse's sides, for he was spurless, Drayton took off after him. A pistol ball went by his head, striking a tree, as he disappeared from view in pursuit of Carver.

Drayton flattened himself against the horse's neck, avoiding branches and thick brush as his horse galloped down a narrow path after the Fifth Monarchy man.

Carver, on the better horse, was well-ahead now. Seeing the woods thinning out, he realized they were fast approaching a crossroad. He slowed his horse to a trot and finally to a stop, swinging expertly down from it. Leading it into the dark woods behind him, he hurriedly secured the horse to a tree and ran back to the pathway to hide himself behind some bracken.

Drayton rode on, sensing that his horse had had a workout that day and was tiring. It looked as if the woods were becoming more sparse ahead. He realized that he should be able to see his enemy ahead of him, unless . . .

There was an explosion of a pistol and Drayton let out an oath as he was knocked sideways from his saddle, falling on his face onto the ground. The horse neighed, tossed its head and galloped away.

Carver replaced the still-smoking pistol in his belt. He heard a groan as he rose from his place of concealment and approached the big man who lay spread-eagled before him, struggling to lift himself. His hat had been knocked from his head and his wig lay partially askew, but his true identity was still hidden.

Carver had drawn a second pistol from the top of his boot.

"Death to the monarchy!" he cried and fired it full-blast into Drayton's back!

The body before him collapsed on the ground and lay still.

Chapter Twenty-six

IT WAS EVENING. LISA, AFRAID SHE COULD KEEP HER ANXIETY NO longer from Mary, had feigned a headache and taken to her room. Now she sat by the window looking out at the garden below her that was slowly being bathed in moonlight.

She could think of nothing but Richard. He must truly love her, she now realized. He had asked her to marry him, although she knew that to wed someone not of his station went against all he had been taught to regard as his family duty. His love for her must then have grown beyond his control and he had felt he must have her, whatever the price. She should have been flattered, but the tactless, insensitive way he had phrased it had only insulted her further. It would all have been so easy if she had trusted him with her secret. Now Richard might never know.

Lisa began to twist her hands in her lap. If all had gone well, he would have returned by now. Something had happened to him. She could sense it. Oh God, why did it have to have been Richard? If only she had given the copy of the bond to the authorities and not to him. But they would have asked too many questions, might not have believed her and she would have been forced to confess her identity, ruining all her plans with Basil Stavely.

Perhaps nothing had gone wrong. Perhaps he was just delayed, that was all. Richard could take care of himself as well as any man—better than most. There was a perfectly good reason for his tardiness.

Perhaps the men had stopped to celebrate their victory over the Fifth Monarchy men at the inn in Watford. Richard could be laughing and drinking there this very minute. But she knew in her heart that this was not so.

She was gripped by a wave of panic so intense that she wanted to scream. Slowly, with great effort, she managed to gain control of herself, deliberately finding tasks about her room to occupy her, but the tension continued to lie just beneath the surface.

It had been a day of disaster. The morning had been gray and dismal, but the sun had broken through the clouds later in the afternoon and Lisa, restless, worrying about Richard, had decided to go for a ride to take her mind off her anxious thoughts.

She was on her way to the stables, when turning the path around the corner of the house, the new manservant, Styles, stepped out from behind some shrubbery and motioned to her.

"May I speak with you a moment, Mistress Manning?"

"Of course, Styles."

She had followed him off the path and behind a large hedgerow where they could not be observed from the house.

He stood for a moment observing her and she detected a growing insolence in his stare. How stupid she had been to let this big man waylay her. No telling what he had in mind. She made a quick move to go back past him to the path, but he laid a large hand on her shoulder.

"Now, just a moment," he said, a lazy smile spreading over his handsome face. "I thought ye should know that Polly has confided her secret t' me," he drawled, noticing that Lisa paled at his words. "Aye, she told me all about ye and Lord Drayton. Not that I needed telling. The other morning, early, I saw m'lord carrying ye back to thy room after a night o' pleasure in his bed. Nay, don't deny it. It will do ye no good. Polly and me—we both know ye been layin' for him and we understands them things we does. The two o' us now, we been thinkin' o' marriage, we have. Wouldn't it be nice, we says to ourselves, if we had our own little inn. Not too big a place, mind, but comfortable-like. We lack only the wherewithal, and that, Mistress Manning, is where ye come in."

Lisa had stood listening to him, two bright spots of color appearing in her pale cheeks. Now she managed, "Polly knows I have little money. It would not be nearly enough—"

"We knows that, sweetheart." He grinned and she winced at his familiarity. "Ye have been right generous with Polly so far I'm told, but m'lord now, we all knows he be a very rich man. I seen the way he looks at ye. Ye could get it from him as easy as rollin' off a log." He laughed. "Or rollin' in the hay, if ye gets me meanin'." He roared at his joke.

"I would *never* ask Lord Drayton for a penny," Lisa said angrily. "You will have to find some other way to finance your inn."

"Ye wish me and Polly to tell Sir Peter and Lady Stavely about the two o' ye?" he sneered. "Sir Peter, I know, thinks ye as sweet and pure as springwater, and Polly tells me Lady Stavely treats ye like a member of her own family. Can't ye just see their faces. Especially now that there be two o' us to back up one 'nother's word."

Lisa said nothing.

"When Lord Drayton gets back from his estate this evenin', ye had best ask him," Styles threatened. "We'll give ye only until the end of the week."

When Richard awoke he was stripped to the waist, lying on his stomach on some blankets on the floor of what appeared to be a wagon. His left shoulder and arm were expertly bandaged with strips of clean linen.

"So you be awake at last," a gruff voice asked, as he pondered his whereabouts. He looked up to see an old hag leaning over him. She had a bright red scarf over her head and two golden hoops hung from her earlobes to brush against her dark, wrinkled cheeks.

"Gypsy," he murmured, his face contorting as a spasm of acute pain swept over him.

The woman nodded. "I am Zada, and lucky you be that I came along when I did. Saw the cursed Roundhead ride off leaving you for dead."

"Thank you," he managed. His lips felt dry and cracked. He ran his tongue over them.

Zada turned him gently and held his head as she put a mug to his mouth. He drank deeply of a liquid that tasted pleasantly cool and sweet.

"I almost gave you up, I did, but you be a strong 'un and I kept the poison from your wounds."

Richard tried to look grateful. He felt too tired to say more. He closed his eyes and his head dropped forward again.

Zada had spent the last several weeks searching for Lisa. She had traveled to Valerie's family home, hoping to find Lisa there and reassure herself that the girl had come to no harm. She had questioned the servants and found, to her dismay, that Lisa had never arrived or even been seen in the area. Where had she gone?

Zada had carefully retraced her journey back to the old campsite from which Lisa had departed and had spent weeks traversing different roads and questioning people along the way.

It was on a hunch that she had started out that day driving her wagon along a little-used crossroad.

She had heard the shot, and seen the rider, whom she recognized by his clothing to be a Roundhead, gallop off down the road.

The scarlet coat he wore made the wounded man easy to find. At first she thought him to be dead, but then she felt a feeble pulse.

She tore off his coat and shirt and saw the wounds. One ball had torn the flesh in the upper part of his right arm, but had passed right through. The other, however, was still imbedded in his back. He had lost a great deal of blood. Zada set about cleaning the wounds as best she could and, using moss torn from the side of a nearby tree, staunched the flow of blood from his back. After she had bandaged him with strips of linen from her petticoat, Zada set about pulling him onto a counterpane she had brought from her wagon.

It was as she did this that his wig was dislodged and she saw for the first time the golden hair.

"A handsome 'un you be," she puffed, "but I wish, sir, that you were of a smaller size."

She had gone back to the caravan and moved it into the woods as close as she could get to the wounded man. Now she let down the tailboard and pulled him on the counterpane up and into the wagon.

The exertion had completely exhausted the old woman and it

was only the thought that she had a human life in her hands that kept her from collapsing.

She had unharnessed her old horse and tethered him close by. Now she set about making a fire. She knew she had only a few more hours of light left and would have to work quickly.

The knife she produced from her voluminous skirts was slim and sharp. She placed it in the flame of the fire for a moment and then climbed back into the wagon.

The pistol ball was deep. She probed at it gently and skillfully. A fraction of an inch to the left and he would have been dead. With a steady hand, she carefully removed the lead ball with the point of the knife. Blood gushed out of the wound and she began to pack it again with mold fungus and clean moss. It was almost dark before Zada had rebound his wounds.

Five days had passed. Richard had been in and out of consciousness many times. For days, as he lay in delirium, Zada had wondered if he would live, but this morning she felt for the first time that he was out of danger. Now, as evening neared, Zada found him struggling to sit up.

The pain was excruciating. Sharp and searing. It was an agony to move his shoulder. He groaned.

Zada rushed forward.

"What do you think you be doing?"

"Get up," he gasped. "Must get up."

"Lie still," she growled at him. "I will prop some pillows behind you."

She did this, placing them against the side of the wagon and helped to partially raise him.

He discovered he could lean no weight against the left side of his back, so he lay at an angle. It was not very comfortable.

"Zada," he looked up at her. His face was deathly pale and his eyes looked sunken and glazed. "How long have I—"

"Five days," she replied. "You have been here five days. The ball was dangerously near your heart. I dared not move you or the wagon. You will take some time to heal."

"Kind. You have been very kind. I promise you, Zada, you will be well taken care of for doing this."

"Mmmm," she said. "I have broth on the fire. Be you hungry?"

"Starved." It took an effort, but he managed to grin at her. The grin was not lost on Zada. How many lasses had fallen for that charming grin, that handsome face? Plenty, if she were any judge, but there was one, especially, who bothered her. He had murmured her name over and over in his delirium.

"Drink this first," she ordered him, handing him a cup.

This time the liquid was not cool and sweet. This time it tasted foul and Richard gagged, but managed to get it down.

"My own medicine," Zada said proudly. "Made with roots and herbs." She took a bowl from a shelf and went out the wagon door.

He must have dozed, for the next thing he knew Zada was spooning some broth into his mouth. He mumbled that he could feed himself.

"You need rest," she said sternly. "You lost much blood."

He swallowed as much of the superbly good broth as he could and then held up his right hand.

"No more, thank you."

Zada went about gathering up the bowl and cup and her back was toward him when she asked. "You have been calling a name over and over in your sleep," she said, turning to face him. "Lisa."

A pained look came into his eyes. "Aye," he said. "I do not wonder she was on my mind. I believe it was she who betrayed me."

Zada's dark eyes narrowed. "Why would she do that? Did you scorn her?"

"Nay! Never! I love her. God help me, despite what she might have done I still love her."

"Perhaps you are wrong then," Zada murmured. "What is your name, sir?"

"Drayton. Richard Drayton."

"And what is this Lisa's full name?"

Drayton turned painfully to study the old gypsy's face and then it came to him where he had heard the name "Zada" before.

"Zada!" he exclaimed. "Of course! Lisa told me about you."

The gypsy's dark eyes flashed. "Then 'tis *my* Lisa you spoke of. Do you know where she is?"

"Aye. She lives at Stavely Manor, this side of Bridgeford. She is a companion to Lady Stavely."

CLOAK OF FATE

"I now know why I was fated to find you," Zada said quietly. "Tell me, sir, does my Lisa love you?"

"Once I believed she did, now . . ."

Richard had awakened in a cold sweat from a nightmare where he had seen Roger, covered in blood, staring down at him accusingly. "Who knew about our plans beside the king and Clarendon? . . . Someone betrayed us. . . ."

It must have been Lisa. Who else could it be? She was the only other person he had told. And they had not parted happily. He had never seen her so angry. Had her anger and resentment of him been so great that she would have betrayed him and all with him? He could not believe that of her and yet . . . Might she possibly have acted from some motive he was completely unaware of? Could she have actually sided with the Fifth Monarchy men, been planted by them at Stavely Manor to captivate and spy on him? Perhaps the copy of the bond she had given him was a ruse to throw him off the track, so the ambush could be arranged.

Lisa was an actress. She could have taken him in very easily, convinced him of her innocence. But would she have gone so far as to give up her maidenhood for the cause she supported?

And what of Stavely? Surely Lisa was not in league with that blackguard. *That* he could not believe of her. Nor did he want to believe any of the thoughts that had sprung to his mind.

He kept seeing her beautiful little face, hearing her soft musical voice. Before he had met her he had been nothing, an empty shell, and she had given him life again. Made the world seem as young and fresh and innocent as herself.

Innocent! He prayed then that she was innocent of the betrayal, for he knew he could never hurt her, no matter what she had done to him.

The man who had tried to murder him was another matter. He would always remember *his* face. He would get his revenge on him if it were the last thing he did!

"If she betrayed you, it would not be for any love of Roundheads," Zada assured him when he questioned her the next day. "Actors nearly starved under Cromwell, and the Manning Shakespearian Players fell on very hard times. Lisa knows how badly her parents fared." She looked at Richard shrewdly. "Nay, if my Lisa betrayed you, Richard Drayton, and

204

I do not believe for a minute she would do such a thing, it is because of what you did to *her*."

Drayton looked up into Zada's piercing black eyes. Could the old woman read his mind?

"Mother of God!" she cried. "Have I saved the life of the very man who stole my child's innocence?"

His lips twisted in his old cynical smile. "Perhaps you should have let me die."

A slim knife was suddenly pointed at his throat. "Did you seduce her?" The dark eyes narrowed. "A man of your looks would not have to take a maid by force."

"And if I said I did, would you plunge that dagger into my gullet?"

The point of the knife scratched the skin, drawing a drop of blood.

Drayton did not flinch. "I cannot answer you, Zada. It just happened. We fell in love, almost, I think, from the first moment we saw one another. When the time came . . . no word was even spoken . . . it just had to be." He paused then and gave a little snort. "How the devil can I expect anyone else to understand. . . ."

"You truly love her," the old gypsy grunted and the knife disappeared within the folds of her skirt.

Chapter Twenty-seven

LISA, FRANTIC AFTER TWO DAYS OF HEARING NOTHING, WAS EAGER to see Peter when he arrived unexpectedly that afternoon at Stavely Manor. Perhaps he might have some news.

It required all of her acting ability not to seem too anxious as they sat down to tea in the gallery. Mary, of course, thought Richard had only left on a visit to London again and she could think of nothing but Basil's impending return.

Peter, Lisa realized, had something else on his mind and he looked at his sister carefully before he spoke.

"I have something of import to say to you, Mary." He cleared his throat and put down his untouched cup of tea on a table beside him.

"There was an ambush attempt made on the king's party on its way to Watford two days ago. A group of Fifth Monarchy men attacked from the woods about five miles south of Watford Heath."

Lisa smothered a cry, but no one noticed her reaction.

"There had been a warning given to the king of a supposed attack at Watford Heath. Because of it, his place and that of his brother was taken by two loyal men who had dressed to impersonate them. One was killed in the attack and the other is missing. The missing man, the one who masqueraded as the king, was Richard Drayton!"

"Richard!" Mary exclaimed in alarm.

"Aye. The story has all come out now. Richard had his regiment gathered at the heath, ready to surround the traitors when they appeared, but someone must have warned them that their plan was known, for they changed their strategy and attacked the party before they reached there."

"What happened?" Mary asked anxiously.

"Over half of the king's troopers were annihilated before Drayton's men could get there to assist them. They had heard the shooting from the heath, and arrived in time to kill or capture all the traitors save one. A man by the name of Thomas Carver, who was apparently rather infamous in the war. Someone had seen Richard, whom they thought to be the king, leap from the coach and grab a riderless horse, taking off after Carver. Neither one has been seen since."

"Has the surrounding countryside been searched?" asked Lisa, unable to control a tremor in her voice.

"'Tis being thoroughly searched at the king's command," Peter said quietly, "and I am afraid they have found some articles that belonged to Richard.

"Articles!"

"The wig he had worn to impersonate the king, and his hat. It had not rained and there was seen on the grass nearby what looked like dried blood."

Mary's thin shoulders began to shake and she put a trembling hand to her mouth.

"Nay, Mary!" Peter soothed her. "Do not upset yourself. Richard must be all right, or his body would have been found there. You see, there was noticed in the same area the tracks of what might have been a wagon. It had moved on, so perhaps someone picked up Richard, if he were wounded, and took him home to care for him."

Lisa sat in shocked silence. So her fears had not been groundless. Richard *had* been wounded—could even be dead for all she knew! How she wished she were a man and could go out herself and join the search for him! How could she simply remain here in this house and go on with everyday matters as if nothing had happened?

"I'm leaving in the morning," Peter was explaining. "I am

joining a troop of the king's men who are camped here in Bridgeford overnight. We'll find him," he said reassuringly to the two women.

Mary was in tears now. "How brave of Richard to take the king's place."

"I wonder who warned the Fifth Monarchy Men that their plan had become known?" Lisa mused.

"That is a mystery," Peter said. "It seems when Richard learned of it originally, he told only the king, who swears Clarendon was the only one with whom he shared the information. Many are casting aspersions at Clarendon since this happened."

It came to Lisa then that *she* had known about the plan. Richard had also confided it to her the night before he left Stavely Manor. Her heart sank. If he were alive was he blaming her? Was he thinking of how angrily she had parted from him, wondering if her anger might have caused her to betray him! She prayed that he would not think that of her, just as she had prayed for his life in the past few days.

"I keep thinking of the name of that traitor. The one Richard went after," Mary murmured. "Thomas Carver. I am sure I once heard Basil mention . . . Oh, Peter, do you think Basil was involved in that awful plot?"

"I don't imagine so, Mary. Basil is still in London. That is the other news I meant to convey to you. Basil has been . . . he has not been well. That is why he has not returned home before now."

"Not well! Is it serious?" Mary asked. "Should I go to him?"

"Mary, Mary, you are too good to be true." Peter got to his feet and went over to her, placing a gentle hand on her shoulder. "That scoundrel does not deserve a thought from you, much less your personal attentions. He has his manservant with him to look after his needs."

"But what is the matter with him?"

"An infectious disease, I am told," Peter said uncomfortably, and quickly changed the subject.

Mary had had conflicting thoughts about Richard ever since the evening he had comforted her and she had practically thrown herself at him. She had had to reconcile herself to the fact that he was a dear friend and would never be anything more. Yet, she knew she would always care for him in a secret little compartment of her heart.

As the days passed with no word of Richard, it became evident to Mary how anxious Lisa had become. Did the girl also care for him? she wondered. Had her animosity toward him made a complete changeabout? It was hard for her to believe. She remembered the way Lisa had glared at Richard the night he had returned from London and had come upon them all in the gallery. Perhaps Lisa had had words with him and now felt guilty for her actions. Could she have spurned him? She and Lisa had become such close friends. She felt hurt that Lisa did not feel free to confide in her. But then, she sighed to herself, she had not confided her feelings for Richard to Lisa.

To get both their minds off their worries, Mary suggested to Lisa that she move from the cramped little room next to hers to a larger one further down the hall. She had picked the room because it was decorated in a soft shade of pink that, she knew, would complement the girl's coloring. Lisa thanked her, smiling for the first time in many days. She moved into the new bedchamber the next day.

It was a full week after the ambush that Zada pulled her bright caravan up before the front doors of Stavely Manor.

She got down from the box and wearily climbed up the steps to the large, impressive doors, pulling heavily on the bell rope.

It was Pottle who answered the door and he waved Zada away with an imperious flick of his wrist.

"Off with you, gypsy. We do not wish your thieving kind about here."

"I wish to see Mistress Manning," Zada announced. "Tell her Zada is here. She will see me."

"Humph!" Pottle sniffed. "Undoubtedly *that* one would have friends like you. Go around to the back of the house, you old hag. I will tell Mistress Manning where to find you."

"Nay! I will stay here," Zada said stubbornly.

"What!" Pottle was not used to having his orders ignored. His eyes bulged from his head and he took a menacing step toward Zada, but just then Mary, hearing the commotion, came running to the door.

"What is it, Pottle?"

"Only an old gypsy woman, m'lady, wishing to see Mistress Manning."

"Pray let her come in."

Reluctantly Pottle stepped back and Zada quietly entered the great hall, her dark eyes darting about her.

"Pottle," Mary said pointedly, "I believe Mistress Manning is in the library."

Lisa appeared seconds later, and upon seeing Zada let out a cry and ran toward her, her arms outstretched.

It was immediately evident to Zada that in the weeks since she had seen her, a great change had taken place in her little girl. There was evidence of a new maturity in her face as well as in her manner. In her absence, Lisa had become a woman.

Lisa at once began asking questions of the old gypsy, but after a moment Zada held up her hand, her golden bracelets jangling.

"We will talk more later." She turned to Mary. "Lady Stavely," she said, "I have a wounded man out in my caravan who asked to be brought to this house."

"Wounded!" Lisa cried. "Is he—oh, Mary, could it be Richard?"

"His name is Richard Drayton." Zada nodded. "I found him shot in the back and near to death. I have been nursing him back to health."

Both Lisa and Mary heard no more but rushed out of the house and down the front steps to the caravan that stood there.

Lisa pulled down the stairs, and mounting them, opened the doors. Mary quickly followed her.

Richard lay on the pallet Zada had fixed for him in the back of the caravan. Even in the dimness, it was easy to see the pallor of his face as he lay on his side, pillows placed against his back to support him. His eyes were closed and to Lisa he looked young and unguarded.

She longed to kneel down beside him and lay her cheek against his, but Mary was grasping her arm, saying breathlessly, "He's alive! Oh, thank God, he's alive!"

Lisa had to force herself to remain where she was, to stay in the role of Mary's friend who was merely acquainted with the wounded man who lay before them. But in that first second, she had become aware by Mary's reaction that her feelings toward Richard Drayton were far deeper than Lisa had ever supposed.

Rushing to the open doorway of the caravan, Mary now called out to Pottle who stood on the manor steps.

"Get the footmen and bring something flat," she ordered. "Bring something on which to carry Lord Drayton into the house."

Under Mary's instructions, Drayton was lifted by Styles, another footman and Ned, who had joyfully appeared to welcome his master, onto the top of a trestle table. He groaned as he was moved, and Lisa realized that he was not only weak, but still in much pain.

Richard's eyes opened once and met Lisa's as they carried him from the caravan. He saw a look that she was unable to mask quickly enough. It cast away his last doubt. Lisa had not betrayed him.

Richard Drayton remained confined to bed in Stavely Manor for the next fortnight.

He was waited on hand and foot by Mary and Lisa, not to mention Zada, who, although she insisted upon living in her own caravan, would not relinquish the care of Richard to anyone else, least of all "that manservant of his who would have given him anything he asked for—even spirits!" She allowed Ned to care for his personal needs, but insisted upon doing all the nursing herself.

It was several days after Richard's arrival that Lisa went to his room one afternoon while Mary was having her nap.

She knocked at the door and it was opened by Ned.

"May I see his lordship?" she asked. "Or is he sleeping?"

"He is awake," Ned said. "I will see."

He half closed the door and Lisa heard the murmur of voices before he returned.

"He will see you," the manservant said, opening the door for Lisa to enter.

Richard was propped up in bed. His face was still very pale, and there was a look of suffering about it, as if the pain had not completely left him. He had always seemed so strong and confident to her; now he had lost that authoritative air and there was something almost pathetic about him.

"Come and sit down," he said, indicating the empty chair by his bed. "Tell me what has been happening at Stavely Manor in my absence. I feel as though I had come back from the dead."

"From what Zada tells me, you came very close."

"I'm aware of that," he replied and motioned to Ned. "You may leave us for now. I will ring if I need you."

The manservant nodded. "Don't be doing too much now," he said with the familiarity of a servant who has been long with the same master. "You are not all that strong yet."

Richard grinned as the door closed behind Ned. Then he looked at Lisa, his eyes going over every inch of her.

"This is the first time we have been alone," he said.

"I know. How are you feeling?"

"Thirsty. That old gypsy nurse of yours forbids me to have anything stronger than tea."

"She is right." Lisa stood up, fluffing the pillows behind his head.

"Brandy would help build up my strength," he grunted.

"So will this." She handed him a mug from the table beside the bed.

He made a face. "Not Zada's medicine again."

"No, you ungrateful creature. Do you realize that her medicine has helped to cure you? This is milk."

"Milk! I am not a babe!"

"You are almost as weak as one."

"Really?" He reached out quickly and grabbed her wrist. His fingers were surprisingly strong.

"Look at me, Lisa." His green eyes darkened as they met hers. He seemed to be searching for something—something she was keeping carefully hidden. He gave a sigh, finally, and his hold slackened on her wrist. She drew it away.

"Zada is a remarkable woman," he said, taking a sip from the mug. "She got me to do things no one else has since my own old Nanny died."

"She has not had an easy life. People seem ever suspicious of gypsies."

"I would like to settle some money on her for all she has done for me, but she has refused to accept it."

"Richard," Lisa said decidedly, "'Tis time you learned that there are some people who do not care to be paid for their good works. It gives them pleasure to help others. That is their reward."

"Hah!" he gave a cynical snort. "I have lived a lot longer than you, Lisa, and Zada happens to be the first one of that species I have ever run into." He sighed and before long his eyes closed.

Lisa sat for a few minutes in silence before she realized that Richard had fallen asleep. She stood up, looking down at him for a long time before removing the empty mug from his fingers and tiptoeing from the room.

Chapter Twenty-eight

IN THE DAYS THAT FOLLOWED, LISA LOOKED IN ON RICHARD AT least twice a day, but she never saw him alone again. There was always Zada or Mary with him, or Ned hovering in the background.

Richard was now insisting upon doing a little more each day. By the end of the next week, he was sitting up in a chair beside the window for a part of every day.

It was there, early one evening, that his eyes were drawn to a man hurrying along the path that circled the house. As he stopped for a moment, below his window, looking about him to see if anyone were following him, Richard recognized him.

It was Styles, the footman that Peter had placed in Stavely Manor to give added protection to Mary. As Richard watched, he darted behind a tall hedge and into an enclosed garden.

Richard grinned to himself. "Ah, a secret assignation!" he thought. He could not see into the garden, but he knew there was a stone bench there. Probably Styles was now seated there, waiting impatiently for his light of love. The new servant was a tall, good-looking man. No doubt the young housemaids were easy prey to him.

Richard continued to watch out the window, expecting to see

a female form appear at any moment, but fifteen minutes passed and then half an hour.

It was beginning to grow dark as a girl came into view, running hurriedly along the path before slipping quickly behind the tall hedge.

Richard did not realize it, but he had risen from his chair to move even closer to the window.

He could have sworn . . . nay! There were other girls about the house; others with long, dark hair. If he could only have seen her face. She had come and gone so quickly.

He sank back into his chair. It could not have been Lisa. What a foolish thought. But, his jaw tightened, the man was handsome. Perhaps he had concentrated his charms on Lisa and not the housemaids.

His thoughts were interrupted by Zada bursting into the room clearly annoyed that Ned had not been there to help him return to his bed. Clucking at him like a mother hen, she rushed out into the hall to summon his manservant.

Peter came and went twice to see Richard. He told him that the search was still on for Carver, but it was as if the ground had opened up and swallowed the man.

One afternoon the king himself made a surprise visit to Stavely Manor.

Free of worry, he was now on his way to Watford for the official visit that he had postponed on Richard's advice. While his party continued on, Charles instructed his coach to stop long enough for him to offer his thanks to Drayton for risking his life on his behalf.

"I also wish to assure you, Drayton, that your plans were not betrayed by Clarendon or myself. From one of the wounded traitors, a man by the name of Brintnall, who is waiting to be hanged with the others at Tyburn, 'twas learned that you were followed to your meeting with your men by Thomas Carver and your plans overheard. He was not aware, however, that you and Francis, poor devil, had replaced James and me in the royal coach. That part of your plan was remarkably successful. Mayhap Carver, if he is in hiding, still thinks he has succeeded in murdering his king." Charles gave a hearty laugh. "Thanks to you, Richard, I am very much alive."

"I was glad to be of service, Your Majesty."

Charles's face sobered. "I appreciate your loyalty more than I can say." He cleared his throat. "Outside of Carver," he said, "there is now only Stavely left of the original plotters who signed the bond. We have had a man watching his movements since you informed me of his involvement, but Stavely was laid up in London at the time of the attack."

"His name on that copy of the bond is all the proof you need."

"But the bond, itself, was never found."

"Stavely has likely destroyed it by now, but he should not be allowed to go free," Drayton said angrily. "I should be well enough in a day or two to go after Thomas Carver. If I can capture him alive, I will get him to denounce Stavely."

"Richard, my friend, let my men handle Carver. There are search parties out all over the country. Just spend your energy on regaining your strength. Perhaps you will feel well enough in a week's time to join the royal party at Ellsbury's estate. Been invited to stop off there for some hawking before returning to London."

Lisa was out riding during the king's visit and missed all the excitement, but Mary told her every detail upon her return. In fact, Lisa heard little else for days afterward.

Lisa and Zada had managed to have several talks. Often Lisa would visit with the old gypsy in her caravan while Mary had her afternoon nap.

From the first, they had discussed Richard. After Lisa's visit alone with him, she had questioned the woman. "He seems to be still in pain."

"He can only sleep for short periods," Zada had said. "He cannot lie on his back, because of his wound there, and so he must lie on his face or his side—both positions putting a strain on his wounded right shoulder."

"I see."

"Do you? Oh, you have been eager to help to care for his physical needs, but what about the needs of his mind and heart?"

"I don't know what you mean."

"I mean that a man who is unhappy is not likely to mend as quickly."

It was the afternoon after the king's visit, and Lisa had hardly entered the caravan before she found herself berated by Zada for her lack of attention to Richard.

"Can't you see, girl, that he loves you dearly," she poked a finger at Lisa. "You love him, so what has come between you?"

Lisa looked away from Zada's piercing dark eyes. "Doubt," she murmured. "Stubbornness. Pride. Oh, there are many things. 'Twas not meant to be, Zada. Love cannot exist without trust and understanding. The only true meeting between Richard and me was with our bodies, not with our hearts or minds."

"Hogwash!" Zada snorted. "You want me to believe that there was never anything between the two o' you but passion and lust?" She shook her head. "You may think, Lisa, that you are all grown up, but you are still my little one and my little one would not give herself to a man except for love."

"Oh, Zada." Lisa put her arms about the old woman as she sat down beside her on the hard bed that served as a sofa. "I do love him, but he is the destroyer of our love. We parted in such anger. . . ."

"Why was that?"

"Because of his arrogance, the condescending way he . . . oh, it doesn't matter now. . . ."

"Have you ever tried to see things through Richard's eyes? I have grown to know that young man quite well in these last weeks. My lord is charming and strong and very brave, but he has his faults. Mayhap his greatest being that he lacks trust. Could it not be that in the past he has been let down by women? He loves you deeply. If you had only been there when he was lying in an agony of pain and calling out your name, you would not doubt his love for you."

Tears glittered in Lisa's eyes at the old gypsy's words.

"Go and see him, child."

There was no one stirring on the second floor of the old mansion. Mary would be resting for another hour, Lisa knew, and the servants were instructed to curtail their activities. She wondered, as she approached his door, if Richard, himself, would be taking a nap. She knocked softly.

"Come in!" said his rich, deep voice.

Richard was seated in an armchair reading. He looked up as Lisa entered.

"Lisa!" He smiled as she came across the room toward him, smiled with that effortless grin of his that was so devastating. How handsome he was, she thought as she stood before him, looking down at him. He wore a dark-green dressing gown and the moustache he had shaved narrow to resemble the king's had now grown back in again. His eyes . . . What was it about those green eyes? They seemed to have lost some of their haughty arrogance. In fact, he did not look at all sure of himself.

"Lisa," he said quietly, "I have had a lot of time for thinking since I have been wounded." He was not a man accustomed to apologizing and this was not easy for him. "You had every right to be angry with me when we parted. I behaved like a bloody, pompous ass." He gave a crooked little smile. "I don't deserve your forgiveness, but—" He put out his arms to her and without a moment's hesitation, she flew into them.

"Richard! Oh, Richard, I shall always forgive you."

Before she knew it, she was nestled on his lap, her arms about his neck. Tears flowed down her cheeks as she told him of her days of anxious worry; of how she had prayed for his safe return; of how she had agonized learning he was wounded and missing. She had had to keep everything locked inside for so long.

"Don't cry," he whispered, kissing away her tears. "Lisa, my love, God's blood, how I've missed you!" he said thickly, kissing her lips, then her throat, drawing her closer to his chest.

"Don't hurt yourself," she protested, thinking of his wounds.

"I won't—not like this," he muttered, and then his kisses became more ardent and his hands began to move over her, rekindling emotions that made them both tremble.

"I want you like the very devil!" he groaned.

She colored. "Hush! Ned will hear you." But inwardly she rejoiced at his desire for her.

"To hell with Ned! Besides, he has gone off to the village." Then he swore. "But Zada . . ."

"In her caravan."

He grinned then, his green eyes flashing wickedly. "That is a very pretty gown, Lisa, but if you are not out of it in two seconds, I'm afraid it won't remain in one piece."

"Richard!"

"I mean it." He pushed her from his lap.

"But you can't. . . . You're not well enough . . . your back . . ."

"My back, my dear, hasn't a damn thing to do with it," he growled.

Laughing, Lisa pulled her gown over her head and when she returned to him she was clad in only a thin chemise and petticoat.

"You are too modest," he murmured. "Where is my naked nymph from the meadow?" He pulled her down onto his lap again and began to place a blazing trail of hot, demanding kisses from her lips down her throat to the full, lush breasts his lean fingers quickly released. He tossed the unlaced chemise onto the floor and drew her closer. She felt his full arousal against her thigh and gave a shudder of delight. It had been so long. . . .

A hand slipped beneath her petticoat, caressing her, probing the very essence of her womanhood. She squirmed against him, clasping her arms fiercely about his neck, nibbling at his ear, pulling open his dressing gown to press a kiss against his chest.

His fingers were enflaming her with their gentle probing and she began to whimper.

"The bed . . ."

"Nay, my love. This will do just fine."

"But how . . ."

Before she knew it, he had pulled off her petticoat and had positioned her astride him, leaning forward to press his warm lips to the deep cleft between her breasts, his hands resting on her hips.

Lisa, her desire fanned by Richard's skillful and unhurried prelude, hugged him to her, feeling that rock-hard length, wanting it deep within her.

Gently, Richard lifted her hips and she let out a startled gasp as he suddenly thrust upward, entering her easily, filling her completely with his wondrous strength as he pulled her tight against him.

For a moment she hesitated, uncertain of what to do, and then she was caught up in the sensual delight that filled her as he moved purposely within her. She began to sway from side to side, rotating her hips.

"That's it," he groaned, and she clutched him wildly as he lifted her up and down, striving upward to the next summit and the next. . . . He was so intensely physical, this man she loved, and the tension in him excited her to madness.

She let out a little cry of abandoned pleasure as she became lost in the harmony of their motion, staring hypnotically into his dark, engulfing eyes. Thrust followed fiery thrust, eyes glazed in passion, mouths opened hot and eager.

Higher and higher Lisa felt herself swept in a growing tidal wave of ecstasy, until at last the final exultant summit was reached and she plunged down, down, into the deep serene sea of satisfaction.

Collapsed against Richard's chest, Lisa heard nothing but the pounding of his heart and then a deep rumble as he began to laugh.

"That was worth being shot in the back."

"It didn't hurt you?" she asked anxiously.

"On the contrary. I will be much better now that you have ministered to me."

"You are impossible, Richard Drayton!" She scrambled off his knee and began to dress.

"Then why are you smiling, Mistress Manning?" He grinned, fastening his dressing gown. She looked more beautiful than ever, he thought, despite her hair being in disarray and a flush staining her cheeks, making her skin glow in the afternoon sunshine.

"Come kiss me," he begged.

But she refused. "I am afraid to get that close to you again."

"Then promise me something." His voice was husky. "Promise me my sweet rider will come again tomorrow."

"Tomorrow and the day after and whenever you want me," she whispered shamelessly, moving to the door.

She did not even see the gypsy woman who had just turned the corner as she entered the hallway, but Zada took in Lisa's appearance and nodded to herself, a wide smile spreading across her wrinkled cheeks.

Chapter Twenty-nine

ALL IT HAD TAKEN WERE A FEW WORDS OF APOLOGY FROM RICH-ard's lips, and she had given in to him again, Lisa thought bitterly. She lay in her bed that night, angry at herself for being so weak. What was the matter with her? Nothing was solved between them. Their liaison was still headed nowhere. She would not be his mistress, nor would her pride let her be his wife. She would have a talk with Richard, and the sooner the better. Something had to be settled between them.

The next day Richard was up and prowling about the house. He had decided he might even feel well enough by the end of the week to travel to Peter's estate and join the royal party.

Calderwood was also on his mind. He had had word from Wren that the laying of the foundation was to take place the first of July. He wanted to be present.

He had settled himself in a comfortable chair in the library when Lisa discovered him in the late morning. She was about to speak to him of what had been on her mind since the night before when they both heard a commotion outside in the great hall.

"Oh, dear God, not Sir Basil!" Lisa murmured, moving unconsciously closer to Richard.

"Don't worry about that swine," he said, rising from his chair.

With that the library door burst open and there stood one of the most beautiful women Lisa had ever seen. She had a classical face framed by hair the color of rich honey and large, languid eyes. She was dressed almost like a man in an amazone, the latest riding habit for women, consisting of a buttoned coat and doublet. But she had chosen to go even further and wore breeches and long riding boots that showed to advantage her shapely legs. A large plumed hat, set at a rakish angle, covered her fair curls. There was an air about her that defied convention and a seductive charm in her smile. Lisa felt instantly wary of her.

"Christina!" Richard growled. "What the devil are *you* doing here?"

"That's hardly a warm greeting after I have come all this way, Richard," she said in her husky voice as she moved toward him. "I heard you were wounded—near death." Her eyes swept over Lisa. "I didn't realize you had acquired such a sweet young nurse."

"Christina, Lisa is not—"

"No need to explain." She waved a hand at him as she removed her gloves. "I'm sorry if I interrupted. . . ."

"No," Lisa said decisively, "you did not interrupt a thing." She started for the door.

"Lisa!" Richard stopped her with his voice. "This is Christina Grenville. Christina, Elizabeth Manning. Lisa lives here at Stavely Manor with Lady Stavely."

Christina critically surveyed Lisa's simple dress and lifted an eyebrow. "As a companion?"

"That's right, Mistress Grenville," Lisa said, her chin automatically rising.

"*Lady* Grenville," Christina corrected her.

"I'm sorry." Lisa again turned toward the door, her cheeks burning.

"I will speak with you later, Lisa," Richard said meaningfully.

"Shall I tell Mary of *Lady* Grenville's arrival?" She coud not resist the gibe.

"That won't be necessary, Lisa," said the soft, sweet voice of Mary Stavely as she entered the room.

Richard made the introductions and Christina added, "My husband died just over a year ago, Lady Stavely, and Richard has been so kind to me. When I heard that he was wounded, I simply had to come and see how he was and if I could be of any help."

"How kind of you, my dear." Mary smiled quite guilelessly at Christina. "I do hope you will stay a few days with us."

"Oh, but I wouldn't dream of inconveniencing you, Lady Stavely. My late husband's cousin's estate is quite near at Greenleigh and I—"

"Greenleigh! My dear, that is miles and miles away. No, I do insist. You must stay with us. We have so few guests and I would love to hear all the latest news from London and"—her eyes darted to Christina's outlandish attire—"what the latest fashions are."

"Thank you, Lady Stavely. I would be delighted to stay a day or two." Christina smiled her most charming smile.

Richard glowered darkly at her, as Mary turned to Lisa who had remained in the doorway. "Pray tell Pottle that there will be another for luncheon, Lisa. And ask Mrs. Pottle to prepare the green room for Lady Grenville."

Lisa nodded and left the room. Her heart felt leaden. What was it Richard had said to her when he had returned from London? "I was not unfaithful with Christina or any other wench while away from you." But if he were through with Christina for good, why was she here? Christina must *still* be living under his protection. He must *still* be paying her bills. She wondered how much the dashing riding habit had cost him.

Had she but known, Christina had watched Lisa retire from the room and had seen the way Richard's eyes had followed her. It was obvious he was enamored with the girl. She was incredibly beautiful, despite her unstylish gown and simple hairstyle. But there was also something else about her—a freshness, an honesty—that Christina found completely foreign and therefore most unnerving.

It mollified Lisa a little, as they sat down to luncheon, to see Richard's obvious displeasure at Christina's presence. He paid little attention to her, although she looked very fetching indeed in a gown of soft peach that showed off her tiny waist, and restrained her full breasts beneath a demure fichu of exquisite lace. Her eyes never left Richard's face as, in answer to her question, he told her in purposely succinct terms how he had been wounded and when they left the table, she immediately moved to take his arm in a possessive manner.

"It appears Lady Grenville will not remain a widow for long if *she* has anything to do with it," Mary murmured. Her remark was so unlike Mary that Lisa found herself staring at her.

Lisa had never felt so plain, so unsophisticated, so unsure of herself as she did beside the beautiful and worldly Christina. It made her realize the vast difference in her and Richard's lives.

In the great hall, Mary excused herself. "I always take a nap after luncheon, Lady Grenville—"

"Christina, please."

"And you must call me Mary. If you will excuse me, I hope to see you at teatime."

Mary started up the stairs and Christina said softly to Richard, "May I speak with you a moment?" She nodded toward the library.

He looked about to say something, but she pulled gently at his arm.

"Pray excuse us, Lisa," he sighed. "We won't be long."

"Of course," she said crisply and started up the stairway after Mary. Then she remembered that Mary had given her a message for Pottle about the supper arrangements and returned to the dining hall.

It was a few minutes later, after seeing Pottle, that she again crossed the great hall. As the library door was ajar, she could not help but hear the clear voice.

"Is Miss Dewey-Eyes your latest, Richard? I hardly think her your style, my love. Much too provincial."

Richard did not answer for a moment. He was still livid with Christina for coming to Stavely Manor. In fact he had just finished a long tirade that seemed to have gone right over Christina's head.

In that moment of silence, Lisa fled up the stairs. It was very clear to her now that if she had become Richard's mistress—even his wife—he would have tired of her very quickly. How could he not help it? Beside someone like Lady Grenville she was dull and uninteresting and yes, Christina was right, provincial. She ran to the safety of her room.

"I thought I had made myself clear to you, Tina," Richard said to her. "Our liaison is finished. Over. Surely by now you have found yourself another lover who will pay your rent. Hasn't young Hetherington—"

Christina shook her head. "He has no money," she admitted, "but even if he had I could not live with him. It is *you* I love, Richard. *You* I need."

As she spoke she moved closer to him, brushing intimately against him.

"No, Christina," he shook his head at her, stepping aside. "You are going to tell Mary that you will be leaving in the morning."

"And if I do not choose to?"

"Then you will force me to reveal to her that you were my mistress."

"*Were,* Richard?"

"*Were,* Christina!"

She bit her lip and looked away from him. "How bitter you have become," she said, crossing the room to the window. "It must be very lonely for you here in the country." For a moment she gazed out over the lawn. "Those long weeks lying alone in bed—wounded—suffering—" She turned back to face him. She had unfastened the fichu of lace. Her voluptuous breasts were now barely imprisoned by the low-cut neckline of her gown. She ran her hands lightly over them, cupping them, squeezing them. "How long has it been, Richard? How many long days and nights since you have known a woman. . . ."

He gave her an insolent grin. "One," he said, the grin deepening.

"You bastard!" Her eyes narrowed. "One of the housemaids, I suppose."

"That's none of your concern," he said calmly. "Our conversation has ended, Tina. You will leave in the morning." He strode toward the door.

"Not so fast!" Something in Christina's voice stopped him. The color in her cheeks had darkened and her eyes flashed dangerously. "I think Miss Dewey-Eyes and I should have a long talk," she smiled, and it wasn't a pleasant smile. "There is so much I could tell her about you."

"Leave Lisa alone," he growled.

"So that's the way it is," she cried triumphantly. "You care for the little innocent." One perfectly arched eyebrow lifted. "She *is* still innocent, isn't she, Richard?"

He didn't answer.

"You *are* a bastard!" she spat.

* * *

Richard met Lisa at the foot of the stairs as she came down for supper. At Zada's urging, he had returned to his room for an afternoon rest, but had insisted upon joining the ladies for supper in the dining hall.

"I must speak with you, Lisa."

"What is there to say, Richard?"

"I want you to know that I parted from Christina weeks ago when I went up to London. She came here at no invitation of mine."

"I realize that," Lisa said quietly. "But 'tis obvious she still cares for you."

"She has promised to leave in the morning."

"I trust you have not left her destitute."

"Of course not. I have been very— Look, why are we—"

"That is comforting to know."

He frowned. "What the devil are you getting at?"

"I am only interested to learn the treatment I might expect to receive when you tire of me."

"Damn it, Lisa, it isn't the same with you and me and you know it. I love you. That makes all the difference in the world."

"I won't marry you, Richard."

"We'll see about that. Right now—"

"Good evening, Lisa. Richard." Mary came slowly down the stairs. When she reached the bottom she stopped and clicked her tongue. "I seem to have forgotten my handkerchief, Lisa. Would you mind running up and fetching me one?"

She had seen the two of them quarreling again. It made her feel like a nursemaid separating two squabbling children.

Lisa left Mary's room a few minutes later, handkerchief in hand, and had only reached the top of the stairs, preparing to descend when Christina appeared beside her.

Lady Grenville seemed even more beautiful in an elaborately trimmed gown that did much to emphasize her curvaceous figure.

"Good evening, Lisa," she said. "Might I have a word with you?" She laid a slim hand on Lisa's arm, the fingers glittering with gems.

"Certainly."

"I thought you should know about Lord Drayton and me. Just in case you have any illusions about him. Richard and I have loved one another for a very long time."

Lisa looked hard at her but said nothing.

"Do you see my diamond earbobs and necklace?" Christina put a hand to her throat. "They are lovely, are they not? Richard gave them to me as an expression of his love."

Lisa fought the jealous thoughts that sprang to her mind—thoughts of what Christina must have given Richard in return.

"I am sorry if I have distressed you, dear. But I felt I should be frank with you. Richard is mine." The last three words were said almost threateningly as Christina moved to sweep down the stairs.

"*Was* yours," Lisa heard herself saying. "He *was* yours, Christina. He loves *me* now."

"You poor child." Christina looked at her pityingly, then her face hardened. "Don't deceive yourself. He does not care a farthing for you. Richard is a very physical man. You were only handy when he desired a willing little body. I understand his needs. He always returns to me."

Christina moved on down the stairs and a few seconds later Lisa followed her. When they had departed, Styles stepped out of the shadows where he had been standing, listening to their conversation. A large grin spread slowly across his handsome face.

Supper had proved to be a bit strained and Richard was almost glad when he was unexpectedly called away from the table.

When he returned to the dining hall, Lisa recognized the gleam of excitement in his green eyes. He had received a message, he explained, that someone answering Thomas Carver's description had been seen in London. He would leave first thing in the morning.

"You cannot go, Richard!" Mary entreated. "You are not well enough."

"Nonsense, Mary. I have been getting my strength back for a week now."

"Nevertheless, you are not ready to ride all that distance."

"Mary," he said in a voice that defied any argument. "I am going to London."

"Then you must take my coach," she insisted. "I will not hear of you riding."

He grinned as he gave her a little bow. "On that I will acquiesce, Mary," he agreed. "And I thank you. Now, if you ladies will excuse me, I will retire early to my bed." He was looking at Lisa.

"Take care," she managed to whisper to him before he turned reluctantly from her to Christina.

"Remember what I said," he told her.

Christina nodded contritely. "Aye, Richard."

Drayton left first thing in the morning, but Christina did not obey him. She stayed on at Stavely Manor after asking Mary sweetly if she might remain until Richard's return.

In the few days she had at her disposal before Richard arrived back, she had to think of a way in which to discredit the girl forever in his eyes. She must retain her position as Richard Drayton's mistress! She must!

Hetherington had not been the only one she had dallied with while Richard was away from London. There had been many fops and dandies who had found their way into her bed, but they had all lost in comparison to Richard. She had yet to find a lover to measure up to him in looks or in skill. His enormous wealth was another factor in his favor. No! She could not lose him!

Carefully, she mused over what she might do, accepting and rejecting ideas, and then a plan began to form in her mind, a plan that was quickly aided and abetted by Styles who came to sell her information about Mistress Manning.

He was not satisfied with the small amounts of money he was getting from Lisa. She had never gone to Drayton, as he had suggested, but he had seen no point in cutting off even this small supply by telling Sir Peter and Lady Stavely about her. Instead, after overhearing the conversation between Christina and Lisa, he had decided to go to Lady Grenville, in hopes of obtaining a second source of easy income.

Soon he was involved in a plan that included both himself and Polly. A plan in which Polly, who harbored an intense jealousy of Lisa, was more than eager to participate.

It was two days since Richard's departure. Mary had retired to her room directly after supper, claiming a headache, and Lisa and Christina sat alone in the gallery.

There had been little conversation in the half-hour they had been seated there and finally Lisa put down the book she had been trying to read and got to her feet.

"Oh, don't go just yet," Christina begged her. "Won't you have a game of cards with me?"

"I don't play very well."

"We won't play for money. Just *one* game."

Lisa sighed. "All right," she agreed. Perhaps it would take her mind off Richard and her concern about him and his safety.

When Lisa was seated again Christina rang for Styles.

"Mistress Manning and I would like a glass of wine, Styles," she told him when he entered.

"Aye, m'lady."

"I don't think—" Lisa began.

"One glass, Lisa, and one game. Is that too much to ask?" Christina opened her hands.

Lisa nodded and soon Christina was dealing the cards.

Styles returned with the wine and after he had poured it and departed, Christina raised her glass. "To Richard," she smiled, a sensuous, catlike smile. "Our mutual lover."

Lisa put down her cards. "Christina, if you are going to—"

"I'm sorry if the thought offends you, my dear, but we have both received the bounty of his passion, have we not?"

"I do not wish to discuss—"

"Forgive me. I speak indelicately." She drank deeply. "Do play a card, Lisa."

Lisa picked up her cards and selected one. As she waited for Christina, she sipped at the wine. It seemed overly sweet but not unpleasant.

The game continued.

Lisa drained her glass. She had begun to feel rather sleepy. She was finding it more and more difficult to concentrate on the cards. Her head felt so heavy. Was she drunk? How in the world had one glass of wine affected her so much?

There was darkness. Lisa's limbs felt numb and yet she was not asleep. She felt herself being picked up from the chair and carried across the room. She tried to speak, but nothing came out of her mouth.

An outside door was opened. Lisa felt the cool night air rush over her and she shivered. Something was thrown over her as she was carried down some steps. She could not credit what was happening to her. Everything seemed so fuzzy. She was thrust onto a seat and a door was slammed behind her.

She was in a coach! She could smell the leather of the cushions against her nose. With a jerk and a rattle, the vehicle moved off.

Lisa sensed that someone was with her in the coach, but she could not discern who it was. They drove along a winding road, and as the coach traveled on and on, its motion made everything begin to grow dimmer and dimmer.

She must have slept, for the next thing she knew, she was aware of a hazy light bobbing back and forth outside a window. It must be the coach lantern, she decided. She tried to lift her head, but it felt far too heavy.

The neck of a bottle was shoved between her lips and tilted upward. More of the heavy, sweet wine filled her throat. She had to swallow it or gag. The bottle was removed.

Again she slept. The next thing she was aware of was that the coach had stopped. She thought she heard Styles' voice ask, "Is she unconscious?" And Christina's laughing reply. "For now, but she'll come awake enough for him."

Darkness closed in again.

It was a half-hour before midnight when he went upstairs to his bedchamber.

His manservant was nowhere in sight, but that was not unusual. Being discretion itself, and knowing that his master was more often than not in the company of a member of the fair sex, this estimable servant made it a point to become scarce, yet always within calling distance should the need of him arise.

He undressed himself with little trouble, tossing the bothersome wig onto a dresser nearby and running a hand through his matted hair.

The heavy red and gold damask coverlet had been pulled back and his nightshirt laid over the end of the canopied bed. As he approached, he saw, by the light of a candelabra on a nearby table, that he was not alone. Someone was lying in his bed!

Walking naked around to the lighted side, he gazed down at a sleeping girl, her dark cloud of hair fanned out over the pillow. What a little beauty she was! Saints preserve us, but his host was generous! Gently, so as not to waken her, he pulled back the covers and slid in beside her.

Lisa felt she was swimming underwater, coming close to the surface but unable to raise her head above it. She felt strangely weightless—drifting almost in limbo.

A deep voice was speaking to her from far away. A man's voice. Soft, coaxing . . .

She was asleep, that was it. But she could not seem to wake up. A hand touched her shoulder. She felt the warmth of it as she was turned over onto her back. She felt lips press themselves to her throat, then rise to her mouth in a gentle kiss. She felt the soft bristle of a moustache.

It was Richard! Oh, dear God, he had come to her! He was seeking *her* arms—*her* bed—and not that of the ravishing Christina.

"You are so beautiful," he whispered.

Oh, why couldn't she see his face? Why were her eyes so heavy? Why could she not hold them open?

She tried to move her leaden arms to embrace him. Everything seemed in slow motion to her.

Hands began to caress her, teasing fingers, knowing so well the soft, intimate spots to incite her. Kisses burned her lips, a fiery tongue seared her mouth.

Her body responded to his expert touch, the heat rising quickly to engulf her. She moaned, pressing herself against him, shuddering in delight at the hard, throbbing length that gently probed for entrance.

"Open to me, love," he murmured huskily in her ear, as he nibbled at the lobe.

She was trembling now, her hands reaching for him hungrily. Thighs fell apart, hips arched as she guided him to her.

He needed no urging. She let out a little cry as he filled her, thrusting himself deep into the welcoming heat.

He took his time, intensifying her pleasure, and at the climax, she cried his name aloud. With a convulsive explosion it was over.

She lay there obscurely aware that something was wrong. Very wrong. Her drug-dulled mind could not tell her what it was.

He had been a perfect lover and she felt warm and fulfilled, lying now in his arms, but some insidious little fear was growing inside her. A fear that she must drag to the surface and examine.

He kissed her cheek and his voice was low and amused as he said, "By the by, my sweet, methinks you should know that my name is *not* Richard."

Chapter Thirty

THE VOICE AND THE WORDS AFFECTED HER LIKE A DRENCHING OF ice water. Instinctively she became aware, although still confused and disoriented. She rose on one elbow to regard him.

She had moved too quickly. Her head swam sickeningly as she looked down with horror at the smiling face—the heavy features—the narrow black moustache—the dark eyes filled with amusement.

"You *aren't* Richard!" her voice croaked.

"No, my sweet. Methinks you crawled into the wrong bed."

She let out a gasp as she looked around her in the dim candlelight. This was *not* her bedchamber. But how had she come here?

Then it began to come back. She remembered Christina and the wine that had tasted too sweet. She remembered being carried and a coach ride and the sound of Styles' voice.

"I—I must have been drugged," she murmured, rubbing a hand across her eyes. "'Tis all coming back to me. But why was I put in *your* bed? Who are you, sir?"

Fearfully, she backed away from him, gathering a counterpane over her breasts.

"You do not recognize me?" He raised himself to a sitting

position, showing his wide bronzed chest, with its matte of black curling hair.

"Nay, I do not. Oh, God in heaven, what have I done?" She broke into tears and as she did so, she felt a comforting arm go about her shoulders.

"Do not cry, little one. I thought you had come to my bed to pleasure me, or I would never have taken you."

"I did not know. . . ." she gulped. "I thought you were someone else."

"So it would seem. May I ask who this Richard might be?"

"Richard is my—he is Lord Drayton."

"Drayton! Drayton is your lover?" he laughed aloud. "'Oddsfish, but the man has become embroiled in my life a good deal lately."

"You know him?" Lisa asked. "You still have not told me your name, sir?"

"It is Charles."

"Charles who?"

"Charles Stuart, your king."

At his words, Lisa collapsed back upon her pillow. "I knew it," she murmured. "I knew I must still be asleep. Oh, thank God, this is only a dream."

He laughed again. "You are very much awake, my dear. Shall I pinch you to prove it?"

"No!" She looked up at him in alarm, clutching the counterpane even closer. Her eyes were wide violet pools of astonishment.

"What is your name?" he asked her kindly.

"Lisa, Your Majesty."

"And you do not remember how you got here?"

She shook her head. "They drugged my wine and brought me here. I was not conscious."

He grinned. "Well, conscious or not, Lisa, my sweet, you know well how to please a man. I thank you greatly for the pleasure."

She blushed deeply. "But I would not have. . . . 'Twas that I thought you were Richard. . . ."

"He is indeed a lucky man. I envy him."

Tears again filled Lisa's eyes. "Oh, what am I to do?"

"I would not worry about it. Drayton is not likely to challenge *me* to a duel."

"No one must know." Lisa looked frantically about her for her clothing. "I must get back to Stavely Manor without being seen." She put a pleading hand on his arm. "Oh, promise me you will keep this a secret. You will not tell Richard."

"You have my word, but—" His voice became more intimate as he raised her fingers to his lips. "Could I not persuade you to stay until morning?"

"Nay!" She drew back her hand and moved away from him, inching toward the edge of the bed. "I must go *now*." She had seen a small pile of clothing on a chair in the corner. "Turn your head," she ordered as she wriggled off the bed and rose to her feet, still clutching the counterpane about her.

He did as he was told, though he could not help but chuckle. After such intimacy, why should the wench be so modest?

Lisa dressed hurriedly in her underclothes, but when she came to put on her gown, she found another one had been substituted for the gown she had been wearing earlier in the evening. Her own had been of plain, blue linen, with a simple white lace collar. This one was of crimson silk, richly embroidered, with a form-fitting bodice and a neckline that half exposed her breasts. It had been created for a smaller woman, Lisa realized, as she struggled to do herself up. Was it Christina's gown? Fortunately, she had been left a shawl and she pulled it close around her.

"I am dressed now," she said.

Charles turned his head to her and quirked an eyebrow.

"You realize you have devastated me, Lisa. That you should prefer Drayton to me is not very flattering." His lips twitched. "Where did you find me lacking?"

"Oh, I did not—" she began, then blushed deeper than before as he let out a roar of laughter.

"I did not mean to tease you," he said, seeing those huge violet eyes becoming luminous again.

"You don't understand, Your Majesty. Until tonight, Richard was the only man who had ever possessed me. Now, I have betrayed him!" She let out a sob as she collapsed into a chair, putting her hands over her face.

"Child, child," Charles said softly, rising from the bed and pulling on his dressing gown. He walked over to where she sat and gently uncovered her face. "You love him very much, don't you?" he asked, looking down at her with concern.

She nodded.

"Are you under his protection, my dear?" He was thinking of Christina Grenville.

She shook her head.

"Then Drayton is a bloody fool! I'll tell him so."

"No!" She raised her tear-stained face to him. "You must not, Your Majesty! You promised!"

"Aye, I promised. All right, sweetheart, we'll get you away from here without being seen. I am an old hand at that."

"Thank you, Your Majesty."

He rang for Will Chiffinch and that poor man at last came slowly into the room, rubbing a painful bump on his head.

He showed no surprise at seeing Lisa, being too busy apologizing. He could not understand why or who had hit him from behind outside in the hallway.

"It must have been Styles," Lisa said. "He knows this house. This is Peter Ellsbury's home, is it not?"

Charles nodded. "Do you know him?"

"Aye." Her eyes were frantic now. "But I must get away from here before *he* is aware—"

"Of course."

The king explained to Will that the girl had gained access to his room by mistake and wished to leave the house as quickly and surreptitiously as possible.

It was at once arranged that the page would obtain a coach from the stable as well as a driver who could be trusted to keep his mouth shut. When this had been accomplished, Will would see Lisa down the servant's stairs and out the servant's entrance to the coach.

The page disappeared, anxious to rectify what he considered to be an unpardonable lapse of duty. Why, what if whoever had hit him over the head had been bent upon taking the king's life!

Charles poured Lisa a goblet of brandy and insisted she drink it. "'Twill settle your nerves."

"But my head is still not completely clear."

"Fie! You can sleep in the coach. 'Tis a two-hour drive at the very least."

He poured a brandy for himself and pulled a chair over beside her. "Poor Will was quite upset. Have you any notion who is behind this little prank?"

"Aye. I believe 'twas Styles who hit your page. He is a

manservant at Stavely Manor and used to be employed in this house, so would know it well."

"Why would this Styles be involved?"

"'Tis a long story. He and Polly, a housemaid, threatened to tell Lady Stavely about Richard and me. I am her companion, you see, and I did not want her to . . . so I was paying them to keep quiet and I—I ran out of money."

"May I ask if Drayton was aware of all this?"

"Of course not. I would not go to him for money."

There was pity in the dark eyes that regarded the young girl. "Is Drayton still residing at Stavely Manor?"

"No. He went to London in pursuit of the man who shot him."

"What! The fool's hardly mended."

"I know." She bit her lip.

Charles was about to question her further when Will Chiffinch returned.

He had discovered, he told them, that there had been three people who had entered the house through the servant's entrance. A man and two women. They had told the king's attendants that it was a joke and that Charles' page was aware of it, which Will now indignantly denied.

The two women had been supporting the girl and the man had gone on ahead, no doubt ready to silence anyone who might cross his path.

"Who would the women be?" Charles asked Lisa curiously.

"Polly would have been one and I am fairly certain of the other," Lisa said, thinking of Christina. But how had Styles and Polly got together with Christina? Lisa's head was still not too clear and she could not make any sense of it.

Will Chiffinch was motioning to her and she got to her feet, dipping a deep curtsy to her sovereign.

"Thank you, Your Majesty," she said softly.

"The pleasure was all mine," Charles grinned, his brown eyes twinkling.

It had taken Drayton two days in London before he had discovered that Carver had escaped him and was reported to be on his way north to Scotland.

He and Ned retraced their journey, taking the main road northeast from London late in the day and planning to return

Lady Stavely's coach to her at the manor before continuing north on horseback the next morning.

Because of darkness, the going was slow and it was nearly one o'clock in the morning when Drayton finally reached Stavely Manor.

Pottle opened the door sleepily to him and Drayton crossed the dimly lit hallway with only one thing in mind. A good night's sleep. The hours on the road had drained his energy. His back pained him and he was forced to admit to himself that he had not as yet gained back all of his strength.

As he strode down the corridor to his room, he saw that there was a light shining from beneath one of the bedchamber doors. It was the room Christina had occupied! Damn the wench, was she still here?

He knocked on the door and turned the latch. It opened to him. Christina was languishing against the pillows on her bed, buffing her nails.

"Richard!" she exclaimed, the color leaving her face. "I did not expect you back so soon."

In truth the sight of him was most unsettling for her. She was expecting the handsome footman, Styles, to come for part of his reward that, she was sure, he had not mentioned to Polly.

"You were to have left here yesterday morning, Christina," Richard growled at her. "What the devil do you mean by staying on?"

"I was not feeling well enough to travel," Christina pouted.

"A likely excuse!"

"You're right," she admitted. "I wanted to be here when you returned." She smiled at him. A smile that was both sensuous and challenging. "Come here, Richard. You look so tired. Let me massage some of the tenseness from your shoulders." She reached out to him, the neck of her robe opening provocatively.

"I presume everyone else is to bed," he said.

"Lady Stavely, certainly, but Lisa . . . ?" Christina gave a significant little shrug, unveiling even more white flesh to him.

"And what is that supposed to mean?" Drayton asked sharply.

"Oh, nothing. Nothing at all."

"Tell me, Tina."

"Well, I'm afraid I caught sight of the girl slipping out earlier, Richard."

"Slipping out?" he thundered. "Where the devil did she go?"

"How would I know?" Tina sulked. "A secret assignation, perhaps—a lover waiting in the shadows—oh, to be so young again. . . ."

His voice was deadly quiet. "Is this true, Tina?"

"Would I lie to you, Richard? Go to her room if you do not believe me. I am sure you will find it quite empty."

"I'll do that." He strode angrily toward the door.

"I'll be waiting," she whispered.

Styles stopped Pottle in the hallway. "Was that the door?" he asked, with an exaggerated yawn.

"Aye, Lord Drayton just returned."

"Lord Drayton?" Styles looked alarmed.

"Aye. You would think he owned this blasted house," Pottle grumbled as he went off down the hall to his rooms.

Styles stood there. He knew immediately what he must do. He and Polly must away from here tonight. They must not be found at Stavely Manor when Lord Drayton discovered what had happened to that wench, Lisa. He had had a bad feeling about this whole thing from the start. Well, that Grenville bitch had paid them a hundred pounds. He and Polly'd make out all right. Too bad he wouldn't be able to claim the rest of his reward, he grinned. He'd have liked to have made that bitch squirm 'n holler beneath him.

Lisa crept up the back stairs of Stavely Manor and quietly made her way down the hall to her room.

The house was quiet. The candles in their tall sconces burned low. Everyone was long in bed. No one had missed her. She sighed with relief.

It had been a night she would never forget. Although it had not been her fault, she still felt guilty and ashamed. She might have lain with the King of England, but it felt no better to her than if he had been a stable boy. She no longer belonged to Richard alone. Other arms had held her—other lips had claimed hers—another body had joined . . . She must forget that! She must!

Her head still pounded with the effect of the drug she had been given. She realized she should never have had the brandy. On top of the potent drug, it had gone to her head, and she had not slept on the ride home.

She opened her bedchamber door and drew off her shawl, dropping it onto a chair.

As she turned from closing the door, she saw him in the light from the candles by her bed, sitting in a chair, waiting for her. Richard!

She stood frozen in her tracks, her body swaying a little.

"Welcome home, my dear," he said, his voice thick with sarcasm. She had never seen his green eyes look so cold and hard. The color left her cheeks as she whispered, "Richard!"

His eyes swept to the gown she wore. It was more revealing than any he had ever seen on her, and her hair was tumbled and loose and wild about her shoulders, as if she had not bothered to pin it up again after her assignation.

"Where the hell have you been in that whore's gown?"

Lisa was stunned. It was a moment before she could find her voice. "'Tis all been a terrible nightmare, Richard. I—I can explain—"

"Really?" he drawled. "By your tongue it appears you have also had too much to drink."

"Don't look at me like that!" Her eyes filled with tears. "You can't imagine what I've been through. I was drugged and kidnapped—"

"Kidnapped?" He got to his feet and in one stride was towering over her. "What do you take me for—a bloody fool!" he cried, gripping her shoulders with his big hands. "Those tears won't work on me. Not now. You were seen sneaking out of the house, going to your lover."

Her violet eyes widened in amazement. "That's not true!"

He was shaking her now, so hard she thought her neck would snap! Oh God, how her head throbbed! She could not think! The room was spinning!

"Who is he, Lisa?" He remembered the scene in the garden beneath his window. "Is it Styles, the footman? Is *he* the bloody bastard?"

Lisa had never seen Richard in such a rage. There were taut white lines around his mouth and a vein throbbed in his temple. He looked as if he could murder her!

"Pray listen to me, Richard. 'Twas not my fault—"

"Liar! Will you at least admit you were with a man tonight?"

"Pray stop! I beg of you! All right. I was with a man, but 'twas not like—"

His hands fell heavily to his sides. She felt the pain in the tops of her arms and knew there would be deep bruises on her flesh in the morning.

His voice was strangely flat now. "Did you let him make love to you?"

She didn't answer, but her pale cheeks gave her away. A scarlet flush spread over them.

"Slut!" He reached out and pulled her roughly to him. For a moment his hands caressed her bare shoulders and then they moved upward toward her soft, white neck. A pulse beat madly at her throat and she felt his fingers tighten there. Then suddenly his hard mouth caught hers in a brutal kiss.

Despite the fact that he was kissing her to hurt, to punish, a warm surge of joy flowed through her and she pressed her body closer to his.

"Little bitch!" he growled. "So you haven't had enough lovemaking for one night."

"Let me go!" she cried, furious at him for condemning her without listening to her explanation.

"I'll be damned if I will!" Deliberately his fingers fastened in her gown and he ripped it from neck to hemline. Her other garments followed until she was standing naked before him, her eyes dark, her breasts heaving now with anger.

"How dare you! You have no right to treat me like—"

"A whore? Isn't that what you are, my dear? Who *was* he, Lisa?"

"Why should I tell you? You cannot call him out."

He laughed ruthlessly. "I have no intention of calling him out. A man duels for a lady's honor. Since it is apparent you have none, why on earth would I exert myself? Who bothers to defend the honor of a whore?"

"How quick you are to believe the worst of me," her voice choked.

But he ignored her, scooping her up in his arms, throwing her across the bed.

He lay over her then, his emerald eyes glittering hard as the jewels they resembled.

Lisa had no idea how lovely she looked with her hair loosened and disheveled, her tremulous lips, the flush on her soft, white skin. She heard Richard draw in his breath sharply.

"Did he kiss you like this?" he asked hoarsely, his mouth

crushing down on hers passionately, demandingly, until her lips could not deny their own desire and opened to him, allowing in his searching tongue.

He smothered her face in kisses and then he was nibbling her neck and shoulder, working downward in a burning path.

His tongue etched circles around her breasts and his lips teased her nipples until they hardened.

"Did he do that?" he murmured, continuing his slow but determined exploration of her body.

The warmth was spreading. He was devouring her with his mouth and his tongue. He was a master at lovemaking and he was using every ounce of his expertise to take her to the heights of pleasure.

With slow, hot kisses, he traced a course down her flat stomach, stopping just above where she had begun to throb, to ache for him. She was infused with heat now, moaning softly, writhing in his arms.

"Did he kiss you here?" His lips continued down the inside of her thigh and back up the other.

"Richard!" she gasped.

But he continued to tantalize every part of her body but where she was the most hungry.

"Here?" he asked. "And here?"

She was alive with desire for him, squirming sensuously under his caressing fingers. Oh God, how she wanted him! The trembling in her loins had spread throughout her body. She couldn't wait! Her feverish fingers tried to reach for him, but he held them away as with his other hand he found the softness between her thighs, his fingers stroking, parting, probing. . . .

The deep, throbbing need rose to a frenzy within her.

"Oh God, Richard, take me!" she cried. She was mindless with desire now. Her fingers clawing, her back arched as spasm after spasm overtook her.

And then he laughed. A cruel, grating, bitter laugh, as he wrenched her arms from where they clung tightly around his neck and left her lying crushed on the bed.

"I think you have had quite enough lovemaking for one night," he said, his eyes blazing with contempt. "I'll say goodnight, now, my dear. Pleasant dreams."

A terrible wave of loss swept over her. "Richard!" she shuddered. "Oh God, don't leave me!"

But he was gone. Striding out of the room and slamming the door without ever looking back.

He had aroused her to the highest pitch—to a madness of passion and desire and then he had left her—burning—aching and throbbing for fulfillment.

"Richard!" she cried in agony. "Come back to me!"

She had never felt this way before—stretched out tight like a bow—crying for release.

She let out a groaning sob and pulled her knees up, rolling herself over on her side. She felt physically ill. That was it. She was going to be sick!

Flinging herself off the bed, she reached for the chamber pot.

Drayton flung open the door of Christina's room. She was still reclining against the pillows.

"What do you want?" she asked, a little fearful of the black scowl on his face.

"You!" he growled, advancing toward her and she saw by his breeches that he was already aroused.

"Then come here," she whispered, quickly divesting herself of her robe and opening her arms invitingly.

He stripped off his clothes and her eyes caught the white scar on his shoulder, before moving to admire his perfectly proportioned body—huge, lean, superbly muscled.

The ones who had come after, the fops and the dandies she had taken to her bed after he had left London, were all lost in comparison—forgotten. Here was a real man. Here was her Richard.

There would be few preliminaries, she knew, viewing his full erection as he came toward her. She did not care. All she wanted was to feel him deep inside her once more.

She parted her legs and then he was upon her, his body a savage, driving instrument as he tried to appease himself of one raven-haired, violet-eyed girl.

It was a quick taking—purely mechanical—without the slightest emotion. Their lips never even touched.

Afterward Richard jerked away from her as if he were disgusted with himself. He left the bed and began to dress.

"You're not leaving?" she asked, her voice rising shrilly.

"I am. I won't be coming back to Stavely Manor."

Christina relaxed. She had won! He was through with Lisa!

"Will I see you in London?"

"I am heading north, Tina. When and if I return to London I expect to see you on the arm of some new protector. Our affair has ended. This little interlude tonight has not changed a thing between us."

As he turned to the door, he stopped and gave her a little bow. "I admit to being guilty of using you tonight, my dear. My abject apologies."

Chapter Thirty-one

Lisa lay awake for most of the night, swept by a sense of desolation. It was as if all meaning had been drained from her life.

She had known Richard Drayton for only two months. Now she could not imagine a world without him. He had come into her life and changed it in so many ways. She would never be the same again.

She alternated between weeping for him and raging at his lack of faith in her. Neither brought her comfort.

As Richard rode north through an early dawn, almost overcome by fatigue and the recurring pain of his wounds, he pictured Lisa over and over again with her handsome lover; pictured her in that gown that had barely covered the nipples of her full, young breasts; pictured him cupping those soft, white mounds and releasing them to his eager lips; pictured a wild and lustful coupling in the secluded garden where he had once seen Lisa run to meet him.

Faithless! The one woman he thought to be different from all the others. The love she offered him true and pure and everlasting. What a fool he had been! How easily that love had been cast aside.

He was aware that he had been the one to awaken her and teach her to enjoy her own sensual capacity, but was she so hot-blooded that one man alone could not satisfy her? How could she come straight from Styles' arms and then respond so easily to him?

He would forget her! He had to forget her!

But in the days that followed, Ned began to despair over him. Lord Drayton, he thought, was clearly overtaxing himself—too little food and sleep and too much drinking. It was always a sign of trouble with his lordship, Ned knew, when he made such indentures. Something was eating at him and if he came upon Thomas Carver in his present state, Ned was afraid of the outcome.

It was the morning after Drayton's departure. Christina had sent her groom for her horse. She paced the front hall of Stavely Manor impatiently, tapping her riding crop against the top of one of her leather boots.

Lisa descended the oak stairway slowly. Her head pounded unbearably.

Astonished to see her, Christina stopped in the middle of her pacing. "You're back!" she exclaimed, without realizing the full import of her words.

Lisa met the surprised blue eyes with a cool composure she did not feel.

"What do you mean?" she asked. "Back from where?"

Two red spots appeared on Christina's pale cheeks. "You know damn well what I mean!" she snapped. Then she seemed to gain more control of herself. The haughty expression returned to her face as she looked at Lisa closely.

"I gather you failed to please His Majesty and he sent you on your way. 'Tis no wonder. You look a sight."

Lisa's eyes narrowed. "I underestimated you, Christina. I just never realized to what great lengths you would go to win Richard's favor again."

"Oh, but 'twas worth it," Christina gloated. "He came to me last night—spent the *whole* night with me in fact." She yawned. "I must look a sight myself this morning. I didn't get much sleep." She gave a little smirk. "Ah, but I don't begrudge a moment. There is no one to equal him, is there, my dear?"

Lisa paled at her words, cold desolation striking her. So Richard had gone straight to Christina's arms when he had left her. If he had meant to continue his punishment of her, he had succeeded. She hated him! She would never forgive him for this! Never!

"Where *is* Richard?" she asked as if unconcerned.

"He has left for the north. He said he would not be returning again to Stavely Manor." She looked impatiently toward the door. "I am leaving myself in a few minutes. Going back to London to wait for him."

Lisa did not go to Zada to be comforted. She was a child no longer and her humiliation at Richard's hands was too great to impart to anyone—even her old nurse. Nevertheless, she did tell the old gypsy what Christina had done to her—the drugging and the kidnapping and what had transpired with the king.

Zada's eyes took on a look of shock at her words.

"Polly!" she muttered. "So that was it!"

"What do you mean?" Lisa frowned.

"Polly came to me a few days ago for something to help her mother sleep, she said. She gave me quite a story about the poor old widow being ill and afraid she might lose her cottage. I told her that a few drops of the extract I gave her would relax the muscles and make her mother sleep. I swear that was what Christina put in *your* wine, Lisa! And more than a few drops, I'll warrant."

Lisa nodded. "You are probably right."

"I will see to that Christina," Zada said menacingly, "and Polly too."

"'Tis no use, Zada. Christina has gone back to London and Polly and Styles disappeared during the night. Mary thinks the two servants eloped, though she has Pottle checking to see if anything in the manor house has been stolen."

"Have you told Mary what happened?"

"No, Zada. I could not do that. I would have had to tell her about the king and Richard."

"Drayton? What had he to do with it?"

Lisa had to admit then that he had seen her come in, still half-drugged and quite dishevelled, and had accused her of being with another man. Their parting had not been pleasant, was all she would say.

Zada was furious with Drayton. She could understand why he had jumped to conclusions, but why had he not let Lisa explain? She decided that he must have been totally shattered by Lisa's apparent faithlessness. She could imagine his hurt—his blind anger. It was a wonder he had not struck her.

Why were these two always punishing one another? Tearing each other's lives to pieces? Pride was their problem. Stupid, senseless pride. Last night, she feared, the final cord between them had been severed. There seemed no way now that their differences could ever be bridged. Their love had been destroyed by too much hurt and too little faith.

"He went to Christina when he left me," Lisa was saying, her beautiful face pale and drawn, mauve smudges beneath her eyes. "He spent the whole night in her arms."

"Did she tell you that?"

Lisa nodded.

"She lied," Zada growled. "I heard him leave myself in the middle of the night."

Lisa looked at her. "Are you positive it was Richard?"

"Aye."

But he must have gone to her, Lisa thought. Richard was not a cold block of ice. She felt sure his body must also have been stirred in the process of arousing her to such heights of passion. He would have craved release and Christina—always eager Christina—was only a few doors away.

She trembled, imagining the scene in her mind. "I hate him, Zada!" she cried, her little hands going into fists. "All I want is to forget he ever existed."

But it was not that easy. In the days that followed, Lisa felt alone and lost and a bleak and hopeless future lay ahead, with nothing to look forward to.

She had suspected that when the numbness wore off the pain would be acute. She had not known it would be unbearable. How could she possibly bear the emptiness of her life?

Mary Stavely had little time to wonder over Lisa's listlessness. Basil had come home.

Complications had incapacitated him for several weeks in London. His physicians had done little for him, finally recommending rest in the country. He still was not well and in considerable pain and discomfort. It was an ugly disease. His manservant, John, was in almost constant attendance.

For the first time since she had met Basil Stavely, Mary felt sorry for him as she looked down at him lying in the big four-poster bed. The big man she had feared so greatly seemed to have shrunk and aged in the weeks he had been away. How long ago it seemed since that dreadful night when he had treated her so despicably.

"How are you, Mary?"

"I am well, Basil."

She looked well. Very lovely, in fact. She was rounder in body and there was a new look of assurance in her face and manner.

"You must be crowing that I got what I deserved," he grunted.

"I would not do that, Basil."

"I could hardly blame you if you did."

She stared at him. She felt for a moment that she did not know this man who was her husband. Had he really changed? She found it difficult to believe, but she vowed that she would look after him. It was her duty as his wife. In his present condition he was hardly a threat to her, but, as she had promised, she sent word to Peter that Basil had come home.

Peter arrived the same day, clearly anxious to see for himself the condition of his brother-in-law.

It did not take him long to assess the situation. At the moment, Mary was in no danger from Basil Stavely, nor was Lisa. However, he made a point of having a private conversation with the man, pointing out to him that if he should ever lay a hand on his sister again, he would have to answer to him.

Peter was most anxious to see Lisa and when he discovered her in the library, he rushed eagerly across the room to her. She looked up at his approach and he was shocked by her appearance.

"Lisa, are you not well?" he frowned. "You look so pale."

She smiled up at him, closing her book. "How good it is to see you, Peter," she said. "No, I am quite well, thank you."

"I have wanted to see you before, but when I came to see Richard, I was only able to manage a few hours and then rush home. The king's impending visit set my house in a panic."

"I quite understand, Peter."

"I've missed you, Lisa." He indicated the place beside her on the sofa. "May I sit down?"

"Certainly."

"Have you—have you thought at all about what I said to you a few weeks ago?" he asked, as he seated himself.

She looked into his anxious face. "I have, Peter," she answered, "but I am afraid I must refuse you. I do not feel ready for marriage."

"I will give you time," he said and then he smiled. "I do not give up easily. I will ask you again."

Pottle had spent an hour with Sir Basil upon his return. It had taken him that long to report to him all the things that had occurred at Stavely Manor during his absence.

As Basil lay about day after day, enjoying Mary's attentiveness, he began to realize what a lovely, desirable woman she was. The one thing that had bothered him in Pottle's recital was an occasion when he had reported seeing Drayton emerging from Mary's bedchamber when she was known to have been alone. He wondered more than once if she had let that handsome bastard make love to her. There was a change in Mary, there was no doubt of that, and if Drayton were the cause of it, he would find out soon enough and deal with him accordingly.

For weeks Lisa had readied herself for Basil Stavely's return. She had planned how she would rush to the local authorities, show them the papers revealing her identity and return with their support to the Manor to confront Stavely to his face.

But everything had gone wrong.

No proof had yet been found in Sir Basil's involvement in the plot to kill the king and so he could not be accused of the crime. Instead, all she would succeed in doing was to throw both him and Mary off the estate. She could not do that to Mary. Basil, she knew, would take out his wrath on her and there was no Richard Drayton nearby to protect her. All Lisa's determination seemed to have fled with him. All her reason for living. Did she really want to possess Stavely Manor with all its painful memories?

In a state of indecision, Lisa allowed the days to slip by until the summer was over. Now she imagined Richard back in London lying in Christina's arms. She found herself bursting into tears over the slightest thing. She had become listless and thin and she did not sleep well. When she did, it was to dream of Richard and she would wake up longing for him.

It was only when she started to feel nauseated in the mornings that she was forced to face the truth. She fought the waves of panic that rushed through her. She was with child! Counting back, she wasn't sure who had fathered the babe that grew within her. Had it been Richard, or the king?

She remembered a conversation she had had with Richard.

"Is she bearing your child?" she had asked him of Christina, and he had answered rather shortly that she was not. "Have you any sideslips at all?" she had continued to press him, but Richard had only grinned at her and said, "Not to my knowledge."

Even after months of sharing Christina's bed and God knew how many others before her, Richard had not fathered a child! But the king! He was well known for his bastards! God in heaven, she was producing another one! She was carrying Charles Stuart's child!

Fiercely proud, Lisa kept this new agony to herself. She did not even tell Zada.

Zada was having her own problems. There was now no real reason for her to remain at Stavely Manor and the servants were complaining of her presence. If the slightest thing was misplaced in the house, it was blamed on "that thieving gypsy woman."

Mary was finally forced to come to Lisa.

"I'm afraid Zada must go," she said. "I know how close you are to her and it pains me to do this, but she is disturbing the servants. Even Trent came to me the other day complaining that she was interfering with his treatment of an injured horse. She had made some poultices of her own out of herbs and plants she had gathered and completely discarded his ointments and bindings to apply them."

"She was only trying to help."

"I realize that, Lisa, and I know she saved Richard's life, but Basil has been demanding she be put off the property ever since his return. He has always had a deep aversion to gypsies."

"Then I am afraid, Mary, that I must leave with her."

"You?" Mary looked stunned. "But Lisa, you cannot go! I need you here. I rely on you so much. You have done so much to help me. Pray don't leave me now."

"I would have to leave soon anyway, Mary. Another few months and it will be evident."

"What will be evident?" Mary was completely bewildered now.

"I am . . ." Suddenly it all burst from her lips. What Lisa had tried to keep from Mary since Richard's departure. "I am having a child," she sobbed, and before she was through Mary knew the whole story of Christina and the drugged wine and Polly and Styles and Lisa waking up in the king's bed.

"The king took advantage of you?" Mary gasped.

"Aye. He thought I had been placed in his bed for his pleasure."

"Oh, my dear . . . oh, Lisa! Why did you not come to me before about this?"

"I was too ashamed," Lisa admitted, "too humiliated."

"But it was something you had no control over. You were drugged. Oh, when I think of that dreadful woman!" She paused. "But why would she do such a thing?"

"I think she thought there was something between Richard and me."

"You and Richard? How ridiculous! She had only to use her eyes to see how you two were always quarreling."

"No doubt mistresses can be very possessive."

"I should have known what she was from the start!" Mary said, angrily. "The way she exhibited her limbs in that brazen manner and the way she looked at Richard—as if she were undressing him with her eyes! I shall never forgive him for allowing a doxy of his to stay under my roof!" Her eyes softened as they looked at Lisa. "Here I am carrying on about something that can no longer be helped and you are sitting here and . . . Oh, forgive me, Lisa, how terrible it must have been for you." She put her arms about the girl.

"You see now why it is better that I leave with Zada," Lisa said quietly.

"Nay, I do not! Where would you go? Oh Lisa, what a strange thing life is. You are bearing a child you do not want, and I—I would give anything in the world to bear a child. Now, I never will."

Lisa looked at her. "Anything . . ." she whispered.

They both stared at one another. Their eyes held and something passed between them.

"Basil would never accept it," Mary's hushed voice was nevertheless tinged with excitement.

"He would accept it happily if he thought it his own."

"But how . . ."

"I will go away," Lisa murmured. "Have the child someplace else."

"But where? You just cannot go to some strange . . . I know! Peter. You will go to him. He loves you. He will take you in and you will have Zada with you to look after you."

They were both silent for a moment and then Lisa nodded. "And you will tell Basil that you are expecting his child."

"But how . . . won't he . . . ?"

"You will gradually start wearing extra clothing and will pad yourself. Then, about a month before the time, you must go to visit Peter."

Mary's face fell. "Basil would never let me go."

"Then you must make up an excuse. Peter has injured himself or is ill and is asking for you."

Mary debated. "It all seems . . . but I could never stay a *month.*"

"Suppose you had false labor pains while you were there? Peter's physician tells you that you must not travel or you may lose the babe. Then, while you are there the child is born. Several weeks later you return to Stavely Manor with your son or daughter in your arms."

"Oh Lisa, you make it all sound so plausible."

"'Tis plausible. I just know 'twill work, Mary!"

"I don't know. . . ."

"'Tis up to you, of course."

"How can I refuse you? But are you sure you will be able to give up the babe that easily?"

"'Twould only remind me of a night I would like with all my heart to forget," Lisa choked, thinking of something quite different from that which Mary supposed.

"As Zada must leave soon, I will send a missive with her to Peter, telling him what has happened and our plan," Mary said.

"Would you let me write to him, Mary?"

"If you wish," the other agreed. "You will stay with me as long as you can, won't you, Lisa? I hate to think of you leaving Stavely Manor. 'Twill not seem the same without you."

"In the past few months you have become a different woman, Mary—stronger, more sure of yourself. I will miss you very much, but I know you will manage well."

Upon receiving Lisa's letter, Peter lost no time in riding over to the manor house. He was shown into the library and was pacing the floor when Lisa quietly entered, closing the door behind her. Peter's anguished eyes swept over her.

"Lisa," he said, opening his arms to her. "Oh, my dear . . ."

She went to him, letting him hold her, comfort her.

"Why did you not tell me about this when I was here before? 'Tis no wonder you have become so pale and wan, carrying this burden around with you."

"How could I tell you, Peter? I did not suspect until recently that I was with child."

"I mean about this—this woman having you kidnapped and drugged," he said, "and the king—"

"I was too ashamed, too—"

"Ashamed! Why should you be ashamed? The king had no right to take an innocent maid! I am going to Whitehall to confront him and—"

"Nay, Peter! You must not. He found me there in his bed. He did not know. He thought I had been put there for his pleasure."

"God's blood, Lisa, if I found a maid in *my* bed I would ask her how she got there. I would not just take a half-conscious—"

"You are not Charles Stuart, Peter." Lisa almost smiled.

Peter looked down at her, his eyes wistful. "I wish you had thought enough of me to confide this whole dreadful experience."

"I did not know how you would feel . . ."

"About you? Lisa, I love you. I love you with all my heart. Do you think so little of me that you would imagine it would make a difference?"

"Oh, Peter . . ." Tears stung her eyes. If Richard had only shown such understanding.

"Lisa, I want you to give up this foolish notion you and Mary have devised. Marry me and I will take the child as my own."

Lisa shook her head. "'Twould not be fair to you, Peter. I am fond of you, but I do not love you and the babe—'twill only remind me. . . ." Her voice trailed off.

"I think I understand."

"Mary," Lisa went on, "will be so happy to have a child to care for and Basil may be kinder to her if he has his heir."

Peter looked at her, his eyes full of love. "Mary found an angel the day you came to live with her."

Lisa looked up Nelly and Matthew before she left Stavely Manor. She did not tell them where she was going or why, and both appeared concerned for her welfare. She tried to reassure them by telling them that Zada would be with her.

"I will be sorry to miss your wedding at Michaelmas," she said, handing Nelly a wrapped gift of two fine linen pillowcases that she had embroidered herself. "I hope you will both be very happy."

"We wishes the same for thee," Nelly answered, wiping a tear from her eye with her apron as she waved goodbye to Lisa.

Lisa had come to Stavely Manor with a firm resolution. She had been forced to pause in acting upon it, but she vowed as she left the old manor house that before long things would be set right.

"Mary, look! I have more lesions on my face!" Basil bellowed at his wife. "I must go to London. That old doctor from the village is useless."

"As you will, Basil." Mary would welcome his departure. The man had been impossible of late.

"Would you"—his voice softened—"would you care to come with me? Perhaps to do a little shopping. . . ."

His remark surprised Mary so much that she stared at him for a moment, open-mouthed. When she had recovered her senses she shook her head.

"I am afraid it would be unwise for me to travel at this time."

"Why?" he demanded.

"Because," Mary began, and then the words came out in a rush, "because I am with child."

Seeing the joy that leaped into his eyes, she felt strangely sorry for her deception. She should not be deceiving him. He wanted an heir so badly. Then, suddenly, his eyes changed—darkened.

"It better be mine," he snarled, "and not Drayton's bastard!"

Two bright spots of color flamed in Mary's cheeks. "How dare you suggest—"

"You haven't answered me," he thundered. "Who is the father?"

"Why you, of course, my lord," Mary said bitterly. "You were always so good at it. Tell me, what is the latest count of your bastards?"

There was a dark silence in the room.

"You would not have dared speak to me in that fashion before I went away," Basil said, his eyes almost bulging from his head in anger. "'Tis that wench—that Lisa—who has made you so bold and defiant. The Bible says that a wife must be subservient to her husband. Don't you ever forget that! Lisa must go! I do not wish her in this house."

"She has already departed, Basil. Several days ago," Mary said sadly.

"Good." His voice rose again. "This may well be my last chance to sire a son. See that you do not lose this child, or I swear to you, you will deeply regret it!"

"And *I* swear you will never lay a hand on me again, Basil," Mary said quietly as she made for the door.

"You should be glad I did, my dear. It appears that the only way you can conceive is to be taken against your will. Aye"— the grin was ugly—"you thought I used you cruelly that night. 'Twill be a strong son who comes forth from such a violent planting. Mark my words!"

Mary blanched and quickly escaped from the room.

How could she have thought for even a moment that Basil had changed? He was still the beast he had always been! Pray God he would never learn she had miscarried that night and could not possibly have conceived a child.

Peter warmly welcomed Lisa to his home. She was installed in a beautiful suite of rooms that had been redecorated in soft blue to match her eyes.

Zada had had to be coaxed to leave her caravan home, but now she was quite used to the small room she had been given next to Lisa's. Lisa had to smile when she saw it. It looked quite outrageous filled with Zada's wild array of colorful belongings.

It was after supper on the day of her arrival that Peter told her about Richard.

"The king has called him back from Scotland," he said.

Trying to appear indifferent, Lisa asked, "Did he manage to catch the man who shot him?"

"Aye, he caught him all right." Peter shook his head. "That, it seems, is the reason for the uproar at court and why he has been recalled to Whitehall."

"I don't understand."

"Neither did I, but it seems that Richard confronted the man in broad daylight in a village square. He must have gone mad—that is all I can put it down to—for he literally hacked the man to pieces with his sword! Right in front of half the townsfolk." He apologized then, seeing how she had paled at his words.

"'Tis all right," she assured him. "Tell me the rest."

"Whitehall feels he gave the king and Englishmen in general a bad name. The Scots did not take kindly to that bold-faced slaughter, I can tell you."

"I simply can't believe it, Peter. 'Tis not like Richard. . . ." She was remembering his gentleness—the softness of his lips—his caressing hands.

"But you never really liked him, did you?" Peter asked her. "The two of you often quarreled."

"He seemed to enjoy provoking me."

"Apparently he did more than provoke Carver. Terrible thing. Terrible. Perhaps all those years on the Continent—all that bloodshed and killing—did something to him. I never thought him a violent man until now."

It struck Lisa then that she had seen the violence in Richard's nature—that last night, before he left. He had put his hands around her throat. He could have strangled her easily, but he had not. Instead, he had decided to torture her. Yes, there was cruelty in Richard Drayton, but she still found it hard to believe he would kill so ruthlessly. Something must have prompted it, she was sure.

"There is a rumor the king is sending Richard out of the country for a time, to Holland."

"Holland? But isn't there still a danger of war with the Dutch?"

Peter nodded. "I imagine Charles feels that Drayton can look after himself. I doubt, though, if he will have a chance to see Calderwood before he sails."

"Have you seen it?"

"Aye. I was there when the cornerstone was laid. They are making good progress with the construction. That Wren is a genuis. 'Tis going to be one of the most beautiful residences in all of England. Let us hope Richard lives to see it."

Chapter Thirty-two

CHARLES HAD FORGIVEN HIM WHEN RICHARD HAD EXPLAINED to the king the circumstances regarding Carver's death.

Drayton and his manservant, Ned, had been lodged for the night in a village inn deep in the lowland country of Scotland. It was early evening when there had been a knock at the door of Richard's bedchamber. He had been in the process of changing from his dusty travel clothes before going downstairs to sup.

"Yes?" he had called out, but there had been no reply.

Ned had opened the door, and as it swung wide, a shot rang out and the servant had fallen dead. A round hole between his eyes.

Reacting instantly, Richard had grabbed his sword and dashed down the narrow staircase in rapid pursuit of the assassin. Shirt open and flying about him, he had run out into the courtyard of the inn, scattering three honking geese before heading down an alley and across a road toward the village square.

A cart had come to a halt just before the fleeing man, which slowed his progress, and Drayton was able to recognize Carver. He was quickly upon him, brandishing his sword like a madman.

Throwing his pistol at Drayton's face, Carver had managed to draw his own sword as Richard ducked from the flying weapon. But Drayton recovered instantly and lunged forward, the tip of his sword catching the hilt of Carver's, flinging it from his hand to land clattering upon the brown cobblestones.

His own wounds at this man's hands—Lisa—weeks of weary pursuit—his fondness for Ned—it might have been one or an accumulation of all of these that made the rage in Richard finally erupt. With a roar that struck fear into all who watched, the wild, half-clad giant struck, hacking at Carver until he fell in a bloody heap at his feet.

Clarendon had not forgiven Drayton. He had wanted Carver alive. There were names he had been anxious to learn. Perhaps Stavely could have been convicted on Carver's word. Now, there was no chance of that.

He decided to send Drayton out of the country for a while, until everything simmered down, and Charles had agreed. Information was required on the Dutch shipping. Drayton could do a great deal to redeem himself if he obtained it.

The king planned a farewell party for Richard the night before he was to sail. Not a large party—only Drayton's oldest friends.

Christina had come on the arm of the Earl of Cranford, a crony from Richard's gaming days. Charles had frowned when he saw the wench. He wanted no altercations tonight. But Drayton, he was relieved to see, only watched in amusement as Christina flirted with this man and that. She kept looking over at him, trying to catch his eye, but he ignored her.

Richard was not interested in women tonight, nor had he been since his departure from Stavely Manor. Week after week he had focused his thoughts on nothing but revenge on Carver, and when he had finally killed the man, revenge had been replaced by sorrow. He blamed himself for his manservant's death. He still did.

By midnight he was quite drunk, and the king, seated near him at a massive carved table, was in like condition.

Christina was now playing some sort of card game with an actress, who was the latest of the king's favorites, and two young gallants.

"Terrible dinner," Charles said to Richard. "Sorry about that."

"Didn't notice," Drayton held out his goblet for a footman to refill.

"I ordered household expenditures be trimmed this autumn, and trim them they did. Cut down the dinner courses to ten."

"Quite enough."

"You think so?"

"Assuredly."

Charles looked over at the table where Christina was playing cards.

"Warned you about that wench. Told you not to stay away too long."

Drayton waved a hand to indicate his lack of concern. "Stopped paying her rent months ago."

"Still has eyes for you, though."

"Faithless wench! Like all of them. Faithless!"

Charles stared at him, his hooded eyes sweeping over the man who sprawled in the carved armchair beside him. One arm rested on the table, the fingers clasped around the stem of a brandy goblet. His neck cloth was askew and his velvet coat hung carelessly open. An unruly lock of golden hair hung over his forehead.

"Whatever happened to that raven-haired little beauty with the eyes?" Charles suddenly asked.

Drayton's brow furrowed. "Don't know who you mean."

"Course you do. Little wench in Essex. Lisa, methinks her name was. Had the bluest eyes."

Drayton sat up in his chair. "How d'you know about her?" he asked thickly.

Charles grinned. "Forgot. Promised her I wouldn't tell you."

"Tell me what?" Drayton's clouded brain was clearing.

"Suppose it doesn't matter now. Long behind you."

"Did you meet Lisa when you came to Stavely Manor, sire?" He was sober now, stone sober.

"Nay, 'twas when I stayed with Ellsbury." Charles stroked his chin. "Damnedest thing. Went to my bedchamber one night and this enchanting little creature was in my bed. Seemed to be fast asleep. Figured Ellsbury had given me a delightful little gift. Should have known. Wasn't Ellsbury's style. . . ." He lapsed into silence.

"Pray go on," Drayton urged, unable to hide his impatience.

"Wench was very drowsy, but warm and—er—not unfriendly. Quite eager, if I remember. But in the middle of it all what does she do? Calls me, 'Richard,' plain as day."

"What!"

"Aye, for some reason she thought I was *you*, Drayton. Came to her senses quick enough when she realized who I was. Quite horrified, in fact. Hardly flattering." He gave a self-deprecating laugh. "Made me promise I wouldn't tell you about it. Seems someone had drugged and brought her there. Put her in my bed. Some kind of prank, I suppose. Got her out of the place without anyone seeing. Sent her back to the Manor. Always wondered what happened to her. Seemed inordinately fond of you, Richard."

The man beside him uttered a groan of anguish. "Oh my God! What have I done?"

"What's the matter?"

"I knew she had been with another man. Wouldn't listen . . . Tormented her . . ."

"Methinks you made a grievous mistake. That one was well worth keeping."

Drayton struggled to his feet. "I must see her. Must explain."

"Impossible! You sail in a few hours, Drayton. Your trunks are already aboard."

"Must write her then."

"There are writing materials in the desk in the salon next door. Don't be long"—he grinned—"or I'll drink all the good brandy."

Richard struggled to express his feelings in the brief missive that he managed to write to Lisa. He asked her forgiveness, told her how much he loved her, begged her to write him immediately. Someone would see that he got her letter, wherever he was. He completed the letter, put seal to it and gave it to a footman outside the door, with a gold piece and the instructions to have it delivered promptly.

Unfortunately, Christina, looking for Drayton, saw this transaction occur and when Drayton had gone back to the party, she approached the footman for a look at the letter.

Flirting freely with him, she managed to see that it was addressed to Lisa, and claiming she was a close friend, she obtained the letter, promising to deliver it herself.

Afterward, it was an easy matter to enter the salon and toss the letter into the fireplace, where a hot fire was burning. Christina watched as it blackened and the edges curled.

"Goodbye, Lisa." She gave a triumphant smile. "Goodbye for *good!*"

* * *

As the months went by, Peter's kindness to Lisa began to win her love. It was not the same sort of love as she had felt for Richard. But Peter gave her a feeling of security and affection which she grew to cherish. There was something so dependable about him. With his dairy herd and farmlands, he belonged to a way of life that had continuity, that depended on the seasons and the weather.

Sitting quietly with Peter in the evening, sewing or playing the few simple songs she knew on the virginal, Lisa wondered whether, if she had never known Richard, she would have fallen in love with this man.

Peter was such a fine-looking man and he had the kindest eyes. He was so solicitous of her welfare and so quick to sense a change in her mood and try to cheer her if she were downcast. Yet, her mind could not help darting back to Richard. . . .

Richard so tall, so prepossessing with his glorious golden hair, his amazing emerald eyes. What they had so briefly shared had been so warm, so happy, so perfect. . . .

On a cold March night, with the wind whistling around the old house and the rain drumming on the windowpanes, Lisa lay on her bed, her knuckles white as she gripped the bedsheet, perspiration pouring down her contorted face.

Zada wiped her forehead. "Not much longer. Bare down again, Lisa. Hard!"

"I can't any more, Zada. I'm so tired. So very tired."

"Just once more for me, child. That's it! That's it!"

Lisa's babe was born in the early morning. A nine-pound boy with a mass of dark hair. When he was placed in her arms, she kissed him and then she looked him all over. With relief she saw that he bore no obvious resemblance to anyone. His skin seemed to be fair, more like hers than the swarthy Charles, but that was all she could tell.

Tears of exhaustion welled up behind Lisa's eyelids. "Here we are," she said silently to her son. "We had rather a hard time of it for a while, you and I, but we came through. We both must continue to be strong, my little son. You see, we are going to lose one another in a few weeks. But you will love your new mother. She will be good to you and love you dearly. As for your new father . . ." Lisa shuddered. "Peter says it is not likely he will live past your babyhood. You will then be heir to Stavely Manor and things will be set right there at last."

Zada took the child from his weary mother's arms.

"You must rest now, Lisa, and sleep."

Lisa closed her eyes. During the months she had carried her child, it had not seemed such a difficult thing to give him up. But now that she had seen him and held him in her arms, she realized how hard it was going to be.

Mary had already been at Ellsbury for a fortnight and now that the child was born, she stayed on for three weeks more. Lisa enjoyed her company, especially as she was forcing herself to see less and less of the baby.

This was possible because a wet nurse had been found. Her name was Mrs. Riley and she was to accompany Mary and the child home to Stavely Manor. She was never told that the babe she nursed was not Mary's own.

Lisa let Mary name the baby and Mary called him James after her father. When she saw Mary's joy in the child, the happiness that filled her eyes when she held him, Lisa knew she was doing the right thing.

Mary thought Basil looked a little better when she returned with the child to Stavely Manor. His disease seemed to be in a temporary remission, but he wore his periwig constantly, due to having lost thick patches of his hair.

It was easy to see Basil's pride when he looked upon the boy. James was a strong child, with a lusty cry when he was hungry.

"I have called him James," Mary told him, "after my father. I think he looks a little like him with those light eyes."

Basil gave a reluctant nod. "But he has my dark hair and strength of build."

Mary only smiled.

Soon after Mary had departed from Ellsbury Manor, Lisa told Peter that she must leave. She would at last obey the wishes of Valerie Manning and go to her adoptive grandparents.

"I won't let you go, Lisa," Peter said. "You told me how you hated them for what they had done to your mother. You will be unhappy there." His eyes, so like Mary's, pleaded with her. "Why won't you let me look after you? I love you."

"I know you do, Peter, and I am honored and grateful. I love you too, but not in the way you deserve."

"If you care even a little for me 'tis enough. I swear it. I will be good to you, Lisa. I won't make demands on you until you are ready. Pray think on it. Take as long as you like."

Lisa did think on it and she realized she was afraid—afraid to make a commitment to him. She had loved Richard so deeply and it had given her nothing but anguish and grief. He had not loved her enough. Now, she felt, she did not love Peter enough. She was afraid she might put him through the same agony.

"Why will you not marry Peter, Lisa?" Zada asked her as they walked in the garden that same week. "I know he has asked you again. He loves you dearly and is so devoted to you."

"I know that, Zada. But I don't love him enough and I doubt that I ever will."

"I wish you could have seen him as I did after the child was born. He came quietly into the room and looked down at you sleeping. He brushed the hair back from your forehead and, Lisa, his eyes were so full of feeling I could have wept. I've never seen such tenderness and love."

"I only wish I could return it."

"Why won't you admit to yourself that you will never see Richard Drayton again. Forget him."

"Forget him?" Lisa cried. "Don't you think I have tried? The trouble is that in my eyes no man will ever measure up to him. Oh, I know he wasn't perfect," she hastened to add. "He was stubborn and quick-tempered and insensitive and jealous, but he was also gentle and compassionate and when he touched me . . . when he . . ." her eyes filled with tears.

"You remind me of your mother when your father died," Zada said quietly.

"Nay! I wish I could be more like her, Zada. Mama was such a strong woman. Strong-willed and proud and independent . . ."

Zada laughed. "And you are *not*, my sweet? Has it never occurred to you why Evan Manning was attracted to your mama or Richard to you? You are as she was—your own woman—therefore a perfect match for a man of self-confidence. Any man worth his salt is only attracted to a woman who has some backbone."

"And Peter?"

"You may never reach the heights of passion with him, but he is a strong man in his own right. He'll look after you—allow for your whims—and he is stubborn in his quiet way—enough not to let you get away with too much."

"I don't love him, Zada."

"You've had that, child."

"But with Peter . . . will it be enough?"

Zada shrugged. "I can't answer that for you."

"Sometimes," Lisa admitted, her voice dropping to a whisper, "sometimes I ache for Richard. Actually ache for his smile and his kiss and the touch of his hands. How can I forget him? My body won't let me. 'Tis as if my heart had been sealed and no one else could ever open it again."

"Are you still hoping he will return to you some day?"

Lisa smiled, a sad little smile. "I'm a fool, aren't I?"

That night, Peter again asked Lisa to marry him. This time, she accepted him.

When she lifted her mouth to his, she felt for the first time the demand behind his gentle kiss, but no fire was kindled in her veins.

She did not mind. She had been burned once by an affair that had been wildly combustible. She wasn't seeking that again. It was over. Finished. She wanted something now that would be the complete antithesis of what she had known with Richard. Something safe and solid. Peter's arms offered her that. Devotion, comfort and security—all she needed—would ever need.

It was a simple wedding, held in the Ellsbury chapel. Lisa's only regret was that Mary could not be present.

Little Jamie, as Mary called him now, had developed colic and was fretful and she would not leave him. Basil was again laid up in bed and it was obvious that Mary had her hands full.

Zada was present to see the beautiful bride that Lisa made. Dressed in creamy lace with an exquisite shawl of the same lace draped over her head, she had never looked more lovely.

As she calmly said her vows, she thought to herself that finally she was putting Richard Drayton out of her life forever. All the torment was over. She would find peace at last with Peter.

Lying that night in the huge master bed, her head pillowed against his arm, Peter kissed Lisa tenderly.

"My wife . . ." he whispered. "I have wanted you for so long. . . . How I love you!"

"Peter," she murmured, happy in the warm glow of his love, "my husband . . ."

He looked down at her solemnly. "I swear before God, Lisa, I will give my life to make you happy."

She put a finger to his lips. "Don't do that, Peter. I want you alive and here . . . in my arms."

"I am the luckiest man in the world," he whispered.

Lisa sighed, letting Peter take her then with exquisite tenderness. He was as she had known he would be, lovingly considerate of her feelings and her pleasure.

Yet she could not help but remember the passion of Richard's savage kisses, how he had torn the clothes from her body, how they had rolled abandonedly in the soft mud of a stream bed, reached ecstasy in the wildness of a summer storm. She did not realize that her thoughts had brought her body to life.

Peter, unable to believe she would respond to him so readily, remembered his first wife's timid reluctance and modesty. Lisa was so warm in comparison, so eager.

Although her body was being aroused by Peter, Richard filled Lisa's thoughts and when the culmination came, although they were both unmindful of it, she breathed his name aloud.

In the morning, Peter made love to her again. He was kind and gentle and adoring, but Lisa knew now that she must resign herself to the fact that it would never be the same as it had been with Richard. Peter did not feed the hunger in her, or seem to want any more than dutiful acceptance. It was fortunate, for it was all she felt capable of giving him.

The spring and summer of 1664 were unusually dry and hot. In early June, the English fleet battled the Dutch off Lowestoft and twenty-four Dutch ships were sunk or captured, temporarily crippling the Dutch navy. Few English seamen were lost and the Londoners celebrated the news joyously with bonfires blazing in the streets and firework displays.

Bad news, however, followed the good. The dread bubonic plague had erupted in the heart of London.

People poured from the plague-stricken city into the country and Peter graciously invited numbers of his old friends to stay for visits that extended through the summer and into September.

Lisa, from necessity, developed quickly into a charming and accomplished hostess. She found herself quite at ease with her husband's titled friends. Indeed, the new Lady Ellsbury, if not completely happy, was serene and content.

Chapter Thirty-three

AT THE END OF OCTOBER, MARY STAVELY WROTE TO LISA, inviting her and Peter to come to Stavely Manor for a visit. Basil, she explained, would not be there, having felt London safe enough now from the plague to allow a visit to his physicians. She spent the rest of the letter extolling the merits of seven-month-old Jamie.

"Would it bother you to see him?" Peter asked her, after reading the letter.

"A little, perhaps," Lisa admitted, "but I must get used to it, mustn't I? Do let us go, Peter."

"We are invited to a Guy Fawkes Day celebration at the Dorrington's on the fifth," Peter reminded her, "but actually their estate is closer to Stavely Manor than to Ellsbury. I'm sure they would not mind if we brought Mary with us. They have invited her and Basil again and again and Basil has always refused."

"How long will we be away?"

"About a fortnight altogether. We'll leave for Stavely Manor the day after tomorrow."

Lisa had Zada pack her most attractive gowns. Since their marriage, Peter had spoiled her outrageously, letting her order dozens of lengths of material and bringing a dressmaker from

London in the spring to stay, as it turned out, for the entire summer. He insisted that his beautiful wife be beautifully attired.

The Ellsbury jewels were now Lisa's. Some were a little ornate for her taste, but observing which pieces she did not wear, Peter ordered them reset to suit her.

He was always sensitive to her every thought and mood, Lisa realized, loving him for it, and yet she often wished he was more open with her.

He never confided his true feelings or his problems to her. Nothing serious was ever discussed between them, because he didn't want to worry or upset her. It made her feel more like a pampered pet than a helpmate.

They arrived at Stavely Manor in the late afternoon. Zada and Peter's manservant were to follow them in a separate coach, with the luggage.

It had been nearly a year since Lisa had seen Stavely Manor. Compared to Ellsbury, it looked dark and small to her.

Dressed in a blue velvet gown and matching cloak trimmed with soft silvery-gray fur, Lisa looked her best as Peter helped her to alight from the coach.

Mary met them in the great hall, her eyes sparkling with happiness at the sight of them. She kissed Lisa first and then stood back to look at her, holding both her hands.

"Marriage agrees with you, Lisa. You've never looked more lovely." She kissed her brother. "I suppose you're still keeping her hidden away in the country. I don't blame you, Peter. Lisa would cause quite a stir in London."

"I am well aware of that, dear sister," he smiled. "We haven't been married long enough. I still want her all to myself." Lovingly, his brown eyes caressed his wife.

"You will want to go to your rooms to freshen up before we sup," Mary said, "but first, I want you to see Jamie, as he will be put back to bed soon."

She led the way up the stairs and down the hall to the nursery. Lisa felt a stir to her heart as Mary pushed open the door and they entered.

This was the room where she had given Richard the copy she had made of the bond. There was the same cradle and the rocking chair. . . . Mrs. Riley, the nurse, rose from it and came toward them, Jamie held against her shoulder.

He was a sturdy little child with a mop of dark curls and when he saw them he grinned, toothlessly, and held out his arms to Mary.

She ran to him and gathered him up, returning to where Lisa and Peter stood just inside the doorway.

"Isn't he beautiful?" Mary said, full of pride, as she held him up for them to see.

A ray of fading sunlight from the window illuminated the child's cherubic face, making Lisa gasp. Her fingers dug into Peter's arm and he put a hand over hers, patting it gently, thinking he should not have brought her, that the sight of this baby she had born and had given away had obviously distressed her.

Lisa was gazing into the little boy's face with growing horror. Jamie's eyes, so big, so bright, were a clear emerald green!

She had no idea later what she had said or done, but she must have made the proper remarks and responses, for nothing had gone amiss.

She was shown to her room, not her old room, but one next to Peter's that had a connecting door.

Automatically, she drew off her cloak and gloves, placing them on the bed, and then sank down into a little armchair.

She did not cry. Gazing dully at the patterned rug before her, she sat completely still. She was stunned!

Jamie was Richard's son, not the king's! She would have known those eyes anywhere! There was not the slightest doubt in her mind. Would she have given him up so readily to Mary if she had known before?

In her heart she knew she would not have been able. She had lost Richard. He was gone from her forever. And now she knew she had given up the only part of him she might ever have possessed. His son.

God in heaven, did Mary know? And Basil? What of him? The child's very life might be in danger at Basil's hands, if he thought that Richard had fathered him. And Peter? Had he noticed and begun to put everything together? He had thought the king had stolen her innocence while she was drugged. What would he do if he knew she had given herself to Richard?

Lisa did not know how many minutes had passed before the door from Peter's room opened and he came in. He had a goblet of brandy in his hand.

"Drink this," he said. "I think you need it."

She took it from him gratefully, taking a long drink. It burned her throat, but she did not care. She took another sip.

"I'm sorry," he said quietly. "I should not have brought you. It has only upset you to see the child." He gently smoothed back a strand of her hair that had come loose from a bone bodkin.

"I'll be all right," she managed.

"If God be kind to us, we will have our own children for you to love," he said softly.

"But not Jamie!" she wanted to cry out. "Not Richard's son!"

Where had he been conceived? She wondered. In a soft stream bed, perhaps, or during a wild summer storm? No! She must not think of that. She drained her goblet of brandy.

"Mary will expect us downstairs," she said. "I must hurry and change."

"I'm afraid our luggage has not arrived," Peter explained. "Something must have delayed the other coach. You look lovely as you are."

"Go down without me, Peter. I will join you shortly."

"As you wish." He patted her shoulder. "There is no reason why you have to see the child again, if he disturbs you."

Lisa rose when he had left and went over to stand before the mirror above the dressing table. Was that white face that stared back at her really her own? The violet-blue eyes seemed so utterly lifeless. Lifting her hands, she began to tidy her hair.

When she was ready to go downstairs, she made for her bedchamber door, changed her mind and turned to the door to Peter's room and opened it. For a moment she stood still in the doorway.

It was Richard's room! The room where she and Richard had made love so often! She stared at the huge bed and remembered the storm and how he had dried her body with the coverlet and made such passionate love to her. She closed her eyes. Why hadn't she noticed the rooms that Mary had given them? She had been too upset, she realized, when she had left the nursery. Oh God, would Peter expect to take her in the same bed? She couldn't bear the thought! She couldn't bear to even be in the room another minute!

As she turned back, she saw the decanter of brandy on a table by the door. She picked it up, taking it back to her own room where she refilled her goblet.

She could face them now, Lisa thought, descending the stairs. Although it had made her feel a little light-headed, she had needed that second brandy to get her through what lay ahead.

The dinner had not been as bad as Lisa had feared. Now, back in her bedchamber, Lisa poured herself more brandy—to help her sleep, she reasoned—and sitting down at her dressing table she began brushing out her dark silky hair.

"Your hair is so beautiful, Lisa," Peter said from the open doorway. "I love to watch you brush it."

She put down the brush and looked at him. He wore a dark plum-colored dressing gown and his hands were thrust deep in its pockets. There was a look in his brown eyes that was full of meaning.

"Come to me," he said very low, before returning to his room.

Lisa rose and blew out the candle on the dressing table. The full moon made the room almost as bright as day. She went through the door into Peter's bedchamber. He had disrobed and was already in bed, lying back against the pillows, his arms crossed behind his head.

"Come here," he murmured.

She closed the door and came toward him. As she got close to the bed, she stopped and slowly, sensuously, she drew off her nightdress.

Peter gave a gasp. Lisa's white skin glowed like marble in the moonlight, as if a goddess of old had come alive and was moving gracefully toward him.

For a moment she stood still in front of him and then he let out a groan and reached for her. He had never felt such a terrible desire. His whole body burned with it!

She smiled tantalizingly down at him as he threw back the covers and drew her into the bed. Then, unexpectedly, with a lithe little movement, she was on top of him, straddling him.

"Let me ride you," she whispered, reaching for the already turgid organ.

"Lisa!" He pushed her hands away. He was shocked beyond belief! "You've had too much brandy! You're acting like a little—"

"Whore," she laughed, and the laugh was soft and husky. "Let me be your whore tonight, Peter. Let me—"

"No!" Quickly, purposely, he turned her over onto her back and then he was pressing himself against her, forcing her to open her legs to him.

"I can't wait," he said hoarsely, his searing flesh demanding entrance.

One of his hands had slipped between her thighs to caress her, and now his mouth covered hers in a hot, demanding kiss. Before she could get her breath, he drove into her, thrusting deep, pumping urgently, faster and faster. She had no time to respond completely before it was all over. She could have wept!

Tonight, she had wanted Peter, wanted him to make her forget Richard and the many times he had made love to her in this same bed. Now, all he had succeeded in doing was to make her long for Richard and remember what a magnificent lover he had been.

"I'm sorry, Lisa," Peter said, still panting from his exertion.

"It's all right," she lied.

"Nay, I behaved like a brute. It was because you acted so . . . wantonly. . . ."

"Wantonly?"

He nodded, pushing back a soft curl from her cheek. "Don't ever talk or act like that again, Lisa. It's not you. I know that. It was the brandy talking."

"But—"

"When a man marries, he wants to be the one to instruct and guide his wife. Only trollops institute the act. A lady merely submits to her husband."

"Is that all you want from me? Mere submission?"

"All? Isn't that enough?"

"Would it disturb you to learn you had married no lady?" She rose up on one elbow, smiling down at him seductively. "I don't want to just submit, Peter. I want to enjoy it too."

"Lisa!"

But her fiery little tongue had darted between his lips and she was reaching for him, her small hands caressing, enticing him, the way Richard had taught her, willing him to harden for her again.

Peter pulled back, pushing her hands away as if they were slimy tentacles.

"How do you know such things?" his voice was rough, shaking. "'Tis more than the brandy, isn't it? Isn't it, Lisa?" His fingers had grasped her shoulders hurtfully. "I thought the king had taken advantage of an innocent maid, but you . . ." His voice croaked. "Have you known others? Have you, Lisa?"

Lisa sighed. This room had evoked too many memories, and they and the brandy had made her go too far. "I can't lie to you, Peter. You are likely to know soon enough. There was one other."

He groaned and sank back against the pillows. "Oh God, who was he? Who taught you such depravities?"

"Depravities!" Her tongue had trouble with the word. "Are simple expressions of love between a man and a woman deprav—"

"Did you love him?" he demanded.

"Do you really want to know?"

"No!" he cried, his voice raw, "but I must be told." He sat up, looking down at her, and her heart constricted at the hurt in his eyes. "Haven't you deceived me enough?"

"I didn't mean to deceive you."

"Who was he?"

"You just assumed it was the king who took my maiden-hood."

"WHO WAS HE?" his voice was a growl now.

"Richard," she said softly. "Richard Drayton."

"Oh God!" his voice broke.

"I loved him, Peter."

"And the bastard took advantage of that love and seduced you."

"Nay! You must not think—"

His jaw worked. "How many times did you lie with that swine? Once, twice . . . ?"

She saw tears of anguish in his eyes. She had hurt him badly. "Don't, Peter!"

"How many times, damn you!"

"I didn't count."

"Damn him to hell!" he cried, and it was more like a sob.

She placed a gentle hand on his shoulder, but he shook it off.

"I thought he was my friend and yet he went after you . . . knowing I loved you. . . ."

"Richard knew me before I met you, Peter. He thought me beneath him. He never knew my true identity."

"Yet he took you. He had the gall to—"

"Peter!" She put her arms out to him imploringly.

The coverlet dropped to reveal her naked breasts and he

thrust it roughly over her. "What was it?" he asked. "What was it about the child that upset you today?" He was fighting to control himself. His voice was ice cold. "What was it that made you need the brandy to forget?"

She said nothing.

"Jamie's hair is dark like yours," he mused. "A little more curly. My God, the eyes! That's it, isn't it? His eyes are green! The same color as Richard's. He is not the king's son, is he? Richard is his father!"

Lisa nodded. "I didn't know. I swear I thought 'twas the king who had fathered—"

His lip curled. "How could you know when you had slept in both men's beds."

There was a moment of silence.

"I suppose I deserved that," she whispered. "Don't hate me, Peter. I could not bear that."

"It might make it easier if I could," he sighed. "But I love you too much."

"I should not have married you. 'Twas not fair to you. You have been so good to me."

Peter did not hear her. "You always seemed to be quarreling with Richard," he was saying, almost to himself, "snapping at each other. I thought you hated him."

"There were times when I did."

"And now?"

"Now it is all over."

"Is it, Lisa?" He turned her face to his. "Then why did it upset you so much to realize the child was his?"

"Mary," she said quickly. "If Basil guesses that Richard fathered the child he believes to be his, he will take it out on Mary. God only knows what he would do to her."

Peter stared at her.

"Mary wanted a child so badly. 'Tis all my fault," Lisa burst into tears.

Peter started to pat her gently and then she was in his arms and he was holding her close against him.

"Lisa . . . Lisa . . ." He tried to soothe her, but she continued to sob, deep, heartrending sobs of despair that had been building up in her since she had seen the child.

"I'm so sorry," he implored. "Forgive me for all I said to you. I did not mean . . ." He stroked her hair.

"Mary has always been so good to me," she gulped.

"I would not worry too much about Basil," he said to her. "Mary told me the reason he has gone to London is because he is much worse. His heavy drinking has not helped. He has had liver problems and something is wrong with his heart. I doubt he has long to live."

"Poor Mary."

"It will only be a relief to her, I am sure." He looked at Lisa. "Did Mary know about you and Richard?"

"Nay." Lisa wiped at her eyes. "She warned me once about him—that he was a womanizer—but I did not listen. I—I thought he loved me."

"How would you know about a man like him? You so young and innocent. Lisa, can you forgive me?"

"'Tis I who should be asking your forgiveness, Peter."

He still held her against his warm body and her own was beginning to respond to his closeness, his nakedness. She moved against him, but he pushed her gently away, laying her down on the pillows, pulling the covers over her and tucking them in about her as he would a child.

"Go to sleep," he murmured. "You are my wife now and you must forget the past and all its unpleasantness. Everything will be all right."

He lay down beside her, not touching her, and closed his eyes.

She could not sleep. The room held too many memories. She lay taut, her eyes wide open, her senses alive. She wanted to throw her arms around him, press against him, reveal her desire. Her body ached for fulfillment. She wanted him so. Needed him to assuage the painful memories of Richard that were plaguing her; needed to be taken roughly, savagely, so she could forget another strong, hard body that had taken her again and again in wild, unbridled passion in this very bed.

"Oh Richard," she sobbed to herself, "why can't I forget you? Why did you use me and leave me to this torment?"

Beside her, Peter also lay awake. He heard her sighs, felt her restlessness, and sensed that her thoughts were not of him, but of a man he had thought to be his friend.

"You and Richard were lovers, weren't you?" Mary accused Lisa the next morning in her bedchamber. When she asked the question, she could not help but glance down at the sofa on which they sat, remembering herself in Richard's arms.

"Yes," Lisa admitted quietly. "I loved him very much."

Mary looked at her closely. "You are a very good actress, my dear. I thought the two of you did nothing but quarrel."

"It was often like that between us. We either fought or we . . ." She bit her lip.

"Why did you not confide in me?" Mary asked. Her soft brown eyes bore the same hurt look that her brother's had the night before.

Lisa looked away. "I thought you would be disappointed in me," she said. Her gaze returned to Mary. "I was right, wasn't I?"

Mary nodded. "I believed your moral standards to be higher," she said primly.

"They were, until I fell in love with Richard. Then, when he held me in his arms, when he told me he loved me, well, nothing else seemed to matter."

Mary's eyes clouded. "I can believe that."

"But I was a fool!" Lisa cried. "I should have listened to you. You warned me about him."

"It still hurts, doesn't it?" Mary said quietly. "You have not forgotten him."

"No. Just when I think I have, something happens. Like—like seeing Jamie yesterday."

"His eyes are very like Richard's, are they not?"

"May I ask when you realized that?"

"A month ago. I have not let Basil see him in the sunlight since."

"Oh Mary, you can't go on hiding it—"

"I can," she said resolutely, "and I will. Basil has not long to live. He knows it and so do I."

Lisa got up and went to stand by the window. After a moment she turned back to Mary.

"Why did you ask me here?" Her voice was very low. "You must have wanted me to know that Jamie was Richard's son. Why did you want to hurt me, Mary?"

"Hurt you?" Mary looked stunned by her words. "But I did not— Oh Lisa, I would never do that. It was because I was afraid that when you *did* see him . . . when you realized . . . you would want him back."

"Back!"

"I love Jamie so. 'Twould be terrible to give him up now, but 'twould be even worse in a year or two or whenever you saw him and learned the truth."

"Oh Mary, I would never take him from you. Surely, you know me better than that."

"But you loved Richard—"

"And did *you* not love him?" Lisa asked, her eyes boring into Mary's.

Mary's soft eyes lowered. "I was very fond of him," she admitted. She took Lisa's hand. "Does Peter know that Richard fathered—"

"Aye. I told him last night."

"How is he taking it?"

"At first he . . . but I think it is all right now. Oh, Mary, he is such a good man—so kind and understanding. I do love him."

"But 'tis not the same as it was with Richard," Mary said perceptively.

"No," Lisa acknowledged. "Perhaps given time . . ."

"I hope so," Mary sighed. "I hope so for both your sakes."

Peter had changed. Even Mary noticed that he seemed quieter. In the days that followed, he began retreating more and more into himself. Lisa soon realized that he was drinking more than usual. He made love to her, it seemed, only when he had sufficently fortified himself with brandy, and yet he was always gentle with her.

The night before they were to leave for the Guy Fawkes celebration at the Dorrington's, Lisa awoke to see Peter standing beside her bed. She could see, in the candlelight, that his dark brown hair was dishevelled, as were his clothes. His soft brown eyes were bloodshot and full of tears.

"How can I?" he asked, his voice slurred from drink. "How can I make you love me?"

"Oh Peter," she cried, sitting up and reaching for his hand. "I *do* love you."

"But not like him. Never like him. What was it about Richard you can't forget? Was he so good a lover?"

Lisa put a hand up to his mouth. "I won't listen to this, Peter. What has come over you? Have I not been a good and loving wife to you?"

"Aye, but you've never been *all* mine. Always been a part of you I couldn't reach. The part that still belongs to Richard."

"Don't, Peter," she whispered, drawing him down to her,

kissing him tenderly as she would a hurt child. Without meaning to, he kept reviving her memories of Richard and now she again felt the loss.

"Make love to me," she murmured.

He tried, but it was no good and he wept again at his inadequacy. It wasn't until he fell asleep in her arms that Lisa let her own tears fall.

She must never again think of Richard and the love they had shared. She must forget the past once and for all. She must think only of Peter. Peter needed her—all of her. He was entitled not only to her body, but to her heart as well. Given time—given patience—one day she might be free of her memories to give it.

Chapter Thirty-four

THE FIFTH OF NOVEMBER DAWNED AND IT WAS A LOVELY, SUNNY autumn day.

"We will depart for the Dorrington's after lunch," Peter declared.

Lisa instructed Zada to pack for her. The party would be followed by fireworks so would end late, and they were invited to stay the night.

Before leaving Ellsbury Manor, Lisa had decided on the gown she would wear. A deep golden silk, it was simple in style, but complemented her creamy shoulders and slender waist.

Zada was in the midst of folding up the petticoats when there was a knock at the door of Lisa's bedchamber.

"Come in," Lisa said, rising from her dressing table.

Mary entered, clearly agitated. "I cannot go with you," she said.

"But why?" Lisa asked. "It has all been arranged."

"Jamie was fretful all last night and Mrs. Riley says he is cutting his first tooth."

Lisa smiled. "'Tis only nautural, isn't it? Surely you—"

"But I cannot leave him! His little head is so hot and his cheeks so red."

Lisa was at once anxious. "Has he a fever?"

"Only a small one. The nurse says it often happens when a child is teething."

"There, you see? There is nothing to worry about, Mary."

"I could not go. I wouldn't enjoy myself. I would keep worrying."

"We were so looking forward to having you come with us, Mary."

"Another time I would love to go," Mary said distractedly. "Now I had best get back to Jamie." She hurried from the room.

"That Lady Stavely," Zada shook her head. "She will never leave that babe. He means everything to her. The child will be badly spoiled, mark my words."

Lisa was still staring at the door that had closed behind Mary. "If anything should happen to Jamie," she said quietly, "I don't know what would become of Mary."

Sir Bruce and Lady Alicia Dorrington had a magnificent home, and the evening had been filled with gaiety. There had been an excellent supper for thirty guests, followed by much laughter as, despite the cool November air, all the guests had ventured forth outside, wrapped in warm cloaks and clutching tankards of steaming cider.

As was customary, a giant bonfire had been lit on the hillside overlooking the village, and an effigy of Guy Fawkes was burned. This commemorated the Gunpowder Plot in 1605, an abortive conspiracy led by Guy Fawkes to blow up the Parliament buildings while King James I and Parliament were in assembly. To end the celebration, a spectacular display of fireworks was set off.

"I'm sorry Mary had to miss the fireworks," Lisa said to Peter, her eyes wide as another glittering panorama burst forth into the clear night sky.

"She will have her own little display." Peter squeezed her hand. "I left some fireworks with Trent at Stavely Manor. He and Matthew are going to set them off on the lea and Mary can see them from the house."

"Oh Peter, how thoughtful of you! The villagers and tenants will enjoy them too." She reached up to give him a little kiss on the cheek. Peter beamed.

The beautiful Lady Ellsbury had attracted a great deal of attention at the party, particularly from the gentlemen, but she had made it clear to one and all that she had eyes only for her husband.

After being slapped on the back by several of his old friends and told how lucky he was, Peter seemed to relax and become more like his old self.

"Matthew says you are to watch out the window at ten o'clock, m'lady," Zada said to Mary, who was sitting rocking little Jamie in a chair in the nursery.

"What on earth for?" Mary raised her head.

"Sir Peter left fireworks with Trent to set off on the lea."

Mary smiled. "How like him not to want me to miss anything. Tell the servants, Zada, if they don't already know. They may want to go outside to watch the display. Do go yourself, if you wish. Take Mrs. Riley. I will stay here and view it from the nursery window." This was all said in a whisper, so as not to wake the child who had finally fallen asleep in her arms.

Jamie woke again just before ten o'clock, howling. Mary rushed over to the cradle where she had placed him and scooped him up.

"Poor darling, there, there," she crooned, rocking him back and forth in her arms. She rubbed her gold wedding band over his inflamed gums and he sucked a little at it before starting to howl again. Mary carried him over to the window and pulled back the heavy draperies.

"Look out there, little one. Watch the showers of sparkling light."

She held the child up to the window as the first explosion occurred, lighting the night sky and the whole nursery with its brilliance.

The baby stopped in mid-cry, blinking his big bright eyes, focusing them in the direction of the exploding fireworks.

There was a sound of a door opening and closing and heavy footsteps as someone crossed the nursery floor.

"So there you are," boomed Basil's voice. "Thought the whole house to be deserted."

Mary started and turned around to him just as another display of fireworks burst forth. This one was even brighter than the first and clearly illuminated Jamie's wide-eyed little face to Basil.

He took a step closer, his red-rimmed eyes riveted to the

child's. "My God, they're green!" he ejaculated. "Green as emeralds! Only one person I've ever known had eyes like that. Drayton! Richard Drayton!"

Basil stood for a stunned second staring down at the baby in Mary's trembling arms, while the veins stood out in his face and the color deepened to an apoplectic purple. Then he gave a roar like an enraged bull, and went for her.

In the same instant Mary moved, darting past him, running frantically for the door.

She had one hand on the latch when he grasped her wrist, wrenching her about. She went down on both her knees, protecting the child with her body for she had seen him draw his sword.

"No, Basil! Spare the child!"

"I'll not raise Drayton's bastard as my own!"

Mary screamed as the sword plunged. It pierced through the skin of her arm and the sharp tip stabbed into the child's shoulder.

High-pitched screams came from the baby as Basil withdrew the bloody blade and prepared to strike again.

In one motion, Mary put down the child and rose, giving a low growl like a mother lion protecting her cub. She sprang at Basil, clawing her fingernails down his cheek, gouging deeply, leaving a bloody trail.

Basil's sword clattered to the floor and his hand went to his face. "You'll be sorry for that," he bellowed. "I was right, by God. You did take Drayton to your bed, you damned little . . ."

Mary would have started for the door again, but she could not bring herself to leave the wounded babe. In that second of indecision, he was on her, his big hands seizing her by the throat, strong fingers closing over her windpipe, pressing brutally.

She tried to break his grip by grabbing his wrists, but it was futile; he only squeezed harder. The fireworks were still continuing outside, but even brighter lights were now flashing before Mary's eyes. Brighter . . . brighter . . . as thick thumbs crushed flesh and muscle.

Mary made a terrible gurgling noise in her throat and her bulging eyes flew to Basil's demonic face, the muscles straining, the teeth bared. It was the last she saw before darkness mercifully engulfed her.

Mary slid to the carpet in a limp heap, her head twisted at an odd angle, all the life strangled from her slight body.

Basil never looked at his dead wife as he stepped over her and reached for his sword. As he straightened up, he heard a noise.

Zada had been the only one to see Basil Stavely coming around from the stables and entering the house. For some reason, Zada felt she must follow him.

Entering the hall below, she had heard the screams from above and had rushed up the stairs and down the corridor to the nursery.

She knew she was too late when she saw Mary Stavely's contorted face as she collapsed on the carpet, but the babe was still alive. He was whimpering. She drew the sharp stiletto from beneath her skirts and picked up the child.

The old gypsy woman had never looked more fierce huddling in the corner by the door, knife drawn, the blood from the child's wound spreading on the carpet before her and dripping down the front of her blouse.

"You've killed them both," she shrieked. "A curse upon you, Basil Stavely! May you die as agonizing a death!"

The half-crazed man turned on her. "Go to hell, you old hag!"

He raised his sword, but something—the dagger, the glitter in the gypsy's eyes, a superstitious fear—stayed his hand, and he lowered it and strode past her out the open door.

Zada sat there, hearing in the distance his heavy tread on the stairs, the slamming of the great front door. Then she moved.

The fireworks display had ended and the laughing men and women were crossing the lawn and again entering the Dorrington's brightly lit home.

Suddenly, Lisa stopped and laid a hand on Peter's arm.

"We must get back to the manor house!" she exclaimed.

"What do you mean?"

"Peter, I beg you. I feel something is wrong. We must go back there tonight."

"But 'tis after midnight."

"'Tis a clear night. How long should it take us?"

"Two hours, perhaps."

"Peter, 'tis not a whim. I pray you, do this for me."

* * *

Lisa sat stiffly beside Peter in the coach as it careened along the country road on its way back to Stavely Manor. Her hands were twisting nervously in her lap.

"I think you are imagining things, Lisa. What could have happened?"

"Jamie. Perhaps something more serious was wrong with him. He had a fever. . . ."

"Nonsense. That child is as strong as an ox. Just like his father."

"Peter, please . . ."

"Sorry. I know I promised. . . . What's that fool coachman doing? I told him to hurry, but that last turn nearly had us in the ditch!"

"He doesn't seem to be slowing down," Lisa murmured. "He's probably been drinking."

The coach suddenly made a sickening lurch to the side and there was a wild yell from the box as the horses were pulled up short, snorting and pawing. The coach had come to a stop in the middle of the road, leaning over drunkenly to one side.

"Lost a wheel," Peter groaned. "Damn fool!"

He opened the door on the high side of the coach and got out. Lisa could hear him giving the coachman a piece of his mind as that man and a footman got down from the box.

"Do you want to stay there or come outside while they repair the wheel?" Peter asked, sticking his head in the open doorway and addressing Lisa.

"I'll come out," she said. "It's a beautiful starlit night and we'll probably be warmer walking about."

He was helping her down from the coach when they heard the hoofbeats of a horse approaching from the direction in which they were headed.

The hatless rider slowed down a little as he drew near them, and Lisa was able to see his scarred face clearly in the bright moonlight. There was dried blood on one of his cheeks and his eyes looked wild.

"Basil!" she cried aloud.

He stiffened as he heard his name called. He knew that voice! In order to get by the coach, he had to skirt his horse carefully around it and it was then that he saw Lisa, standing beside it.

There was the wench who had caused him so much grief!

Mary had been an obedient and docile wife before *she* had come to Stavely Manor! It was *she* who had ruined everything!

Abreast of Lisa now, he halted his horse and from beneath his cloak he brought forth a pistol and in one motion cocked and fired it straight at her!

Seeing his movement and the gleam of his weapon, Peter quickly threw himself in front of his wife. He took the full charge from the pistol in his chest!

Lisa screamed as Peter fell back, and tried to catch him as he crumpled against her. As Basil galloped off, she went down on her knees on the muddy road, cradling her husband's head in her lap and moaning, "Peter! Peter!"

He said only one word to her and that was to whisper her name. Lisa knelt there, stroking his hair, murmuring over and over, "I love you. I love you." But he could no longer hear her. Peter was dead.

The coachman had managed to get a shot off after Basil, but Stavely had escaped into the night. Now cold sober, the servant came over to examine Sir Peter.

He spoke to Lisa quietly. "He's dead, m'lady. Nothing we can do." He nodded to the footman. "We'll put him on the seat in the coach," he said. But the two of them almost had to pry him from Lisa's arms. She did not want to let him go.

After they had closed the coach door, the coachman suggested to Lisa that she get up on the box while they worked with the wheel. She shook her head.

She was in shock, her mind numb with disbelieving horror. Her face was a chalky white in color, her blue eyes enormous and yet strangely blank.

She got to her feet and stood by the side of the road, staring with unseeing eyes as the two men rolled back the wheel they had lost. Fortunately, the axle had not broken and they had but to find a stout tree limb with which to pry up the side of the coach so they could replace the wheel.

Lisa watched the hurried proceedings without saying a word, but when the coach was ready, she walked over to it and got in, sitting down on the seat across from where Peter lay. She reached over and gently closed his eyes and then the tears came. She sobbed uncontrollably all the way back to Stavely Manor.

* * *

It was nearly dawn when they arrived at the manor house, but one look at it and Lisa knew something was wrong. Lights were burning throughout the whole mansion.

Mrs. Pottle met her at the front door. She had been crying, and it was so unusual to see her express any emotion that Lisa stood for a second staring at her.

"What is the matter?" she asked the woman finally.

"'Tis her ladyship . . ." she began, and was again overcome for a minute, putting her apron up to her eyes.

"What has happened?" Lisa's voice had risen to almost an hysterical pitch.

Mrs. Pottle looked at her, her eyes widening at the sight of the blood splattered over her cloak.

"She's gone, m'lady."

"Gone? What do you mean?"

"The master came back while the fireworks were on and we were all outside watching them. He came back and went up to the nursery. Perhaps it was his illness—who knows what it was—but something caused him to go completely out of his head! He must have been raving mad, for he strangled her ladyship and thrust his sword into the babe!"

It was too much for Lisa. She crumpled to the floor in a dead faint.

Zada came into Lisa's bedchamber and stood with hands on hips looking at her mistress propped up in bed.

"'Tis been over a month. Don't you think it high time you left this room? You stay in here brooding from morning till night, taking all your meals on trays, never even bothering to get dressed. The only time you seem to come alive is when the child is brought to you." She walked over to the windows and pulled back the velvet draperies.

"Look," she went on, "the sun is shining. 'Tis a lovely winter's day." She walked over to the armoire and pulled open its doors. Leafing through the clothing hanging there, she brought forth a mauve wool gown. "Put this on," she ordered, "and come downstairs with me."

Lisa was outraged at her actions.

"*I* will decide what *I* will do, Zada," she said angrily.

Zada looked at her. "That's the spirit!" She grinned. "About time you took charge. Since the Pottles left after the funeral, claiming they would not stay in the house of a murderer, I've been having the devil's own time running this place."

"You have been running . . ."

"Who else? Nelly has had her hands full with the maids to look after as well as the cooking. Matthew has been forced to take Pottle's place and there's only been one manservant since Styles left."

"I didn't know. . . ."

"How would you know? You cut yourself off from everyone and everything."

"I needed time. . . ."

"I know that. You loved them both very much and you blamed yourself for their deaths. How many times you have said to me, 'If only I had not . . .' 'Twill not bring them back, Lisa, you must realize that."

"I still can't believe I will never see them again," Lisa murmured. She sat in the big bed, looking very childlike with her long, dark hair hanging loose about her shoulders. "I still think of things I want to tell Peter, and when Jamie does something new, I still look around for Mary—to share it with her. At first I was numb and then the feeling came back and 'twas even worse. 'Twas that way when Papa died and Mama . . ."

Zada's dark eyes had clouded at her words, but her voice was resolute. "You've had too many deaths for one so young, but the time for grieving is over, Lisa. The time for living has begun again."

It was not until the morning after the murders that Lisa had seen Zada. The gypsy woman had spent the night with the wounded child. After staunching the flow of blood and cleaning the puncture in his shoulder, she had drawn the flesh together and bound it tight. Little Jamie was a strong child, she had told his stunned mother. He would recover.

Matthew and Trent had gone straight to the authorities in the village after Sir Basil had ridden off into the night. An alarm had been sounded throughout the countryside to be on the lookout for the murderer, but in taking the quiet country roads instead of the main thoroughfares, Basil Stavely had managed to elude all his pursuers.

Lisa had been forced to tell the details of Peter's death to the authorities and Zada, as the only witness to Mary's death, had related what she had seen.

The funerals had been a nightmare. Mary and Peter's two sisters and their husbands had come to Stavely Manor and Lisa in her glazed state had had to deal with all the arrangements as well as these grieving relatives, who were completely shattered by what had happened.

Lisa no longer had Peter's strong shoulder to lean on. In death he became even more dear to her than he had in life. His love had given her something to live for after Richard had left her. Now that he too was gone, she was devastated.

She had collapsed, the day after the funeral, and had retired to her room. Since then she had never left it and had seen only Zada and the child. Jamie had been brought to her twice a day. He was all she had and like Mary before her, he had become her only reason for living.

Now, Zada had made Lisa realize that she was needed in this house. She could no longer hide away in her room.

She swung her legs over the side of the bed, and with the gypsy's help, began to dress for the first time in nearly six weeks.

"I've heard loud hammerings and bangings today," Lisa said to Zada. "What are the servants doing?"

"I will show you. Come downstairs with me."

Lisa hesitated a moment before following Zada from her bedchamber. She moved, almost reluctantly, down the corridor after her. When they reached the upper gallery, Zada gestured about her.

"Do you see what we have done?"

She and the servants had decorated the house with holly and mistletoe, rosemary and laurel and ivy. Woven garlands of cedar had been draped around the high ceiling posts of the stairway and down the bannisters. Candles were ensconced at intervals among the foliage. All had a festive air.

"'Tis only a week until Christmas," Zada said.

"Is it really that close?" Lisa asked in surprise.

"Aye, Nelly has already baked the mince pies and plum pudding and cakes."

"For whom?"

"Lisa, there have been many friends and neighbors who

have wanted to call upon you. They were told to wait until you would feel up to seeing people again. What better time than at Christmas?"

"Oh Zada, I don't know whether I . . ."

"You *must* make the effort."

As Lisa met the gypsy's determined eyes, her own became wet and then she was throwing her arms about the old woman. "The world still revolves, doesn't it? I suppose I can't hide from it forever."

It was after two o'clock on the afternoon before Christmas. The Dorringtons had stopped by to see Lisa and had stayed with her for luncheon. Now they had made their departure, and as Lisa turned back to the dining hall, her eyes caught sight of the dark red wine stain on the delicate white tablecloth that she knew Mary had embroidered. Sir Bruce had carelessly knocked over his glass while describing a race at Newmarket.

This would never have happened in the Pottle's time, Lisa thought. The cloth would have been instantly removed as soon as the table had been cleared. She removed it now herself, folding it up in her arms. She felt a compulsion to get it down to Emma in the laundry before the stain had set. As a child, she had seen Zada pour boiling water through a wine-stained cloth to remove the spot.

Intent on her task, she was hurrying across the hallway when the front door was flung open and a draft of frosty air entered the great hall.

Lisa looked up, and the color drained from her face as the door slammed shut.

"More laundry?" a familiar deep voice said. "This has always been the most deucedly clean household."

Chapter Thirty-five

"RICHARD!"

The laundry fell to the floor, and Lisa would have followed it, except that two strong arms were suddenly steadying her.

"I only just heard. I had to come," he said, his green eyes sweeping over her.

She was thinner, but even more lovely than he remembered. There was more depth in the violet eyes. That aristocratic quality was even more apparent in her bearing as she strove to gain control of herself.

"Wh-when did you return to England?"

She had forgotten how big he was, how that positive, forceful manner always made him seem larger than life. His very nearness set a storm battling within her.

"Only a few days ago. I rode straight to Calderwood. 'Tis nearly completed now," he said proudly. "I encountered Matthew on the road and he must have spoken to Zada. She came to see me yesterday. Told me everything." His strong features had softened in a look of compassion.

"Then you know about Basil and the terrible things he—"

"Aye," he nodded quickly, as if to silence her. He grasped her elbow. "I have something I wish to say to you."

She let him lead her almost blindly across the hall and into the library, where he removed his cloak and carelessly threw it with his hat and gauntlets onto a nearby chair before turning back to her.

"I think you should know," he said, placing his hands on her shoulders, "that before I was sent to Holland, the king told me all that had happened between the two of you that unforgettable night." He gazed deep into her eyes. "I wrote a letter to you, asking your forgiveness, pouring out my heart and soul to you. I had no reply, though for a while I kept hope—"

There was a look of astonishment on her face. "But I did not—"

"I know that now," he said, interrupting her. "But at that time, after months in Holland, the first news I had of you was that you had married Peter. I felt that you had fallen in love with him and that was the reason I had had no answer from you. 'Twas Zada who told me yesterday that you had never received my letter."

"That's true," she looked stricken. "I did not. I heard that you were thinking of remaining in Holland. Peter had asked me to be his wife many times," she went on. "He had been very good to me. I loved him, Richard. I would not have married him if I had not. But it was not . . . not the same. . . ."

"No," he said softly. "Nothing could be, could it?"

Their eyes spoke for them and suddenly he was pulling her close, murmuring something about wasted time and stupid pride, kissing her cheeks, her eyelids, her throat, before at last finding her lips.

"How brief a time we had," he growled, "before you cast me into the nearest thing to hell a man has ever known."

"Cast *you!*" Anger blazed up in the violet eyes. "Do you remember how you left *me* that night? Do you?"

"Aye," he nodded. "It has tortured me sometimes."

"Has it? I would have thought Christina quite capable of assuaging your passions, or didn't you take her with you? Perhaps she is a thing of the past, too."

"Christina! That conniving bitch! When I think of what she put you through. . . . Damn it! I'll warrant it was *she* who saw to it that my letter never reached you!"

"Doubtless you have had many other women since."

He shook his head. "There has been no one since you."

She raised a disbelieving eyebrow. "No one?" she asked quietly.

"No one who counted."

He drew her closer to him, his lips crushing her mouth. He could feel her body straining for release. She was fighting him. He merely tightened his grip. She began to hammer at his shoulders with her fists. Her teeth bit his lip, but his mouth only pressed down more fiercely, moving until her lips at last surrendered beneath his. She no longer had the strength or the will to fight him. Her whole body went limp.

He swept her up into his arms and calmly walked out the door, across the great hall and up the wide staircase, oblivious to the wide-eyed stare of a little housemaid whom he passed on the way.

He strode along the corridor toward his old room and with one booted foot kicked open the door and crossing to the big bed, dumped her onto it.

"No, Richard!" she murmured. "Don't do this unless you truly love me."

"I have always loved you, Lisa."

"But there is so much that must be explained between us—so much—"

"Will you be quiet?" he grunted, and then his huge shoulders blocked out the light.

Impatient to claim her, he undressed her quickly, but his hands slowed as they began moving over her, as if they were discovering her body for the first time.

It was like the night of the thunderstorm. Unable to deny him, Lisa found herself melting in his arms, responding as always to his every caress.

His lips crushed hers, forcing hers to open, his tongue questing and probing until he felt her soft and eager response.

She gasped for breath as he raised his head and she looked deep into the gleaming emerald depths, now so dark with passion.

"'Tis been too damn long, Lisa," he groaned. "I can't wait."

Hurriedly, he divested himself of his own garments and returned to her, settling his long, hard frame over hers.

Conscious of the scent of him, the wonderful feel of his lean, muscular body pressing against her, she let him draw her closer, trembling to know again his tender-fierce possession.

She was warm and soft and yielding in his arms, filling them as if she had been made for them alone. Only Lisa had the power to quench the fiery ache that now possessed him. Only Lisa . . .

Hungrily his lips and hands moved over her, arousing her to fever pitch as they traveled down over her smooth skin, hardening the upthrust nipples, filling her with an agony of throbbing anticipation.

She writhed against him, feeling him full and heavy with desire. It had been so many long months. Despite everything he had done to her, despite his lack of faith and trust, she loved this man above all else. Only Richard could make her want to cry aloud with the delight of his touch. Only Richard could incite the well-remembered sensations that now engulfed her. Only Richard . . .

She was wild for him, telling him without words what she wanted, arching her body, moaning as she twisted beneath him.

For a brief, jealous second, he wondered if she had given herself as abandonedly to Peter. No! He knew with a certainty that bore no arrogance that he was the only man who could awaken her full wealth of passion.

Their frenzied bodies strained against one another, throbbing with need.

"Now, Richard!" she cried, unable to stand it a moment longer. "Oh, love me, love me!"

He gave a husky laugh as he plunged deep into the seething depths, filling her fully, moving with strong, hard thrusts of passion as he buried himself ever deeper within her.

She wrapped her legs about him, arching high as their bodies came together with feverish intensity.

Lisa was aware of nothing but the joyous driving force that was causing wave after wave of ecstasy to break over her, building, building, as he swelled within her.

The tempo quickened as with wild abandonment they both strove for fulfillment.

When at last the glorious shattering explosion came, they convulsed together, his seed unleashing deep within her.

Gasping, she clung to him as the tremors slowly subsided.

Richard cradled her against him, whispering soft words of love in her ear as they lay intertwined, half-drunk from the blazing pleasure that had consumed them.

"What fools we were," Lisa murmured, looking up at him through tear-filled eyes.

He kissed her soft, sweet lips. "*I* was the fool," he admitted, humbly grateful that he had been given another chance at happiness with this beautiful young woman. "You've got to teach me how to love and trust without question. I grew cynical at such a young age, Lisa. Especially about women." He buried his face in her silken hair. "I love you so much," he groaned. "Living without you was like dying. I swear I'll never let you out of my sight again."

"What does your lordship intend to do with me?" she uttered softly.

"Mmm. Methinks it will take a whole lifetime to show you."

Whispering of their love for one another, they almost did not hear the discreet knock on the door.

"Damn!" Richard complained. "Who the devil is that?"

"It's Zada," came the gypsy's muffled voice.

"What is it, Zada?" Lisa cried impatiently, struggling to sit up.

"'Tis time for you to see Jamie," came the reply. "Do you wish—"

"Who is Jamie?" Richard growled. "Tell him to—"

"No!" Lisa put a hand over his mouth. "I want you to see him." (Zada had apparently not told him of the child).

He shrugged and she took her hand away, only to have him brazenly call out to Zada. "We'll be there directly."

"Richard!" she hissed. Then she shook her head. "Once I would have blushed at that. Now I want to shout out our love for all to hear, flaunt it for all to see."

"Nevertheless, my shameless hussy"—he nuzzled her neck—"I fully intend to make an honest woman of you. What do you think of a wedding on Christmas Day?"

"Tomorrow? But I'm barely a widow. What will people think?"

"To hell with what people will think!"

He kissed her fiercely and then she pushed him gently away from her and struggled to rise.

"Where do you think you're going?"

"To see Jamie."

He pulled her roughly back down to him.

"Let him wait," he said hoarsely. "I'm not through with you yet."

"But Richard, we haven't time. . . ."

"We have all the time in the world, my love. Would you deny a starving man?"

It was more than a half-hour later when they finally emerged from the bedchamber. Lisa was radiant with love and happiness as she led Richard down the corridor until they stood before the nursery door.

"In here," she said, taking his hand.

Jamie had been fed and was happily propped on his nurse's knee playing a little game of clap-hands. As Lisa drew Richard across the room to him, Jamie gave her a wide grin and held out his chubby arms to her.

Lisa reached down and picked him up, cuddling him close against her.

"You may go for your supper now, Mrs. Riley," she said.

"Thank you, m'lady."

Richard's eyes had never left the child since he had first entered the room, and when the woman had departed, he asked of the dark-haired little boy in Lisa's arms, "He's yours, isn't he?"

Lisa nodded. "Aye, he's my son."

"How old is he?"

"Nine months old."

"He was born before you married Peter?"

She nodded again. "Would you care to hold him?"

She held Jamie out to him and the child stared up at the big man unblinkingly as he was lifted chest high. Richard's strong hands clasped Jamie beneath his arms as he looked down at him.

"He has your eyes," Lisa said, her own filling with tears as he drew the child close and somehow gathered her to him as well.

"Why didn't you tell me?"

"You never came back."

"Didn't you think I had a right to know?"

"At first I wasn't sure that you *were* his father."

"What!"

"That awful night . . . the king . . . the boy was dark like him."

He looked down at her tenderly. "It appears that you have been through a great deal, Lisa. I'm so very sorry."

"It has not been easy," she admitted. "Especially giving Jamie up."

"You gave him up!"

"To Mary. Mary was bringing him up as her own. Oh, Richard, 'tis a long story. I will tell you all about it later."

"I think you have much to tell me," he said. He was again gazing down at the child in his arms. "My son," he murmured, almost in awe, "Jamie."

"Mary named him after her father. *His* name was James."

"That's odd. 'Twas also *my* father's name."

"I'm glad of that," she smiled.

"Look how straight he holds his back."

"He's a strong child. Peter thought him very like you."

"Peter knew?"

Lisa sighed. "That's another part of the story."

By the time they went downstairs to dine, the candles had all been lit along the decorated stairway, illuminating the great hall below.

"'Twill be my happiest Christmas, Richard," Lisa smiled softly.

He squeezed her hand. "And mine."

They dined in the flickering candlelight, waited on by the one manservant left at Stavely Manor.

Lisa had changed from her black mourning dress to a gown of soft green. Having lost weight she had had to add a sash of deeper green to pull the gown in at her waist. Her skin looked very white, except for the faint blush of color in her cheeks. She looked every bit the gracious lady of the manor.

"What did you do in Holland?" Lisa asked Richard as they began to eat.

He laughed. "I was sent to spy on the Dutch. A very poor choice on their part. I am not exactly inconspicuous when I enter a room and despite the fact that I told them I was exiled from my own country and intended to settle there, the influential members of the Dutch court were not falling over themselves in order to tell me their secrets."

Lisa laughed with him. "What did you do?"

"I decided that I would get no information from those in high circles, so I went down to the docks and posed as a sailor. Managed to get word of the size of their fleet back to England before I found myself pressed into service on a Dutch ship for four months.

"Pressed?"

"That's right. Knocked unconscious and taken forcibly aboard. It didn't take the captain long to realize I was no sailor, but my size helped me there. After the second mate was stabbed in his bunk one night, I took over his position. Didn't take too long to gain their respect." He rubbed his knuckles.

She did not doubt that for a moment.

"I was with the Dutch when they encountered the English fleet at Lowestoft. Fortunately for me we were crippled early in the battle and were forced to limp back home. I could never have brought myself to fire on an English vessel. When we reached port, we were not allowed to come ashore. Some of the sailors on the other ships had come down with the plague. Thank God, our ship was free of it, but after two weeks of inactivity, I got impatient. Dropped over the side one night and swam ashore. Took me weeks, but I made my way to France. I still have friends there and they helped me. Got me back to England."

"Thank heaven you escaped the plague."

"I gather London got the worst of it."

"You once told me of the filth of the city. Now they are saying that the open sewers and the unhealthy conditions helped to spread the plague. Thousands perished. We were lucky to be in the country. Peter and I housed many of his friends over the summer."

They had completed their meal and were lingering over their

wine before, at his urging, Lisa told Richard all that had occurred in his absence.

"When I discovered I was with child and even after Jamie was born," she said, "I thought him to be Charles Stuart's son."

"And 'twas not until you came here in November that you realized he was not sired by the king?"

"Aye," she nodded. "It upset me greatly when I realized he was your son. . . . Jamie's eyes were so distinctive . . . so obviously yours. I think 'twas why Basil . . . why he killed Mary and tried to kill the child as well."

"You don't mean that he thought that Mary and I . . ."

"I believe that he did. Oh Richard, I have been so burdened with guilt. It has been almost unbearable."

"But why have you stayed on here in this gloomy house with its bitter memories? Wouldn't it have been better to have taken Jamie back to Ellsbury?"

"Peter and Mary's sisters came for the funeral. Their oldest sister, Jane, is married to a naval officer. He was wounded at Lowestoft, and has been forced to retire from active duty. They have never been very well off. They have one son and he was always Peter's favorite, as well as his namesake. I insisted they take up residence at Ellsbury. With Jane's husband away so much, Peter had been urging them to do so for years. Now they have gratefully consented. I want it to be their home. Jane's husband will be able to take charge with the help of Peter's excellent estate manager. I want Ellsbury to remain in the family."

"That is very generous of you, Lisa."

"Nay, not generous. It helped a little with the guilt. I have given the two sisters the family jewelry, except for a few personal pieces that Peter gave me."

"And you planned never to return there?" he asked, amazed.

"'Twould have been too painful."

"But is not Stavely Manor just as—"

"Stavely Manor is my home, Richard."

"Nay, Lisa. Legally it still belongs to Basil."

"It has *never* belonged to Basil!"

"What do you mean?"

"Do you remember Sir Edmund's will that you saw in the chest in the library?"

"Aye, I do."

"This estate was left to his wife and his children."

"Correct, but they are all dead."

"Not *all*, Richard. I am Sir Edmund's daughter. I am Elizabeth Stavely!"

"My God!"

"I did not come to Stavely Manor by accident. I was told of my birthright by the only mother I can remember, Valerie Manning, before she died. It seemed that after my own mother died, my brother and I were taken in by a relative, a neighboring squire. Shortly afterward, his house was fired by Cromwell's troopers.

"The Manning Shakespearean Players had been allowed to camp on the squire's property, and the very night the house was burned, I wakened and ran out of the house and found my way to their camp. I cannot remember it, Richard. I cannot remember anything of my life before going to live with the Mannings. Zada says I have purposely blocked it all out of my mind, and yet, when I first came into this house, it stirred something in my memory. I knew I had been here before."

Richard sat staring at her in amazement.

"The Mannings made inquiries about me and were quick to realize that they should tell no one that I, the remaining member of the family, was still alive. They were afraid there would be an attempt on my life if it became known. They took me in as their own child. I was raised as Elizabeth Manning."

"But why did you not—" Richard began, but Lisa went on, "Basil usurped these lands that were rightfully mine. When I overheard his plans for regicide and copied the bond, I felt he would be branded a traitor and I would then claim my heritage. Instead, the bond was never found and it could not be proved he was involved. I foolishly continued to keep my identity a secret, because of my regard for Mary Stavely and the hurt and embarrassment 'twould have caused her to be thrown out of her home. You of all people know how proud she was to be the mistress of Stavely Manor."

"But why did you not tell *me?*"

"I wanted to. Oh, *how* I wanted to. I wanted to shout at you, 'My blood is as old and as pure as yours, Lord Drayton!' And then my pride took over and I thought if you did not love Elizabeth Manning enough to make her your wife, why should you love Elizabeth Stavely any more?"

"What can I say . . . ?"

"Peter did not care about my background," she said, and there was still a hint of bitterness in her voice. "But I had to tell him who I really was when I agreed to marry him. He was the only one who knew my true identity, outside of the vicar who married us."

"Naturally you had to give your rightful name to be legally married." He shook his head. "Odd, I would have thought Peter would have done something then."

"I begged him not to, Richard, for Mary's sake. Jamie was being brought up as Basil's son. He bore the Stavely name. He would inherit Stavely Manor eventually. The wheel of fortune would go full circle."

"But Basil—"

"He was not expected to live long. He developed severe complications with his disease. Liver and heart problems. Mary said he was often in pain. I was getting my revenge after all."

"You are quite a woman, Elizabeth Stavely Ellsbury," Richard said quietly.

"Nay. My judgment has not always been good. I hurt so many people without meaning to."

"And gave the same people a great deal of happiness. You told me yourself how happy Mary was with Jamie. If it were not for you she would never have had those months. And Peter. I wonder if I will always be a little jealous of what he meant to you."

"You need never be." She met his eyes.

"Would you care to prove that to me again?" he whispered, getting to his feet. In the candlelight, his green eyes gleamed quite wickedly.

Back in Richard's bedchamber as the evening deepened into night, they made love again and yet again. When, at last, they were fulfilled, Lisa lay in Richard's arms, knowing a peace such as she had never known before in all her life.

It was not the way Richard made love to her that made the act so wonderful, she realized, for Peter had been just as loving and considerate; it was her love for Richard that made the difference. They shared a love so strong that nothing had been able to destroy it.

It would be the first time she would be able to sleep the whole night through in Richard's arms and when she awoke it would be her wedding day! It was hard for Lisa to believe that she was finally to be allowed this happiness.

Chapter Thirty-six

IT WAS AS SHE WAS DOZING OFF TO SLEEP THAT LISA heard the noise down the hall. She was instantly alert. Was it Jamie?

She slipped from Richard's arms and, drawing on her dressing gown, crept from the room.

Her bare feet made little sound as she hurried down the corridor and quietly opened the nursery door.

Jamie was sound asleep in his cradle, and Mrs. Riley was snoring gently in her bed across the room from him.

Lisa closed the door and was about to turn back to Richard's bedchamber when she again heard the noise.

It sounded like something slamming shut and it came from the other end of the corridor—from Mary's old room!

Nothing had been touched in Mary's bedchamber since her death. Lisa had not been able to face going through her things. Now, someone was in there!

She crossed the upper gallery. The candles had not been extinguished and the stairway and hall below were still brightly lit.

As she approached the bedchamber, she could see a dim light showing from beneath the door. Opening it silently, Lisa saw, at the far end of the room, a dark shape going through the articles in Mary's armoire!

Some instinct must have warned the intruder that someone was there for she had made no sound.

"All right," he growled, "step forward!"

He turned, and she saw in the light of a candelabra placed beside him that it was Basil Stavely!

Horror and revulsion struck Lisa as she stared at him. He looked so ugly and grotesque that he was barely recognizable. His face bore a jagged scar and was mottled with skin lesions above a matted beard. An even more matted and filthy periwig covered his hair. Hanging on him as if several sizes too big, his clothes were torn and badly soiled. But it was his eyes that made a shiver of terror run through her. Bulging at the sight of her, they now glittered with a wild, unearthly shine. She knew with quiet certainty that she was looking into the eyes of a madman!

Lisa managed to take a step backward before he leveled a pistol at her.

"So 'tis the little bitch," he laughed and the laugh made Lisa's blood run cold. "Don't move! I tried to kill you once, but this time there is no one else to die for you."

He came menacingly toward her.

"Where are Mary's jewels?" he demanded. "Did you steal them?"

"No. They are mine to keep, *Cousin* Basil."

"Cousin?" For a moment he looked confused. "What are you saying, wench?"

"I am saying," Lisa said, raising her head proudly, "that you are my cousin, Basil Stavely—a distant cousin to be sure—but you did wrongfully usurp my rightful lands and honors. My name, sir, is Elizabeth Stavely."

"Elizabeth Stavely? 'Tis a lie! She is dead—she and her brother died in childhood!" cried Basil hoarsely.

"I might have been dead if I had not wakened the night the squire's house was fired by Cromwell's troopers—doubtless on your express orders—and managed to escape. Stavely Manor is my rightful home and Mary's jewels—the Stavely jewels— belong to me."

"What care I who you are? I only know you have caused me nothing but trouble since you came here. You are the reason my wife is dead and the child she bore. I should shoot you between those lovely eyes right now!"

Lisa felt the room spinning as the blood rushed from her veins, leaving her body as cold as ice.

But then Basil laughed and lowered the pistol. "Nay, that would be too easy. Far too easy. I want you to suffer as I have suffered."

Lisa gasped. He was mad, raving mad, and he was striding toward her now. The pistol again raised was pointed at her forehead.

"Onto the bed!" he ordered. "Take off that gown!"

"No!" she screamed.

"Do as you are told, wench!" The pistol pushed her back. He was staring at her with a chilling intensity. "I want to see you naked."

She did as she was told, her fingers trembling as she parted the dressing gown and dropped it to the floor.

Basil's breath came faster and his feverish eyes glistened excitedly as they roved over her nudity. He came closer, staring down at her hotly, prolonging the chosen moment.

Then he began fumbling awkwardly with his one free hand at his breeches. Exasperated by his efforts, he tossed the pistol onto the carpeted floor, where it slid under the bed.

Lisa was ready for him. As he loomed above her, she drew up her knees and kicked out at him as hard as she could.

Her feet caught him in the chest, and he reeled backward against the armoire. He didn't go down and as she jumped from the bed and grabbed for her robe, he was on her again, forcing her back, his big hands gripping her soft white shoulders.

He grinned. "Here 'tis, bitch. Here is what you deserve."

Lisa's eyes opened in terror as he revealed his abhorrent manhood to her, not stopping to remove his clothing. She tried to squirm away from him, but he held her fast with one hand while the other held his organ.

With one knee he wrenched her thighs open. Lisa thought she was going to faint as he reared over her his grinning lesioned face a loathsome mask of hate.

Drayton was across the room in two strides, grabbing Stavely by the back of his doublet and yanking him up, slamming a big fist into his face.

As Stavely crumpled to the floor, Richard turned to Lisa.

"You're all right? I heard you scream."

She nodded. "He didn't touch me."

He reached down and handed her her robe, not noticing in his anxiety for her that Stavely was inching his way across the room to where his hat and sword lay on a chair.

Slowly Basil extracted the blade from its scabbard and jumped to his feet, triumph spreading across his ugly face.

"Watch out!" Lisa cried, seeing the flash of steel. "Richard, he's drawn his sword!"

Drayton whirled about, diving for the fireplace as Basil charged at him. On his knees, he managed to grab an iron poker in time to ward off Stavely's fatal blow.

"No!" shouted Lisa to Basil as he lunged again. "He is unarmed."

"Stay back!" snapped Richard, on his feet now, again using the poker to counter the attack.

Steel rang out against iron. The two men began circling each other in the space between bed and window.

Lisa's heart was filled with fear as she stood watching them. She must do something, but what? Where had the pistol gone? She looked frantically about for it on the floor.

Pure hatred was written over Basil's face as he lunged. Richard's jaw was set as he parried the blade once more.

The door! Lisa thought. If she could slip by them and gain the door, then she could run back to Richard's room and fetch him his own sword. She must try!

But the men were circling again, completely blocking her way. She stood at the foot of the bed, as if paralyzed to the spot. She had drawn her robe close about her and her hands clutched it so tightly that the knuckles showed white. She found it almost impossible to breathe.

"Dear God," she prayed. "Let nothing happen to Richard. Not now. Not when we have finally found one another again."

She watched the grim concentration of the two men. Basil thrust out and Richard countered, until in a sudden backward step to parry Basil's jabbing blade, Richard's right leg was hampered by the long dressing gown he wore and Basil took his advantage. His sword pierced the sleeve above the left elbow with a tearing sound, slicing into Richard's arm.

Basil smiled disdainfully, stepping back, completely sure of himself, feeling in perfect control of the situation.

"Take it off, Drayton," he said magnanimously. "It impedes you and you need all the advantage you can get."

Richard shrugged out of the garment, not trusting Stavely, transferring the poker, never letting it go.

He stood bare-chested now before his opponent, the dark red blood from the slash running in rivulets down his left arm. He had only taken the time to pull on breeches and dressing gown before going in search of Lisa, and she felt a new fear rising in her as she saw the easy target his wide, muscular chest presented.

"I'm going to kill you, Drayton!" Basil growled, his hate-filled eyes narrowing. "Kill you for bedding my wife and making her bear your bastard!"

"I did not bed your wife, Stavely," Richard said quietly.

"That's right," Lisa cried out. "The child is mine. Mary wanted a babe so badly that I let her—"

"Liars! Both of you. Liars! Pottle himself saw you leaving Mary's bedchamber, Drayton. You planted your seed in her and she bore your son. I saw his eyes. Green they were—as green as yours!"

He gave a wild lunge in Richard's direction, but it was expertly countered.

They fought on. Basil attacking and Richard defending himself the best he could with only the poker for a weapon, sidestepping and ducking beyond the reach of Stavely's sword.

Basil's face betrayed his growing frustration and lust for blood. He became more violent, his thrusts forcing Richard back toward the door.

Drayton fought on grimly as they entered the hallway, the battle raging back and forth between them. The tempo of Basil's attack seemed to be growing even more furious. How long could Richard hold him off? Lisa wondered, as she followed the two fighting men back to the upper gallery.

"Ha!" Stavely laughed, "I have you running before my sword now, Drayton. It won't be long."

Richard said nothing as he parried a furious lunge and danced easily away on his bare feet.

Basil was breathing heavily now, relentlessly wielding the heavy sword, the rage bellowing up in him.

The tension seemed to increase by the second. They were at the top of the stairs now.

Richard's left arm was red with blood and his right was just able to turn aside the flashing blade. He knew he was tiring and all his energies were concentrated on avoiding that final deadly thrust.

Suddenly, he saw his chance. In a last desperate attempt, he darted to his left, turning his back to the tall arched window. Basil turned with him, and with a yell to Lisa to "Run!" Richard threw the poker straight into Stavely's face.

It happened so quickly and unexpectedly that Basil did not see it coming until it was too late. He took a futile step backward to avoid the flying rod, clutching wildly for the stairpost and then he was falling . . . falling . . . his hand tearing the cedar garlands from the high post close to him, bringing the lighted candles down with them, setting the brittle boughs instantly aflame as they trapped and encircled his body!

Desperately he clawed at them as his clothing became ignited and like a blazing ball of fire, he rolled over and over down the stairs, the trailing, burning cedar licking at the dusty wall hangings, the dry wooden posts and bannisters!

Basil's screams echoed down the stairs as he descended and Lisa put her hands to her ears and turned away.

As Stavely hit the bottom step, his neck snapped back and broke, mercifully, before he was totally consumed by flames.

Richard stood still viewing the conflagration below him. The whole stairway was ablaze now and as he watched, the front door was flung open from the outside.

Trent, on his way home from having some Christmas cheer at a tavern recognized Stavely's horse at the front of the manor house and fearing trouble, burst in the front door.

There was a violent roar as the sudden draft caused the fire to leap across the great hall below. Trent slammed the door shut, but now the downstairs was totally engulfed in flames!

Richard did not wait. Turning quickly to Lisa he instructed, "I'll get Jamie and Mrs. Riley. You go to the servant's stairs, and hurry!"

Great orange flames belched from the faceless windows of Stavely Manor and black smoke climbed high about it in a lurid winter sky that gleamed as bright as day.

It was a scene that would be repeated and greatly enlarged upon a few months later in the great fire of London, but now a little group stood huddled on the lawn, watching as the old manor house was consumed by flames.

Lisa held her sleeping son close against her, rocking him

gently. Zada had managed to save a few things for her mistress and Lisa was now dressed in warm clothing, but some of the servants had not been so lucky and were shivering in their night clothes as they watched the fire leap higher and higher into the sky.

"They should go into the stables to keep warm," Lisa said to Zada.

"They won't leave here, but I'll get some blankets from my caravan," Zada said, hurrying away.

The old, part-timber structure was burning like tinder. The fire had spread so fast that Richard and the other men who had been working at a bucket brigade on the side of the house nearest the river finally gave up their futile efforts. It was plain to see that Stavely Manor could not be saved. All they could do was to stand there and watch it burn to the ground.

The fire had lit up the countryside for miles around and by now some of the villagers had arrived with blankets and flasks of ale to warm the homeless occupants of the manor house.

Richard, his face and hands smoke-blackened, joined Lisa at the front of the house.

"'Tis no use," he said. "We cannot save it."

"Are you all right?" she asked, noticing he was warmly dressed, albeit the clothing ill-fitting. "Your arm—"

"Is fine. Just a flesh wound. Mrs. Riley insisted upon bandaging it." He indicated the blazing house. "I'm sorry, Lisa."

She looked at him. "I don't think I am," she murmured. "It had few good memories for me."

"There were some," he said softly, putting an arm about her shoulders.

"Aye," she agreed, "there were some." She reached for his hand. "It came back to me tonight, Richard," she said, trembling at the memory. "'Twas the fire, of course, that made me remember."

He regarded her closely.

"I was trying to get down a corridor to David's room. David was my brother. But the corridor was filled with smoke and flames and it was all sweeping toward me. I just turned and ran. I ran and ran. . . . Down the back stairs and out the side door and across the courtyard and through the trees until I reached the open fields beyond. Tonight, I found myself doing the same thing! I had the same terrible feeling of panic! It was Zada who stopped me, or I would have run off into the woods again."

"Oh, my dear," he whispered, brushing at a tear on her cheek. "'Tis all over now, Lisa. All over."

"But," she asked, drawing the child closer to her, "where will we go?"

"To Calderwood, of course," he said. He nodded toward the servants. "If they agree, we'll take them all with us. 'Tis only right they should be present at our wedding."

"Our wedd— Why, 'tis now Christmas Day!" she exclaimed.

"Aye, 'tis Christmas. The time of peace and good will and new beginnings. This Christmas will be a new beginning for both of us and our son."

Lisa held Jamie out to Richard. "Will you take him now?" She gave a little sigh at the weight of him. "I do believe he is going to be as big a man as his father."

Richard grinned as Lisa transferred the sleeping child into the crook of his uninjured arm. The other arm went about her waist as they started off across the lawn, never looking back, leaving the smoldering manor house and its grief and unhappiness behind them.

ELEANOR HOWARD, a Canadian author, has published numerous articles combining her interests in travel and history. *Cloak of Fate* is her second book.

Tapestry

HISTORICAL ROMANCES

Breathtaking New Tales

of love and adventure set against
history's most exciting time and
places. Featuring two novels by the
finest authors in the field of roman-
tic fiction—<u>every month</u>.

Next Month From
Tapestry Romances

IRON LACE
by Lorena Dureau

LYSETTE
by Ena Halliday

POCKET BOOKS